# With Neighbors Like This

## TRACY GOODWIN

sourcebooks
casablanca

Published by Sourcebooks Casablanca, an imprint of Sourcebooks
P.O. Box 4410, Naperville, Illinois 60567-4410
(630) 961-3900
sourcebooks.com

Cataloging-in-Publication Data is on file with the Library of Congress.

Printed and bound in Canada.
MBP 10 9 8 7 6 5 4 3 2 1

*For my husband, Greg, and our children, Zachary and Emma.*
*I love you…always and forever.*

# Chapter 1

AMELIA MARSH HALTS MIDSTEP, STRICKEN BY THE LAUGHTER AND squeals of a half-dozen children racing towards her.

"Incoming!" Grabbing her daughter and son, she wraps them in her arms, turning just in time to avoid the melee. One for the win column! Sure, those children appear to be sweet and innocent clad in their frilly dresses and formal ties, but she knows better. Amelia is a mom after all, and this is war—playground style. She's got the superpower of keeping her children in check. Like the Hulk/Bruce Banner, those powers come and go. Some days, Amelia is a master, while other days…well, not so much.

The playground is surrounded by trees and lush green grass; however, its pretty setting is *this* parent's nightmare. Kids of all ages shout, wrestle, and run like they're all on one heck of a sugar high. While she's scoping a group of younger boys wrestling in the kiddie play mulch underneath the jungle gym, Amelia's eldest tugs at her arm.

"Mom, can we play?" Her son, Jacob, asks, looking up at his mom with his signature bright smile. At ten years old, he is a charmer. What's worse? He knows it. One flash of his megawatt smile and he receives free cookies at his favorite bakery, or snags extra stickers at their local supermarket.

A little girl rushes past them, dressed in a pink tutu with a bunny tail that hangs haphazardly in the back. The child's faux tail bounces with every step she takes, and her bunny ears remind Amelia of their mission: today, they are attending their community Easter egg hunt and taking pictures with the Easter Bunny.

This is their first major outing since the big move back to Amelia's hometown of Houston, since her divorce, since their lives drastically changed. The last thing she wants is her children running around in the sweltering Texas sun, then taking pictures with some costumed cottontail while they sweat profusely with tangled hair or—worse yet—covered in mulch. She glances again at that same group of boys, who now have pieces of mulch stuck to their clothes and in their hair. The chances of more than one shower needed: likely. Drain-clogging potential: high. Just what Amelia's trying to avoid.

Crouching in front of her son, she ensures that her long skirt is covering her legs, then reaches for the hands of Jacob and his sister, Chloe. They're twenty-two months apart, the best of friends on most days, and bicker like nobody's business the rest of the time. "Why don't we take pictures with the Easter Bunny first, then you can run around. Deal?"

Jacob wrinkles his brow, considering his mom's offer. He's not buying what she's selling, and Amelia's glad that she didn't go all out like some other parents. Contrasting the once-pristine girls and boys wearing their best attire and ruining their special outfits, her kids are wearing clothes of their own choosing—cargo shorts and a polo shirt for Jacob, while Chloe wears leggings and her favorite ruffled shirt with a pink flamingo on it. No fancy shoes, either. Just socks and sneakers.

Picture-taking Marsh style is practical by necessity, because their family is cursed when it comes to family photos. Without fail, the better dressed her children are, the worse the picture. There could be fifty photos taken, and not one would include both of the kids smiling or looking at the camera at the same time. But, when they wear comfortable clothes—their favorite clothes—voilà! It's like a Harry Potter moment with magical smiles and happy memories.

At this community event, she seems to be the only parent with this mindset, seeing the abundance of children once dressed to impress now getting dirty, sweaty, and screaming louder than the audience at a Metallica concert.

"I promise you can play after—"

"They have cookies! Can we have cookies, Mom?" Chloe, her eight-year-old spitfire tomboy, points to a little boy eating a large cookie, then sprints toward the clubhouse, followed close behind by Jacob. When all else fails, cookies will do the trick and, thanks to a little boy covered in grass stains, a trail of cookie crumbs is leading Amelia's children away from the lure of a crowded playground.

"Save some for me!" she calls to them, walking close behind until they reach the pool clubhouse, also known as their community's "aquatic center." It's a fancy name for a small in-ground pool and a building with bathrooms.

Their subdivision of Castle Rock is a newer one, situated in the northern suburbs of Houston in a town named Timberland, Texas. Here, in what is known as the *Lush and Livable Timberland*, where natural pine trees that were once in abundance are rare thanks to the building boom, residents pride themselves on their thick green lawns and blooming flower beds.

Under the shade of the clubhouse and its covered patio, Amelia spies tables accentuated with spring-themed tablecloths whipping in the warm breeze, upon which plates of cookies with colored icing and cups of lemonade are arranged around stuffed-animal bunnies and Easter decorations.

She's traded sweat and dirt for icing and lemonade. Given the fact that her kids used to hate any and all imaginary figures in costumes, from Santa to the Easter Bunny to their school mascot, Amelia will take whatever photos she can get. Cargo shorts? Sure. Flamingo shirt? Done. Icing turning their tongues blue like Smurfs? She'll deal.

Such is the single mom in her. Always trying to please, to make the kids happy, and to find her own sense of satisfaction. Without her ex-husband, Daniel. It was his choice to start a new life with his mistress. Did it hurt? Yes. Because he walked out on their children and because he caused them pain. Though Daniel may have wanted out, he also wanted everything that he valued—their house, their money, their investments. What he didn't value are Amelia's biggest blessings: Jacob and Chloe.

Granted, she's no pushover. With the help of a brilliant attorney, Amelia fought for what her children and she deserved. When the divorce was finalized, it was time to remove her children from the situation and give them a chance to heal—near some of Amelia's best friends.

Today, she's on her own, with her children—who are scarfing down cookies like they haven't eaten in days. "Slow down, sweeties. Let's take a break from the cookies."

Mom rule number one: never let your kids overeat and throw up. As a matter of fact, avoid vomit at all costs. Gross, but true.

"Hello there." A saccharine-sweet voice and a terse tap on Amelia's shoulder grab her attention. "I'm Carla, from the community's management company. I don't believe we've met."

"Nope, not yet." Amelia would remember Carla, who is a sight to behold with teased red hair, full makeup, and a pristine pantsuit. How is this woman not melting in today's heat? In her light maxi dress and messy bun, Amelia is already perspiring, but Carla's heavy makeup remains flawless. Is she human or is heat endurance *her* superpower?

"Hi, Carla. I'm Amelia Marsh. These are my children, Jacob and Chloe." Her daughter waves while her son gulps more lemonade before flashing his signature grin.

Carla narrows her eyes, staring at Amelia's children, seemingly immune to Jacob's charms. In turn, Jacob smiles wider, arching his brow. With still no response from Carla, Jacob gives up and studies his feet, while Amelia gives him a reassuring pat on his back.

"Where's the Bunny?" Chloe asks.

"He's coming. How about you line up over there?" Carla points at the seating area where four carefully arranged lawn chairs remain empty, and a line has already formed, full of flushed and disheveled children. Parents are doing their best to right the damage done by playtime. *Good luck with that.*

Amelia's children look to her for approval, and she nods. Jacob smiles, his teeth blue from the icing. "That's my boy!" Amelia encourages him with a thumbs-up.

Mom rule number…who knows, since there are so many mom rules that she's lost count, but this is one of the most important rules of all: you can only control so much. Amelia has traded the messy, sweaty, grass-stained debacle for blue teeth. The glass half full theory is that the blue might not show up in the picture.

"Keep drinking, buddy." She smiles as Jacob takes another sip of his lemonade, then she turns to Carla. "What's the difference between the HOA and the management company?"

"The Homeowners Association consists of Castle Rock residents, some of whom preside on its board of directors. The management company, for which I work, handles the logistics, enforcing the bylaws—in other words, the community rules, and—"

"Collecting the annual dues," Amelia adds with a smile. Now she understands. "I know my dues are paid for the year. I took care of that at closing."

Studying Carla, Amelia notes that the woman has a half smirk/half grin plastered on her face. Just like her makeup, it isn't moving.

"I'm sorry about the letter arriving so soon after you moved in. But rules are rules, you know."

Amelia's catches the woman's exaggerated grimace. "Letter? I'm lost. Why would I receive a letter when I paid my dues?"

"Oh, no. You haven't read it yet." Carla gasps, her hot pink nails matching her lipstick as she covers her mouth with her hands.

"Nope, I haven't received it yet. What's in this letter? It sounds ominous." Amelia's humor falls flat on the stoic-faced Carla.

"There are rules."

"Right. You've repeated that. Three times, I believe. Possibly four." Shoving her sunglasses on top of her head, Amelia refuses to break eye contact with Carla, whose expression remains serious. "Rules like what, exactly?"

Carla shifts, then whispers, "Your gnome."

"My what?" Is *gnome* some sort of code word for one of her children? Amelia's head snaps immediately to her kids. Jacob laughs while Chloe chats with him, probably reciting one of her famous knock-knock jokes. The kids are safe, so her attention returns to Carla. "Did you say my 'gnome'?"

"Your garden gnome. The one in your front yard," Carla counters.

Amelia laughs. She can't help it. Carla's mock horror that this new resident finds her comment amusing quickly fades into impatience, her eyes emanating frustration and disapproval, the lines around them deepening.

Clearing her throat allows Amelia time to keep her expression neutral, her tone calm, and her snark to a minimum. "Do you mean my tiny, hand-painted garden gnome hidden within the bushes, flowers, and mulch that comprise a small portion of my front yard? You can barely see it."

Carla scoffs. "I see everything. It's my job to inspect the front yards. I drive by intermittently, so I can ensure our community remains up to the standards set in the bylaws."

Of course she does. The fact that Carla *sees everything* is a bit alarming. Sticking to the topic at hand, Amelia explains, "My children made me that gnome for Mother's Day last year." Before the divorce. Before their move. It was displayed prominently in the front yard of their old home. That gnome represents her children's only request when moving to Houston: that she'd place it in their new front yard. It helps them feel at home.

"You must remove it, I'm afraid. Rules are rules, and some people's trash is others' treasure, so to speak." Carla grins, seemingly oblivious to the fact that she just insulted Amelia and her beloved gnome.

"Trash?" *Carla. Did. Not. Just. Say. That.*

Carla nods. "Not that I find your troll trashy, of course. Playing devil's advocate, the truth is that you may like it, but your neighbors may find it tacky. Besides, the ban is in the bylaws."

So, this woman has called her kids' gnome *trash*, *tacky*, and a *troll*. For any mom, especially Amelia, those are fighting words. "Who bans garden gnomes that you can barely see in their bylaws?"

"Your HOA. If you don't like it, I invite you to attend your next quarterly Homeowners' Association meeting. You just missed the last one, but I'll send out an email blast to all residents, signs will be posted at the entrances to the neighborhood, and an announcement will go up on the community website approximately ten days in advance of the next meeting." Applause drowns out Carla, and Amelia turns to see the Easter Bunny waving at the kids.

"Time for pictures! Have a good day." And just like that, Carla dismisses Amelia, sauntering away to schmooze with other residents.

Amelia blinks. *What the heck?* Gnomes are off limits, but bunnies are okay? She scans her surroundings which, like most front yards in her subdivision, are decorated with colored ribbons, bunny cut-outs, and enlarged egg décor. Yeah, bunnies on full display are fine, yet one tiny, beautiful gnome—the gnome that her kids made for her—must go? The same gnome that makes their new house a *home*.

The Easter Bunny high fives Jacob and Chloe, and Amelia makes a beeline to them, just as her daughter begins hiding behind her brother. Apparently, Chloe hasn't gotten over her fear of fake bunnies after all. This one is cute, sporting a purple suit jacket, a yellow vest, and a rainbow-colored bow tie. Though this event is held weeks before Easter, beads of perspiration trickle down Amelia's spine, causing her to pity the poor soul who drew the short straw and must wear a furry costume in this heat and sticky humidity. Hopefully, his or her costume has a fan.

"Hi, Bunny!" She smiles and high fives the faux fur paw of whoever is in the costume.

Nodding and swaying to the beat of Taylor Swift's "Shake It Off", which is blasting through the pool speakers, this rabbit is in character. Amelia needs to shake Carla off, since her blood pressure is still high from the woman's lack of tact and the accompanying ban notice. Over a gnome? Really? So, Amelia takes Taylor's advice, singing and dancing with her children in line. The Easter Bunny must be a Swiftie, too, because the person in the costume dances over to the chairs before taking a seat.

When it's their turn for picture time, Amelia hands her cell to a man standing next to Carla, who will take the picture for them. Carla… ugh. The sight of her after that catty "tacky" comment makes Amelia's heartbeat pound like an anvil.

Normally, Amelia would have let Carla's comments about the letter go. Who knows? She might have even removed her gnome. But Carla insulted Jacob and Chloe's art, even after Amelia explained the importance of it.

One simple, passive-aggressive comment is all it takes for her to decide that she can't let it go. Instead, Amelia may drive the kids to Target, Walmart, or both after they spend time at the playground and buy out their entire garden gnome department. If she's lucky, maybe they'll be on sale, and she'll display an extended gnome family on her front lawn. If the HOA wants to send her a letter, she might as well earn it.

As they approach the Bunny for their picture, Chloe hides behind Amelia's skirt while Jacob charms the fluffy cottontail immediately with a knock-knock joke. No matter which way Amelia turns, her daughter won't come out from hiding. Amelia half expects Chloe to hide *under* her skirt any minute. Every time Amelia moves, so does Chloe, taking her mom's dress with her. "Sit on my lap, Chloe. Let's take the picture together."

With Jacob on one side, and Amelia and Chloe on the other, they pose with the Bunny.

When the man holding her cell prompts them to smile, Amelia instructs her kiddos to smile, adding, "Say 'garden gnome!'"

"Garden gnome!"

*It's official. The Bunny must think I've completely lost my mind.*

On the bright side, the kids smiled, laughed, and took a great picture. Add to that the fact that Amelia's got a plan.

The HOA better look out, because this mom protects her gnomes at all costs.

# Chapter 2

THANKS TO A BROKEN FAN IN KYLE SANDERS'S COSTUME, HE'S about to suffer heat stroke by rodent impersonation. It's not exactly the way he expected to go, but hey, if you're going to sweat to death, why not do so wearing a goofy Easter Bunny costume? Go big or go home, right? Sure, it'll be humiliating, especially when it hits the local news. And it would traumatize a lot of children.

*Oh man! The kids…*

In an effort to hide his demise from the neighborhood children, Kyle darts into the cleaning closet of the Castle Rock community's pool house, desperate to cool off. Struggling with the top of the costume, a muffled curse word escapes his lips as one of his pawed feet lands beside a bucket and a mop slams against his bunny forehead. It's Kyle against a cottontail costume, in a cage match, or in this case a closet match. His opponent—a bulky, furry rabbit costume—is a modern-day torture device that's currently winning.

*Why did I ever volunteer for this?*

Taking a step to the side, his oversized furry foot lands in the empty bucket. Still, Kyle manages to use his floppy tail to leverage himself against a wall. "The things I do for this community. Come on!"

Managing to free his face from the bunny head, Kyle tosses the thing onto a small table taking up too much space. He then rips the Velcro at his back and frees both arms, sliding the costume down to his waist. Drenched with sweat, he grabs his sports drink and takes several desperate gulps from the large bottle.

Though his foot may remain stuck, at least he won't die of dehydration. Limping over to the small table with the decapitated rabbit head, Kyle narrows his eyes, staring at the bunny's face which remains frozen in place, that wide, toothy grin taunting him along with its glossy eyes and fake wire-rimmed glasses.

Kyle mutters under his breath while placing the bottle on the table before attempting to yank his enlarged rabbit's foot from the yellow bucket. It still won't budge. Kyle once considered a rabbit's foot to be good luck, but in this cleaning closet of horrors, it's anything but.

Blood-curdling, high-pitched screams cause him to jump, as his eyes dart to the closet door, which is now open. Standing in the doorway is the cute mom wearing the casual dress who has covered her daughter's eyes, gaping at Kyle as her son yells, "The Easter Bunny isn't real! He isn't real!"

"I'm sorry!" It's all Kyle can manage. Repeating it louder, over the screams, doesn't do much.

*I've traumatized this woman's children! I've destroyed their innocence.* It's all he can think as his neighbor—Kyle doesn't know her name because they've never met—leads her kids into the closet and slams the door shut in an attempt not to traumatize anyone else's children, he supposes.

"Jacob, Chloe, it's okay," she says in a soothing voice, caressing her kids' shoulders. "This is the Easter Bunny's helper. Think about it. EB can't be everywhere at once, right?"

She wipes her little girl's tears as her son surveys Kyle with a skeptical expression. "You're the Bunny's helper?"

*Sure, why not?* Right now, Kyle would agree to anything that will calm the kids. "Yes, I am." He glances to their mom, who nods at him, as if encouraging Kyle to elaborate. "Your mom is right. The Bunny is busy painting eggs, making baskets, buying candy—"

"He buys candy? From where?" This little boy asks a lot of questions.

Kyle shrugs. "A candy store."

"What does he pay you?" the kid asks him.

"Not enough." It's the first thing that comes to mind. In truth, Kyle doesn't make a dime for this. He's a volunteer, donating his time so the community can save money as opposed to hiring a professional hare. He's also the community's Santa. Multitasking is his thing. Along with running his own business, he is the acting HOA board president, also on a volunteer basis, which means residents yell at him about the cost of their annual dues (in spite of the fact that the cost of dues hasn't risen once in Kyle's four years as president), letters they receive from the management company prohibiting decorations in their front yards and criticizing the height of their lawns, and all other concerns. Meanwhile, he sweats in a rodent costume on an eighty-plus-degree day for kids who don't belong to him. It's a thankless task. One he was reelected for, because no one was willing to run against him. There's only one poor sap in Castle Rock willing to torture himself, and he is currently being interrogated by a kid.

The boy scratches his head. "I want to drive a Ford F-250 when I grow up, have a Mercedes transit van, and a Tesla. My mom says I need to make a lot of money to pay for all of it."

Talk about a change of subject. "That's ambitious. You'll figure it out, though. You've got time." Kyle winks at him, hoping he's appeased the little boy's curiosity.

All he wanted was to cool off in a cleaning closet. Now Kyle is giving advice on a kid's future career path and vehicle ownership. This is way too much. Especially since it's cramped with the four of them in the tiny space, and the walls seem to be closing in. Or it could be Kyle's claustrophobia. Fun times.

"What's your name?" the boy asks Kyle, jerking him from his concerns regarding the confined quarters and heavy costume still covering the lower half of his body.

"My name?" That's an easy one. "Kyle Sanders. What's yours?"

"I'm Jacob Marsh, and this is my mom, Amelia Marsh. My sister, Chloe Marsh, is there," he points at the little girl, whose red cheeks are tear-streaked.

She nods. "Yeah, I'm Chloe Marsh, and this is my mom and brother."

"Got it." Chloe, Jacob, and Amelia. *Amelia Marsh.* A brunette with a killer smile, Amelia is luminescent, wearing minimal makeup and exuding a natural glow. Her dress is sleeveless and floor length, but when the breeze blows in the right direction, sandals that lace around her ankles attract Kyle's attention. She's left him breathless, or maybe it's the lack of oxygen in the cramped closet.

"Mom, I've still gotta pee." Jacob doesn't hold anything back.

Amelia steps forward. "We were looking for the restrooms. I'm sorry—um..."

"Kyle," he reminds her. "The men's room is one door down; the ladies' room is two doors down that way." Pointing to his left, Kyle stands stock still. With his annoying costume foot still stuck in the bucket, he isn't going anywhere.

"Right. Let's go, you two." Amelia opens the door a crack and ushers her kids out, before adding, "I'll be right back."

As she closes the door behind her, Kyle is left to stand in silence for what feels like forever. Just when he begins to think she's abandoned him, Amelia returns wearing a sweet grin. "Sorry, I had to make sure the bathrooms were single stalls, and that my children were safe behind locked doors. You look like you could use some help."

"Nope. Just chilling." Kyle places his hands casually on his hips, ignoring the fact that the rough interior fabric of his costume is causing him to itch. "This is how the Bunny's helper rolls."

Shaking her head, she laughs. "You're not rolling. You're trapped, from the looks of it. Here I thought rabbit's feet were good luck."

Kyle shifts his weight to his free foot. "I know! That's what I've been told."

"They lied to us. Unless…" Amelia smirks, tilting her head to the side. "The truth is that messing with a rabbit's foot *is* bad luck. I don't need any more of that. Perhaps I should pass?"

"No, please!" Kyle's plea is urgent. "It's not bad luck if the rabbit's foot is stuck in a snare and still attached to the rabbit. Besides, I didn't break a mirror."

"Duly noted." Amelia bends down, shoving a stray lock of hair from her face as she studies the bucket. "I was kidding, you know. I wouldn't leave you here, stuck like this."

"Good to know." Kyle exhales, watching her lips upturn into a wry grin. "You've got a sense of humor."

"So I've been told." Amelia reaches for the bucket and struggles to free Kyle's foot. "I've almost got it." She gives it another hard yank and Kyle's foot is free, though Amelia lands with a hard thump beside him.

Kyle offers his hand and helps her to her feet. Face-to-face, their eyes lock and he notices the gold flecks in her deep brown eyes. They're mesmerizing. He inhales, overcome by her intoxicating scent—a floral perfume with hints of musk. Those traits alone would make her attractive, but add the fact that Amelia just saved him from the ultimate humiliation, being forced to ask Carla for help…

Chills travel up his spine. He would never have lived that down.

"Thanks for coming to my rescue. Freeing me from a pail and convincing two traumatized children that I'm the Easter Bunny's helper takes skill."

She averts her gaze from Kyle's. "I did what anyone would have. Except a lot less gracefully."

"You're speaking to the guy who got his foot stuck in a mop bucket." Kyle raises his brow.

"I'm not one to judge." Her eyes shine with amusement and something more. *Is she flirting with me?* Before Kyle can fully ponder that thought, Amelia turns towards the closed door.

"In spite of your humility, I do owe you a debt of thanks." He offers her his hand, and she shakes it. Her skin is soft.

"Anything for the Easter Bunny's helper." She extracts her hand from his, then opens the door. "You okay?"

"I feel great." It's true. Kyle can't stop smiling. "Thanks again for the save."

"You're welcome. Now I've got to find my children before they do something not approved by Mom. Bye, Kyle." Amelia darts out the door, and Kyle peers around it in time to see her peek over her shoulder—long enough for him to note that her cheeks are bright pink as she studies his chest.

She just checked him out. One could argue that he's her man candy, and he wouldn't mind one bit, which is a first. Truth be told, Kyle checked her out, too—her ring finger, that is. She doesn't wear a wedding ring. Normally, Kyle would ask her out in a heartbeat. There's one problem, though—he doesn't date women who have children.

That one rule of his has never been so inconvenient, but it's a rule Kyle never breaks. At least not since its inception. Then again, he never thought he'd be wearing a bunny costume. Funny how life throws you a curveball.

A child cries outside the door and the jarring sound jolts Kyle back to his senses. *Don't go there.* Some rules aren't meant to be broken. For Kyle, this is a nonstarter—and for good reason.

# Chapter 3

As Amelia watches Jacob and Chloe play on the jungle gym, she sneaks a peek at the Bunny posing for yet another picture. Who would have thought that inside that cute costume would be Mr. Abs for Miles? She could have gotten seriously distracted by Kyle's abs, had her kids not been screaming about the Bunny not being real. That brought her back to earth big time. As did Chloe's tears. And the fact that Amelia has no room in her life for... *What are they? A six-pack? A twelve-pack? All of the above?*

Whatever they may be, Amelia has no time for abs, or men. Nope, she is too busy making sure Jacob and Chloe are adjusting to their new life, new home, new routine. It's kind of nice to recognize that her divorce didn't kill everything inside her and that she can at least appreciate an attractive male specimen. Not that she is looking to get involved with one again.

A split second is all it takes for Jacob's laughter to turn into an exasperated sigh. "I don't want to play that game, Chloe!" he snaps at his sister.

Amelia's shoulders tense. She's on alert, ready to referee an argument or watch them work it out by themselves. Which will it be this time? Anticipation mounts as she watches Chloe halt midrun.

"Come on. Please?" When Jacob won't budge, Chloe sighs. "You never want to play what I want to play."

The tears will follow. Amelia knows it, as she takes a step forward.

"Don't cry, Chloe. We'll play it later, okay?" Jacob hugs his sister.

*That's my boy.*

Nodding, Chloe wipes her eyes. "You promise?"

Jacob smiles his famous megawatt smile, and all is forgiven as they kneel in the mulch and begin stacking pieces of it like they're Legos. Amelia's heart swells with pride and with love. There are times, many times, that the kids can't work things out without her, but this time… Well, this is a huge Mom victory and she savors it, watching her children smile and laugh. Probability of mulch in their clothes: high. And it's worth it.

Wails from the clubhouse grab her attention, and Amelia turns to see that Kyle has finished taking pictures with all but one of the children. This last one is young and won't stop crying as the Bunny rocks him gently. His poor mom clutches her cell, pointing the camera at the scene with an angsty expression, while Carla and the man who was taking the pictures earlier are nowhere in sight.

Glancing at her children, who are enthralled with the playground mulch, Amelia instructs them, "Stay here and be careful, please. I'll be right back."

Walking under the shade of the covered patio, she approaches the new mom. "How are you doing?"

"Not well. How do parents get good pictures? I don't understand." She walks over to the Bunny and Kyle hands the little boy with hair the color of spun gold over to her.

Rubbing his back, his mom, who is also a beautiful blond, grins, though her lips quiver. The child continues to cry as tears well in her eyes. Amelia can recognize a sleep-deprived woman when she sees one. Heck, she's been one many times over. "May I try?"

She nods and hands Amelia the little boy. Rocking the child, Amelia's expression is animated. "Look at how handsome you are. I remember when mine were this small."

Her reason for holding the young boy isn't because Amelia has a knack of calming children, or that his mom did anything wrong. It's because the young woman needed a break, and Amelia can relate. It's something she's experienced herself, along with the guilt that comes with the feeling. Between the little guy's time with his mom and Amelia, he has stopped crying. Though Amelia wishes she could take credit, the reality is that the little boy is exhausted, and costumed characters are kind of creepy.

"Hey, little one. I know you're tired, and this bunny is large, right? Looming over you." She's attempting to rationalize with a baby. Familiar territory, to be sure. "It's okay, though. Why doesn't your mom pose with you? I do that with my kids all the time."

The child watches Amelia intently, and so does Kyle—the Bunny's wide eyes ever present. The costumed head tilts to the side, like Kyle's caught up in Amelia's conversation with a child who is too young to hold up his end of the chat.

Turning to the baby's mom, Amelia suggests, "Why don't we switch. I'll take the cell and you can take this little guy. Maybe stand behind the Bunny. Holding him—the baby, not the Bunny. Obviously."

The young woman kisses her little boy on his forehead, then inhales a deep breath.

"We've all been there, you know," Amelia assures her, certain this is her first child. She recognizes how overwhelming it can be. "They don't warn us about the tantrums, or fear of Santa, the Easter Bunny, and elves. It should be in the handbook."

Amelia's last comment makes the blond laugh. The baby notices the shift in his mom's emotions and smiles.

"There you go. We've got a happy little guy."

Sighing with relief, the young woman whispers, "Thank you."

Tentatively, she approaches Kyle, who remains stock-still. Everyone is holding their collective breath, trying not to upset the little one.

"Ready?" Amelia whispers in an effort not to break the peaceful spell that's been cast.

Both the Bunny and the mom nod, then Amelia takes somewhere between ten and twenty photos. "There are some great shots in here."

The mom smiles, reclaiming her cell. "Thank you so much. Um, what's your name?"

"Amelia."

"I'm Sophie and this is Stephen. Hopefully, we'll see you again."

Amelia nods. "I'm on Royal Court. I have a tacky troll in my yard. Apparently, you can't miss it. Stop by sometime."

"We live a block away and walk down that street all the time. I haven't noticed a troll, but I'll look out for it. I love gnomes." Sophie is a smart woman with great taste, and Amelia likes her already. It's nice to have an ally in the neighborhood.

Though she has local friends, each of them live in different subdivisions. Amelia wonders if Sophie has a support system.

"What's your cell number?" She programs it into her iPhone and texts her name to Sophie's cell. "If you ever need anything, call me or text. I work from home, so I'm available."

Sophie smiles. "Thank you so much. Take care."

Glancing at Jacob and Chloe, Amelia notes that they've moved on to that Pokémon game with lots of hand gestures—the same game Jacob refused to play earlier. Chloe has been obsessed with this game, and Jacob humors her most of the time, or at the very least, more often than not. Amelia studies them, in awe of how well they seem to be handling all of the changes in their lives. As she knows from experience, looks can be deceiving.

"You're doing something right." Kyle's muffled voice is low beneath the costume, his presence all-consuming as he stands beside her. "They're great little people."

"Thanks." Though Amelia would like to think that it was his compliment which sent a shock wave through her system, she knows better. Still, she resists, pushing such thoughts aside. She shouldn't feel anything for Kyle, let alone attraction, because rebound relationships never work, and Amelia's not your casual sex kind of girl. She never has been. That's why she's only ever been with one man—her ex-husband. They were college sweethearts, marrying after graduation. Sex was something Amelia never thought she was very good at, and that was before he cheated.

Sure, Kyle's hot, but that isn't what currently has Amelia smiling. It's his kindness, the gentleness in his husky tone. And the fact that Kyle sees it, too…the genuinely good souls that are Amelia's children. It's validation, even coming from a stranger in a bunny costume.

Friend-zoning Kyle, Amelia claps him on his shoulder, noting the fur is matted. "Well done, Bunny."

Managing a thumbs-up, he waves and disappears, presumably into his closet. Where he'll remove his costume, and his abs will be on full display once more. Abs that Amelia must never think of again.

"Can you believe what her children wore? I mean she's single, but still. Can't she go to a thrift store and buy them proper Easter attire?" The voice is shrill, all too familiar, and middle-aged mean girl. As Amelia's learned, mean girls have nothing on mean women. Unsurprised, she recognizes that voice as Carla's. "What can we expect from someone who puts that monstrosity in front of her home? No taste whatsoever."

Following the soft sound of smothered laughter, she finds Carla taking a drag on her cigarette at the far side of the clubhouse.

"Carla, I'm glad I found you. I wanted to thank you so much for welcoming me to the neighborhood today." Amelia's voice is calm. She doesn't let people know they're getting to her. It would grant them power over her, and Amelia refuses to do so. Instead, she's well versed in her ability to shower them with kindness, knowing how it bothers them. She learned that art during her divorce, and it unnerved her ex-husband to no end.

Silence hangs heavy as Amelia slides her cell from her pocket and unlocks the screen with her thumb. *Camera app... Open.* "Let's take a selfie to remember this day. Shall we?"

On the spot, Carla nods.

"Smile, ladies." Amelia takes their photo—her, Carla, and Carla's friend, who Amelia doesn't know and doesn't care to know.

As she heads towards the playground, Amelia glances at the picture she just snapped. Carla has a cigarette in hand, standing beneath a sign that states in bold letters NO SMOKING. She must be breaking a bylaw, if not an actual law. Amelia plans to tuck that in her arsenal.

"Oh, Amelia!" Carla calls, causing Amelia to glance over her shoulder. "There's a community garage sale tomorrow. Benefitting a Houston animal shelter. I hope you'll donate." Carla's tone is sugary sweet.

"Absolutely. Count me in." Amelia plasters a smile on her face, all the while clutching her cell in a tight grasp, before marching past Kyle, who's now in a T-shirt and jeans as she gathers Jacob and Chloe.

"Are you okay?" Kyle asks, walking beside her as she unlocks the doors to her SUV with a remote key fob.

Waiting until her kids are inside and out of hearing range, Amelia mutters, "No, but I will be."

She hops into the driver's seat, turning her key in the ignition and blasting the air. Good thing she parked in the shade. Lowering the windows, Amelia allows the engine to idle as Jacob and Chloe snap their seatbelts in place.

Kyle stares at her, his eyes wide. "What happened?"

*Carla is a witch.* Amelia bites her tongue, tapping her fingernail against the steering wheel.

Women like Carla don't hurt her...not unless they drag Amelia's children into it. That's the mistake Carla made, and it's a big one. Does she tell a guy she met in a cleaning closet about it? Of course not. Amelia knows nothing about him, except that he is a stranger who wears a bunny costume on a Saturday afternoon and compliments her children.

"It's nothing that you need to worry about." She manages a terse smile, but his narrowed gaze proclaims he isn't fooled.

That much is clear when he places his palm on her shoulder. "What did Carla do?"

Amelia stares at his hand, flattened against her flesh. No man has touched her, not since Daniel. Kyle's hand is warm and strong. Their physical connection causes Amelia's pulse to race.

Kyle jerks his hand away. "Sorry. I shouldn't have—wh—um—what did Carla do this time? She annoys most of us residents, you know."

"You live here?" Mr. Abs for Miles isn't a stranger, per se. He's a member of Amelia's new community. "Please tell me Carla doesn't live in Castle Rock, too."

"No, she doesn't. Why?" His dark brows furrow. Like he senses that Amelia is about to unleash psychological warfare upon Carla and her bylaws. Is Amelia overreacting? Probably. So, she inhales and exhales, first one breath, then two, followed by a third.

"Uh-oh. She's going Zen," Jacob announces from the backseat. Loud enough for Kyle to hear.

He turns to Jacob. "What does that mean?"

"Someone messed with the wrong mom," Chloe and Jacob say in unison. Amelia's children know her too well.

"Dad always said she should have been a lawyer." Jacob meets his mom's eyes in the rearview mirror.

"Yeah. He never won an argument. Mom is magical," Chloe adds.

Kyle scratches his chin, his smooth jaw tense. "Magical?"

"Logical," Amelia explains, clutching the steering wheel at the memory. "My ex used to say I am logical to a fault."

Averting her eyes from Kyle with that embarrassing admission, Amelia views her children through the rearview mirror. "Seatbelts on?"

"Yes, Mom!" the kids answer in unison.

She knew the answer before asking, but used the question to distract Kyle, her new neighbor, from the words her ex-husband used repeatedly to intentionally hurt her. As if being logical and presenting a clear argument is an insult. Only Daniel would see it that way. Then again, Daniel had a warped sense of fidelity, honesty, and family.

"Thanks for helping the Bunny, Kyle." Placing her palm on the gear shift, Amelia waits for Kyle to back away before safely reversing.

*And thanks so much, Carla, for putting things in perspective.*

New home, new neighborhood, the same catty gossip. If only Amelia had listened when her husband was the talk of their old community. She wouldn't have been blindsided by his betrayal. But there's no going back.

Live and learn, that's her motto. What did Amelia learn? That Daniel did get something right: she *is* logical. It's time she researches some bylaws. But first, a respectful revolt involving some garden gnomes is in order.

Operation Game of Gnomes has begun.

# Chapter 4

"Mom! Where do you want this one?" Jacob holds a medium-sized gnome in the air.

Amelia halts, carrying a larger one. They were in stock and half price. *Take that, Carla!* "Your choice, dude. Go for it."

Jacob places his gnome beside the tree in the middle of their front yard.

"Come here, you two. This is the last one…" Jacob and Chloe run to Amelia, and she gives her large gnome a Vanna White flourish with her hands. "Where do we put this guy?"

The children ponder her question, searching different parts of the front yard.

"Bunny man!" Chloe shouts, pointing to the street.

Amelia turns and sure enough, Kyle has parked his truck in front of her house. He's wearing the same T-shirt and jeans as when Amelia drove away from him earlier.

"Hi!" Jacob and Chloe say in unison before Jacob adds, "You drive a Ford F-250. What is your job? Wait…" Jacob reads the decal printed on the passenger door. "*Sanders Construction.* Is that your company?"

"Yeah, it is." Kyle smiles at him. "Maybe you can own one when you grow up."

"Do you have a Mercedes transit van?"

Kyle shakes his head. "Afraid not."

"Huh. I really want that Mercedes van."

"The Tesla, too," Chloe adds.

Placing her free hand on Jacob's shoulder, Amelia adds in a teasing tone, "Jacob is committed to his choice of vehicles. If he were to give you the complete list, it would tally at about two dozen and it grows almost daily."

"Ambitious." Kyle opens his passenger door and hands each of the kids a baseball cap with his company logo on them, before returning his attention to Amelia. "Can I talk to you for a second?"

"Sure. Why don't you two decide where we should put this last guy," Amelia suggests, realizing she's still holding a large ceramic gnome. Between the way she behaved before pulling away, and now the gnomes, Amelia is certain that she must appear to be a hot mess.

"I'm sorry about what Carla said." Kyle cuts to the chase, meeting her eyes. His are the color of moss and are surrounded by subtle lines when he frowns.

"You have nothing to be sorry for." Amelia leans in, so her children can't hear. "Carla insinuating that I'm poor, trashy, and can't dress my children properly had nothing to do with you."

Kyle stiffens. "Wait—what?"

"Oh. She didn't tell you about that?" *Oopsie.* "I thought that was what you were referring to."

"No. I was talking about Carla telling you to remove your gnome." He shuffles his feet, shoving his hands in the pockets of his jeans. "She actually said all of that other stuff?"

"Yep. So, why are you here, Kyle Sanders of Sanders Construction? My instinct tells me this isn't your average neighbor saying 'hi' visit." Her tone is teasing, but anxiety has coiled within Amelia's abdomen.

"Um. I don't know how to say this…" He studies the ground.

Her anxiety has now twisted into a tight knot. This can't be good. Funny how she immediately goes to the worst-case scenario. Once upon a time, Amelia used to be a glass-half-full person. Not anymore. Not since…

No matter how hard she tries, Amelia can't pinpoint precisely when it began. Perhaps it was the moment she discovered Daniel's infidelity, his secret life.

Hugging the gnome as if shielding herself from the onslaught of whatever Kyle's about to say, she waits with bated breath for him to say something, anything.

"I see your gnomes have multiplied. Is this some kind of convention?" His smile is tentative. Like he's not sure how she'll respond.

Amelia laughs. "'Gnome convention.' That's a good one. No, it's not a convention. Though I don't know what they do when we're sleeping. Isn't there some sort of folklore about gnomes coming to life at night, or was that in one of the Harry Potter books?"

Kyle shrugs, his smile widening as he waits for a real answer.

"Actually, I'm making a statement to our HOA, or is it our management company? One or both deemed a little gnome my kids gave me for Mother's Day as an eyesore. So, I'm protesting their bylaws."

"By breaking those bylaws in abundance. You think that's wise?" His eyes hold hers, and there's an intensity burning within his gaze. He's not judging Amelia, but there's something behind his question... Concern, maybe.

Glancing at her children, who are sitting in the grass out of earshot, Amelia whispers, "Look, I understand the HOA has a job to do, same with the management company. Here's the thing: my kids lost their dad, their home, and the feeling of security they once felt when my ex-husband walked out on us. That so-called trashy, tacky gnome was outside our home—the home my ex-husband now shares with his pregnant mistress. When we moved here, my children asked me for one thing—that I put that gnome in our new front yard. How can I tell them that the gnome they painted for me last Mother's Day isn't worthy of being in our front yard, according to some bylaws? Or that Carla thinks it's ugly? Or that I was in such a haze after their father's betrayal, during the divorce and our move, that I didn't read the fine print about a gnome hiding in the bushes being banned before I made that promise to them."

"Oh," Kyle mutters, exhaling an exaggerated breath. "You can't. Well, you could, but you'd break their hearts."

"Right? That's why I'm protesting." Placing her free hand on her hip, Amelia adds, "This neighborhood is teeming with Easter décor. Half the homes on this block have some form of the Easter Bunny in their front yards. How is my gnome different?"

"Theirs is for the holiday only. They are supposed to take their décor down after Easter, just like Christmas. It isn't permanent."

"Okay. Your clarification is noted and appreciated." She can use that to buy herself some time.

Kyle shoves his dark hair out of his eyes. It's black, and the contrast between it and the green of his eyes is striking. Enough to cause Amelia to stare, then look away, attempting not to stare. This guy throws her off-kilter, and she doesn't have the time or inclination to be off-kilter. Not for him, or anyone.

"You're going to think I'm the biggest jerk when I say this, but you can't keep the gnomes."

She meets his eyes again, her confusion heightening, simmering just below the surface. "Why not? If I do my research and make a compelling argument—"

"None of it will make a difference. The developer created the bylaws, and we're beholden to them. I can't make an exception for you, no matter how much I want to."

*I can't make an exception for you…*

There it is. The *I*. The exact thing her subconscious has been dreading since this conversation began.

"*You* can't?" Gripping the gnome she's holding with all her might in an attempt to center herself, Amelia's knuckles begin to ache. "You're one of them?"

*One of them*—that came out wrong, and much more accusatory than she meant for it to sound. "I mean, you're a part of the HOA?"

"Yeah, I am. The HOA board president, to be honest. I'm not proud of it right now, and I wish I could do something to help you." A crease etches deep within Kyle's forehead as his lips purse in a frown. "Believe it or not, that's why I accepted the board position. If it were up to me, I'd change the bylaws and let you have your gnome, but I can't. Not until the builders sell all of their inventory and we're free of them and the developer."

He studies Amelia's house, concentrating on the gutters. One of them is clogged. The fact that he noticed reminds her that she needs to hire someone. Great, in addition to upholding the HOA's gnome ban, Mr. HOA President is noting everything wrong with her property. She'll probably get another letter. Maybe two.

"I'm sorry," Kyle's baritone is brimming with sincerity. At least Amelia thinks it is. She's been wrong before, though. Hence her divorce.

"Don't be. Rules are rules. This is my fault. I made a promise to my children that I can't keep, unless I fight the rules. And though it may be a losing battle, I won't give up without a fight. I can't." That's the crux of it. Why Gnomegate will continue. Because she owes it to her children to at least try to keep her word. "So, these will be Easter gnomes by tomorrow. No violations here."

Kyle snaps his head from the line of sight of her gutter to Amelia. "I didn't mean—"

"Nope. You said it. You gave me the idea." Amelia raises her finger in the air. "No backsies."

Rubbing his jaw, which has become tense, Kyle mutters, "You're going to be a pain in my—"

"Swear jar." She interrupts. "We're kid-friendly here. You curse and it costs you money."

Expelling an exaggerated sigh, Kyle purses his lips before adding, "Backside. You're going to be a pain in my backside, aren't you?"

Amelia nods. "I expect that I'll be the largest pain in your...backside." She was about to curse, which would mean putting a quarter in the kids' swear jar.

If she had a dollar for every time she added to that darn jar, she'd be rich. Some would ask how that's possible when she doesn't curse in front of Jacob and Chloe. Well, Amelia goes by the honor system. Even when her children aren't around, if Amelia curses, the quarter goes in. That's typically how the jar fills.

As Kyle opens his mouth to speak, she waits for a retort. One that never comes.

"Would it help if I admit that I derive no pleasure from being a pain in your you know what?" she asks, half joking.

"No." One word. From Kyle, who is currently wearing a determined frown.

She softly says, "Sorry," to him, then proceeds to her front porch, where she places the large gnome directly in sight of the street.

Remembering what Carla said about the quarterly HOA meetings, Amelia breaks the heady silence between them. "Carla mentioned that I can take the matter up at our next HOA meeting. Expect me to be sitting in the front row, prepared to argue my case."

"You just missed one, I'm afraid. They're quarterly."

"She mentioned that. It gives me time to prepare." And prepare she will.

Kyle stifles a laugh. "Prepare? Holy..." His eyes meet hers. "Swear jar. Yeah. Never mind."

Based upon Kyle's tightly clenched jaw and the vein that is visible in his neck, this is torture for him. Amelia would find it cute if her gnome situation wasn't so serious.

"I'd expect nothing less." His words are precise, slow, and chosen with care. This guy is in control of his temper.

"Less than what, Mr. Bunny Helper?" Chloe asks, wearing the cap Kyle gave her as she and Jacob run towards them.

Chloe is faster than Jacob. It's the tomboy in her, combined with the younger sister who must compete with her older brother. It motivates her.

Reaching for the brim, Kyle adjusts her cap. "Let's just say that I'm sorry that I can't be more help with something. It's nothing for you to worry about, though."

"As long as you try hard, that's what matters." Jacob adjusts his cap to match his sister's. "Mom taught us that."

Exhaling, Kyle appears to be at a loss.

"Go inside, kiddos. Mr. Bunny has a lot to do, and you need to wash your hands, please." Amelia waits for the front door to close behind them. "So, what's next on your to-do list? Steal candy from kids? Issue tickets like the gnome police?"

Amelia's isn't using her usual snark, which is her defense mechanism. Instead, her tone is playful, since Kyle hasn't been a jerk in the least. Instead, he's gone out of his way to be nice when he didn't have to be, and she's attempting to cheer him up.

"Nope. I'm heading to the bookstore." He studies the gnome that started this mess, the one her children made for her. "There's got to be a book on dealing with a pain of a neighbor with an unhealthy obsession with trolls."

Gasping, Amelia chides him. "They're gnomes. All kidding aside, though, what I admitted to you about my divorce isn't common knowledge, and it's not easy for me to discuss. Had I known that you were on the HOA board…" She wouldn't have told him. There's no need to complete her sentence. He understands.

Why did she tell him? Because in addition to being the Bunny's helper, this guy seems genuine. Like someone she'd be friends with. Or more…if Amelia was ready, which she's not. Or maybe she could be, with the right guy. Regardless, Kyle isn't the right guy. Instead, he's on the opposite side of Gnomegate.

"My protest isn't personal." It's her olive branch, though not entirely accurate. Amelia confided in him, which she doesn't do much with people outside her inner circle of best friends. That's a lesson she learned the hard way. Even before Daniel. It was easy today with Kyle. That in and of itself should have been warning enough.

After clearing his throat and commanding Amelia's attention, Kyle shoots her a wide grin. "Just for the record, stealing candy and issuing gnome tickets are Carla's hobbies. Not mine."

"Well played, Mr. Bunny." Amelia pauses. This guy is charming. He's also her adversary. She refuses to forget that. "It's a shame we're on different sides of Gnomegate."

"Gnome what?" Kyle laughs.

Amelia shrugs. "It was between that and Game of Gnomes."

"You are a handful. Heaven help me." Running his hands through his hair, Kyle expels a deep breath.

"At least we share a sense of humor." Her tone changes, from joking to dripping with remorse, though he probably won't notice, so she adds, "I do regret that we're on opposite sides of this, but I'm not giving up without a fight."

"That's what I was afraid of." He turns, shouting over his shoulder as he walks to his truck, "I'll see you around, then. In the front row. Next quarter."

"Bye, Kyle." With a wave, Amelia enters her house and closes the heavy oak and glass door with a loud thud. Through one of the glass panels, Amelia watches as Kyle sits in his truck. He drives forward a foot or so, then his brake lights illuminate for a brief moment, as if he might park and return. He doesn't, though. Instead, he drives away.

Surveying the entrance to her new home with its polished cherry hardwood floors, her home office to the left accentuated with interior French doors, like most of the houses built by this builder, and a long corridor that leads to her kitchen, living room, and the rest of the house, Amelia thinks of the extended family of gnomes sitting in their front yard. When she considered taking on the HOA, she never thought that would mean taking on the Easter Bunny's helper. And Amelia never considered that she would regret that decision. For one brief moment, she does…until her children run down the hall.

"The front yard is so cool!" Jacob announces as Amelia sits on the hardwood floor. He hugs her, while Chloe climbs on top of her lap, joining in on their hug.

"I'm the bread," Chloe says of what Jacob calls their sandwich hugs.

"And I'm the tuna," Jacob adds.

Amelia giggles. "What does that make me?"

"The lettuce," Jacob replies, with a tone that conveys it's obvious.

Chloe nods. "Yeah, you're the lettuce."

Amelia squeezes them tighter. "Did you have a good day?"

"Yeah!" both children shout in unison.

"Decorating with the gnomes was awesome. Can we get some more?" Jacob asks.

Rubbing their backs, Amelia kisses her daughter, then son on the tops of their heads. "I think we've made our point with the ones we have."

"What point?" Jacob's curiosity leaves his ability to question anything and everything second only to his list of the different cars and trucks he wants.

"We're home." Two words. A sentiment Amelia doesn't fully feel yet, but she will. Once she's able to keep her promise to them about their gnome or, at the very least, try her hardest to do so.

After squeezing her kids in a tight hug one more time, she texts her best friends. It's a group text.

SOS. Need to whine. Pizza for all.

With that call to arms, her cell begins to vibrate. Amelia's group of friends have her back.

Oh, bring some Easter ribbon. Please.

One of her friends types back in record time. On it!

"I just thought of something." Jacob looks at his mom, then his sister. "We have a gnome home."

Chloe erupts with laughter. "A gnome home. That's funny!"

They both smile and Amelia tickles them, causing them to shriek with laughter until it fills the open floor plan.

Yes, they are home. This is just the beginning of their new chapter.

# Chapter 5

No sooner does Amelia send her SOS than her friends come running—Bridget Reilly and Lily Young. Between them, they make an eclectic group if ever there was one. Bridget has the no-nonsense personality, and in addition to being a best friend, happens to be the best teacher Amelia knows. Lily is a chic real estate agent with a love for DIY crafts, and has brought enough Easter accessories to dress the front yard gnome community in style.

The three of them are the friends who remained in Texas after high school, and though they once scattered throughout the Lone Star State for college, all three wound up back in Houston with children who are close enough in age to enjoy playdates and be each other's best friends. Just like their moms.

"Pizza is on the table!" Amelia announces, as all of their children run to the dining room table, where the paper plates and napkins are already laid out for them. The table is large and takes up most of the space next to the kitchen. Decorated in a country chic motif, the oak and whitewashed wood table has both chairs and benches to accommodate Amelia, Jacob, Chloe, and their extended family—that same circle of friends who rushed to chat when she needs it the most. It seats children and adults, though this evening the children will be dining on pizza at the table while the moms talk in Amelia's garage. After all, Amelia has a community yard sale to prepare for that Carla just told her about, and boxes stacked in her garage which must hold some donation/community yard sale items in them.

They serve the children their pizza. There are seven ravenous kids between the three of them, and the talking ceases once the kids start taking large bites of the warm, cheesy slices.

"Love you," Lily says to her two girls as she grabs a box and heads into Amelia's garage.

Bridget follows close behind, carrying the two bottles of wine she brought with her. One red, one white. Even though Amelia has plenty on hand for any given SOS text, Bridget still brings her own. It's one of the rules she lives by—*you must bring a gift, even if you're going to a friend's house to hear her whine.*

As Amelia places the paper plates and napkins on one of two end tables that she hasn't decided if she's selling yet, she jokes, "As usual, I'm keeping it classy, ladies."

Bridget laughs, plopping the bottles of wine beside the red Solo cups and plates. "We are nothing if not classy."

Lily opens the box, the aroma of a supreme pizza causing Amelia's mouth to water. "Umberto's. There is nothing better than New York pizza."

"God bless them for moving from Manhattan." Amelia grabs a slice, and dishes the others out to her friends.

"And for delivering." Amelia hands the electric wine opener to Bridget, who pops the cork.

"This was the best Christmas present I ever received. I use mine on a regular basis," Bridget says.

"Don't we all?" Amelia shoots Bridget a wry grin. She gave the same high-tech bottle opener to each of them when she moved back, as a better-late-than-never Christmas gift, and bought one for herself.

"True that." Setting down the bottle of red, Bridget repeats the process with the white as Lily pours wine into their Solo cups.

Holding her cup in the air, Bridget proposes a toast. "To us. The classiest, smartest, sassiest single moms I know." Her toast is always the same. It's Bridget's mantra.

They all toast with their plastic cups, and Amelia clucks her tongue as a fake clink.

"So, what's this SOS about?" Lily takes a large bite out of her slice of pizza. "Not that I mind. My girls have complained at least three times today that they wish they had a brother. Being around their friends might keep their complaints to a minimum tomorrow."

"Poor girls. You could always adopt a puppy," Amelia suggests as she reaches for a box marked MASTER BEDROOM and peels the cardboard to reveal purses.

"Don't even…" Lily holds up a finger to silence Amelia, as if she doesn't need any more noise in her life, especially when it comes to a canine. "Now, what's with the SOS, Amelia?"

Bridget grabs a fuchsia tote from the box that Amelia's riffling through, slinging it over her shoulder. "I like this. Can I have it?"

"Sure." Amelia nods. "Though the money raised during this community yard sale will benefit a Houston animal shelter."

"Way to guilt me." Bridget reaches into her own purse, and hands Amelia a fifty-dollar bill.

Placing the cash in the pocket of her shorts, Amelia announces, "Sold to the gorgeous redhead."

Bridget winks at her. "So. About the SOS… It's time for you to spill."

Amelia inhales another deep breath, savoring the aroma of their delicious Italian food, before recapping the events of her day. Gasps fill the garage when she reaches the part where Carla called her gnome names.

"She did not!" Lily whispers, her eyes wide and jaw clenched.

"Her exact words were 'one person's trash is another's treasure.'" Amelia pauses for a gulp of wine. "That Carla woman makes me want to curse. Big time."

"What a witch." Lily's voice is raspy, spoken just loud enough for them to hear, and low enough for their children to be oblivious to the non-curse word. Even though they are in Amelia's garage with the interior door closed and the exterior garage door wide open.

"The kids can't hear us, Lily," Amelia announces as she sorts her purses into two boxes, one marked SELL and the other marked KEEP.

"God, I hate HOAs. They're like PTAs, but worse. Because it's your home and you can't escape," Bridget mutters, reaching into another box, and tugging on a negligee that Amelia has yet to unpack. Yep, she's found Amelia's intimates box, which Amelia has had no need for. Even before her divorce. That's why all of the tags are on. They were gifts from Daniel. For being an insensitive jerk. Who knew his mistress worked at Victoria's Secret? It had been news to Amelia.

"I am respectfully dissenting," Amelia answers with a wink to Lily. "And your Easter décor will be my salvation for at least a couple of weeks. Until I think of something else." Amelia has a lot of work to do. She'll need to stay one step ahead of Carla, who will be out to get her.

"So that explains the group of gnomes outside. I wondered." Lily plops her half-eaten pizza slice on the plate. "Do you want me to decorate the gnomes? Please."

She doesn't have to ask Amelia twice. "Go for it. Thanks!"

After Lily marches onto the well-lit front yard and begins decorating, Bridget smiles in encouragement, brushing her long bangs from her eyes. "Good for you. I would protest, too."

"Well, the die was cast when Carla trash-talked me to a friend of hers—"

"Whoa. Wait!" Bridget raises her hands in the air, a black lace baby-doll nightie swinging from her fingers. "She said what?"

Amelia's rage has morphed into indignation. "I'm not going to repeat it. What I will say is that I hate neighborhood gossip, and got a taste of it today, though technically she isn't a neighbor. It took everything in me not to engage. Between her cattiness and the fact that I made a promise to Jacob and Chloe, I have to protest, right? It's my own fault, though. I signed those bylaws at closing. As for my defense, I needed a home, and I was concentrating more on the kids' transition and the fact that their father abandoned them."

"I'm sorry, Amelia." Bridget's empathy knows no bounds. She shoves her hair into a bun atop her head, then dives into a china box.

"This entire box can go in the SELL corner. It's my wedding china. I will be glad to see that go."

Grabbing a brand-new-with-tags nightie dangling from Bridget's forefinger, Amelia tosses it into the SELL pile. It was another gift from her ex. Never worn. Tags still on. When their marriage had already deteriorated.

"This whole box is unused and has tags on every item. All of these are going." After dumping the entire contents in the SELL box, Amelia pauses. "It is appropriate to sell Victoria's Secret lingerie at a yard sale, right? Or should I donate them to Goodwill? Do I really want my neighbors seeing my unworn lingerie?"

"The tags are still on them. Besides, sex sells, and it's for a good cause. Think of the shelter dogs and cats." Bridget reaches for another box.

There aren't many boxes left since Amelia already donated most of the things that reminded her of Daniel to Goodwill before she moved. She's still not sure why she kept the intimates...

"So, you're going to at least try to fight the bylaws and show your kids that you did your best to keep your word." Bridget rifles through the last box, which isn't labeled.

"That's my plan. I thought taking on the HOA was best until Mr. Abs for Miles stopped by, gave baseball caps to my kids, and admitted that he is president of the HOA. Then he apologized because he couldn't help me and seemed so sincere that I've felt guilty ever since."

"Wait!" This time Bridget raises her forefinger. "How do you know this man, let alone the fact that he has abs for miles?"

Slack-jawed, Bridget stares at Amelia. "Oh my! You saw his abs."

Amelia shushes her.

"Explain yourself. Now," Bridget demands in a no-nonsense whisper.

"Kyle—that's his name—Kyle was in the bunny costume. Jacob opened the wrong door, and there was Kyle, wearing only the bottom half of his costume." Heat rushes to Amelia's cheeks. "I couldn't miss his abs. They were on full display, tanned and glistening with sweat. He was hot—it was hot—um, he was hot."

"How about his face?" Lily asks, placing an Easter egg ribbon around the neck of the gnome next to the driveway.

"Forget his face. Go back to his abs." Bridget's snark rivals Amelia's. "Tell us more."

As Amelia recalls precisely what happened, she comes to realize it was a fiasco. "At least they still believe in the Easter Bunny."

None of them are prepared for their children to lose that precious bit of innocence. Somewhere along the way, their children stopped calling them "Mommy" and moved on to "Mom." Amelia and her friends aren't prepared to lose the Easter Bunny, Santa, or the Tooth Fairy. Not yet.

"Well played." Bridget lifts her red Solo cup in the air as if to applaud her friend, then takes a sip of wine.

"Later, after the kids and I bought the gnome family, Kyle stopped by. Baseball caps were given, apologies were made, and Mr. HOA President is my new nemesis in Gnomegate. Actually, I'm not sure what to call it, nor can I pinpoint why I feel so conflicted. I mean, I am guilty of breaking the bylaws. I know that. And he did tell me I can't keep my gnome in the front yard, but he was nice about it even though I was frustrating him to no end."

Lily reaches for Amelia's arm. "You feel guilty because he was kind."

Leave it to Lily to be right. "Kyle was too nice to me, and remorseful. At least I think he was. I doubt myself now, you know? Ever since Daniel cheated."

*Daniel.* "Never did I fool myself into thinking we had a great marriage, but I didn't even consider that he'd be unfaithful. Me…a smart and strong woman, missed all the warning signs, and there were a lot of them. He couldn't have been more obvious if he had hung a neon 'I'm Cheating' sign in his man cave."

"Daniel is an idiot, and I say that with a heavy heart. You, Jacob, and Chloe deserve better." Bridget removes more thongs from her box. "What about the Bunny's helper?"

"Besides the fact that we're in the middle of a War of Gnomes, Kyle wasn't the least bit confrontational when he stopped by. He actually seemed concerned—and exasperated with me, though he tried hard not to show it." Amelia stands near the opening to her garage door, the warm breeze a welcome distraction from her current train of thought. "That's not possible, is it? For a man to be heartfelt, after having met me the same day. I mean, I knew Daniel for years and he was still a jack—dang it."

"He was a Jack Russell terrier?" Bridget prompts.

"Nice save. Thanks." The swear jar won't get a quarter out of Amelia tonight, with a little help from her friend. "What's wrong with me? I used to believe in good guys. I used to believe in love. I used to believe in working hard to make relationships work."

Scanning her friends' faces, Amelia is met with the same expression: sad eyes and grimaces.

"My children asked for one thing, and I made a promise to them. I may not win the fight, but at the very least, I've got to try." Her heart feels heavy, her stomach churning, her own face crestfallen. "I just don't like fighting Kyle on this."

Bridget shrugs. "It doesn't have to be contentious. Let's face it, he doesn't make the rules. He simply helps to enforce them or hires that Carla person to enforce them."

"Kyle said something similar, but it doesn't make me feel any better." Amelia catches a thong that Bridget tosses at her with a tag still on.

"That isn't going in the SELL box," Bridget announces, tossing a second at Amelia followed by a third. "Neither are these. You may have need for them yet."

Rolling her eyes, Amelia stretches one of the thongs out in front of her. "Real mature—oh, holy s—sweet potato."

Jogging on her sidewalk, in full view, is Mr. Bunny himself, Kyle. Shirtless, he stops, tugs out one of his earbuds, and says, "Hi."

"Holy Chris Hemsworth, you weren't kidding about his abs," Bridget whispers, waving to Kyle. "Hi."

His eyes rove from Amelia to the thong she's holding. Which Amelia quickly wads in a ball with the others and tosses into the SELL box.

"We're preparing for tomorrow's community yard sale," she says, as if it's no biggie that her neighbor just caught her with a lacy thong in the middle of her garage.

Kyle shoots Amelia a puzzled look. "The community yard sale is the weekend after Easter."

"Carla told me—oh!" *That witch tricked me!* "Well, I'm getting a head start. With my friends."

She motions to the ladies who are now crowded in a small group beside Amelia, staring at Kyle with rapt attention. "Kyle, these are my friends, Bridget and Lily. Gals, this is the HOA president."

Bridget's hand has stilled in the air, while Lily stares at the man's abs. Both remain silent.

"Say 'hi,'" Amelia mutters through a forced smile.

"Hi!" Her friends awaken from their trances, and manage a combination of "How are you? Nice to meet you. Great jogging weather." In unison.

"Nice to meet you, too. Have a good night." Kyle sticks his earbud back in his ear and jogs down the street.

"If that wasn't the most awkward encounter ever, I don't know what was," Amelia mutters.

Bridget grabs her arms. "Okay. His abs are worth the price of admission."

Amelia studies her KEEP and SELL piles. "I need another box for donations, because all of those intimates are being donated to Goodwill. There's no way I'm ever wearing a gift from Daniel, and no other neighbors will ever see a thong of mine."

"On it!" Lily begins moving the items into an empty box.

Clenching her hands into tight fists, Amelia's anger reaches a crescendo. "Carla tricked me! Had I not seen Kyle tonight, I would have set up for a yard sale weeks too early and looked like a fool. That woman is trying to humiliate me. That is so not cool."

"You're right." Bridget nods. "It's cruel."

*This is my neighborhood now.* Amelia knows it. This is her home, and her children deserve a place free of drama, and of petty pranks. They deserve a community, one that comes together, not undermines each other. Especially when Carla isn't even a resident. Who is she to play a prank like this?

Surveying the distressed wood that comprises her end tables, Amelia is reminded why she decorated her living room in shabby chic to begin with—so her kids could be kids. She traces a scratch on the top, one that Jacob made with a Matchbox car, and realizes that the imperfection is what makes it perfect. Because of her children.

"I'm not just doing battle with the HOA anymore. No, I'm taking down Carla. And I'm keeping my end tables," she says with a flourish of her hands. "This is war. Suburbs style."

Bridget pats Amelia on her back. "You've got this."

"Darn right," Lily adds, standing beside them. "Plus, we've got you."

"We love you." Bridget smiles. "Now where's the candy? The kids must have collected candy during the Easter egg hunt, right?"

"Oooh, let's raid their stash!" Lily is all for it.

Amelia's head darts from Lily to Bridget, then back to Lily. "We can't do that. Can we?"

"No!" They all laugh in unison.

"Can we crash the Bunny next year?" Lily catches herself. "That didn't come out right."

"Yes, it did. I was considering the same thing. I haven't seen abs in miles. At least not abs like those." Bridget takes a sip of wine, clearly satisfied with her innuendo.

They laugh louder, until Amelia's eyes tear and her cheeks hurt from smiling. After eating more pizza, drinking a little more wine, and closing her garage door, they enter Amelia's home to the sound of their children playing in the other room, with a Disney movie blaring.

Amelia's heart swells with satisfaction, as she puts today in the win column. Her life may have its highs and lows, but by her calculations, the wins are beginning to add up.

# Chapter 6

AMELIA'S STILL NOT HOME, SO INSTEAD OF WAITING FOR HER, Kyle has set up his ladder and is in the process of fixing her gutter. There's always a possibility that her SUV is parked in the garage and that she ignored him when he rang her doorbell, but that's highly unlikely. Given what he's seen of her, Amelia's not the type of person that hides. Kyle may not know much about her, but that much was clear when he met her.

A horn blares, not once, but twice from the street. It's the sound Kyle dreads, the same sound he'd recognize any day of the week. That sound means Carla has arrived, and when Kyle finally turns, he will see her expensive Lexus sedan parked behind his truck.

Kyle glances to his left, and sure enough, Carla's parked right where he expected. She is nothing if not predictable.

Descending from his ladder, Kyle exhales a ragged breath. The last thing he wants is Carla's complaints right now or, worse yet, her opinions on how things ought to be. Carla has a difficult time staying in her lane. She tends to go beyond what's in her job description. It's something that Kyle has warned her about on numerous occasions, and he isn't in the mood for another such conversation today.

Even on a normal day, Kyle dreads seeing Carla. Though he tries to see the good in people, Carla exudes negativity and lacks empathy. After learning what she said to Amelia, his dislike of Carla has grown tenfold.

Sure enough, she rolls down her window and calls Kyle's name, probing for details about why he's here at what she has dubbed "the eyesore," which causes Kyle to cringe. He's cautioned her repeatedly since the

Easter egg hunt to stop calling Amelia's home an eyesore, but Carla hasn't heeded his warnings yet. She has a tendency to take any bylaw infractions as a personal affront, which is problematic. He'll need to discuss her lack of tact and inappropriate behavior with the other members of the board.

"You're doing the rounds, I see." It's all he says to her.

Carla nods. "What are you doing here, Kyle?"

Her knuckles grip her steering wheel so tight that they turn white. It bothers her to see him here, at gnome central. That much is obvious.

"Hank asked me to take care of that clogged gutter before the sale closed. I'm just now getting around to it."

Hank is the previous owner of Amelia's home. Kyle used to help him with things like clogged gutters, trimming trees, replacing exterior lightbulbs, and other handyman work. Hank was a good man, with no local family. Kyle would do anything for him. Hank did ask for Kyle's help with the gutter, but then the house sold before Kyle could honor his request. No one gave Kyle an expiration date on fixing the gutter.

"Hank asked. I couldn't turn him down, could I? There are no regulations against being a good neighbor."

Pursing her lips, which are bright red today, with some of the pigment bleeding into the deep lines around her mouth, Carla pouts. "Do you see what she's done? The gnomes are wearing bows and little bonnets. I've never seen anything like it. Ms. Marsh is doing this to defy me, isn't she?"

Kyle attempts to defuse Carla's frustrations. "I don't think she's defying you, Carla. She's probably trying to make her kids happy. They did move recently. It's got to be hard on them. Besides, why would she want to defy you?"

There's nothing like putting Carla on the spot. Though Kyle would love for her to admit to being mean to Amelia, Carla never will, and Kyle would never betray Amelia's trust or say too much. Only enough to hopefully cause Carla to see things in a different light. Heaven knows she could use some enlightenment.

As for Amelia's change of tactic with her gnome colony, it's no surprise, since Kyle's last conversation with her. He has a nagging suspicion that after Easter, she will then decorate her gnomes, at least the most important one, for the next holiday, which happens to be Memorial Day. Then the next, Fourth of July, and so on. It's a brilliant plan, and he admires both her tenacity and her ability to make the best of what was a losing situation while making Carla frazzled.

"What do you suggest I do, Kyle?" Carla asks, leaning over her passenger seat. "How do I handle this?"

"Just let it be. The owner of this home is in compliance and has decorated for Easter, as have many Castle Rock residents. Amelia Marsh has no violations." Carla's grimace is all the encouragement Kyle needs. "Now, why don't you finish your drive through the neighborhood and I'll finish up the gutter? Oh! One more thing: please stop calling this home an eyesore. I don't want to hear that again, okay? I've asked you too many times. The next time I do—if there is a next time—it will result in a formal warning."

Carla's eyes widen, clearly affronted. Kyle just pulled his HOA president card, and she knows it. The Homeowners Association consists of a management company, which Carla works for, who assigns a property manager/subdivision manager to do periodic drive-throughs, take photos of bylaw infringements, send letters to property owners, answer questions, process residents' yearly dues, and all other administrative duties. That management company reports to Castle Rock's resident-run HOA board, led by Kyle.

The subdivision's board is comprised of three residents, though Kyle seems to do most of the work, which is why he's the one Castle Rock residents call and email when there's a problem, even though they can contact Carla directly.

The board approves or denies requests for home improvements, subdivision improvements including sidewalk and landscaping, spraying for mosquitos, finding the best prices for subcontractors, scheduling the Easter Bunny and Santa to visit their Rec Center, to mention just some of the duties.

As he explained to Amelia, until the remaining lots build out to one hundred percent, the board can't change the bylaws. The builders want to sell homes, want consistency and certain standards kept in place to attract potential homebuyers and sell out their lots. Those standards differ greatly from Kyle's, but until the developer has built out and packed up, his hands are tied.

"All right, then. I'll email you the latest list of infringements once it's ready." Carla's tone is terse.

"Can't wait." Kyle's monotone answer is just quiet enough. Kyle doesn't care what color someone's mulch is. As a matter of fact, he still can't believe that's a thing. Or that residents must have shrubs of a certain height to hide the concrete slabs beneath their homes, instead of choosing to plant a palm tree and flowers. Both look great. That's what the HOA should care about.

After waving goodbye to Carla, he heads over to the gnome that started this whole mess. "What a pain in my ass you are."

The gnome stares back at him with a sly smile on his bearded ceramic face, as Kyle crouches in front of him. "Don't tell anyone I cursed. Apparently, there's a swear jar."

He studies the DIY hand-painted gift from Amelia's kids. "You're actually kind of cute. In a Travelocity gnome meets Happy of the Seven Dwarfs kind of way."

It's obvious to Kyle that Amelia's kids have seen *Snow White*. There is definitely a Happy vibe with this one.

"Do you always converse with banned gnomes?"

Kyle's muscles tense as he rises, shoving his hands in the pockets of his jeans. Of course, he'd be busted by Amelia, who drove up when he was having a tête-à-tête with her garden gnome. She must think he's nuts.

Wearing a smile, Amelia's tone is teasing as she shuts the car door behind her. "If I didn't know better, I'd say that my trashy gnome is growing on you."

"I plead the Fifth," Kyle says, playing along. This banter between them keeps him on his toes.

"Surely, there must be a rule against you interrogating my gnome. Along with trespassing—I know there are laws against trespassing." Amelia tilts her head to the side, leaning against her SUV. "Precisely why are you trespassing on my property, Mr. Bunny Helper Sanders? Talking to my gnome and working on my gutter has got to break some bylaws. Should I call Carla?"

"He—" He clears his throat, catching himself before cursing, which is absolutely ridiculous. There are no children present, after all, and he's already changing himself. For what?

For Amelia.

With an exaggerated drawl he doesn't normally possess, he answers, "Heck no, ma'am. She's got unkempt yards to find and errant garbage pails to take photos of."

"Nice Texas twang, Mr. Sanders. You don't hear that much from native Houstonians."

Amelia's right. Houston is the fourth-largest American city and is a melting pot of Texans and transplants from across the country. As a state with no state income tax, Texas is a big draw, and southern drawls are becoming harder to find in Houston. Kyle lacks one, as does Amelia.

"So, you're a native Houstonian then," Kyle surmises, bridging the distance between them, until he's standing a foot in front of her. Amelia's

Explorer is an older model, from when they first became less boxy, less like a truck and sportier.

Speaking of sporty, Amelia's rocking that look, wearing a white button-down blouse, cuffed jeans, and lace-up sandals. Her hair is down today, and her golden highlights shimmer within her long brown waves, causing a birthmark just above her upper lip to appear more pronounced. She's still got very little makeup on, and wears several charm necklaces of different lengths. The one with a small compass rests between the soft swells of her cleavage.

"Carla takes photos of garbage pails?" Amelia asks, slinging a small purse over her shoulder. The strap crosses over her breasts, making them more pronounced. She's got a white bra on, that much is obvious through the light fabric of her shirt and between the buttons. She laughs. "Well, I'd say that's karma."

Kyle nods. Not because he lacks an answer but because Amelia's left him awestruck.

"Well, Kyle, you never did answer my all-important question. What are you doing on my front lawn? With a ladder of all things?"

"Today is Monday. I trespass with ladders on Mondays. It's part of the job description." He grins at her. "What are you doing here?"

Tugging on her purse strap, she hooks her forefinger through it. He makes a concerted effort not to look. Instead, he meets her eyes, reminding himself not to look down. Total guy move. Doesn't he deserve points for trying to be a gentleman? "You haven't answered my question. What are you doing here? It's a Monday afternoon, after all. Do you work from home?" He doesn't know anything about her, really. But he *wants* to, which means one thing: Amelia's already stormed past his guarded, self-imposed wall. Not good. Not good at all.

"Well, this is my driveway, and therefore my home, so I have a right to be here. However, to answer your question, I do work from home.

Today is, as you have informed me, Monday, and I meet my kids for lunch at school on Mondays." She shifts her weight. "It's one of the perks of running your business from home. Oh! And before you get me on the 'no businesses allowed to operate from one's residence' bylaw, mine falls into the category of self-employed with no clients meeting me in my home. I'm a web designer."

"A web designer and someone who has clearly been doing her research on our community bylaws." Kyle usually hates talking about bylaws, but when Amelia mentions them, his interest is piqued.

Amelia tilts her head to the side. "You sound surprised."

"No, impressed actually." Kyle's tone and wide smile fails to hide it. "Going up against you is going to be interesting."

"Well, I have been doing my research, but I can't share any of that information with you. You are the enemy, after all."

"Right." Kyle almost forgot they're at odds. *Almost…*

"It's nice that you meet Jacob and Chloe for lunch." Kyle pauses for a moment, before adding, "You're very close to them. That much was obvious at the Easter egg hunt."

"They've been through a lot, and Mondays are usually difficult for children anyway. Returning to school after a weekend, getting back into the routine. Add a new school to the mix in a new city, and I have lunch with them as a way to be there for them and give them something to look forward to."

"How is school going overall?" Kyle asks, genuinely interested.

Amelia grimaces. "Well, I drive them back and forth because Jacob was teased on the bus. That's another reason I meet them for lunch. Thankfully, they have friends. That's why we chose this subdivision… It is in the same school district that my friends' children attend. The women you met the other night."

"Oh!" Kyle exaggerates that one word. "Them."

"Come on. They weren't that intimidating." Amelia chuckles.

"You're right. Besides, I wouldn't really know. I was too busy eyeing your lingerie."

Her cheeks turn a bright crimson. "I had hoped you missed that."

*How could anyone have missed that?* He changes the topic. "Your friends seem nice, just not very subtle."

"That's true. But they are supportive and very resourceful, which is why my gnomes are now Easter gnomes." She motions to her yard with her hand. "I'm sorry if I was being irrational the other day when—"

"You were protecting your kids? That's not irrational." His eyes remain locked with hers, those same brown eyes he noticed the other day on her front lawn during that whole gnome storm. They're a rich, smoky brown with amber flecks that glow in the sun.

"Why, Kyle Sanders, you have compassion. Don't tell Carla or she might toss you from that cushy board position." She winks at him.

Kyle's hooked on their banter. "Hey, I was elected by the residents of Castle Rock, our fine subdivision. Besides, I don't get paid."

"It's volunteer?" Amelia's eyes widen as Kyle nods. "Why? Are you a glutton for punishment?"

"Carla certainly made an impression on you."

"Yes, she did, and you never answered my first question: Why are you here, cleaning out my gutter?" Amelia studies his ladder.

"I promised Hank that I'd fix the gutter."

"You did not." Shaking her head, Amelia is adamant. "Would you like to know how I can be certain of that? Because I negotiated a small sum from his asking price due to that very gutter you are currently fixing."

"Nope. He asked me before the sale, and I'm just now getting around to it. I honor my commitments."

"Are you sure this isn't charity?" Amelia's voice is rough. "You aren't bound by your agreement to the previous homeowner after closing, you know."

"I do know, and no, this isn't charity. Like I said, I honor my commitments, though this may also be a peace offering. Since I can't do anything about the gnome, I wanted to help with the gutter." It's true.

Amelia's full lips curl into a smile. "Thanks for that. It wasn't necessary, but thank you."

"You're welcome." Are they making headway? The excitement Kyle feels at the prospect causes his heart to beat erratically. *She has kids*, he reminds himself. That alone is enough to sober him.

He's dated women with children before. Doing so has left him far too invested and inexplicably broken-hearted when the romantic relationships ended, which they always did. Kyle's just no good at keeping relationships going. No matter how hard he tries. Especially when he's the rebound guy, and based upon what he knows about Amelia's divorce timeline, that is exactly what he'd be: *her* rebound guy.

On that note, he decides to wrap up their chat. "I'm just about done with your gutter. Is it okay if I finish?"

Nodding, Amelia proceeds to her tailgate and Kyle studies the streetlight. *Don't look. Rebound guy.* That's all it takes to set him straight.

She grabs a couple of bags from the back of her SUV and he helps her shut the tailgate.

"Would you like to come in for coffee when you're done?"

Though her offer is tempting, Kyle has other plans and also remains firm in his resolve—no dating anyone with kids and no coffee with any woman who has kids. No more banter with Amelia, who has children and is on the rebound. "I've got to get back to my office. I have an appointment with an architect this afternoon. The only reason I'm in the neighborhood now is that I was checking on a nearby project, but thanks for the offer."

"Thanks for your help with the gutter. Maybe some other time." Amelia walks to her front door, which has one of those coded locks. Kyle turns away while she types in her code. After opening her door, she returns her attention to him.

"I owe you another thank you. For the Easter décor idea." Amelia stares at him. Kyle can sense it. She's waiting for a sign, a hint that he might have given her the idea deliberately.

Kyle clutches the ladder, then climbs to the top. "Don't mention it."

"Why did you give me the idea?" she asks.

*Why?* Kyle wishes he could say it was because he wanted to defend her, like he's some knight in shining armor, which he's not. Even if he were, something tells him that Amelia is no helpless damsel in distress. No, she gets things done and probably kicks butt while doing it. "Honestly, I was just trying to explain things to you. There was no ulterior motive."

Like the fact that it didn't feel right to be on separate sides in this, even though they are.

"You still drive me crazy with your community of gnomes, especially since I've already answered to Carla once today about them. Don't worry, though. You're in compliance." Kyle concentrates on the gutter, avoiding Amelia's rapt attention.

"I drive you crazy? That's a compliment, or at least that's how I'm going to take it. You seem like the type who doesn't get easily frustrated. Am I right?"

Kyle's tone is rough. "You've got me." Her assessment of him is dead on.

"Want to know a secret?" Amelia's whisper grabs his attention, and he turns towards her. She's leaning against her doorframe.

"Sure. Why not?" He already seems to know too many secrets when it comes to his new neighbor. What's one more?

"I knew the gnome rave would bother Carla." At that admission, Amelia flashes him a mischievous grin.

"Who is it you're going to war with, Amelia? The HOA, Carla, or both?" Kyle dreads her answer.

"Let's just say I have a plan and leave it at that."

*Oh no.* "I'm not going to like this, am I?"

"Don't worry. I have it all under control. You have a good day and don't be late for your meeting. Thanks again, Kyle." She flashes him that bright smile once more, the same smile that makes the world seem sunnier and warmer.

"Okay, terrific." It's his automatic response when things are beyond his control. It's also his call to arms. "Take care, Amelia."

It's all he offers as she enters her home, and he finishes working on her gutter in record time. As he drives away, Kyle turns up the radio. Switching stations, he tries to find a song that distracts him. Kyle settles on an eighties station. "Mony Mony" is playing and he taps the steering wheel in sync with the beat.

He's helped many a resident with gutters, changing porch lightbulbs, and other things. It's what he does for his neighbors. What makes Amelia different is that he felt an urgency to fix her gutter. In record time, after their last conversation about her gnomes and her divorce. After all of her admissions, he was desperate to make sure she didn't think ill of him. But why?

Kyle turns up the volume even more, letting Billy Idol drown out his conscience, which is questioning everything he thought he knew about himself. Everything he had accepted, long ago.

His doubts are unacceptable. Because he's not a dad or stepdad material. Just ask his ex-girlfriends with kids. Even though he grew to love them, and thought there was a future, his girlfriends never saw the stepdad potential in him. It's Kyle's cross to bear, which makes Amelia Marsh off limits.

Not even Billy Idol can stop his train of thought, so he shuts the radio off with an exasperated breath.

"Of all the subdivisions in all the communities north of Houston, why did Amelia Marsh have to move into mine?"

# Chapter 7

AMELIA IS AWAKENED BY A BUMP AGAINST HER HEAD. GRUNTING, she reaches for the object that jolted her half awake to find Jacob's bare foot resting against her temple.

Her mattress rocks up and down as Jacob readjusts, now splayed over Amelia's abdomen, his weight pinning her down. She manages to reach for her cell, noting the time. Eleven at night. That's about right. This is what happens when Jacob wakes up and climbs into her bed at night. He's a restless sleeper at best, and the only fourth grader she knows who has a full-size bed. Always tall for his age, Jacob had outgrown his twin bed early on and fell out of it more times than she can count.

Jacob's offending foot is no longer near her head, but his body is now contorted, lying across her. He flails his arms again and his hand smacks her cheek. She manages to move just enough to where she can place her palm on his back, rubbing it in gentle circles in an attempt to soothe him.

"You're awake." Jacob's voice isn't the least bit rough with sleep. He's been waiting for her to wake up, for one of their middle of the school-night talks, which means something is troubling him.

Stifling a yawn, Amelia manages to sound semicoherent, shrouded in shadow. "Yes, buddy. I'm awake. What's been keeping you up?"

"I wanted bedtime cuddles." He crawls to her pillow and rests his head in the crook of her neck.

"Bedtime cuddles. This must be serious." She caresses his cheek. "Do you want the light on or off?"

Jacob sighs. "Off."

"Off it remains. Talk to me, you can tell me anything." She kisses his head; his short, buzzed hair has grown longer, meaning it's time for a trim.

A heady silence engulfs them. Amelia knows that Jacob will open up when he's ready... She also knows that the last time she checked on the kids was around nine, and neither was awake. He must have come in shortly after she fell asleep.

"I can't play basketball," he admits in a whisper.

Amelia grins in the darkness. "Neither can I. But that's okay. We can learn."

Her son burrows deeper. "I suck at it."

"Hey, don't be so hard on yourself. You haven't learned how to play yet." Heaven knows his dad never taught him, and Amelia's own basketball skills are nil. Though she did score an occasional shot when she was a child, it was pure dumb luck. In the end, the law of averages was always against her. Ratio of attempts to actual baskets made: one in twenty is being generous.

"The kids in gym say I suck. They call me 'Sucky Jacob.'"

Cradling her son tighter, Amelia's abdomen recoils. Children can be so cruel. She thought having friends in his new school would help, but none of the kids Jacob's close to are in the same classes. "I'm sorry, sweetie. Just remember, the problem isn't with you, it's with them."

Amelia's neck is wet with his tears, though he uses the sleeve on his sweatshirt to wipe his eyes. "I wanna be good at it. I don't want to suck anymore."

"First off, please stop saying you suck. You don't suck, you just need practice." Amelia squeezes her eyes shut, thinking hard on what to say next and how not to say anything against Daniel's lack of parenting, or reveal her absolute rage against her callous ex-husband through her cadence or her body language. "Tomorrow is Friday, and you don't have gym, do you?"

She slides her palm to his shoulder, squeezing just hard enough for him to feel safe and loved.

Jacob shakes his head, his "No," a mere mumble and ragged.

"Then you and I are going to learn how to play basketball together. This weekend. I'll start googling how to play basketball when you go back to sleep, and I'll purchase a basketball when you're at school. We can practice all day on Saturday at the playground. Just you and me, while Chloe has her sleepover playdate with Lily's girls. Sound like a deal?"

"Okay. Just don't tell Chloe, okay? She worries about me and…"

That sentence, left dangling, causes Amelia's every nerve to stiffen, before pulsating with dread. "And what? Spill."

"Chloe and I protect each other."

"Right." Amelia knows this. But how? "Keep talking, sweetie. I won't be angry."

Another long silence follows, before a jagged sigh from Jacob. "She heard a boy making fun of me in the car rider line and got into a fight with him. She almost hit him."

Amelia's heart plummets. Her little girl is starting fights to protect her brother. Her mind swirls with thoughts of the school calling her, a visit with the principal or vice principal, suspension, or worse, expulsion.

*Wait.* "You said almost?"

"I stopped her. I didn't want her to get into any trouble or hurt. He is taller than she is by, like, a lot." Jacob wipes his eyes again. "I'm sorry, Mom. I'm not good at anything—"

"That's not true. You are a great big brother, and the best son I could have ever asked for. You're smart, you're kind, you're funny, and you're loving. That's just the beginning of a very long list of the many things that make you remarkable." Amelia kisses his hair, her own eyes welling with tears.

"What does remarkable mean?" Jacob asks.

Amelia ponders his question. In kids' terms… "Remarkable means that there is no one like you, and I am proud of you. I'm also so very lucky to be your mom. And Chloe's."

After a long pause, allowing her words to set in, she adds, "I'm going to email your principal and teacher, and let them know what's going on—"

"Please don't! It will make it worse."

She knows the drill. When someone is making fun of her children, they typically don't stop. "I'll do what's best for you, always. Let me handle it through the proper channels. In the meantime, don't let this boy see that he's hurting you. That only gives him more power. If you show no reaction, it won't be fun for him."

"Huh." Jacob yawns. "I never thought of it like that."

How Amelia wishes Jacob and Chloe never had to think of such things. "Do you feel better?"

Jacob nods, stifling another yawn.

"Good. Now give me a hug." Turning on her side, Amelia wraps Jacob in her arms and holds him, until all of his tension dissolves and his muscles relax, until all of his tears are shed. "Do you want to sleep in here tonight?"

"Yeah." His sleepy response is all she needs as she releases him, and Jacob rolls onto his other side. Soon his breaths become deep, a sure sign that he has at last found slumber.

While Jacob is hopefully having sweet dreams, Amelia's mind races with all she has learned. Boys are making fun of Jacob, Chloe is about to start a fistfight with a boy who is probably twice her size, and Amelia needs to learn basketball fast. Oh, and first things first, Amelia must stop her daughter from drop-kicking anyone—any child—at her school, or even making an attempt to do so.

*Why did I ever allow Chloe to take karate lessons?*

Because her daughter wanted to learn the art. Little did Amelia know that she was creating a bodyguard, a superhero for her brother, and a danger to bullies everywhere, or at least mean kids who make fun of her brother.

Sliding out of bed as slowly and quietly as she can, Amelia reaches for her cell and unplugs the charger, then tiptoes to Chloe's bedroom, the hardwood floor creaking beneath her feet, interrupting the silence that has befallen the house with the AC fan resting.

Peeking into her daughter's room, Amelia sees her little girl wrapped in her favorite pastel zebra blanket. Her light is on, full force.

Oh, how Chloe would cry as a baby. Nightlights on, nightlights off—nothing made a difference, until the little girl was old enough to stand up in her crib, reach for the light switch on her bedroom wall, and turn on her overhead light. From then on, she slept soundly, always with the light on. Some things don't change—like her daughter's independence, even if that means defending her brother with brute force.

Amelia will talk with Chloe before school. She'll also text Bridget, who teaches at the children's school, and ask her to be on the lookout. Bridget has been watching out for Jacob and Chloe ever since they started attending Lakewood Elementary, but Amelia will still let her know what's going on.

Once Amelia reaches her front office, she opens the French doors and flips on her dim desk light, for nights when she's working late. Or researching, like this one. Tonight, it's basketball research, using her desktop computer.

Google and YouTube are this mom's friends, so she navigates the new-to-her question: *how to play basketball*. Then *how to dunk a ball in the basket*. Turns out, dunking is the wrong word. Good to know.

"Let's begin with something simple," she mutters to herself, typing into her search *how to dribble*. That search leads to a video about performing a layup. So much terminology. But she watches more videos, and prepares for their weekend lesson. Psyching herself up, Amelia becomes hopeful that she can teach her son how to make a layup, a.k.a. sink the basketball in the basket. Fortunately, their community playground has lots of baskets to practice at, so they'll be all set come Saturday.

Yawning, Amelia glances at the time on her computer. It's now four thirty and her alarm will soon go off, meaning it will be time to shower, prepare the kids' breakfast, and ready them for school. Stretching, she waits for her Keurig to warm up, then brings her piping hot mug of fresh coffee to her front office windows. It's a bank of three, which offer prime light during the day. She forgot to close the blinds the night before.

She studies her neighbors' houses, bathed in the safety of the streetlights lining their block. A figure catches her eye, on the sidewalk, jogging. Her cell alarm goes off, the generic tune much too loud as she reaches to silence it. Her attention then returns to the sidewalk.

The jogger is Kyle. That guy jogs a lot. He's kind, athletic, and owns his own business. What a catch, if he's single, that is. He probably has a girlfriend. A super-hot girlfriend. Guys like that usually do.

Kyle looks her way and waves at her. Amelia waves back, or as much as she can with her cell phone in her free hand. It is still illuminated with her home screen—a picture of her children smiling.

Short of that one passerby, her road remains quiet, the only sounds being her air conditioning fans cycling on, then off. Silence can be a blessing, and a curse. On this morning, it's a little bit of both. Sometimes, Amelia just wants to stop thinking, stop worrying, but today isn't one of those days.

Shower, dress, wake kids, have breakfast, talk to Chloe, text Bridget, and drive them to school. That's her plan, not necessarily in that order, followed by work and a trip to the store for a basketball. Her alarm goes off again.

There's no prolonging it. The day has officially begun.

*Please God, don't let anyone make fun of Jacob. And please help me with Chloe.*

Teaching basketball pales in comparison to helping her daughter with her propensity to protect her brother at all costs.

*Please help me say and do all the right things, today and every day.*

Such are her mom goals, and on this day, they feel staggeringly out of reach.

# Chapter 8

TODAY, AMELIA'S WEARING HER USUAL BOHO CHIC, WITH A billowing blouse, jeans, chunky-heeled booties, and the layered necklaces and rings featuring crystals and gemstones she always wears. They signify important events in her life, like Jacob and Chloe's birthstones, and a compass that reminds her where she's going while not letting her forget where she's been.

Her ex-husband told her on more than one occasion that she looked like Stevie Nicks, though she dressed the part of the executive's wife when required. Now Amelia has fully embraced her inner Stevie. Call it her declaration of independence from Daniel.

Upon entering Chloe's room, she finds her daughter sprawled on top of her bed, tangled in her favorite blanket.

"Good morning, sunshine," Amelia prompts in her singsong morning voice.

Her daughter doesn't move, her profile sweet and serene while her naturally curly brown hair is untamed. She's adorable, especially now, when Amelia can still recognize the baby who has grown into an incredible little girl.

Did Amelia take for granted that Chloe was handling things with her father better than Jacob was? Perhaps. It's something she won't do again.

Sitting beside the little girl on her bed, Amelia repeats her greeting. Chloe moans and pulls her blanket over her head. "Five more minutes," she grumbles.

"Not this morning. Today, it's time to wake up." Amelia removes the blanket, and her daughter opens one eye.

"Why?" she whines with a large yawn. "I'm tired."

It's tough to be a growing Chloe. "I know you are. I am, too. But today is a school day, and you and I must talk beforehand."

At the last statement, Chloe sits upright, her eyes narrowed. "Talk about what?"

"Well, the fact that you love your brother and want to protect him." Amelia brushes Chloe's messy curls from her eyes. "Is there anything you want to share with me?"

"Ugh! Did Jacob tell on me?" Chloe mutters.

Amelia takes her daughter's hand. "He couldn't sleep and was upset last night. He told me what was going on with the boys at school, and that you defended him."

Squeezing her mom's hand, Chloe shakes her head, her hair haphazardly falling into her eyes. "They are so mean to him, Mom. Why are kids so mean?"

Good question. "I don't know, sweetie. Most times, we will never know. But being teased is never fun. It also happens too often. Even I experienced it when I was your age."

"You did?" Chloe's eyes widen in disbelief.

Nodding, Amelia continues. "Some children tease others because they feel bad about themselves, or because something is going on at home. We don't know, right? I try to give people the benefit of the doubt."

At least, Amelia used to. When she was Chloe's age.

"That doesn't make it right that they make fun of Jacob." Chloe's anger is rising, her eyes narrowing.

"You're right. It also doesn't give you free rein to get into a physical fight with anyone." Amelia's tone is forceful.

"But Mom—"

"'But' nothing, Chloe. Please let me handle it. I'm going to email the principal and Jacob's teacher, as well as yours. Your job is to come to me, talk to me. I'll take care of it. That's what I'm here for." Amelia pauses, letting her words sink in. "You have every right to tell these kids to stop, so does Jacob. If they don't, go to your teachers. Go to Aunt Bridget. Definitely come to me. But don't fight them. Violence is never the way to end an argument."

"Those boys make me so mad!" Chloe's determined expression belies the tears brimming in her eyes.

Amelia wipes her daughter's eyes with the pads of her fingers. "I know, baby girl. But it's not your responsibility to handle everything. Let your teachers and me take care of it. You and your brother stick together and tell us what's happening, okay?"

"Okay." Chloe leans in for a hug, and Amelia wraps her in a tight embrace.

"How are you holding up?"

Chloe exhales before placing her head on Amelia's shoulder. "Okay, I guess."

"You guess? How are your friends treating you?"

"Good. Jacob, Liam, and Seth hang out with me a lot on the play-ground, and Britney in my class is nice. She's the girl who moved from Colorado." Liam and Seth are Bridget's sons, and are in Jacob's grade. They have recess at the same time as Chloe and Jacob. Her friend from Colorado has been busy settling in.

Amelia pats her daughter's back. "Do you think Britney is ready for a playdate?"

"Ooh! I know! I can ask her!" Chloe's excitement is off the charts.

"I have her mom's number, so I'll text her." Add that to Amelia's to-do list. Standing, she offers her daughter a hand. "You ready to wake your brother? He's in my bed."

"Jacob!" Chloe runs out of her room and into the hall, making a beeline into Amelia's master suite. "Wakey, wakey, eggs and bakey."

It's Chloe's personal wake-up rhyme for her brother and he immediately smiles as they enter the bedroom. The little girl jumps on Amelia's bed and tickles her brother. "It's time to wake up."

"No! Stop tickling me!" Jacob squeals.

Amelia's cell vibrates as the alarm goes off. "Do you want cereal or breakfast in the cafeteria today?" She hopes they want the cafeteria breakfast, because exhaustion is setting in from the sheer emotion her convo with Chloe stirred within her.

"Cafeteria!" both children shout in unison. "We want French toast."

Thank goodness it's Friday, which is French toast day. "How could I forget how much you love those French toast sticks? Make sure you eat fruit with them please."

Both siblings agree, while Amelia uses her mom voice. "It's time to get going. Let's get teeth brushed, faces washed, clothes on, and…" Amelia cups Chloe's face in her palms. "We need to tame that mane, little miss. Would you like a ponytail or messy bun today?"

"Two ponytails. One on each side." Chloe smiles.

"Two it is. Now hop to it." Amelia and her children scramble with the rest of their morning routine.

As they're finishing up, she places the kids' insulated lunch boxes in each backpack and loads them all into the car. She selects the kids' morning playlist, and Kidz Bop starts playing through the speakers as they head to school, singing the whole way.

By the time they reach the drop off lane, the kids are in a great mood.

"Be good, be kind, and have a great day." Amelia turns and gives each child a kiss as they lean forward in the back seat. "I love you."

They exit the car and sprint into school, chaperoned by the teachers who have drop-off duty. As Amelia drives away, she changes to her own playlist, as a twinge of pride seeps into her soul.

Another morning, another drop-off complete.

She begins to sing with Xtina's "Fighter" at the top of her lungs. Driving the kids to school has its perks. Thanks for making *this mom* a fighter.

# Chapter 9

KYLE ARRIVES AT THE PLAYGROUND EARLY, LONG BEFORE ANYONE would be playing there, with wasp killer in hand. Sure, the subdivision has its own exterminator, but Kyle got a call last night from a resident that a wasps' nest has taken hold on the jungle gym roof, and he's not making the community pay an exterminator emergency rates when he can zap the suckers with a can of Raid and have his morning coffee on one of the benches until it's safe for him to clean up and let the kiddos play.

He rounds the sidewalk to discover he isn't alone. Amelia and Jacob are already taking hoop shots, and between Amelia's loud grunts each time she misses a basket and the bored look on Jacob's face, Kyle's certain that neither is having fun.

"Good morning. I didn't expect to see anyone here so early." Kyle's cheery tone hides his confusion, as he sets his coffee and bag of bagels on one of the tables.

A cooler rests on another table—he assumes it belongs to Amelia. Along with the supersized thermal cup with the reusable straw sticking out of it.

"Kyle!" Jacob yells. "Where's your truck? What are you doing here?"

Amelia offers Kyle an exasperated sigh and slight smile. "Hi. Nice to see you. How is your morning going?"

She's dribbling the ball, until it gets away from her and rolls into the grass. Based upon her eye roll, his morning is going a lot better than hers.

"I'm here to tackle some wasps in the canopy of the jungle gym. I thought I'd beat the crowds." Kyle studies Amelia's crestfallen face as she picks up the basketball. "Do you want to take a break and sit at the picnic table while I spray the jungle gym? Just to be safe."

"Yes!" Jacob's already off and running. Clearly, he wanted out of his current predicament, just as Kyle thought. They were safe where they were, but both mother and son looked like they needed a break.

Amelia follows Jacob, placing a bottle of water in a Koozie before handing it to him. She then offers him a sliced apple in a clear Ziploc bag. Kyle can hear their conversation in between blasts of the obnoxious wasp killer he's aiming at a nest. It's Houston, and wasps' nests pop up everywhere. So, he braves the wild playground and kills one nest at a time, until all of Castle Rock's children are safe. Though noble, it isn't on his resume. To be honest, most never notice this particular contribution.

"May I join you?" he asks, marching over to the tables once he's done.

"Yes!" Jacob answers, making room for Kyle on his bench.

Amelia smiles. "Please." She hands Kyle a bleach wipe for his hands. "Wouldn't want you poisoned by wasp killer."

Laughing, Kyle quips, "Look at that… You don't want me dead. Is Gnomegate a thing of the past?"

"Not a chance. Call that bleach wipe an olive branch and let's leave it at that, shall we?"

Nodding, Kyle returns his attention to Jacob, then halts in the process of offering him half his bagel.

"Is it all right, Mom?" Kyle asks. "Plain, buttered. From New York Bagel in town center." He's checking for allergies with his explanation.

"Only if we can match your offer with a cinnamon raisin with cream cheese from the same place. That's Jacob's favorite." She smiles through the tension, though her eyes have lost some of their usual spark.

"Hey, Kyle. Let's swap. You try mine, I'll try yours." Jacob offers him half his bagel, and they each hand one half over to the other. Kyle almost expects the kid to double dog dare him from pure excitement.

Taking a bite, Kyle makes some "Yum" noises, in spite of the fact that he hates cream cheese. Ever since he was a kid, he usually can't eat it, but for this little boy, he not only dives right in but tells him how delicious it is.

"So, what are you both doing here so early? And where's Chloe?" Kyle asks, wiping his mouth with a napkin and taking a large gulp of coffee to wash down the cream cheese.

Amelia sips her coffee. "Chloe is at a sleepover with Lily's girls, while I am attempting to teach Jacob the art of a layup. I'm failing miserably, aren't I, buddy?"

Patting her son's hand, Amelia watches him intently as her son shrugs. "You're not that bad."

"You're too sweet, trying not to hurt my feelings. But be honest."

Jacob expels a deep breath. "You suck as much as I do."

"I guess we know who you inherited that gene from." Amelia tries to make a joke of it, but it falls flat—at least for Kyle. The pain emanating from her eyes and her frown are proof of it.

"What's going on, Jacob? Why this need to learn basketball early on a Saturday morning?" Kyle asks, turning from Amelia, aware that she's blinking quickly, deflecting tears.

Setting his bagel on his paper, Jacob shrugs. "Kids in school have been making fun of me because I suck, and my sister is close to going all Thanos on them. Mom thought she could teach me. But she—"

"Sucks as bad as you do. Got it." Kyle turns to Amelia. "Is 'suck' a curse word? If so, we all owe that swear jar a lot of money."

"Technically, it is not, however I would like Jacob to stop using that word. He doesn't know how to play. There's a difference." She wraps her hands around her thermal cup, in spite of it being a beautiful seventy-degree morning with clear skies. "I made the mistake of researching all night, thinking that between Google and YouTube, how difficult can it be?"

Ah, that explains him seeing Amelia's silhouette from her front windows before dawn when he was jogging. "In defense of YouTube, it's an easy mistake to make. They have piano-playing cats, after all. If you can't find a how-to video there, where can you find one?"

Amelia grins at him and mouths "thanks." That one joke isn't enough, though, and Kyle knows it.

"I'm no expert, but I do have a friend who I play basketball with down at the gym. I learned a lot from him. I'm not great or anything, but maybe I can help you?" He searches Amelia's eyes, then Jacob's, whose large brown eyes are alight with hope.

"Really? You mean it?" Jacob asks.

Kyle turns to Amelia. "If it's okay with you."

Tilting her head to the side, Amelia studies him for a moment, then asks, "When can we begin?"

"How about now?" Kyle suggests and Jacob jumps from his bench and grabs his ball, heading for one of the hoops in record time.

Following close behind, Kyle asks Amelia if she's okay.

"I don't like failure. As a matter of fact, it's not an option, yet I seem to be failing a lot lately." She turns to him, arching her dark brow. "But sure, I'm fine. I have no choice."

Though he may not have known his new neighbor long, he does have intuition, which is screaming that this is not Amelia Marsh. She's no quitter. "Well, you do have a choice when it comes to learning how to play basketball. What you're going to do is learn, and crush it."

"If this is some motivational, reverse psychology, Yoda attempt at bringing out my inner basketball Jedi, it's a losing battle."

"Actually, this is a *stop feeling sorry for yourself and let's have some fun* talk. So, get with the program, Marsh," Kyle challenges her.

"You are such a pain in my—"

"Swear jar!" Kyle points his hand in the air. "Ha! It's my turn to use that. I like the power it invokes."

Amelia shakes her head, her tone sinister. "I've created a monster."

Stretching his arms outright, Kyle mimics the Frankenstein walk. "'There can be no community between you and me; only enemies,'" he says, quoting *Frankenstein*.

"The doctor said that, not the monster." Amelia rolls her eyes again, though this time she's suppressing a grin.

Kyle drops his hands. "You know your literature. Impressive."

"Can we not be enemies?" Amelia stops, rounding on Kyle. "For one day. Please? Because if so, I think today is that day."

She places her hand out. Kyle studies it long and hard before accepting it. "I'd be happy to call a truce. For today." He shakes her hand as Jacob calls for them to hurry.

"I hope your mad skills are all they're cracked up to be and more." Amelia's expression turns dead serious. "Jacob and I need all the help we can get."

*No pressure. None at all.*

Suddenly, Kyle feels like he bit off more than he can chew.

# Chapter 10

AMELIA WATCHES KYLE IN AWE AS HE EXPLAINS HOW TO AIM AND toss a ball into the basket. It's all about control, about precision, and Jacob's height is an advantage that Kyle teaches him how to use in his favor. It still takes Jacob at least a dozen tries before his first successful layup, and Kyle supports him with lots of cheers, positive affirmation, and high fives.

He's good with children, Amelia notes. Kind, patient, with a great sense of humor, Kyle is great with Jacob in particular. They joke, and soon Jacob's tension recedes, replaced with jovial laughter and then confidence. It's a sight to behold.

After Jacob makes his third basket in a row, he runs over to Amelia. "I can do it. I don't suck."

Wrapping him in a hug, Amelia reminds him, "You never sucked. You just didn't know how to play."

A family of six gets out of their car, and Kyle heads to the jungle gym with a garbage bag to remove the dead remnants of the wasps' nest he eviscerated earlier. Amelia uses this time with her son to compliment him.

"You did great today. You really did." She runs her hand through his spiky buzzed hair that she trimmed last night. "At school, you just need to relax, remember what Kyle taught you, and take the shot. Believe in yourself. You can do this. You saw that today, right?"

Jacob smiles, his toothy grin wide and brimming with pride. "I did it, Mom!"

"Yes, you did!" Amelia embraces him tightly until three kids come over and ask if he wants to play.

Kyle is behind them, trash bag in hand. "It's safe."

"Have fun." Amelia winks at Jacob as Kyle takes a seat across from her, watching the kids run over to the swing set.

"Are you sure you don't want basketball lessons? I bet you can be just as good as Jacob."

Amelia laughs. "No thank you. That's not a deficiency I need to tackle at the moment. I've got my hands full as it is."

"Well, Jacob seems ready to take on the world."

"He does, but it still scares me. Those kids were so mean that Chloe almost hit one of them." Amelia adjusts her ponytail.

"'Thanos.' Jacob's Thanos remark was about that?" Kyle asks, his tone one of surprise, but without a hint of judgment.

"Who knew my daughter would snap bullies out of existence if she could."

"You're getting hit from all sides, aren't you?" Kyle's eyes hold Amelia's. She forces a grin. "I'm not perfect, no matter how hard I try."

"No one is." Kyle places his bagel wrapper in his trash bag. "Can I confide something in you?"

"Please. So far, it's been me spilling my guts. I'd love to know something secret about you." Amelia's sass makes her sound all too eager, which she kind of is.

"I hate cream cheese." His admission hovers in the air.

Amelia gasps. "Why did you eat half of Jacob's bagel?"

"Because it meant so much to him, and it was obvious he needed a confidence boost, not to mention some comic relief. You both did."

"I thought I covered well, or at least I tried to," she admits solemnly.

"You did an admirable job." Kyle smiles at her. "The reason I hate cream cheese is because when I was a kid, my mom used to mix my antibiotics in cream cheese."

"Oh no."

"Yeah, it tasted disgusting. I haven't enjoyed cream cheese since."

"I can understand why." Amelia offers him an understanding glance. "Your mom didn't know better?"

Kyle taps his forefinger on the table. "She thought it would be better than ice cream. Thicker. And that the bagels would hide the taste."

"Please don't tell me that she fed you cinnamon raisin bagels." Amelia's heart sinks at the thought.

Kyle doesn't admit it, but Amelia knows it to be true.

"That must have been torture for you this morning. I'm so sorry." This guy ate a food that reminds him of a disgusting childhood memory to help her child. That makes him amazing in her book.

"Don't be sorry. My point is that my mom tried her best, and I didn't fault her. Her intentions were good. As are yours. Don't be so hard on yourself."

*Easier said than done.*

"Jacob knows you love him, and that you're trying your best. Look on the bright side, you haven't ruined cream cheese for him, so there's that," Kyle teases.

"You've set a high bar for me. I don't know how I'll ever be able to meet it." Amelia's sarcasm is back, as is *her* confidence. This guy would be a phenomenal motivational speaker. Or coach. "You must be a great boss."

"Wow. A compliment from the Gnome Queen... What did I do to deserve such an honor?"

Wrinkling her nose with a grin, Amelia answers, "You ate a cream cheese cinnamon raisin bagel, all for a boy you don't know well. That, and the fact that you encouraged him to no end. Those are skills, Mr. Sanders. I imagine you're a tremendous team leader."

"Team builder. I'm also humble," he adds with a wink. "With as many people as I deal with on a daily basis, from employees, clients, subcontractors, architects, building officials... I have to be. It's my job."

"Spraying wasps isn't, yet you do it anyway."

He shrugs. "It saves the community—"

"Money. Yeah. I know." Something tells Amelia it's more than that, but she allows Kyle to keep that secret to himself. For now. "Do you have plans for Easter? It's tomorrow, you know."

"That fact hasn't escaped me, and I do have plans. I'm spending it with friends. How about you?"

"Same." Amelia wonders if Kyle really does have plans. He's never mentioned friends. Just work, and community stuff. "If your plans fall through, you're welcome to join us. What's your cell number?"

Amelia programs his number into her cell and texts him. "Now you have my phone number. Feel free to join us. If—well, if your plans fall through."

"Do you honestly think we can coexist under a ceasefire for two days straight?" Kyle says in mock horror.

"Stranger things have happened. Like getting along with the HOA president at the opposite side of Gnomegate." Like beginning to like the HOA president. "Besides, no one said this can't be an amicable—"

"War of gnomes? I believe someone might have hinted at that." Kyle picks up his trash bag and stands. "That person might have been me. Just sayin'—bye, Jacob."

Jacob waves goodbye, and Kyle winks at Amelia. "Bye, Amelia. Happy Easter."

Did he just allude to *I told you so* without saying *I told you so*?

Amelia watches him saunter away with that cocky *I told you so* demeanor.

Her cell vibrates. It's a text from Kyle: I told you so.

*Son of a biscuit!*

Just when a truce seemed inevitable, it's now so not. As a matter of fact, Gnomegate is steaming full force ahead, speeding down the tracks.

He had to go there. If Amelia didn't know better, she'd think that Kyle likes going to battle with her.

Well, she'll have the last word. She's a mom, after all, and this mom will get the last word, especially where Kyle Sanders is concerned.

# Chapter 11

EASTER IS A DAY THAT BEGINS WITH CHURCH, FOLLOWED BY Easter baskets for the kids, and Jacob asking Amelia to text Daniel a picture of the kids with the Easter Bunny and a reminder of his call with them after a Zoom with Amelia's parents. Follow that up with an early dinner and movie with Amelia's friends and their children at her home, and it all equates to the Marsh family's new normal.

Amelia studies her children and tries to anticipate what they're thinking and feeling. So far, neither Chloe nor Jacob has said much to her and are currently playing in their rooms with their Easter basket treats, which include lots of Legos.

Amelia checks the time on her laptop. Her parents are late—at least some things remain the same. She texts them and waits for a response.

"Stop bossing me around." Jacob stomps into the living room, his arms crossed over his chest. "I'm not a baby, Chloe. I'm older than you are."

Bickering, though annoying, is also normal. "Hey, bud. What's up?" Amelia asks.

Jacob plops beside her on the sofa. "Chloe keeps telling me what to do. I don't want to play with Barbies. Why can't I play with Matchbox cars like I want to?"

"You can play with Matchbox cars while Chloe plays with her Barbies. Barbies drive, right?" Amelia rubs her son on the back.

"Yeah, Barbies have planes, and cars, and elevators!" Chloe announces with a flourish of her hands, proud of herself, as she sits on the other side of her mom.

Amelia takes her daughter's hand. "The important thing is that you work through this together. Remember what I taught you about flexibility?"

"Yeah," Jacob and Chloe answer in unison, their voices flat and devoid of emotion.

"Oh, am I boring you?" Amelia jokes, noting that both kids are staring at the laptop screen and the message that states it's waiting to connect.

Jacob leans forward. "Did Dad text us back?"

This explains Jacob's attitude. "No, he didn't. He is supposed to call us, and I sent the reminder like you wanted. Let's give him some time, okay?"

*Please let Daniel call them on this holiday.* It's Amelia's silent prayer.

"All we do is give Dad time," Chloe chimes in. "He never calls when he's supposed to."

"What do you know, Chloe?" Jacob snaps at his sister.

Amelia wraps her arms around both children. "Hey. I understand that you miss your dad, and that you want him to call. It's hard on both of you in different ways."

The kids nod.

"Listen, you don't have to play together, you know. You can take some alone time." Every single time Amelia says this, neither child listens. They either like playing together or hate playing together. But they never want to separate, even when she makes it a mom order. "If you choose to play together, you both have to be flexible."

"Why do I always have to be flexible?" Jacob asks, planting his palm against his forehead. He should win an Oscar for this performance, or at least receive a nomination.

"It's all about sharing, and Chloe is flexible, too." She tickles both children until they squeal with laughter. "You are each other's best friend. Always and forever. So, work this out, and give each other credit for trying. Please."

"Okay. You can play with Matchbox cars, Jacob," Chloe says, compromising.

Before Amelia can high five her daughter, her cell rings and a picture of her parents illuminates the screen.

*Speaking of flexibility...* "Hi, Mom, or is this Dad?"

"It's both of us," her mother answers. "We're on speaker."

"We hate Zoom. Let's just talk to the kids," her dad adds, his voice as jovial as usual.

Though Amelia sets up these Zooms so that the kids can *see* their grandparents, and vice versa, her parents end up backing out and choosing to talk. Pressing her speaker button, she prompts Jacob and Chloe to say hello to their grandparents.

There's a brief discussion about the Easter Bunny, during which Jacob admits that they are good friends with him. Amelia's parents laugh, like he's making it up, never questioning if indeed their grandson and granddaughter met someone dressed like the furry cottontail and befriended the costumed human.

Though Amelia loves her mom and dad, they were never easy to approach or speak with while she was growing up. That's especially true now that they're over a thousand miles away, in Fort Lauderdale living the retirement dream.

"We have a golf game, but hopefully, we'll see you soon, darlings," her mom says.

Clenching her jaw so Amelia doesn't say what she's thinking, like *you would have seen us today if you'd entered the Zoom chat I invited you to*, or *you'll see us next summer when we visit annually*, or *you could see us if you'd ever visit us*, Amelia simply says, "We love you. Happy Easter."

Jacob and Chloe echo her, and she disconnects the call.

"See?" Amelia studies her son first, then her daughter. "Flexibility at its finest."

Jacob notes the time on Amelia's laptop. "Dad didn't call. Did he leave a voicemail while we were talking to Grandma and Grandpa?"

Wearing her calm expression, even though her heart is beating a mile a minute, Amelia checks. "No voicemail."

"Did Dad text us?" Chloe asks.

Amelia pulls up her texts. "No, he didn't." Though her text to him says that it was read. Daniel has disappointed the kids again.

"The day isn't over yet, right?" Amelia smiles, hoping being with their friends, their extended family, is enough to get their minds off their father.

With that, their doorbell rings and both Jacob and Chloe shout, "They're here!" Their excitement alleviates some of Amelia's stress as they all head down the front hallway.

Answering the door together, they shout "Happy Easter" and welcome the Reilly brood inside.

Bridget hands Amelia a vase of lilies. "Happy Easter and thank you for hosting this new tradition. I am so glad you're back in Houston!"

Jacob and Chloe hug Bridget's children—Ava, Seth, and Liam—then run down the hall to their bedrooms chatting with glee, while the two moms converge in the kitchen.

"It's so good to see you." Amelia places the vase on her kitchen island and takes the store-bought cheesecake in a plastic container from Bridget. "How are you?"

"Well, church service with my parents and Sean's was…you know." Bridget exhales as Amelia gives her a hug. "My parents want me to move on, while Sean's don't. Though they're not debating it like they did last year, it's still tense. How are you?"

Sean is Bridget's husband—was Bridget's husband. He passed away about five years ago.

"I'm sorry, Bridget. I can swap places with you next time, if you'd like."

"So, the Zoom went that well?" Bridget places her purse on the counter.

Amelia checks the oven, the aroma of honey ham wafting through the kitchen. "If you count my parents being later than usual, the quick phone call, and 'gotta go play golf' as going well, followed by Daniel ghosting the kids, then sure."

"Yeah, let's trade next holiday. I can totally handle that. I'll also tell Daniel where he can go." Bridget winks at her friend and helps set the table.

Lily arrives with her two daughters and the side dishes. Dinner is filled with lively conversation and much laughter. Amelia studies her children. They've returned to their happy, outgoing selves. Having an extended family has its perks, and this holiday definitely falls into that category.

After dinner, the women help Amelia place the dirty dishes in the dishwasher, while the children gather in the living room to watch *Hop* with James Marsden.

"I love me some James Marsden," Bridget confesses as she places the clean wineglasses in Amelia's cabinet, after Amelia hand-washed and dried them. They've got a system going.

Lily sighs. "He made *Sonic the Hedgehog this* mom's favorite movie."

"Mine, too." Bridget laughs. "Then again, I've been a fan since his *X-Men* days."

"While I'm a James fan, Hugh is the *X-Men* for me." Amelia dries the counter with a dish towel, then places it over her drying rack. "Hugh Jackman is my everything. And he sings."

"Dances, too," Bridget chimes in. "So, how did the kids do with their Easter baskets?"

"Great," Lily answers.

Amelia leans against her counter. "You'll do even better."

Her friends study her with skepticism.

"Let's just say my backyard is a mom's playground. Who's ready for a Mom Hunt?" Before the words escape her lips, Amelia's friends have raced out the back door and are running through the backyard, chatting and laughing. Miniature bottles of wine and bags of candy wrapped with raffia bows are hidden in the lawn, bushes, and flowers. Amelia makes sure the kids are set, then joins her friends just as Bridget dives for the last of the Dove chocolate, her arms full.

Handing them each their own adult basket with scented hand cream, body wash, and bubble bath, Amelia smiles. "I should have handed these out before I told you what was waiting outside."

"The chocolate was worth it. Oh! I think I have a grass stain on my dress." Bridget laughs, kneeling in the grass.

Lily has already opened her bag of Dove chocolates. "This is heaven," she whispers, savoring the dark chocolate.

Sifting through her loot, Bridget notices the bottle of bubble bath. "Oh, if you take the kids for a sleepover and I can use this, that grass stain will be so worth it."

"Done." Amelia smiles.

Lily halts, holding a bag of truffles. "How are the kids? We ran out of there fast."

"They're fine. We did have one adult in the room, and I told them where we'd be," Amelia assures her.

"Hey, you've got gnomes." Bridget eyes Amelia's backyard. "Gnomes with no Easter décor."

"That's correct. Easter is officially over today, so I decided to move these to the backyard." They're the new gnomes, but one remains in her front yard—the all-important gnome. "The gnome made by the kids is still in my front yard, but he is now holding an American flag."

Bridget arches her ginger brow. "How patriotic."

"Did you know that flags—United States and/or Texas—are not subject to HOA bylaws?" Amelia announces.

Lily takes another bite of chocolate. "Someone has done her homework."

"Impressive," adds Bridget.

"I'm just keeping one step ahead of Carla, and getting one day closer to the next HOA community meeting."

"How is Carla?" Bridget stands, holding her basket against her chest like it's a treasure that someone could steal at any moment.

Amelia shrugs. "I don't know. I haven't seen her recently. Something tells me she'll make an appearance at next weekend's yard sale, though."

"Oh, I am so there!" Bridget jumps at the chance to stand up to a mean Carla. "My kids will be with my parents, and I love causing trouble."

"No more trouble." On this, Amelia is adamant. "I'm doing enough of that with my defiance. And the fact that Gnomegate is also *Get Rid of Carla Gate.*"

"You have a lot of gates," Lily mutters between bites. "We're here for all your gates. You know that."

Bridget looks around. "I just wish Mr. Bunny was waiting for us out here."

Laughing, Amelia shakes her head. "No, you don't. He's too much trouble."

"Good trouble, you mean," Bridget announces. "Oh! Speaking of… I brought dessert!"

Lily turns to her, wearing a skeptical expression. "You baked?" she asks.

Bridget feigns indignation. "You know I don't bake. I bought a cheesecake. It's in Amelia's fridge."

"Well, seeing as there's no bunny, let's go inside and have cheesecake with James Marsden and our kids," Amelia suggests, then follows her friends to her back door.

Her cell vibrates, and she checks her texts. Though she'd hoped to see Daniel answer the children, it's from Kyle instead.

Happy Easter, Marsh! 🐰

Just as she's about to type, she notes the three dots indicating that Kyle is typing something else. Sure enough, a second message comes through.

Do you miss me?

*That man is a pain in*—her swear jar almost got more of her money, but she managed to stop her thoughts just in time—*my grass.*

Yep, Kyle is one big pain in her grass. So why is she smiling? There's only one answer: that man *is* trouble. And as her late grandmother taught her, when it comes to men, there's good trouble and bad trouble. What kind of trouble is Kyle? And does Amelia really want to find out?

In a rush, the children race into the backyard, all noise and commotion.

"Hide the chocolate!" Bridget stuffs a piece in her mouth.

Amelia smiles. "Okay, dudes and dudettes. You have some eggs to find. Over there." She points to a manicured line of shrubs against the far side of her fence, where multicolored plastic eggs have been placed in the mulch.

"No more candy. Please." Lily stands. "They're going to be bouncing off the walls."

"Stamps! Mom, look!" Violet, one of Lily's daughters, runs over, showing her mom an ink stamp with a flower on it.

When all of the children have gathered, they're stamping the backs of their hands with flowers, lady bugs, and even zoo animals.

"Just remember not to stamp walls, furniture, carpets, counters, electronics…" Amelia's voice trails off as she tries to remember what else is off limits.

"Don't stamp your clothes either," Lily adds.

Amelia raises her hands in the air. "Don't stamp anything not mom approved. Deal?"

"Deal!" the kids shout in unison.

Chloe shrieks, pointing to the mulch in front of the shrubbery lining Amelia's fence, "Look! There's a frog. Isn't he cute?"

"Mom, there's another frog. We saw two of them!" Jacob is as excited as his sister.

"Can we keep them?" Chloe looks at Amelia with wide eyes, filled with emotion. They want a pet, and Amelia has said that now isn't the right time.

Amelia bends down and offers Chloe a hug. "Those frogs belong out here. I hear them croaking every night."

Coming up to her, Jacob joins in a group hug. "Really?"

Amelia nods. "Yes. They croak to one another. Clearly, they like being outside and are happy. We don't want to take them away from that, do we?"

Both kids shake their heads.

"So, where did you leave off with the movie?"

Seth, one of Bridget's sons, answers, "The best part."

"Let's go, moms. James Marsden awaits." Bridget's all in, carrying her basket with a heartfelt smile on her face.

"Who is James Marsden?" her daughter, Ava, asks.

"He plays the Easter Bunny's helper," says Chloe, her stature straight and smile wide, clearly proud of herself for answering a question asked of the adults.

An "Ah!" escapes Jacob's lips. "Like Kyle. He's the Easter Bunny's helper, too."

*Apparently, all roads lead back to Kyle. With neighbors like him...*

"Now can we watch the rest of *Hop*?" Jacob smiles, a mischievous one at that.

Amelia rubs his back. "That we can, buddy."

"And we can have dessert. Who wants cheesecake?" Bridget's like a cheerleader prepping the crowd. The moms are on board, the kids not so much.

Lily adds, "We've also got ice cream."

That the children are eager for.

"And James Marsden," Bridget whispers, while the group of moms laugh.

Friends 'til the end, this group of women are Amelia's family. No catty gossip, no competition, just friends supporting one another. This is life, Amelia's new life. And for today, it feels right.

# Chapter 12

CASTLE ROCK COMMUNITY YARD SALES ARE A NEIGHBORHOOD staple. For those who want to take part, it's a nice way to raise money for a local animal shelter, and for those who don't, it's a great way to meet your neighbors, chat with the community, and possibly purchase some stuff from them. As for the cons, well there was the time that someone stole all of the signs and cost the HOA a lot of money. That was a definite con, and left Kyle reconsidering his decision to devote so much of his time to the community. He was reminded of something his mother would say growing up: *there's no such thing as perfection—just do your best.* That advice, told to a little boy before his parents divorced, remains with him to this day.

As HOA president, it's Kyle's responsibility to put the signs up first thing in the morning, at each of the community's three entrances. Being a minimalist, he never has anything to sell. Instead, Kyle does the heavy lifting by helping his neighbors prepare for the upcoming traffic. As for the cause, he privately donates money to it.

Driving through the sunny streets of Castle Rock with his windows down, Kyle stops here and there to help some of his neighbors and catches up with others. When he reaches Amelia's block, he drives even slower than the speed limit, hoping to see her. Sure enough, she's in her driveway with her children, who are setting toys out and wave as soon as they see him. Her friend—Bridget is her name, if Kyle recalls correctly—is with them.

"Hey, everyone. How's it going?" Kyle asks, getting out of his truck to say hi. Something he does for every neighbor. Nothing to see here. Nothing special. Except he did drive extra slow in the hopes of catching Amelia's attention. That's a first for him.

Jacob and Chloe run to Kyle, with the former announcing, "Kyle! We're selling stuff for the cats and dogs."

"Yeah. Can we see them?" Chloe asks.

Amelia walks up to him. "Hi, Kyle."

"Hi." The last time Kyle spoke with Amelia was at the playground. He did text her, though she never answered him. That should have been enough of a red flag, but here he is making small talk.

"Chloe and Jacob want to see the animals we're helping." Kyle grins at her.

"Oh, really?" She glances at her children. "Is that all you want to do? Because I'm pretty sure we wouldn't leave the shelter until you asked for a cat or dog of your own."

Jacob shakes his head. "We wouldn't do that."

"I know you both, remember?" Amelia arches her brow. "You once tried to capture a gecko in our backyard because you wanted a pet so badly."

Bridget laughs. "I remember that. Your mom walked outside, and it ran up her leg."

"No!" Kyle's eyes widen. "How did Amelia handle that?"

"Like a pro." Bridget winks at Amelia. "This stuff happens a lot with her. She's this magnet for pets, children, and chaos—not necessarily in that order."

Chloe yanks her mom's arm. "That wouldn't happen this time, Mom, because we already have one."

"Excuse me?" Amelia glances from Chloe to Jacob and back. "You already have what?"

Jacob leans into his sister, muttering, "That was our secret, Chloe."

"Rewind. You already have a what?" Amelia crouches down to her children's eye level. Neither will meet her stare, instead each studies their shoes. "Hello! Jacob… Chloe, you already have what? A gecko?"

"No, a kitten!" Chloe blurts out excitedly, while her brother does a full-on facepalm.

"Are you serious? Where did you find a kitten—wait, where is this kitten?" Amelia searches her children's faces.

Chloe turns to her brother, who shoots her a *you got us into this mess* look.

"Seriously, start talking now. Where's the cat? You *are* sure it's a cat, right?" Amelia is using her stern mom voice. It's a valid question as far as Kyle is concerned.

The silence emanating from Amelia's children is deafening, and even Kyle begins to question whether this is a cat or a small mountain lion cub, or perhaps a skunk. You never know.

"Show me. Now." Amelia's voice is firm, her finger pointing to her front door.

She follows her kids into their house to see if this so-called cat is in fact a cat. Bridget nudges Kyle forward.

"You before me. Get moving, please." Her words are clipped. Bridget is freaked out. Heck, her tension is starting to wear on Kyle's nerves. How is Amelia so calm?

Chloe leads their group to her room, where a castle sticker with her name printed on it is placed dead center in the middle of her closed door, along with a hand-written piece of paper with several letters written backwards that says *knock first*. Standing and waiting, the kids watch as Amelia opens the door with great care. Sure enough, curled in a ball on a round pink rug in the center of Chloe's room is a black and white tuxedo cat. Emaciated, with matted fur and large eyes, he or she lifts its head with a faint *meow*.

"She said hello to us. Isn't she cute?" Chloe squeals.

Amelia heads over to the kitten, who is surrounded by teddy bears and Barbies along with several Matchbox cars. "How long have you had this cat?"

"Since this morning." Jacob sits on the floor, legs crossed. "We found her in the backyard. She was hiding in the bushes and came right toward us. We were going to tell you, Mom. You were just so busy with the yard sale."

"Nope. No, sir. I'm never too busy for you to bring an animal into our home. What if it bit you? It didn't bite you or scratch you, right?" She searches their hands, arms, faces, and every other appendage for signs of a struggle.

Meanwhile, the ball of mangled fur rises and head bumps Amelia's leg.

"She's so sweet!" Chloe can't stop smiling as Amelia lifts the kitten into her arms.

"It's not a frog, Mom. It's a cat, and she doesn't belong outside all alone," Jacob explains to his mom.

"Jacob. Please grab my cell. It's on the kitchen counter." Amelia strokes behind the cat's ear.

Shaking his head, Jacob pleads, "Please let us keep her, Mom."

"Please!" Chloe chimes in.

Clearly outnumbered, Amelia studies the cat. "We will talk about that later. First, we need to take her, or him, to the vet. I need my cell to find one that has office hours on Saturday."

"There's one next door," Kyle offers, pointing east.

Amelia narrows her eyes. "The woman who does yoga in her driveway?"

"No. That's Mrs. Bass." Amelia is right. Mrs. Bass works out in her driveway at least three times a week. "Dr. Bass's wife likes to exercise on the driveway. Dr. Bass is a local vet."

"Does Dr. Bass have office hours on Saturday?" Amelia asks.

"I can do one better. His car is in the driveway, and he makes house calls. For VIPs." Kyle winks at Jacob and Chloe.

Chloe turns to her brother, a confused look marring her features. "How do we get a VP?"

"Yeah, I want a VP," her brother agrees.

"You *are* VIPs," Kyle assures them. "And I'm pretty sure Dr. Bass is home, taking part in the yard sale."

The kids race to the garage as Amelia, Bridget, and Kyle follow close behind.

"Bridget, I need you to keep the kids busy while I talk to our resident vet." A line of concern is etched in Amelia's forehead.

"Sure thing." Her friend nods, her messy bun flipping forward and back with the motion.

"Why are you worried?" Kyle's been told that he reads people well, and it's true. Especially when it comes to Amelia.

She leans into him, the floral and musky scent of her perfume awakening his senses. "If the kitten is sick, or belongs to someone else…" Her words trail off, and she grimaces. "This is no newborn, though. He or she is worse for wear. I just don't want the kids to lose someone else they love."

Kyle never even considered that risk.

"We'll keep them busy. With the yard sale stuff. They'll be safe and distracted. Not a problem." Bridget offers a smile to her friend, then meets up with the kids and tells them to help her organize the toys section.

After introducing Amelia to Dr. Bass, Kyle joins in the *let's keep the kids busy* chore with Bridget. When cars arrive, Bridget tells Kyle what to charge, and she chats with Jacob and Chloe about school and every topic other than the cat. Apparently, Jacob's ability at making baskets in gym class has appeased the mean kids, and they've let up on him.

Before Kyle can respond, Carla drives up and pulls to a stop, blocking Amelia's driveway.

"Kyle. I didn't expect to see you here." Carla has a Southern drawl that comes and goes. It's usually at its most prominent when she's feeling snarky. Today, it's a full-on drawl as she proceeds to the table next to which Kyle is standing.

He smiles, though he's not overly friendly. "Isn't today your day off, Carla?"

"Yes. But I'm looking at houses in the neighborhood. It's a buyer's market."

Seriously? Is Carla really considering moving in to Castle Rock? The neighbors might riot if Carla moved in to the neighborhood. Very few people like her due, in great part, to her many violation letters.

"That's not a good idea, Carla. Unless... Are you being reassigned?" Kyle asks.

Carla scoffs. "Of course not."

"Wouldn't it be a conflict of interest for you to live here and act as our management representative?" Yeah, that's it. Make Carla choose. She'll take her job and the power she wields any day of the week.

"This is just one of the many communities I'm looking at today. But your point is well taken." She surveys Jacob, Chloe, and Bridget—the last of whom has become very interested in Carla, who returns her attention to him. "What are you doing here, Kyle?"

Before he can answer, Bridget holds out her hand. "Hi. I'm Bridget, Amelia's best friend. In truth, she's like my sister. It's so good to put a face to the name, Carla."

Each syllable of that name is exaggerated. Intentionally, Kyle suspects.

Carla shakes Bridget's hand, though Amelia's friend fails to release it.

"You made a big mistake when you told Amelia that the yard sale was the weekend of the Easter egg hunt." Bridget's tone is sweet as molasses, though her eyes are narrowed and unforgiving in spite of her tone. "Thank goodness she caught your error. I'd hate to think of my friend setting up for a yard sale on the wrong day. Can you imagine?"

Clearly, Bridget wants Carla to know she's got Amelia's back and that she is well aware of Carla's behavior towards her friend. Rather commendable, if you ask Kyle.

"I—I didn't realize." Carla turns towards him. "I don't make mistakes like that. Perhaps Ms. Marsh misunderstood?"

"Nope. Amelia understands everything." On this Bridget is adamant.

"My mom's got superpowers." Jacob joins the conversation.

Not to be outdone, Chloe adds. "She's like the Scarlet Witch. Only she isn't a witch and doesn't have magic."

Jacob nods.

"Yeah. Mom knows every time we hide something from her," Chloe admits.

Jacob releases an "Ugh. That's because you told her about the kitten."

This entire conversation is so amusing that Kyle tries not to laugh as he adds, "I think your mom would have busted you regardless. I mean, how long could you hide a cat in your bedroom?"

Jacob does another facepalm against his forehead.

"Well said, Kyle." Bridget smiles at Kyle like he passed some test.

Carla clears her throat. "What cat?"

"We found a kitten and the veteran is with Mommy." Chloe's jumping up and down, vibrating with excitement.

Jacob smiles at Carla, like he's trying to charm her. "Kyle said we're VPs." The boy exudes a Tom Cruise vibe, and Kyle would bet his smile affects most people.

Tilting her head, Carla studies him with her brows furrowed. Jacob smiles wider, like this kid's done this before—charming the socks off the ladies. He even raises his eyebrows. Jacob is giving his all even if his unspoken message of *aren't I cute* falls flat on Carla.

Before Kyle can correct him, both kids shriek, "Mom!" Carla flinches at the noise level, and Kyle's smile widens.

"How is she?" Jacob asks.

"I want to name her Sabrina," Chloe announces. "Hi, Sabrina!"

Dr. Bass shakes Kyle's hand. "Hello, sir. Doing some community service, I see." Dr. Bass likes to joke, so Kyle chuckles.

"Always. What can I say?"

After a long pause, Dr. Bass acknowledges Carla with a curt nod, then turns his attention to the kids.

"I'm afraid I have some bad news."

Kyle's heart sinks in his chest. *Oh no, the kitten is sick.* He watches Chloe and Jacob as his blood pressure skyrockets, pounding against his temples like a sledgehammer.

"Your Sabrina is a Steve," Dr. Bass announces.

Kyle laughs, understanding straight away.

"I don't get it," Jacob says, staring at the veterinarian.

Amelia kneels in front of them, cuddling the kitten her arms, close to her chest. "Sabrina is a boy, so you'll need to name him something other than Sabrina."

"We can keep him?" the kids shout, and Carla jumps in horror.

Nodding, Amelia assures her children that they can keep the stray. "There's no chip, and Dr. Bass said he seems healthy. I'm scheduling a vet visit for tomorrow, but we can keep him."

Jacob and Chloe high five each other.

"Slow down there, you two." Amelia cuddles the cat close to her chest. "Having a cat is a huge responsibility and there will be rules you must follow, which we'll discuss later. In the meantime, please take the bag Dr. Bass gave us inside. He's given us everything we need to take care of our kitten formerly known as Sabrina until I get to the store tomorrow."

Jacob and Chloe follow instructions with Bridget's help. Kyle sees a small bag of litter, along with dry cat food, as Amelia thanks her neighbor. "It's nice to finally meet you. Your wife is sweet. We've spoken during her workouts."

Having firsthand knowledge on just how much Carla hates those workouts, and the fact that Mrs. Bass goes out of her way to Jazzercise on days that Carla is inspecting the community (for the sole purpose of annoying Carla), Kyle is certain hearing such a compliment is torture for the rep to witness.

When Dr. Bass returns to his driveway, Amelia surveys what little stuff is left.

"You and Bridget sold a lot while I was gone." She turns to Carla. "Carla. How are you? Oh, I know. You must be surprised to see the yard sale today since you mixed up the dates when I saw you at the bunny hunt. Good thing Kyle is such a great HOA president. Very communicative."

Amelia turns towards her gnome. "And look! My gnome is a flagpole, for the American flag. Though small, that gnome is mighty, and per our state law, flags of all sizes are allowed in subdivisions since state law supersedes bylaws. Bless Texas, am I right?"

Staring at the small flag attached to Amelia's gnome, Carla is stunned into silence.

"I'll still be at the next HOA community meeting though. So nice to see you today." With a wink, Amelia says goodbye to Carla and Kyle, then walks into her house, the cat still sleeping in her arms.

She just handled Carla like a pro. Kyle can't hide his admiration as he shifts his weight. "Well, I should see if anyone else needs my help. Don't you have some other neighborhoods to look at? I hear the subdivision near the middle school is nice."

Carla scoffs. "No, schools are much too noisy. But I do have other communities to look at. I'll speak with you soon, Kyle."

Kyle nods, watching her drive away, then collecting the empty boxes and cutting them down for recycling. Kyle will help other residents as soon as he's done helping Amelia. Did he get rid of Carla by dismissing her? Yes, he did. He's also got zero regrets.

Amelia meets him on her driveway. "Please. I can do this. I just wanted to make an impactful exit. Thanks for playing along."

"Honestly, I wasn't playing at anything. I was impressed with the way you handled Carla." There's a bit of awe in his voice. Enough for Kyle to notice, though he doubts Amelia does. "Nice move with the flagpole idea, though I doubt that will fly for long. It's a tiny flag, and from the looks of it, the flag is taped to your gnome."

"Good guess." Amelia studies the gnome that started Gnomegate. "I thought it would buy me more time. It's clear tape, so I don't know if it will survive one rainfall."

Kyle chuckles. "It's a good thing today is sunny." This woman is brilliant. Carla's got her hands full, and as the HOA president, so does he.

"Thanks for introducing me to Dr. Bass."

"The cat's okay?" Kyle asks.

Amelia nods. "I will be combing him for fleas, and he will sleep in our guest bath for a little while to make sure he can use the litter box, but he's old enough to eat dry kitten food. He's mangy, emaciated, a total oddball, and all mine."

"Your kids might argue that he's theirs."

"They definitely will, but welcome to my world." Amelia adjusts her ponytail. "Thanks again for your help today."

Kyle should say *you're welcome* and leave it at that. He should, but he doesn't. "You didn't text me back."

"Very astute, Mr. Sanders. No, I did not text you back." Her wry grin is on full display.

He plays along, "Why didn't you text me back? Were you at a loss for words?"

"Me? Never." Amelia winks at him. "I've let you have the last word twice now, and in doing so, I've lulled you into a false sense of security. Just like Carla. It's all part of my master plan."

Goodness help him, there's the mention of her plan again. "The plan I won't like?"

She backs away, heading towards his truck. "I've got a few plans you might not like. Don't you need to get going?"

She opens his truck door for him. "Don't let me monopolize your day. There are lots of other neighbors who would love a visit from you."

*Other neighbors.*

So, Amelia loves a visit from Kyle, too. Good to know, especially since she doesn't acknowledge her slip-up.

Kyle leans against his truck, about a foot away from Amelia. "What's the hurry? Afraid our truce won't last?"

"Oh, I know it won't." Amelia steps aside, motioning Kyle to his driver's seat. Once in, she closes the door. "Especially since I got another letter from Carla, this one about a flower that she thinks is a weed in my front yard. I've already emailed her to point out the error."

"You didn't confront her today?" Kyle is surprised.

Amelia shakes her head. "Nope. I emailed her. Documentation is always necessary, especially when it seems like she's targeting me in particular."

He starts his ignition and presses the button for his window. Just as he's about to speak, Amelia beats him to it.

"For the record, I'm no pushover, Kyle Sanders. Carla will learn that the hard way. So will you."

Leaning against his open window, Kyle answers clearly, "I already know it. How about you come to my barbecue next weekend and meet some more of our neighbors?"

"Careful what you wish for." Amelia backs away and saunters towards her driveway.

"Should I take that as a yes?" Kyle shouts to her.

She turns. "You can't handle this, Kyle."

"Try me," Kyle adds before driving down the street.

A text message alert pops up on his display, and he presses the button. It's from Amelia. Two words:

You're on.

Challenge accepted.

# Chapter 13

SUNDAY EVENINGS ARE USUALLY HECTIC, BUT AMELIA DECIDES TO spend some quality time with Chloe by painting her nails a neutral color while Jacob's showering.

"So, how's school going?" Amelia asks, as she applies the pale pink to her daughter's short nails.

Holding Chloe's hand still, she waits for an answer.

"It's good. Britney is nice, and I had a fun playdate at her house yesterday. Thanks, Mom."

Amelia smiles. "I'm glad you had fun. We'll invite her over soon, okay?"

Chloe laughs. "Yes! I'd love that!"

"So how are you adjusting? There have been a lot of changes, and you never complain." It's true. Chloe's upbeat and always supports her brother, who has been openly struggling to fit in at times. "You can talk to me, you know. You don't need to be strong all the time or hide how you're feeling from me."

Sighing heavily, Chloe's hand quivers slightly. "I think I have it easier than Jacob, because I have you. You're my mom, and the one who always spent time with us. You picked us up, dropped us off, and were at every class party and science fair. Dad never went."

"True. But it's okay to miss your dad, Chloe."

A heady silence engulfs them, until Chloe whispers, "Is it okay not to miss him?"

Amelia's hand quivers and she paints Chloe's finger, instead of her nail. "I'm sorry." She removes the wet nail polish with a tissue, then closes the cap on the bottle.

Studying her daughter's worried expression, Amelia caresses her little girl's cheek. "Is that really how you feel, honey? You don't miss your dad?"

"He was never around." Chloe studies Amelia with her beautiful blue-green eyes that she inherited from Daniel. "When he was, he didn't spend time with us. I don't feel as bad as Jacob does because I still have you, and nail time."

Chloe waits in silence, possibly for Amelia's approval, which she readily provides. "It's okay to feel what you feel. There's no right or wrong, just as long as you talk to me. I am here for you."

"I know. You're happier here and we have more fun," Chloe admits, her voice solid, as if this is her truth and she's no longer afraid to voice it.

"Even in school?" Amelia arches her brow. "Tell me the truth now."

"Sometimes. I like my class, and Aunt Bridget's kids are great, so are Ivy and Violet. I like sleeping over at Aunt Lily's house with them. Britney is a new friend, but I like her. I just don't like the boys that made fun of Jacob."

"They stopped, right?" Amelia asks. Her emails were quite clear, and she was promised by the principal and teachers alike that the behavior towards Jacob wouldn't be tolerated.

Nodding, Chloe adds, "I still don't like them."

"That's understandable. There are some people we don't like, or who don't like us. We just need to be kind, respectful, and leave them alone." Amelia's hypocrisy isn't lost on her. She's fighting the HOA and their bylaws, after all. Then again, Carla is sending more letters, about nonexistent violations, which is not professional at all. Amelia amends her last statement. "Try to leave them alone, and don't hurt them. Take me and Carla, for example. I'm doing the research to fight for our gnome. There's nothing physical, and I'm nice to her when I see her."

"I don't like her at all. But I'm nice to her, too." Chloe smiles.

Caressing her daughter's cheek, Amelia winks at her. "See? That's what you should do with the mean kids at school."

Her daughter places her hand in front of Amelia. "Can we finish my nails before Jacob's out of his shower?"

Amelia complies and adds a fast-dry top coat, finishing up just as Jacob jumps on Amelia's bed in fresh pajamas, the scent of shampoo and soap filling her nostrils, replacing the nail polish odor.

"What are you talking about?" he asks, wanting to be a part of manicure time despite the fact that he doesn't get manicures.

"I was asking your sister the same thing I'm going to ask you: How are you, Jacob? Is everything okay at school?"

He rolls onto his back. "It's better. I made some new friends, and we play at recess sometimes."

Not a glowing endorsement. "Do you miss Dad?" Chloe asks.

Studying her son, Amelia notes his eyes have lost some of their luster. "Yeah, but it's okay. We have Mom, right?"

Amelia hugs her son and daughter. "Always and forever. And I'm here whenever you want to talk. Especially about your dad. I know it's difficult for you."

"Can I…" Jacob's faint voice trails off.

Amelia kisses the top of his head. "Can you what?"

"Record a text for Dad? Please?" Jacob's tone conveys his desperation.

Reaching for her cell, Amelia opens her texts and records her son's message to his absent father:

"Hi, Dad, it's Jacob. I missed talking to you on Easter. Chloe and I have a cat." An already litter-box-trained Prince jumps onto Amelia's bed, distracting Jacob for a moment while the boy scoops the furball into his arms. "His name is Prince and he's black, white, and the cutest cat. He looks like he's wearing a tuxedo. He might be British royalty, but I'm not sure. Anyway, call me so we can talk."

Jacob nods to his mom, who stops recording and presses Send. "It has been delivered," she announces in a playful voice to cheer Jacob up. He didn't say *I love you* to his father, which speaks volumes to Amelia.

"Would you like to send your dad a recording, Chloe?" she asks.

"No thanks. I think we should hug." The little girl is trying to cheer her brother up, along with Amelia. "Just don't ruin my nails. Deal?"

"Deal," Amelia and Jacob agree in unison, and they have a group hug including a very sleepy Prince, after which Jacob tickles Amelia. Since Chloe doesn't want to mess up her nails, she supports Jacob by yelling, "Tickle Mom! Go, Jacob."

Laughing, Amelia tickles her son back, and it's on. Tickle fest, Marsh style. There's nothing like tickles to change a dark mood, and that's just what they all needed. Laughter fills Amelia's master bedroom as the fun continues.

Daniel is missing out on two exceptional children and memories Amelia will always cherish. It's his loss, though he will never realize it. Amelia appreciates it, which makes it even more special.

Her children will get through it all.

With her by their side. Always.

# Chapter 14

A MAN'S HOME IS HIS CASTLE, OR SO THE SAYING GOES. BEING A general contractor, Kyle was able to spruce up his particular fixer-upper, though the truth is that no matter how much of himself he pours into this former foreclosure, his two-story with a brick and stone exterior feels comfortable, but not like home—at least not the home he truly wants.

With four bedrooms, two and a half baths, and a downstairs home office, there's plenty of room…more room than he needs. That's part of the problem: if he looks at his life and past relationships, he thought he'd be married by now, and that his home would be filled with love. Still, by purchasing this house when he did, it was a solid investment, one Kyle couldn't pass up. Especially if he ever wants to flip it and make a profit. One of the perks about living in Timberland are the housing prices. You get a lot of room for your money. When it's a foreclosure and a fixer-upper to boot, it becomes a buyer's dream.

Many of the homes in Castle Rock have similar floor plans depending upon the builder, which Kyle is reminded of as he passes his home office. Like so many of this builder's homes, it has a front room jutting off the main hallway on the first floor. Proceeding to the kitchen, which overlooks an open-floor-plan dining room and great room, Kyle stares out his glass back door.

This is why he stays in a house too big for only himself—the view from his living room and master bedroom. Not of his backyard, but beyond the wood fence, where large pine trees loom tall and sturdy. To find a home in this subdivision with no neighbors behind you is rare. To have an unobstructed view of pines is even more unlikely. In a typical subdivision, where houses are built close together, overlooking no one else is a solitary heaven for Kyle.

His living room is another reason. It's the place where he relaxes and can be himself. It also represents who he is, the Kyle very few people ever see: the man who loves music and plays guitar in his free time. Only his close friends know this about him. Kyle's eyes rove his collection of guitars hanging on the wall above his worn leather sofa. Across from it hangs his big screen TV. Beneath it, on a table he built out of distressed wood and pipes, sits an old-school turntable with an MP3 converter and shelves accentuated with his collection of vinyl albums.

After today's busy day, during which every obstacle was thrown at him and his office staff was hustling almost as fast as he was, music isn't going to cut it tonight. Heading into his master suite, he changes into his workout clothes and places his earbuds in his ears, before setting off on his nightly jog. Billy Joel is his companion as he rounds the corner on his usual route. Between songs, the sound of a garage door opening makes Kyle turn. He's in front of Amelia's house.

*Do all roads in Castle Rock lead here to Amelia's driveway?*

Wiping sweat from his forehead with his T-shirt, he watches as Amelia rearranges some storage tubs on a shelf in her garage. It's been a while since they last saw each other. When she drags a ladder over to her shelves, Kyle clears his throat. "Do you need help?"

"Oh! You scared me." Amelia clutches her chest, adding in an exasperated whisper, "I need one of those containers, but there are books in them, and they're heavy. I'm trying not to wake the kids."

As Amelia attempts to walk up the ladder, she slips, and Kyle reaches out to steady her. "May I?"

"Gladly." She steps from the ladder. "What are you doing out here? It's late."

Kyle reaches for the storage container she pointed to, the plastic tub with a lid. "I was jogging. After a long workday, I needed to clear my head. Man, this is heavy. What's in here? A dead body?"

Amelia offers him a sly grin. "It's so much worse than that. It's full of books. I did tell you that. Nice to know you were paying attention."

"Did you say something?" he jokes.

Rolling her eyes, Amelia remains silent. That look says it all.

"Do you have an entire library in this one tub? To say this thing is heavy is an understatement." Kyle manages to plop the large plastic bin on the garage floor minimizing the sound and Amelia immediately opens it. Inside, it's filled with black heavy-duty garbage bags with zip ties. "You wrap your books up tight."

Gasping, she mocks Kyle. "Don't tell me that you dog-ear pages. I'll have to ban you from my property."

She stacks the bags neatly in the corner of her garage and carries the empty tub out of her garage, heading towards her back gate, which Kyle opens for her.

"So, what's going on?" he asks, doing his best to sound nonchalant, when his new neighbor is dragging a large storage tub to her backyard, under the light of a full moon.

After placing the tub next to her hose on her back patio, Amelia picks up a flashlight from her outdoor dining table and walks over to her massive birdbath. "I have frogs."

Kyle blinks. "Is that code for something?"

She aims the flashlight at her birdbath. "Yes, it's code for *I have frogs.* Or at least I have tadpoles which will grow into frogs, if I don't kill them first."

Leaning close, Kyle notices tadpoles of various sizes swimming in her birdbath.

She illuminates her face with the flashlight, very Halloween horror movie-esque. "First the stray cat, and now frogs, or soon-to-be frogs. It would appear I am a magnet for creatures with no homes."

Laughing, Kyle is reminded of his conversation with her friend. "Bridget said something similar."

"Did she now?" Amelia studies the tadpoles. "I'd ask what else she said, but I'm kind of busy trying to rehome amphibians."

"You're going to do what, exactly?"

"I plan to fill the bin with water, and transfer the tadpoles to the storage bin." She leans down and opens a large container of spring water, pouring it into the tub, followed by another.

Kyle tilts his head to the side. "Silly question: why are you doing this?"

She reaches for another bottle of spring water. "Because I googled it, and tap water isn't good for tadpoles. Luckily, I stock up on spring water for hurricane season."

"Okay, that explains the abundance of spring water. Now, how about the rehoming of tadpoles?"

"Because in addition to finding a cat, my daughter found tadpoles while playing in the backyard this afternoon and has told me how cute they are, while she and her brother both explained the life cycle of frogs ad nauseam. I have no choice but to take care of the little creatures, at least if they survive. Living in the birdbath will not equate to their survival." She pours the rest of the water into the container.

Lifting a finger in the air, she shushes Kyle, even though he didn't say anything. "Listen. I've heard these frogs croaking for months. I didn't know they were mating, or that they expected me to be foster mother to their spawn."

"Look on the bright side," Kyle teases. "Your children think you're the Scarlet Witch."

"If only." Amelia stands, meeting Kyle's eyes for the first time in the dim light of the backyard. "Did Carla place a spell on me? How else can all of this be happening?"

"Just lucky, I guess." Kyle smiles. Amelia is this whirlwind of energy and a controlled chaos that would normally have him running in the opposite direction. But her chaos is actually fascinating and—dare Kyle admit it—fun.

After placing leaves and branches in the tub of water for food, she returns her attention to the birdbath. Since there's no pool skimmer, let alone a pool, Kyle helps Amelia scoop out the tadpoles with his hands and transfer them into the bin, along with some more leaves to eat and some branches. "There will be plenty of mosquitos for them to eat."

"True. I had to order a new zapper. It arrives this week." Amelia's attention remains on the tadpoles.

"I still can't believe your kids found a cat and tadpoles in your backyard. All the previous owner discovered were geckos and mosquitos." Kyle holds the flashlight as Amelia scoops the last tadpole.

"Between you and me"—Amelia arches her dark brow, her voice a whisper—"if Jacob and Chloe find a snake, I'm going into witness protection. Snakes and I don't mix."

*Got it. She's afraid of snakes.* "How about you call me. I'm great when it comes to getting rid of snakes."

"Thanks." She smiles, cupping a larger tadpole in her hands. "Oh no! This last one didn't make it. The kids can't know it died. What do I do? Do I flush him like a fish?"

"Sounds like as good a plan as any." Kyle opens her back door, and she leads him through her bedroom to the master bath.

After saying a little prayer for the unnamed tadpole, Amelia flushes it and washes her hands. Kyle follows suit, and she offers him her hand towel.

"Your backyard looks great. Granted it was in shadow, but I like all the shrubs you planted." She's made improvements since moving in. It works. Kyle can easily imagine Jacob and Chloe discovering tadpoles in their bird-bath. The scene in his head is comedic, then again so is Amelia. She's got an energy that fills the room and makes his heart feel a little lighter.

Their new kitten enters the bathroom with a loud *mew*, and Amelia picks him up. "Hey, Prince. You remember Kyle, right?"

The cat is unimpressed with Kyle. Instead, he purrs loudly and buries his face beneath Amelia's hand as she pets him. "So, he's a Prince?"

"As in 'the artist formerly known as'…or 'Prince Charming.' It was between that and 'Sonic the Hedgehog.' I didn't want to give the poor thing a hedgehog complex." Her eyes sparkle with mirth.

"Good call," Kyle teases as they walk into her living room, decorated with distressed wood and lots of beige and light-blue furnishing and drapes.

Her open floor plan is decorated casually, and Kyle loves her natural wood vibes.

"Would you like a glass of ice-cold water?" she asks, her voice low, as she places the kitten on her sofa and then heads into her kitchen. "It's a reward for helping me rescue those tadpoles."

"Sure." Sitting beside the kitten, who yawns, as if Kyle's keeping him awake, Kyle decides to move to Amelia's loveseat, giving the little furball free rein on the large sofa.

"He is taking over my house. It's his diabolical plan." Amelia hands Kyle a bottle of cold water and plops beside him. "The kids already out-number me. Now I've got a cat and amphibians to contend with. And another letter from Carla. This time I had three weeds that have grown near my fence. Say what you will, but that woman is relentless."

Running her hand through her long hair, Amelia looks radiant, even in the dim recessed lighting of her living room.

"Sorry about the letter. As for the rest of it, is this what mom chaos looks like?" Kyle asks, truly interested.

Amelia exhales. "Oh, you haven't seen chaos yet. Trust me, this is just the tip of the iceberg."

Suddenly, Kyle would like to see more. Amelia is willing to transfer tadpoles to a bin in the middle of the night for her kids. That's something special, something that makes him want to break his own rules and get to know her better.

His gaze lingers from her eyes, a smoky brown in the dim lighting, to her high cheekbones the hue of a light petal pink, then to her grin, and down to her T-shirt. White, and wet. It's transparent. Her bra can be seen beneath it.

Kyle averts his eyes, though he's never been more tempted to stare. Not once. Not like this.

"What?" she asks.

Pointing to her shirt, he manages the word "wet." One word is all he can muster as the bulge in his shorts becomes painful.

Though he tries to defuse his craving for her by reminding himself of those well-intentioned rules, all Kyle can think of is the fact that Amelia will do anything for her kids. That's downright sexy.

Amelia excuses herself to change shirts, and Kyle places a light-blue accent pillow on his lap. "Get it together," he mutters to himself.

Prince perks his head up and stares at Kyle.

"What?" His voice is gruff with guilt, as Kyle adjusts the pillow. It's as if the cat knows what he's thinking. But not even Kyle knows. Or does he?

*Ignore these feelings…whatever these feelings are.* It's easier said than done, though. Because he can't ignore Amelia no matter how hard he tries, and he is trying. Desperately so.

Single mom be damned, Kyle's rule book has taught him nothing about how to handle Amelia Marsh.

# Chapter 15

AMELIA DARTS INTO HER BEDROOM, TOSSES HER WET T-SHIRT onto her bathroom floor, then leans against the door of her walk-in closet, after pretending to ignore Kyle's erection. From a damp white T-shirt worn by *her*. Even though she's not wearing sexy lingerie, any makeup, or heels, Kyle is aroused by just plain Amelia Marsh, with her C-cup postpregnancy breasts in a plain white cotton push-up bra, also known as her go-to mom bra.

"Amelia Angelica Marsh, pull yourself together. He's nothing special. Just a guy." She mutters under her breath, but she knows better. Kyle is a guy, that's true, but he's also a guy who is aroused by Amelia. That's a feat even her ex-husband was incapable of.

Reaching for a hanger, which snaps and is now wedged between the others, Amelia struggles to free it. "Damn it!"

A knock on her open bathroom door causes her to jump.

"Do you need help?" Kyle asks from the doorway. "I heard a curse word."

"Dang it! I owe the swear jar," she moans.

Leaving her shirt dangling on the broken hanger, Amelia reaches for a tank on the shelf, and dresses in record time. She exits her large closet to find Kyle with his back to her bathroom, like he doesn't want to look.

"I'm good. Thanks for checking on me." She passes him in the doorway.

"You were taking a long time, and I was worried the tadpole came back as a zombie, or something."

"That would be my luck." She escorts him back to her living room, where he pauses in front of her fireplace mantel, studying the many framed pictures that rest upon it, in various sizes. Pictures of Jacob and Chloe. First as babies, then now. Also of prominence are two pictures of Amelia and her friends. One is from their high school prom, wearing colorful gowns, holding balloons. The other is from present day. Before and after photos, they highlight how much each has changed, how much their lives have evolved.

"Look at this," he says, pointing to the prom picture, her throw pillow nowhere in sight.

Yep, his attraction to her has done a disappearing trick, replaced by small talk. "It's an oldie but goodie. We went stag, just the three of us." They were all that each other needed.

"That's you." He points at a younger Amelia. Fresh-faced, full of excitement and wide-eyed innocence.

"It is. Bridget is the red-headed knockout next to me. Lily is the dazzling brunette." They haven't changed, she notes.

"What are you?" Kyle asks.

Amelia turns to him, her confusion obvious with a "Huh?"

"Bridget is a knockout, Lily is dazzling… What are you?"

Tough question. One she's never considered. "I'm just me."

Turning to the present-day photo of Amelia, Jacob, and Chloe with Kyle's Easter Bunny, Amelia sees happiness in her eyes. It's because of her children. They make her happy and are her life. Do her eyes still hold that same spark of hope they once did? Maybe not, but there's more to her than wide-eyed innocence now.

Kyle reaches for the Easter picture of the kids, Amelia, and him as the Bunny's helper. "This is a great photo. You look amazing, and your personality shines through."

That shouldn't come as a surprise, because she's complete with her kids.

"*You're* a knockout. *You're* mesmerizing. *You're* amazing." Kyle's voice is rough, and he clears his throat.

*Knockout. Mesmerizing. Amazing.*

"Me?" Her whisper is raspy.

She studies his profile as he continues to avoid her gaze. He's dead serious, Amelia notes with a twinge of surprise. When he turns and his eyes hold hers, they simmer with a burning intensity.

"You don't give yourself enough credit." His tone is raw with unchecked emotion.

Reaching for her, he caresses Amelia's cheek with his thumb. She can't help but lean into him. Kyle is magnetic, and she's not immune to his appeal. Far from it. They're mere inches from one another, and Amelia senses he wants to kiss her.

She holds her breath, waiting for Kyle to make his move. She wants it, and is pretty sure he does, as well. He tilts his head down, and his lips hover over hers. The scent of his perspiration mingled with the faint remnant of cologne awakens Amelia's senses, makes her shudder with anticipation.

"To heck with it," she mutters, reaching for him as she stands on her tiptoes, tugging him closer as she parts her own lips.

Splaying his palms against her back, Kyle's warmth fills Amelia and encapsulates her in his tight embrace. Closer they move, then closer still until—

"Mom, I want water."

Kyle releases Amelia so quickly that it causes her to sway. She turns to find Jacob, eyes closed, leaning against the hallway that leads to his and Chloe's bedrooms and bath. Crossing the living room in record time, Amelia reaches for her son. "Come on, sweetie. You're half asleep."

Guiding Jacob when he's half asleep is a task at which she's become proficient. Gripping his shoulders, Amelia directs him back to his room, trying to avoid all walls, corners, and furniture until they've reached his bed, where he collapses. He used to have night terrors when he was a baby, then as he grew older, he would sleepwalk. Now he gets out of bed when he's half asleep, asks for water, then goes back to sleep and doesn't remember a thing the next morning. Such has been their routine since the move. The stress of a new school is a part of it, as is the absence of his dad.

Amelia places his blankets on top of him, then kisses his forehead. "I love you, Jacob. Always and forever. Sweet dreams."

He sighs, and his lips upturn into a grin.

Interrupting her when she's about to kiss their new neighbor is by no means routine. Nope. This is uncharted territory. Thankfully, Jacob won't remember a thing. Amelia, on the other hand, will never forget it. Or the fact that Kyle is still waiting for her. What in the world is she supposed to do next?

By the time she's closed Jacob's bedroom door, checked on her sleeping Chloe, and exited the hallway that leads from their bedrooms and bath, Amelia enters her living room to find Kyle placing money in her swear jar, which sits on the half wall that separates her kitchen and living room.

"Is that a five-dollar bill? That's too much." She laughs.

Shrugging, Kyle whispers, "I'm spotting you. Besides, if I slip up, then I've prepaid. I own a construction company, after all. Cursing is almost part of the job description."

His lopsided grin makes her smile wider. Then she returns to her senses. She's a mom of two who can't let just anybody in, no matter how compassionate he seems.

"I shouldn't have tried to kiss you," Amelia admits, as warmth travels up her cheekbones. "I… I can't date anyone. Not now, not yet. It took months for the kids to reach this good place, if you can call it that. At least it's better than Austin. The kids had some dark days there, bumping into Daniel in the grocery store and having him treat them like strangers was brutal. Even though he worked a lot and they had gotten used to him not being around, they still hurt from his absence. I know it, and we're working through it. That's why I can't date anyone."

"'Date'? Isn't that a little presumptuous?" Kyle teases her with a wink, as if she didn't just suffer from a severe case of TMI, as if she didn't just make a fool of herself.

In spite of her best efforts to control it, Amelia's heartbeat quickens from that one wink… That's all it takes. "Forgive me for being presumptuous, but I don't do the nondating benefits thing either."

"That's a relief, because neither do I."

Kyle's admission floors her. "Really? You?"

"Yes me." He tilts his head to the side, faking indignation.

"But you're…" She swallows hard. "Never mind."

"I'm what?" he asks as he heads to the front door, causing her to follow. Once he reaches the sturdy oak and glass, he places his palm on the door handle before meeting her eyes again. "What am I, Amelia?"

"Hot." Did. She. Just. Say. That?

Kyle smirks. "Really? You don't say."

Amelia sighs. Good thing Kyle placed a five-dollar bill in her swear jar, because she's got a lot of curse words racing through her mind right now. "Well, you're always jogging, helping children, and helping neighbors. I bet you rescue puppies in your spare time. You're a catch and something tells me you could have any type of relationship you want."

Way to rationalize. The thing is, it's true. Kyle is the Webster's definition of a good guy. His picture is probably in the illustrated kiddie version of the dictionary.

"I'm just a guy," Kyle notes with humility. "Come to my barbecue and you'll see that. Friendship isn't a bad thing, as long as quality, not quantity, is the main factor."

He's insightful. Add that to his list of traits that make him a catch.

"Okay. I'll be there." Did she really just agree to go to his barbecue?

His brows rise. "I thought that it would be more difficult to convince you."

"I am close to taking back my RSVP. The sheer number of violation letters I continue to receive from Carla is making me reconsider. Go, now, before I change my mind." Amelia turns the lock to the left.

Opening the door, Kyle leans into her, whispering in Amelia's ear. "I'd like to be friends with you. It's better than Gnomegate enemies. Oh! We could be frenemies. I've never had one of those."

"'Frenemies?' Really?" Amelia bites her lower lip, trying not to laugh. "Out. Now. I'm starting to feel like this is an episode of *Gossip Girl*."

He hands her another five from his shorts pocket. "For when I leave. Something tells me you'll have a lot to say once I'm gone."

Kyle's wry grin…no, his smirk, infuriates her. It also makes her laugh. Grabbing the cash, she retorts, "Where I come from, that's a challenge."

"Make no mistake. Here in Timberland, it is a challenge, too." He saunters through her doorway. "Good night, Amelia."

Exiting through her door without another word, let alone another glance, Kyle is gone in seconds. When the door quietly closes, the battery-operated motorized hum of her front door lock grabs Amelia's attention. She stares intently, watching as the lock turns in place.

Kyle just pressed the exterior *Brinks* key on her front door and locked it. It doesn't take a code to lock the door from the outside and, as a contractor, he must know that. This guy just made sure she and her kids are safe. She couldn't even get Daniel to check if the garage door was closed.

Random acts of kindness are Amelia's weakness. Much more than sexy abs, or lust, or sexual tension. Kyle is a kind man. And she just wants to be friends. No, it's more than that... Amelia needs to be friends and only friends with him—for Jacob and Chloe's sake.

If it were just Amelia, she'd take a chance with Kyle, but not where Jacob and Chloe are concerned. She can't afford to make another mistake. Trusting her ex-husband was tragic enough. They're still paying the price. His distance from the kids has been ongoing, long before their divorce, but it is only getting worse. How can it not negatively affect Jacob and Chloe?

It's like the calm before the storm. Amelia knows something is brewing, and that things with Daniel will come to a head. So, she must stay the course. Family comes first. They're why she will continue to fight the bylaws, fight Carla, and, as always, her number one goal is to take care of Jacob and Chloe. That's her plan. But having a good guy as a friend can't hurt... if she's careful.

It's time for more research in her office. She's progressed from researching the HOA and bylaws to management companies and their representatives. This is her battle, among others. And she's giving it her all.

Prince accompanies her into her office, lying down on his favorite spot on her throw rug. As her desktop powers up, she thinks about Kyle. A neighbor like him might make her wonder what could have been, but it's a brief thought. Nothing more. Because Amelia will never have regrets. Her children come first. Now and always.

# Chapter 16

"YOU'RE GOING TO A BARBECUE. WHY ARE YOU WEARING THAT?" Bridget studies Amelia's sleeveless maxi dress like it's the most atrocious thing she's ever seen.

Amelia glances at herself in Bridget's floor-length bedroom mirror, listening to the children whooping it up in Bridget's media-/playroom. "What's wrong with my dress?"

"It covers everything up, except your arms."

Scoffing, Amelia adjusts the fabric that plunges at a V just above her breasts. "That's the point. It covers my stretch marks, and my other imperfections. I've given birth to two children. I am not one to wear crop tops and daisy dukes."

Bridget disappears into her walk-in closet, and returns dangling a hanger with a short sundress. "Put this on."

"It's the same thing—"

"No, it's not. This one isn't floor length." Thrusting the hanger at Amelia, Bridget's tone is serious. "You have great legs. Don't cover them up."

"What I have are cankles. No one likes those."

"What is wrong with you?" Bridget slings the dress atop her pristine pastel bedding, narrowing her eyes as she approaches Amelia from behind. "It's a friendly neighborhood barbecue. What am I missing?"

"Thanks for allowing Jacob and Chloe to sleep over tonight." Amelia changes the subject, hoping Bridget doesn't push.

"Don't mention it. This is your chance to meet the neighbors, and my kids love it when yours sleep over." Bridget sits on her mattress, her legs tucked beneath her. She's wearing trendy black leggings and a cold-shoulder tee in red. The shade should clash with her natural ginger hair, but not on Bridget. She's radiant, always.

"Will Kyle be there?"

*Annnnd* Bridget just went where Amelia dared not venture in record time.

"I would hope so. It is *his* barbecue, after all." It will be the first time Amelia's seen him since their almost kiss and her admissions about not dating.

"You're going to Sexy Bunny's house!" Bridget adds in a singsong voice. "Oh—wait. Is that why you're all covered up?"

Amelia turns and plops beside Bridget on her bed. "What do you think? The guy isn't human—at least not usually so. I don't think he has a flaw, physically or otherwise."

"That's good, right?"

"No. It's not good. Because we almost kissed, and I had to admit that I can't date, which was awkward. Especially since I already have a lot of conflict with a great guy."

"That's right. 'Gnomegate.' What's next? Clash of the Castle Rock residents?" Bridget scoffs. "And you think I'm corny."

Though Amelia's nervous about seeing Kyle again, she makes a joke. It's her attempt at deflecting. "My Game of Gnomes is serious business, Bridget. It's about breaking the wheel."

With Amelia's *Game of Thrones* reference, Bridget peals with laughter. "Whatever you say, Khaleesi. Or should I say Amelia of the House Marsh, queen of her castle, domestic goddess, and mother of two cutie pies."

As she tosses a ruffled pillow at her friend, Amelia's expression is animated. "That was so good!" Bridget is witty and funny, which are just some of the many reasons she makes such a wonderful friend.

"Are you having a pillow fight?" Jacob asks, leading four children into Bridget's master bedroom: Chloe, Bridget's daughter, Ava, and her twin sons, Liam and Seth. All are quick on Jacob's heels, speaking at once.

"I want to have a pillow fight," Chloe chimes in.

Ava adds, "Me too!"

"We're not having a pillow fight, but we are giving away free tickles to children. Want some?" Amelia knows her kids will be game. Sure enough, they begin to laugh, their high-pitched shrieks ear piercing. You'd think she'd be immune to the sound by now, but it's unlike any other, and still makes Amelia's ears ring. It also makes her smile, so she tickles them more.

Ava joins in, as does one of Bridget's twin boys. The other backs away, shaking his head. How to tell Bridget's twins apart, since they're identical? Seth wants to be part of everything, while Liam is shy and reserved.

"Come on, Liam. There's room for one more." Bridget lies on her back, with two of her children squirming and squealing on top of her.

"Let's tickle Mommy!" Seth's idea gains traction, and Liam piles on at last.

"No. Help!" Bridget and Amelia have started a kiddie revolt.

"Wait! Marshes!" Amelia commands her kids. "We must rescue Aunt Bridget."

Sure enough, Chloe and Jacob jump at the chance and begin to tickle Bridget's children. Shrieks and laughter escalate to a crescendo, until the children decide to storm Bridget's playroom with the large-screen TV.

Breathless, Bridget and Amelia collapse on the mattress as the hanger digs into Amelia's back. "Ouch." Picking up the hanger, she places the sundress on her abdomen. "Maybe we're not so bad at this parenting thing after all. I mean, our children are happy."

Bridget nods, staring at her ceiling. "Their happiness is what matters.

Ours will come soon enough. I mean, they make us happy, but we will find it again with an adult male. With someone worthy. Someone sexy—"

"Is that why you want me to wear this outfit? To find happiness, or share some sexy time with a buff bunny?" Amelia jerks her head in Bridget's direction. "That sounded much more normal in my head."

"Nope. You caught me dead to rights." Bridget rolls on her side. "I want you to lay Bugs Bunny. Is my dastardly plan working?"

"Nope." Amelia sighs. "Daniel let his own children down. How can I risk hurting them again by dating someone? I can't."

"Kyle might be different."

"And he might not. Either way, why are you giving Kyle—a man you just met—the benefit of the doubt?" Amelia asks her friend.

"Because you seem to trust him, and you have great instincts."

Amelia disagrees with Bridget's assessment, but is shushed.

"You're the one who told me Mr. Three was a narcissist, and you were right."

Bridget has been attempting online dating through an app. They've named the men by numbers, because they can't keep track of how many terrible dates she's had. Amelia swears that her friend is choosing the worst men just to have more jokes in her arsenal. "Okay, so I was correct about Mr. Three. I'm great when it comes to your love life. I fail miserably when it pertains to my own."

"Who mentioned 'love'?"

Amelia raises her forefinger in the air. "Oh no you don't. Don't go there. Chalk it up to a poor word choice."

"You should trust yourself more. You did save me from wasting my time on Mr. Three. If Kyle was a Three, you'd know it," Bridget imparts as sage advice.

"Kyle's definitely not a three. A ten, sure. A twenty, yep. Easily a twenty." Amelia fidgets with the gold compass charm that she always wears. It was a gift to herself after the divorce, to ground her and remind her of what's important. It hangs on an eighteen-inch matching chain around her neck, and rests near her heart.

Returning her attention to the short sundress, Amelia grimaces. "Are you sure I can pull this off?" She traces a seam with her pink fingernail.

"Stop doubting yourself! You are beautiful, and it will be fun. Friends can have fun, you know. Just look at us."

Bridget stares at her friend as Amelia listens to their kids chatting and giggling in the playroom. Their happiness is infectious.

No matter how many doubts Amelia has, especially since the divorce, about her abilities as a parent, she loves her kids. The best things to come out of that failed marriage aren't inanimate objects. They're two sweet souls—her children.

"I think we excel at being parents." Will she doubt her abilities tomorrow? Yep. Will Bridget? Probably. But for now, Amelia places this day in her imaginary win column.

"You're changing the subject, Amelia Angelica Marsh. Don't you have a party to get to?" Bridget snaps Amelia back to the present with the use of her middle name.

"Why am I so nervous?" Amelia twists her long waves in a knot. It's her coping mechanism. "It's just a neighborhood party. I've got nothing to feel self-conscious about, right?"

"You're exiting your comfort zone. New neighbors, new activities." Bridget's assessment is correct.

Nothing is the same as it was this time last year, or the year before that, or ever. "Starting over has been tough on all of us. I've shuffled my own insecurities to the back of my mind and given myself completely to Jacob and Chloe. Now that they seem to be settling in, it's catching up to me. It's my turn to process everything. I don't know how else to explain it, Bridget."

"I understand." Bridget expels a ragged breath. "I've been there. Trust me."

Bridget's circumstances are drastically different than Amelia's. She lost her husband in a car accident. In one instant, he was gone.

"I wish you hadn't gone through losing Sean." Amelia takes Bridget's hand in hers, knowing the excruciating pain Bridget has endured. "I'm sorry. I am being incredibly selfish complaining to you."

Bridget squeezes Amelia's hand. "You're not selfish. You've never been selfish. What you are is the rebel with the garden gnome in her front yard, who is afraid of being hurt again. You're also attending a party alone, wondering if people will like you."

"Let me guess... You've been there."

"No. I don't give a darn if people like me." Amelia's best friend winks at her, subtle lines etching her bright eyes. "I do care about you, so cut yourself some slack. Be kind to my friend, the one I'll always be here for. If anyone else doesn't appreciate you, then to heck with them. I've got your back, the way you've always had mine. So does Lily. Remember that."

Grinning at Bridget, Amelia counts her blessings, which include an incredible group of strong women, and though they're not related by blood but by the bond of friendship, they are still family. "That's just what I needed to hear."

"Then slay this thing. You can tell me all about it tomorrow morning when you pick up your kids." Bridget thrusts the sundress at Amelia. "Get changed. You've got this. Now, show me how tough you are, Marsh."

"Right. I've got this. It's just a party," Amelia mutters, grabbing the dress and her purse before heading into Bridget's bathroom to change. Catching her reflection in the large mirror above the sink, Amelia inhales a deep, cleansing breath.

"You've got this," she says aloud.

Repeating her statement for a second time, then a third as she gets dressed, doesn't halt the quivering sensation in her abdomen, nor does it stop her hands from shaking. Still, Bridget's right.

*I am tough. I've got this.*

This is just another step in the direction of a new life, a post-divorce life.

Amelia drives home feeling positive, feeling pretty, feeling independent. It's her turn to control her destiny. With Amelia's newfound confidence and positivity comes a surge of adrenaline coursing through her veins, causing her every nerve to tingle.

Yeah, she's got this. For the first time in a long time, Amelia is excited for the future.

Tonight, this girl just wants to have fun.

# Chapter 17

To say Kyle hosts a plain old barbecue would be an understatement. His backyard gathering is a full-fledged event, complete with a karaoke machine and even live music. As for who plays this live music? Kyle! He plays the guitar, which is info that he keeps only to himself and his closest friends. It's... What did he refer to it as? His stress reliever. There's more to this man than jogging, the HOA, and his construction business. That's for certain.

Amelia had no clue how many layers there are to Kyle Sanders, but she's beginning to understand and appreciate just how complex he is. His backyard is further proof. Kyle's covered patio is striking, with ceiling fans on full blast, it overlooks immaculate landscaping. Kyle must have the nicest backyard in the Castle Rock subdivision. Along with mood lighting, gas lamps, outdoor speakers, and an outdoor flat-screen TV, it contains the most comfortable patio furniture Amelia's ever sat on. There's also a fire pit, though it's not needed tonight, when it's warm and humid with a slight breeze.

His friends and neighbors are an eclectic group of people who love to talk movies, music, and anything else that's fun and escapist. They talk and eat Kyle's delicious barbecue, as an ice breaker. Once done, and everyone has helped Kyle bring dishes into his kitchen, the karaoke begins. There are some great numbers, and Amelia cheers at the top of her lungs. Her cheeks hurt from smiling and laughing.

"Amelia, it's your turn," Kyle's friend Wil Davis announces into the karaoke microphone, after he just killed Guns N' Roses "Sweet Child O' Mine." He's one tough act to follow.

Seven other friends of Kyle's are present, and they hoot and holler for Amelia to join Wil where the karaoke machine is set up. The other guests consist of two couples, along with two of Kyle's employees, and recent single dad Wil, who is Kyle's best friend. They cheer as Amelia approaches Wil, knowing full well he won't expect her to pick a rock song. In truth, she was going to choose Gloria Gaynor's "I Will Survive," until Wil rocked the house. Now the bar has been raised and Amelia is nothing if not competitive, especially when it comes to karaoke.

Amelia whispers to him what song she wants to sing, and Wil asks if she's sure.

"Heck, yes. I'm a carpool karaoke queen. Just ask my kids." Kyle's friends cheer louder. It's a good thing they live next door to him or there might be a noise complaint, though it's only dusk. The sun is setting in the west, and there are still bright pastel hues on the horizon as it sinks lower.

Little do they know that Amelia was in choir all throughout her tween and teen years. Church choir, high school chorus, you name it. She may not have a fabulous voice, but it will do. Especially with this song. It's kind of her post-divorce anthem, and she has the emotional range to make up for any deficits in her voice.

"You ready?" Amelia asks, knowing there is no real intro for Evanescence's "Call Me When You're Sober," just a few piano notes and a pause which then repeats. This song will start with Amelia, and it's all her. Is she nervous? Not at all. Because singing is *her* stress reliever.

With the first piano notes, several of Kyle's friends gasp as Amelia belts out the first line. Her voice is low and strong. There's a look of shock on several faces, including Kyle's.

This song, about realizing someone's deception and in the end, telling him to get out, hits home with Amelia. That's why she doesn't need the microphone. She's belting this one out.

"Oh! She's going there." Trevor, one half of the Mitchell couple, claps. His wife, Vanessa, smiles. "She's going to grab your title, Wil."

"Yes!" the other couple cheers, laughing as Wil shushes them.

Somewhere after the first chorus, Kyle starts strumming along with his guitar and Amelia sings with him. His look of shock has been replaced with a wide smile and eyes full of encouragement. It allows Amelia to concentrate on him—his guitar, his support—as well as his friends. When the song ends, there's a standing ovation. She doesn't fully deserve it, since she did hit some off notes, but Kyle and Amelia put on a great show.

"I had no idea you sang." He walks up to her, holds up Amelia's hand, like she's some sort of champion.

"Funny. I had no idea you played guitar."

"Touché. Guess we don't know each other that well after all," Kyle admits, as his friends stand and crowd them.

Wil shakes Amelia's hand. "Where did you learn to sing like that?"

"I told you, I'm a carpool karaoke queen. My children and I sing all the time." Amelia smiles. "They want to learn to play an instrument now, and it's been narrowed down to the drums or guitar—"

"Guitar!" Wil and Kyle say in unison.

Amelia's eyes widen.

"Trust me." Wil offers her a reassuring smile. "I know from experience, drums cause headaches. My son loves his drums."

"Got it. Guitar, it is." Amelia turns to Kyle. "Can you recommend a guitar teacher?"

"I'll do you one better—I can give Jacob and Chloe lessons."

"I—I can't let you go to all that trouble." Amelia's at a loss for words.

Kyle winks at her. "That's what friends are for."

"He gave our son lessons," Vanessa adds, patting Kyle on the shoulder. "They play *Guitar Hero* when Kyle babysits."

"You babysit?" Amelia can't hide her surprise.

Trevor nods. "We have no family in town, and Kyle is great with him. Our Joey is twelve, and wants to be a rock star."

"That's not my doing." Kyle places his guitar on an empty chair. "I've advised him to own his own company. Working for yourself is rewarding."

"Kyle is our resident entrepreneur," adds one of his other neighbors. Amelia can't keep track of all the names. She needs to take notes.

Employee One raises his hands in the air. "I'm all for that, though I do have to get going. I've got a date."

His other employee adds, "Double date."

They say their goodbyes, and Trevor and Vanessa tell Amelia how nice it was to meet her. They've got to drive their high school babysitter home before her curfew.

The other neighborhood couple follows suit and soon it's just Amelia and Kyle, alone in his backyard. Dusk has turned the sky to an onyx veil, dotted with stars and a moon partially hidden behind some drifting clouds.

Kyle's dim lighting and gas lamps make the atmosphere inviting, as he leads Amelia to a hammock. "You don't think they're trying to play matchmaker, do you?" Kyle asks, lowering his eyes, refusing to meet Amelia's, as if fearful of her response.

She hadn't even considered that scenario until now. Sitting beside him, taking care to adjust her skirt and not flash him, Amelia chuckles. "I would hope not. We agreed to be friends, right?"

"Yep." Kyle meets her eyes, his appearing darker in the dim light. "But here's the thing. Friends know each other and we don't, at least not really. So, I think we need to get to know one another before taking the next step to friendship. You game?"

Amelia nods in spite of herself. Why does she feel naked and vulnerable? Kyle is a friend, and he's right—they don't know enough about each other. The least she can do is let him in, and hopefully discover more about him.

At least, that's her rationale as the hammock gently rocks back and forth. With Kyle facing her, holding her gaze. Searching for something...

*Friendship*, Amelia reminds herself. *We're friends. Nothing more.*

So, why is she nervous? A crowd of strangers listening to her belt out karaoke didn't frighten her in the least, but soul searching with Kyle terrifies her. Because she wants more than friendship. And that's the scariest part of this equation.

"Are you ready?" Kyle asks.

Unfortunately, it's too late to turn back. Let the interrogation begin.

# Chapter 18

"*DIE HARD* IS NOT A CHRISTMAS MOVIE." ON THIS KYLE IS ADAMANT.

Amelia shakes her head. "That's debatable, and I'm on the *it is a Christmas movie* side. It's got Christmas décor, Christmas music, and a happy ending with a family reunited. Oh, and Alan Rickman. It's a Christmas movie."

"Now you're grasping at straws. The late, great Alan Rickman doesn't a Christmas movie make."

"Seriously?" Amelia stares at Kyle with a *don't go there* expression. "Alan Rickman makes everything amazing. And one could argue that the first *Harry Potter* movie has some Christmas elements, not to mention that he was in *Love, Actually*—a definite Christmas movie. He was such an amazing actor."

"Okay." Kyle holds his palms in the air. "You win for now. But my favorite Christmas movie is an actual Christmas movie. It's called *A Christmas Story*. There's no debate with that one."

Sighing, Amelia fiddles with one of her necklaces. A gold compass, drawing attention to her cleavage though nothing is visible, leaving everything to Kyle's imagination.

"You've got me there. Here's a tough one: favorite movie line. Go," Amelia issues her challenge.

"This is easy. 'Randy lay there like a slug, it was his only defense.'" Without a doubt, an incredible line. It all comes back to that movie for Kyle. "Seeing that chaotic family—with their ups and downs—come together for an unconventional Christmas dinner at the end is something special."

"Yeah, it is." Amelia grins. "Is your family conventional?"

Now things are getting personal. "My mom lives in San Antonio. She and my dad divorced when I was a kid, and that's where I went to high school. My dad lives in Dallas, so I went to college and settled in Houston—kind of in the middle. Where I can be independent, but close to both."

"Close enough that you don't take sides." Amelia's assessment is spot on.

"I try to keep the peace between them," he admits.

Amelia studies him, her eyes intense and unswerving. "That's nice."

Kyle scoffs. "'Nice.' Gee, thanks."

"No, I mean it. It's sweet of you. To care so much about them, to sculpt your future to suit both of them." She shoves a stray lock of hair behind her ear. "It's also rare, in my experience."

Something tells Kyle that Amelia's referring to her ex. "How bad was it? Your marriage and your divorce? You don't have to answer if you don't want to." She is tough and can answer or not. Kyle knows that much about her.

"Oh, in the end, it was horrible." Diving right in, getting to the heart of it, Amelia straightens her shoulders, crossing her arms over her chest like a shield. "I met Daniel in college. He was my first boyfriend, lover, all of it. I fell for him hard, not because ours was this passionate love affair, but because it was comfortable. At the time, I didn't know there was supposed to be more to a relationship."

Her sheer honesty is humbling. Kyle experienced her fierce determination and strength from the moment they met, but her answer makes him respect her more than he already did.

"You are fearless." His voice is barely above a whisper.

"I married a man I loved and had children with him. I wouldn't classify myself as fearless. Naive yes, fearless no. We weren't really happy, but I rationalized it based upon my own parents' marriage and knew that sharing your life with someone takes work." She tilts her head to the side. "I discovered after Chloe was born that I was putting more effort into our relationship than he was. He was slick, though. Every time I would pull back to reevaluate our relationship, he'd give me just enough attention to make me try harder. Until I caught him cheating on me. By the time of our divorce, all pretense was gone. Did it hurt? Of course, but that pain was something I could deal with. Replacing our children, hurting them was inexcusable and something I will never forgive. Of course, I keep my feelings from Chloe and Jacob, and I protect them with everything I am and everything I have. Always will."

"I don't care what you say—you are fearless. And I'm sorry." His eyes refuse to release hers. In her deep golden-brown gaze, Kyle sees both her anguish and her strength. "I really am. You didn't deserve any of it. Neither did Jacob and Chloe."

"Yet it was the hand we were dealt. That's life, isn't it?" She studies her wrist, pretending to glance at an imaginary watch. "Would you look at that? It's subject-changing time. As far as favorite movie lines go, it's technically two lines from the same movie for me: 'I love you' and 'I know.' They're from *The Empire Strikes Back*. I am a self-proclaimed nerd and was a huge Han and Leia fan as a kid. Harrison Ford was my first crush."

"You're a *Star Wars* fan." Kyle laughs. "I never would have guessed."

"I *was* a *Star Wars* fan until the seventh movie. I won't spoil the plot, in case you haven't seen it, but I will say that I had hoped that love would conquer all."

She adjusts, and Kyle can tell that Amelia's getting ready to leave. "This was fun. Thanks for inviting me."

"Of course." Kyle straightens, sitting beside her as the hammock sinks, and his hand brushes against hers. An invisible force between them pulls him closer to her, while the air surrounding them becomes more charged than ever. Strong and relentless, this current produces a connection Kyle can't untether, fusing his soul with hers.

Then she places her hand atop his, her warmth and softness filling Kyle's heart until he feels like it will overflow. For the second time in less than a week, he wants to kiss her. Though they agreed to be friends, though his conscience all but screams that he shouldn't, he wants Amelia so much that it's painful—both physically and emotionally.

Turning to face her, Kyle cups Amelia's face in his palm, their eyes meeting once more. Amelia studies him, her gaze smoky with desire. As he traces the curve of her neck, her breath hitches. This one tiny action coveys that Amelia is aching for this kiss as much as he is.

There's this push-pull, like a wave to the shore, ever present, pushing them closer, then tugging them apart.

"I know that we agreed to be friends, yet I can't help but want to kiss you." He caresses her palm, his fingers strong and steady, as is his grip. "I know we shouldn't do this, but I can't not do this… I'm not making sense."

"Join the club. Like I've made much sense? If you ask me, I've botched this whole thing since I met you and challenged you to gnomes at dawn."

"See? That right there is the problem. It's why I can't walk away from you."

"My snark?" Amelia tilts her head to the side. "Out of all my impressive and downright irresistible attributes, my snark is the one reason you can't walk away?"

"I admit it. I love your sass. I want more of that sass."

"No, you don't. It's incurable. I should know. I've suffered from it since high school. My sarcasm was my only defense from mean girls. Until I met my small but mighty group of friends. That's why Carla strikes a chord." Amelia's honesty is as refreshing as a light spring rain.

"Whatever it is, I want more of it. Along with your many irresistible attributes." Kyle leans closer still. "I want more of you—I want all of you. It terrifies me just how desperate I am for you."

"Just in case you missed it, I'm a package deal. My children will always come first, and with that being said, it's too soon for me to let you in. No matter how amazing I think you are, it's a risk I can't take." Amelia places her forehead against his. "I won't subject them to anyone who doesn't appreciate them, who doesn't want them as much as I do. I've got to be certain about you before taking the next step."

"You think I'm amazing?" Kyle teases.

Amelia sighs. "That's your takeaway from everything I just confided? You are such a man."

With a chuckle, Kyle leans in closer. "I may be a man, but I also know how devoted you are to your kids. That's another reason I can't seem to distance myself from you…because you are one heck of a mamma bear. It's why we shouldn't be together, but also why I want to."

Kyle inhales, filling his senses with her scent, her nearness, her warmth. "I'm being presumptuous now, aren't I?"

"Yes, but I don't mind. Because if I were to take the risk with anyone, it would be you." Amelia's hushed whisper is almost inaudible due to the crickets and other noises filling the warm night air.

Flattening her palm against his cheek, Amelia moves closer to him, then closer still…until she brushes her lips against his. It's a gentle kiss, an intimate kiss. It's achingly powerful, so much so that his hands tremble and the world feels lopsided.

"Ouch!" Amelia utters.

Pain emanates from his elbows and arms, jarring Kyle back to his senses, just after they hit the ground, with him atop Amelia.

Rolling off her, Kyle asks, "Are you okay?"

Amelia's laughter peals as she covers her face with her hands. "We fell off the hammock."

There, lying in the grass, with the hard ground beneath them, Kyle can't help but join in and laugh even harder. "It's always something, isn't it?"

She rolls on her side, facing him. "I think the universe is trying to tell us something."

"That it was one heck of a kiss, though much too short?" Kyle brushes a stray lock of hair from her face, then trails his thumb across her jaw line.

"I can't argue with that, but I think the universe is telling us that we should be friends first. We need to take this slow, Kyle. If you can't, I understand." Amelia studies his reaction.

Kissing her forehead, Kyle whispers, "You're worth the wait. So, friends it is."

A chiming emanates from Amelia, along with a vibration. It's a pattern. Chime and vibrate-pause-chime and vibrate-pause.

"I'm so sorry. It's got to be about the kids." Amelia yanks her cell from her pocket.

"Bridget, is everything all right?" She sits upright, listening to her friend. "Okay, I'll be right there."

"What's wrong?" Kyle stands, offering her a hand.

Amelia rushes to grab her purse. "Jacob's throwing up and he has an earache. Those are his telltale signs of an ear infection. I've got to go."

"I can drive you," Kyle offers, following Amelia through his back door and locking it behind him.

Amelia pauses, with keys in hand. "That's too much to ask. I'll be calling his pediatrician, going to a twenty-four-hour pharmacy, and there will be barf bags. You don't need to experience that."

"Your son is sick." Kyle rushes to his kitchen and grabs a handful of heavy-duty garbage bags. "The least I can do is drive you."

"Okay, but we take my car. Trust me on this," Amelia insists while Kyle locks his front door.

As they reach Amelia's Explorer, she grabs his arm. "Are you sure about this? You're about to experience a crash course in my life, including a vomiting child. It's not pretty."

"I'm certain," Kyle insists, getting behind the wheel.

That's what friends are for.

# Chapter 19

AMELIA MEETS BRIDGET AT HER FRONT DOOR WITH A COFFEE CUP, handing it to her posthaste. "Good morning!" After kissing Chloe, she gives her daughter a tight hug. "I missed you, sweetie. Jacob is watching a movie in his room. He's feeling better and can't wait to see you."

Bridget sips her coffee and sighs, as her brood follows Chloe into the main hallway. "The same for you three... Just no running around, okay? I know Jacob bounces back quick, but I want him resting today. Deal?"

Chloe and Bridget's children all nod in unison, then run to join Jacob, as Amelia turns to her best friend. "Thank you so much for letting Chloe stay the night. I didn't want to wake her, and drag her through the whole ear infection thing."

"Not a problem. I love her, and Jacob. You know that. Now on to the juicy stuff. I assume that was Kyle sitting behind the wheel of your SUV which was parked in front of my house last night." Bridget follows Amelia into the kitchen.

It's Amelia's third cup of coffee, and her headache is pounding in her temples due to lack of sleep. She never sleeps well when one of her children is sick. Besides, Jacob shared her bed, and even on a normal night Amelia wouldn't be able to sleep through his tossing and turning.

"You look exhausted."

Rubbing her throbbing temple, Amelia takes a sip of her hot coffee before answering. "I am, but Jacob's doing well."

Prince weaves between her legs, rubbing his head against her calf. When Amelia fails to give him immediate pets, he climbs up her leggings with his claws. "Ouch!" Placing her mug down with a thud, Amelia grabs the little stinker and holds him in her arms. "How many times must I tell you that I'm not a tree to be climbed. Besides, patience is a virtue. Wait for pets."

The feline purrs, nestling in her arms. "You are so cute, I can't stay angry with you. Still, I bought you a cat condo that was much too expensive. Climb that, please."

"Speaking of cute, how are the tadpoles?" Bridget asks as Amelia sits beside her on the cushioned wood, metal, and leather barstool at the half wall that separates the kitchen and living room.

"Oh, it's the circle of life in my backyard. I bought an aerator, and those amphibians are thriving." Amelia holds Prince in one arm, reaching for her coffee mug with the other. "There are tadpoles in all forms of the life cycle. Some with legs, and one very small frog that jumps onto Chloe's hand every time she visits them, which is almost all the time. She's writing a science report on them, complete with pictures."

"Good for her. Girl power."

Yep, Chloe is the little tomboy who touches frogs, while Jacob is more a cat-loving kid. He shows interest in the tadpoles, but hasn't touched one yet. "Between the tadpoles and the cat, my children are being kept busy."

"Small talk aside, how was last night? And what brought Kyle with you to pick up Jacob?" Bridget's whisper sounds like she's using a megaphone.

Amelia takes a larger gulp of her coffee. "Last night was a lot of fun. The food was delicious, the neighbors were quirky—totally my type of people—and the karaoke was top-notch."

"And Kyle?" Bridget asks in her suspicious tone.

Amelia takes another gulp of coffee, savoring it as she watches Bridget's impatience rise. For once, she's living vicariously through

Amelia's personal life and the turnabout is kind of fun. Just when Bridget is about to speak, Amelia answers with, "I learned a lot about him last night—like he plays guitar, has a lot of empathy, especially when it comes to his family, and driving me to Jacob was..."

Listening to Prince purr, Amelia can't quite put into words all Kyle did for her. "It was unexpected, yet completely in character from what I've learned about him. Kyle offered to come with me, knowing that Jacob was ill...like, throwing up ill. Still, he played chauffeur, allowing me to sit with Jacob in the backseat and hold him through his dry heaving, took us to pick up the antibiotic and nausea medication that Jacob's doctor called in. He checked on us through the rearview mirror as I stroked Jacob's hair in my back seat, soothing him until he drifted to sleep."

"Wow," Bridget mutters. "He's a great guy, huh?"

Nodding, Amelia adds, "He even carried Jacob inside and placed him in bed. Then he asked if I needed anything else...like all that he did wasn't more than enough."

"So why are you somber?" Bridget asks, her voice rough with emotion.

Something tells Amelia that her friend already knows the answer. "He's everything my ex-husband wasn't, and while it's nice to know that men like Kyle exist, I can't help but be reminded that Daniel has yet to answer a text or email or phone call from the kids, specifically Jacob. Daniel is another reason I can't move on, and though I'm trying really hard to forgive, I can't as long as he ignores our children."

"But you want to move on?" Bridget is relentless.

Amelia looks down at Prince, whose ears have perked up and whose eyes are now open. "Do you want to get down?" She sets him gently on the hardwood floor.

"You're avoiding my question. I knew it! You kissed Kyle!" Leave it to Bridget and her powers of deduction. At least she was subtle, and no kids are within hearing range.

"I did kiss Kyle. But—"

"Why is there a 'but'?" Bridget wrinkles her forehead.

"Three reasons: first, we fell off a hammock; second, you called; and third, I already explained." Expecting her friend to disagree with her, Amelia steels herself for a tough discussion. Fortunately, a light knock against her front door draws Amelia's attention away from the conversation at hand.

Proceeding down her front hallway, she opens the door to come face-to-face with Kyle. He's freshly shaven, and his eyes sparkle when they meet hers.

"Hi. I hope I'm not disturbing you. I knocked as opposed to the doorbell because I didn't want to wake Jacob if he's napping." Kyle shoves his hands in his shorts pockets, as if he's nervous.

Amelia invites him in. "Jacob's feeling better. He'd love to see you. He's been talking about how the Bunny's helper rescued him."

Kyle shifts his weight, studying his sneakers. "I didn't do anything. Last night was all you."

"You were a huge help, so accept our thanks." Amelia's mom voice is on full display, and Kyle meets her gaze once more.

"Yes, ma'am." Kyle stands straighter, his full lips upturning into one of his signature smiles. Brighter than sunshine, his smiles warm Amelia's heart. "It's good to see you."

His voice is rich and decadent, sending pure energy pumping through her veins. This guy is an adrenaline rush like nothing else. Who needs coffee when Amelia's got Kyle, sweet-talking Kyle?

"Hi, again, Mr. Bunny," Bridget teases, having walked towards them in her super stealth mode.

Kyle's eyes widen. "I'm so sorry. I didn't know you had company."

"Yeah, I parked across the street. Nice to see you again." She holds out her hand, which Kyle promptly shakes.

Silence engulfs them, interrupted only by the central air kicking on and the soft purr of the air circulating through the vents.

"Would you like to join us for coffee?" Amelia asks Kyle, though she's pretty sure he'll decline her offer.

"Actually, I'd like to mow your lawn."

Amelia blinks. "Totally not what I was expecting you to say."

"Well, with Jacob sick, I thought I could help." Kyle grins.

"I do usually mow my own lawn, but I would love your help if that means you'll come inside afterwards. I make a mean iced coffee and pour a tall glass of Gatorade like nobody's business. Your choice."

Kyle laughs. "Sold."

"Okay, well, my electric lawn mower is in the garage." Amelia hides her grin.

His voice is low, his expression one of horror. "Please tell me you didn't buy an electric lawn mower."

"Of course not. What do you take me for? A city girl?" At Amelia's joke, Kyle's eyes deepen, their color now the spring green of lush lawns or leafy trees.

"That's a relief," he retorts. "I might have been forced to unfriend you."

Escorting him outside, Amelia types the code to her garage and Kyle fiddles with her mower. "I'll see you when you're done?"

Grinning, Kyle nods.

When she enters her home and shuts the front door, Bridget rushes into Amelia's office, staring out her front windows with her coffee cup in hand. Together they watch as Kyle starts the mower and begins working on the front lawn.

"Why does he have to wear a shirt?" Bridget lifts her mug to her lips. "I want to see those abs again."

Laughing, Amelia sets the record straight. "No more abs. We're friends. Nothing more."

Bridget gulps more of her coffee. "I may need ice. Is it hot in here or is it just the sight of Mr. Bunny mowing your lawn?"

"Bunny. Lawn," is all Amelia can manage as she studies Kyle, her thoughts swirling, her mental checklist ticking off items in rapid succession.

- Kyle is kind: check.
- Kyle is responsible: check.
- Kyle is funny: check.
- Kyle cares about her children: check.
- Her children like Kyle: check.

"What is it?" Bridget asks. "You have that serious expression, the one that means you're worrying big time."

"Kyle's more than I expected. I thought I'd take this slow and keep the kids out of it, but instead it's like a cyclone, picking up speed. Especially with the kids wanting to spend time with him." She rubs a knot in her neck, her tension rising.

"You're scared. I get it." Amelia's friend rubs her back.

"Scared and scarred." That's her current mental state. "Will friendship be too confusing for Jacob and Chloe? I don't want them to think Kyle is a replacement for their dad."

"Just explain that to them." Bridget acts like it's simple.

Perhaps it is.

They have adult friends—namely Bridget and Lily. Why is Kyle different? Because he's a man? That doesn't make him less friend material. He's a great person, and could be a role model for Amelia's children. "Jacob and Chloe need to see that men can be kind. I don't want them growing up thinking all men are like their dad. Kyle's friendship could help with that. He *did* offer to give the kids guitar lessons."

"Friendship sounds like something all of you could use." Bridget flashes Amelia a wry smile. "It's a shame, though. Those abs are worth the price of admission."

"I don't know if I'm woman enough to handle abs like that."

"Who is?" Bridget mutters.

Amelia sighs, reminded of her C-section scars and stretch marks. She'd never be perfect enough for a guy like Kyle. "Friends it is, but let's be realistic. Can I really keep my children from getting hurt? In their lives, they'll each suffer broken hearts. I wish it weren't true, but it's part of life. Love, loss, acceptance, and rejection. It's about surviving those rough times and appreciating those who still love you, those who you love. To try to protect them from hurt means I'm just delaying the inevitable, right?"

"You are. That's okay, though. It's what you think they need right now." Bridget winks at her friend. "You're a great mom. You've got this, and whatever else arises. Life isn't perfect, and neither are we. We just try our best to protect our children and be good moms."

Smiling at her friend, Amelia hugs her, taking care not to spill Bridget's coffee. "I don't know what I'd do without you."

"Hashtag *friends for life*?" Bridget teases.

"I like it." Amelia pauses. "We should print T-shirts. We could be 'matchies,' as Chloe says."

Welcome to mom life, where *it's complicated* has nothing to do with a relationship status on social media. It's Amelia's world, summed up in one pithy little catchphrase.

# Chapter 20

ONCE KYLE HAS MOWED HER YARD, HE PUSHES AMELIA'S LAWN mower into her garage, puts it away, then starts the weed whacker, edging her yard. Whenever he's struggling with something, Kyle sweats it out. That's his go-to stress reliever. It's why he jogs regularly, because his job is hectic. Owning his own company, being responsible for his employees and their families, making sure all projects are executed to precision when there are obstacles thrown at him on a daily basis. Stress equals jogging. Add the HOA and endless residents' texts, calls, questions, complaints, and concerns...well, he jogs a lot. When not jogging, he's landscaping during his free time.

A dark-haired man crosses the street and heads over to Kyle, with his brown bulldog unleashed and striding by his side. Walking a dog unleashed is against the law, though Kyle won't say anything. Instead, he turns off the weed whacker and says, "Hi, Andy."

"Hey. Nice to know you make house calls. You want to mow my lawn next? Save me from another letter?"

Kyle chuckles, but the resident who lives a few blocks away has a grimace firmly planted on his face. "I supposed you're going to complain about my dog being off leash, too, right? Another letter?"

"I don't complain about you, or any of the Castle Rock residents, regardless of what neighborhood gossip says. Should you leash your dog? Yes, because it's county law. But I have no control over what you do or the letters you receive, Andy." Sweat drips into Kyle's eyes, and he wipes them with his shirt. "If you think something is unfair, email me or text me. I'm here, and my mind is open. I've made that clear at every HOA meeting since I was elected to serve on the board."

"Yeah. Right," Andy adds, walking away. The guy's always got to have the last word.

When Andy is out of earshot, Kyle mutters under his breath, "Just another day in the neighborhood." He then powers up the weed whacker and takes out some frustrations. By the time he's finished Amelia's front and back yards, Kyle is a sweaty mess. Amelia meets him in her garage, and hands him a cold bottle of Gatorade.

"I hope you like the orange. It's Jacob's favorite. Along with the blue. My son always winds up with a blue mustache, so orange it is." She grins as he takes several large gulps. "Are you okay? Or are you rethinking everything we discussed last night. Because if you're having second thoughts—"

"About our friendship? No. Not at all. It's just… Well, I'm in awe of you." She doesn't react to his brutal honesty. Instead, she waits for him to elaborate.

"You're such a good mom." He pauses, taking a gulp of Gatorade. "You knew exactly what to do for Jacob last night. And you didn't ruin cream cheese for him."

He smiles, as does she. "He still loves cinnamon raisin bagels, too. Though he hasn't had one today."

"You remembered?" Kyle asks.

"I remember a lot. Thanks for carrying Jacob into his bedroom for me."

Kyle taps the plastic bottle of Gatorade. "His room was cool. I love how it's decorated with trucks and has an old-school repair garage vibe."

Yeah, Jacob's room was something. Logos of cars reflected from his walls, as did a clock in the shape of a chrome tire rim.

"Nice change of subject." Amelia tilts her head to the side.

She's got him there. "You thanked me last night for everything I did, and again today. Like someone being kind to you is a rare event."

Her cheeks turn pink. "It's something I'm not used to. That and the fact that you stuck around, even after the barf bag was in play."

"I like to be helpful. It's very rewarding." Kyle pauses once more, before making the most personal admission of all. "Especially with you."

Amelia's breath catches. She's surprised, that much is clear, so Kyle adds, "Last night, I realized just how difficult parenting is, though you make it look simple."

"That's what it's all about. Making things look simple, when in fact I'm hanging on for dear life."

Kyle wipes the perspiration from his face with his wet T-shirt. "You have friends. A group of them, me included. We'll catch you if you fall."

"With neighbors like you on the HOA board, you're making it more difficult for me to fight those bylaws. Not that I'm giving up. Because I'm not, just to be clear. I've been doing more research, and will even have handouts."

"I'd expect nothing less." Kyle clears his throat in an attempt not to laugh. Leave it to Amelia to offer handouts.

Amelia notices the blond from the Easter egg hunt stopping in front of her house with a stroller, and walks towards her as Kyle follows.

"Hi, Sophie! How are you and Stephen today?" she asks.

Sophie smiles. "We're good. He's sleeping longer, which is a godsend. Thanks for the tip. As it turns out, he likes the light on full blast, like Chloe."

"I'm so glad." Amelia turns to Kyle. "Sophie and I have been keeping in touch and texting."

With a grin, Kyle nods to Sophie. "It's good to see you."

"Amelia might not feel that way." With a grimace, she holds out an envelope. "It's from the management company. The postal worker placed it in my box by accident."

"Well, it brought you to see me, and that's worth another piece of mail from Carla." Her voice sounds jovial, yet Kyle knows Amelia is sick of these letters.

"I have to go, but we'll talk soon. Oh! I love that your neighbor placed a gnome in her lawn. I'm going to do the same. In solidarity."

Amelia glances at the Bass house. "I hadn't noticed. Wow!"

"You're doing something right." Sophie waves and heads back down the street.

After saying goodbye to Sophie, Amelia opens the letter as Kyle stands behind her, looking over her shoulder, to see another violation. This time it's for her car registration.

"Come on! I renewed my car registration online and am waiting for the sticker to come by mail." Amelia sighs. "Doesn't this woman have anything better to do? Now I have to email her proof that my vehicle registration has been renewed. This is beyond ridiculous. I can't even back into my own driveway without a violation."

"I'll talk to Carla," Kyle offers, almost as angry as Amelia.

Shaking her head, Amelia sighs before answering, "It's my problem, not yours. But it is escalating—Carla is escalating it beyond one small gnome. As if I don't feel imperfect enough, she has to keep trying to remind me that she doesn't think I'm good enough to live in this community."

"I think you are, as do your neighbors. The Basses wouldn't have added a gnome to their front yard if they thought you weren't. Neither would Sophie." Kyle is reminded of his interaction with Andy earlier. "Look, I'm not the management company, you know, but many residents think I am, and complain both to me and about me. One came over while I was edging your lawn."

"I'm sorry, Kyle."

"Don't be." He shrugs. "My point is that believe it or not, there are people in Castle Rock who don't like me—namely the residents who let their dogs run loose without leashes or ride on four-wheelers down the street or get a letter from Carla about their garbage cans in front of their houses. Every time they're called out, they assume it's because of me. There are some neighbors who love to gossip, and that gossip mill churns big time when it comes to the HOA president."

"Kyle Sanders, I am shocked. Not everyone likes you?" Amelia fakes a stunned expression. "You aren't perfect after all."

"Did you miss the fact that I'm taking flack for other residents calling animal control or the sheriff's office?"

"Nope. I understood every word and sincerely apologize for that. Still, it's nice to know you aren't perfect. Give me that, okay?"

"Well, if you want imperfect, take a look." He holds out his right hand, pointing to his middle finger, where his knuckle is somewhat displaced. "This was a high school football injury. One of many, I might add."

"Well, now you're just showing off. That doesn't hold a candle to my C-section scars or my stretch marks." Despite her jovial tone, Kyle senses that this subject is something Amelia might be self-conscious of.

Taking a step closer to her, Kyle speaks clearly, his tone full of emotion. "Every scar or stretch mark represents who you are and how you got here. Those C-sections represent two incredible kids that you brought into this world. That's not an imperfection in my book."

"Wow." Amelia exhales, a ragged breath, as they stare at one another for what feels like a long while, squinting in the bright sunlight. "You know how to give one heck of a pep talk."

The front door opens and Jacob runs out, followed by Chloe.

"Hi, Kyle!" Jacob shouts.

"Kyle! You have to see our tadpoles. They're so cute!" Chloe chimes in at the same time.

"I'm a sweaty mess, but I've got a change of clothes in my truck."

Nodding, Amelia adds, "That's great. You can even take a shower and stay a while if you'd like. We're about to watch a movie in the living room, if you're free."

"What about Bridget?" Kyle asks, noting for the first time that the Expedition that was parked across the street is now gone.

"She and her kids bailed when you were mowing my backyard. She asked me to tell you goodbye."

"Seriously?" Somehow, Kyle imagines that Bridget said a lot more than that.

Amelia laughs. "I'm keeping her message G-rated."

"Okay, then. You've got it. But only if the kids show me those tadpoles. They're growing fast. It must be the aerator I saw that you added."

Chloe and Jacob jump up and down. "Mom added the aerator!"

"They will be thrilled to show you. As a matter of fact, I guarantee they will drag you onto the back patio as soon as you enter the front door."

"Then it's a deal." He smiles at the kids, just as Jacob wraps his arms around Kyle's legs. Kneeling in front of the child, Kyle gets the biggest hug he's ever experienced. "Thanks for taking care of me last night, Kyle."

Kyle's heart swells. "I can't take the credit. Your mom is the one who took great care of you. I simply drove you around."

"You took care of my mom, and she took care of me," Jacob whispers, like it's their little secret. "She wasn't alone this time."

The kid's statement slices to Kyle's very core. Amelia's been alone, has been the only one her children can count on. As young as Jacob may be, he understands that. Kyle thinks about the fact that his kindness, as small as it was, means so much to her little boy.

"Three guesses about our movie." Chloe grabs Kyle's attention.

"Say *Cars*," Jacob mutters.

Chloe turns to her brother. "No fair. He was supposed to guess."

"It's all right." Amelia steps in, defusing the situation. "Let's let Kyle get his clothes and shower. I'll prep, and you two get the floor ready."

"The floor?" Kyle asks.

"Movie time is major. Just you wait." With a wink, she disappears with the kids into the house through the front door.

As Kyle walks to his truck, Jacob's statement nags at him. Friends or not, Kyle cares about Amelia and her children. He cares about his friends, and his neighbors, too. So, what's different? He's unsure—or is unable to contemplate the complexities. All he knows is that a little boy and girl need their mom, and their mom needs support.

Especially now, with Carla clearly targeting her, and her ex causing the kids more pain.

Sure, Amelia is strong and capable. But Kyle still wants to help, to be there for her. What's wrong with caring about her? They're not dating, so there's no chance of heartbreak. Friendship is best. Amelia was right.

No heartbreak is exactly what Kyle wants. More importantly, it's what Kyle needs.

It's simple, really. Know their boundaries, and don't go any further. What could go wrong?

# Chapter 21

As Kyle takes a quick shower, Amelia begins prepping movie popcorn. No butter, no big bowls. Even though Jacob bounces back quick from ear infections, easy does it. That's Amelia's motto. While she's rummaging around in the cabinets, a popping sound emanates from her microwave, and the aroma of popcorn makes her realize that she hasn't eaten all day.

Entering the room, Kyle makes a comment about the kids' blankets and pillows being on the floor facing the wall with the big screen. "You look comfortable."

"What would you like to drink, Kyle?" Amelia asks.

"Gatorade is good." He winks at Jacob, who echoes his order.

"Gatorade and popcorn it is. Would you like water, Chloe?" Amelia's open floor plan has its benefits when it comes to communication.

"Water with ice please." Chloe stands. "Come on, Kyle. Look at our tadpoles! They eat leaves and mosquitos. How cool is that?"

He follows the kids, saying, "Cool, as long as you aren't a mosquito. I was careful not to disturb them when I was mowing the lawn."

"Please don't let Prince out," Amelia calls to them, relief rushing over her as they shut the back door. Prince is an indoor cat. The last thing her children need is to lose someone else they love, and Amelia is protective. Some would say too much so, but they have no idea how catastrophic—pun intended—the loss of that feline they've grown so attached to would be.

When they return, noise fills the house.

"Did you see that tadpole jump on my finger, Kyle?" Chloe asks.

Jacob groans. "You reached in the water. It had nowhere else to go."

"Wash your hands please," Amelia insists.

"I'll wash my hands, then I'm getting my stuffies. Jacob, do you want yours?" Chloe calls to her brother, racing into their hallway and their bathroom to wash her hands.

The little boy glances at Kyle, as if waiting for his approval or his judgment.

Kyle offers him a nod. "Stuffies are good. You can't watch a movie without them, right?"

Jacob smiles. "Yeah. Coming, Chloe!"

"The tadpoles are doing great, and the kids love them. I can see why you couldn't get rid of them." Kyle meets Amelia in her kitchen. "What can I help with?"

She already has two bowls on her countertop and some candy. "You've already helped. Thanks for confirming that stuffed animals are okay. Jacob's dad didn't approve, and while Jacob's okay when he's with me, when others are around, he feels self-conscious." The microwave beeps and Amelia opens the steaming bag of popcorn and pours it into two bowls.

She adds M&M's to one bowl and mixes them in. Not too many, though. "Would you like candy in your popcorn?" she asks in a teasing tone.

"As if you have to ask." Kyle smiles, his sparkling eyes conveying his excitement. "Jacob can eat this, after last night?"

"Kids are resilient. At least mine are. They can be sick in the morning, and running around in the afternoon. You notice there's no butter and not much candy in the kids' bowl. Call it my Jedi Mom trick."

"Maybe that's how you can battle the bylaws—use your Jedi mind trick."

Amelia runs the water, lathering her hands with soap. "It's a Jedi Mom trick, not a mind trick. I don't think it will work on the HOA. Is it strange that you're my friend, considering I am fighting the HOA and the management company? I want Carla out, you know."

"I figured you would want her out. You're not alone on that front."

"That's good to know." Amelia dries her hands with the dish towel. "Where *is* Prince?"

Before Amelia can answer, Chloe enters the kitchen carrying the tuxedo cat. "Mom! Prince is hungry."

Reaching for the cat, Amelia brings him over to his food and water bowls. "He knows where to eat and drink, Chloe."

The cat takes one sniff of dry kitten food recommended by Dr. Bass, then prances away. "He is clearly not hungry. Why don't you finish getting your stuffies? Popcorn is coming."

"What's a spay day?" the little girl asks as she arranges blankets and comforters on the living room floor in front of the coffee table.

"A what?" Amelia asks, watching her daughter set up her stuffed animals.

Chloe stands with a stuffed unicorn in her hand. "A spay day. Aunt Bridget says she needs one."

"Oh. You mean a spa day. That's when moms get pampered." Amelia shoots Kyle a wry grin as she chats with her daughter.

"No, Aunt Bridget wants a spay day." Chloe is adamant as she settles on her comforter. "We should give her one."

Handing Chloe a cup of ice water, complete with a lid and washable straw, Amelia pats the little girl's head. "The last thing Aunt Bridget needs is to be spayed, honey. But we can make a *spa* day happen for her."

It's a comedy of errors, and Amelia can only imagine what Kyle thinks.

Though Amelia stressed the word 'spa,' her daughter announces to Jacob, "We're giving Aunt Bridget a spay."

"Okay, fine. Whatever you want to do." Jacob may have agreed, but he's checked out of this convo and is more interested in gulping his Gatorade.

"Take it slow. No more throwing up." Amelia reenters the kitchen and meets Kyle's gaze, whispering, "Welcome to my world. Where poor Prince will be neutered in the not-so-distant future."

Prince mews and rubs against Amelia's legs. As if that will save him from that particular vet visit. "Nice try, adorable, but you're not getting out of it. I don't care how cute you are," she says to the cat.

"Hurry up, Mom!" Chloe calls from the living room. "We're ready."

"Would you mind carrying our drinks?" Amelia asks Kyle as she grabs the bowls of popcorn and sets one down on the comforter between Jacob and Chloe, who are propped up against pillows on the floor, sandwiched between blankets and comforters. Jacob hugs his stuffy while Chloe has arranged hers in sitting positions. Prince lies in between the two children, biting his tail.

"Use your napkins please." The kids nod and Amelia turns to Kyle. "We've got the sofa all to ourselves, and the cat, of course."

"Has he overthrown your rule of the house, yet?" Kyle takes the bowl, while Amelia sits.

She rolls her eyes. "You have no idea. But he's sweet and the kids love him."

That's what's important, as Amelia hits play on the streaming service.

Jacob turns to Kyle. "I told you it was *Cars*. And I left you something." He motions to the sofa, where a Lightning McQueen plush toy is resting in the corner beside Kyle.

Her son let Kyle borrow a stuffy. Amelia could swear her heart's about to burst. And here she thought that Jacob and Chloe already filled her to the point that her love is overflowing, but Jacob just released the dam. Amelia studies Kyle's reaction, hoping he'll be kind.

Kyle winks at Jacob. "This is awesome. I always wanted a Lightning McQueen toy."

Jacob smiles his familiar megawatt smile, then settles in and watches Lightning McQueen do his thing.

"Thank you," Amelia whispers to Kyle.

Shrugging it off with a grin, Kyle sits with Lightning McQueen on his lap, like it's no big deal. But it's a huge deal. How important and valued he made Jacob feel, how he validated her son's insecurities.

Friendship has its benefits.

# Chapter 22

SHOWER TIME: DONE. PJs: ON. LIGHTING: DIMMED. SCHOOL clothing: chosen and hanging up on the closet doors for tomorrow's morning rush. Bedtime is T-minus thirty and counting. But first, a chat between Amelia and her children.

"Can Jacob and I have a sleepover tonight?" Chloe asks, staring up at her mom, her long lashes fanning her beautiful blue-green eyes.

If this were a weekend night, Amelia wouldn't be able to resist. "Tonight's a school night, honey. How about on Friday?"

"Okay." Chloe follows Amelia into Jacob's room.

"Have a seat on the bed. Let's chat." Jacob scoots over, and Amelia sits beside him, wrapping her arms around him and his sister.

"It was fun having Kyle over." Jacob, that little stinker, knows what Amelia wants to talk about. He's smart, too smart for Amelia's own good. Jacob puts both the CIA and MI6 to shame. He's watched *Cars 2* way too many times, and would make a great spy.

"It was. What did you think, Chloe?" Amelia waits for a response, allowing her daughter to voice her feelings on the matter first, without mom's influence.

"Kyle's nice. I like him. Can we see him more?" Chloe asks.

"That's what I wanted to talk to you about. You know how Aunt Bridget, Aunt Lily, and their children are our friends?" She pauses, reading Jacob and Chloe's responses. Both are nodding. "Well, Kyle has become a friend to us, too. He's offered to give you both guitar lessons if you want."

"Yes!" Chloe squeals, which is always a good sign.

Jacob, on the other hand, wrinkles his brows. "Is Kyle your boyfriend?" he asks.

"No, buddy. He's not. We're friends. Nothing more." Amelia kisses the top of Jacob's head. "What are you thinking?"

"I want him to be your boyfriend. He's nice to us," Jacob whispers, his voice rough with emotion.

Amelia holds him tighter.

"Me, too," Chloe adds, resting her head on her mom's lap, where Amelia strokes her hair.

"I know it's hard, but no one will ever replace your dad—"

"Dad was never around. He isn't around now. He never calls us, or answers our texts or emails. He doesn't want us anymore." Jacob's statement shatters Amelia's heart, as her palpable rage still simmers just beneath the surface towards her ex-husband who has made Jacob and Chloe feel this rejection, who reads their texts but never replies. But now, a heavy anguish causes her limbs to feel like she'll be crushed under the weight of it all. It's as if she's absorbed her children's sadness, pain, and anger.

"I'm sorry, Jacob. I'd do anything to change your father's behavior." Her throat is dry and hoarse, the sorrow swelling, causing a lump so large that she's certain it will asphyxiate her if she lets it. But she won't allow it. Instead, she swallows hard against it and inhales a deep breath.

"Both of you deserve better than what your father did, or how he continues to behave." Amelia hasn't bad-mouthed Daniel, nor has she blamed him. But she's never hidden the truth from her children. They knew it was Daniel's decision. "If I haven't said it enough, none of this is your fault. And I love you so much. Your dad does, too, in his own way."

Jacob scoffs, clearly not having any of this.

"Okay, you're right. I don't know how your dad feels, or how he could do this to you." Amelia doesn't release her children. Instead, she holds them tighter. "I choose to believe that he loves you in his own way. What I do know, beyond a shadow of a doubt, is that you both are my everything, and I love you more than there are stars in the heavens and fish in the sea."

"Infinity?" Chloe asks.

"Oh, baby girl. Infinity times infinity." Amelia admits the one thing she fears the most. "I love you both, and I don't ever want to fail you. Not ever. I'm sorry about your dad, and I'm trying to make it hurt less. I hope by loving you as much as I do, it will somehow make up for his absence."

"It's not your fault, Mom." Chloe pats Amelia's leg. "You love us, and we love you. Right Jacob?"

"Yeah." Jacob's thinking hard, staring at his chrome clock, the one shaped like the rim of a monster truck tire. "Will Kyle leave, too? Is that why he's not your boyfriend?"

After rubbing their shoulders, Amelia asks them to sit up. "Criss-cross apple sauce. Look at me. Both of you."

Holding their hands, caressing them with her thumbs, Amelia gently squeezes until both meet her eyes. "You are wonderful, and you are loved. Kyle isn't my boyfriend, because we're friends. Right now, I think it's what we all need—both of you and me. I wish I could promise that Kyle won't ever leave, but I can't. It's a part of the risk we take in any type of relationship. Here's where choice comes in: we can be his friend and that friendship might last a long time, or we don't take the chance and we'll never know. Either way, whatever you choose, I want you to know that not every man is like your father."

"We know," Jacob says. "I want to be friends with Kyle. Can he give us guitar lessons this weekend?"

Amelia waits for Chloe's response.

"Real friends are important." She is repeating what Amelia once told her. "Having a handful of real friends is better than a hundred meanies."

Okay, not exactly what Amelia told her, but close. It's not about the quantity of friendships you have, but the quality. Kyle said something similar, and it's too true.

"Just know, no matter what, you come first. Always and forever. I love you." Amelia gently caresses each child on the cheek, her tone solid and unswerving.

*Always and forever...* It's their thing. Amelia's told both of her children that she loves them *always and forever* since they were babies. And she does. More than they will ever know.

"So, do you think Kyle will give us guitar lessons soon?" Jacob grips his mother's hand. "I'm ready to risk a new friend if you are."

Leaning into him, Amelia kisses the top of his thick head of hair, then turns her attention to Chloe.

She smiles, her adult teeth in various stages of growing in. "I think he's a real friend, Mom."

"Yeah. Kyle's nice to you, and us." Jacob's voice is louder and more forceful this time.

"Are you sure?" She gives them an out.

Both children nod in unison.

Reaching for them, Amelia tugs them in a tight embrace, kissing each of them. "I love you both so much."

"Always and forever?" Chloe asks.

Amelia squeezes harder. "Always and forever."

"We love you, too, Mom. Always and forever." Jacob is caring and mature beyond his years.

So is his sister, who repeats, "We love you always and forever, Mom."

It's official: they're adding a new friend to the mix, and guitar lessons.

There can never be too much noise in the Marsh home, or too many people who are kind to Jacob and Chloe, right? Besides, always and forever, Amelia has got them.

# Chapter 23

WORKING LATE INTO THE NIGHT IS USUAL FOR AMELIA, AND HER front office allows her to listen to Jacob and Chloe reading a book to one another between the wall that separates their rooms, then ensure that they go to sleep, as opposed to laughing and keeping each other awake. Does it always go as planned? Nope. More often than not? Occasionally. Tonight, a quiet hush quickly overtakes the house, and the clacking of Amelia's typing on her keyboard soon becomes the soundtrack to her worknight. After finishing some coding updates for a client's website, she then checks email once more before powering down her desktop computer. There's always more work to be done, which, for an entrepreneur with two children, is a blessing and why she carries her laptop into her bedroom.

After checking on Jacob and Chloe and making sure they are in fact actually asleep—they have been known to fake it from time to time—Amelia double-checks all locks before heading into her bedroom, where Prince is lying on one of her pillow shams like royalty.

"Hey, can we share?" The feline shoots her a one-eye-open look with a pronounced yawn, then goes back to sleep.

"Nice chat, buddy." She moves the pillow with Prince atop it to the other side of the bed, props the remaining pillows behind her, and sets her laptop down, prepared to make some changes to a client's graphics.

Flipping channels for background noise, she stops when she finds Bruce Willis's battered and bloody body in full action-sequence mode on a premium-cable channel, meaning there will be curse words. She lowers the volume in an attempt not to corrupt Prince, as her cell vibrates on her nightstand.

The text is from Kyle: Guess what I'm watching?

Dialing him, she doesn't wait for him to speak. "Don't you dare say *Cars*."

"No, it's not *Cars*, though I did like what we watched this afternoon." His voice is low and sounds sleepy. Like her children have exhausted him, which they very well might have.

"That's good. My children will expect you to watch the sequel with them. You've been warned."

"You never did guess…"

Right. "Could you be watching *Die Hard*?"

"How did you know? Wait, let me guess: you're watching the same thing?"

A sleepy Prince climbs up her arm before snuggling against her neck while she pets his soft fur. "Yep. Just me and Prince. Though he's purring through it while I'm working."

"Your work is never done, is it?" Kyle's tone is teasing.

"You're one to talk. What are you doing?" Amelia's skeptical that Kyle is just watching television. He always seems to be multitasking.

Kyle sighs. "Answering emails, along with boring construction stuff like working on an estimate and some submittals."

"I knew it!" Amelia laughs. "We're a fine pair. Hey, thanks for today. Jacob and Chloe had a great time."

"So did I." Kyle sounds surprised.

Amelia can't help but smile. "My children make great company."

"Yes, they do. To be honest, though, your popcorn and candy didn't hurt."

"Well, now that you've experienced the full range of my culinary expertise, it's all downhill from here." Amelia opens Photoshop and pulls up a graphic that one of her clients wants changed per his email to her this evening.

Kyle chuckles. "You sell yourself short. A lot."

"Sarcasm is just one of the many services I offer," Amelia responds.

"Got it."

An explosion on television grabs her attention, though Prince is unimpressed and remains content, purring loudly. "Speaking of services... Jacob and Chloe would love guitar lessons. Does the offer still stand?"

"Yeah. Absolutely." Kyle sounds excited. "When do they want to start?"

"Are you free next weekend?" Amelia asks, moving her cursor, and selects the color replacement tool.

There's a long pause. "I'm checking on a job site Saturday morning. How about in the afternoon? That gives me time to shower and change before heading to your place."

"Sounds good. They'll be thrilled. Oh! And just a warning, Chloe wants to be the next Taylor Swift."

"Who's Taylor Swift?"

"She's a singer/songwriter who plays four instruments." Amelia remembers the Easter egg hunt. "'Shake It Off' is one of her songs. You danced to it, or the Bunny's helper danced to it before taking photos."

"Okay. Well, Chloe's on her own with the singing-songwriting part, and the other three instruments." Kyle laughs. "Do your kids do anything halfway? Between Jacob's long car list and Chloe's desire to tackle a band, they're unstoppable."

Amelia stares at her laptop screen. "No wonder I'm fatigued all the time." She's only half joking. Exhaustion has been her constant companion of late, along with overthinking everything, and that's not an exaggeration.

"You've got your hands full, that's for sure."

"How can I repay you?" Silence hangs heavy between them. "For the guitar lessons, I mean."

Of course Kyle knows what she refers to. Here she goes, overthinking things again.

"Not a dime." On this Kyle is adamant. "That's what—"

"Let me guess, that's what friends are for."

An explosion rocks the Nakatomi Plaza, and Amelia's attention is drawn to her television. Is this an omen? Fictional as it may be, could the explosion be a hint of what's to come to their new friendship?

"It just occurred to me that I just missed a chance to ask for you to cancel Gnomegate."

"That's never going to happen. I've done too much research to give up now." Amelia remembers what Kyle admitted today—that many residents are hard on him. "I hope I'm not making your life more difficult. I had no idea that residents give you such a difficult time for being on the board."

"It's nothing I can't handle. I'm a big boy; besides, if you do manage to oust Carla, I wouldn't be heartbroken. She gets on my last nerve, and I'm a pretty patient person." What an admission!

Prince's claws dig into Amelia's shoulder as be slowly slides from her neck. "Ouch!" She picks him up and places the furball beside her.

"Are you okay?" Kyle asks.

Amelia rubs her shoulder, as Prince climbs back up her arm. "Prince has a grip. And a fascination with sleeping in the crook of my neck."

"The cat's got the life and is one lucky feline, even if his goal is to take over Timberland."

"Kyle Sanders, is my sarcasm rubbing off on you?" Amelia strokes Prince's soft little head, scratching him between his ears.

After a scoff, Kyle manages, "As if. You're not the only sarcastic resident of Castle Rock, or Timberland, Texas, for that matter."

"Duly noted. See you Saturday?"

"I'll bring the guitar, you supply the kids. Deal?"

They'll be some happy kids, Amelia notes silently. They might even consider her to be mom of the year after their lesson.

For the first time in…well, ever, Amelia begins to think she's slaying this single mom challenge. A little voice inside Amelia's head warns her not to get cocky. So instead, she chooses positivity.

She can succeed at all of it: being a mom, a business owner, raising a cat, rehoming tadpoles, and keeping her children happy. Things are looking up, and hope fills Amelia's chest until she's certain it might burst.

Giving Prince a few more pets, she bids Kyle good-night and returns to work, reminded of the saying *hope springs eternal.*

"Just keep going, keep moving forward, and you'll be fine," she mutters to herself.

It sounds easy enough, but Amelia knows from firsthand experience that nothing comes easy. No, happiness comes at a price, and a steep one at that. She, more so than anyone, understands to be careful what you wish for.

# Chapter 24

KYLE ARRIVES AT HIS OFFICE BEFORE ANY OF HIS EMPLOYEES. IT'S his usual routine: be the first one to arrive and last to leave. Situated in the heart of Houston, on what locals call "the loop," Kyle's office is convenient to most of the Houston vicinity without being situated downtown where prices are high and traffic is a nightmare. Its location also allows him to commute easily, so when he's needed in the neighborhood, he can fit it into his tight schedule. Also convenient is that he has a few small projects in Timberland.

His projects range from office buildings to K-12 schools, universities, and medical buildings. Never one to brag, Kyle has instead let his work and stellar reputation speak for him, and though his office isn't downtown, it is decorated with a minimalist vibe accentuated with pictures of his projects—with one exception: at the front entrance, on the wall behind his administrative assistant's desk, where his company logo hangs.

After passing through to the main corridor, visitors are met with a large sepia canvas of the Houston skyline, where a skyscraper Kyle built is visible. It hangs across from the conference room. Equipped with a long table and chairs, in addition to several large whiteboards and a projector, it's where he meets with architects, subcontractors, clients, and his own employees.

To the right, down a hallway, are cubicles where Kyle's project managers, estimators, and superintendents work. His business manager also has an office back there.

Across from the bullpen is Kyle's office, where framed sepia photos of his company's completed projects hang between more whiteboards, upon which every project is written along with the project manager and superintendent's names and other pertinent information. Kyle keeps a tight grip, and has that steady personality that his employees rely on. As for the space itself, it's his and it's impressive without radiating that *trying too hard* vibe.

He opens his laptop just as his cell rings. The name on his screen shows that it's one of his clients. At this time of day, this call can't be good. "Hi. How are you, Justin?"

"Where are your guys?" Justin's terse tone proves Kyle right.

"Tim is on-site." Tim is one of his superintendents assigned to the Charles Street school construction site.

"No, he's not, Kyle. And I can't reach Ben, either. Meanwhile, the drywall contractor is on-site and broke a sprinkler head on the third floor. Water has flooded that classroom, down the hall, and has rushed all the way down the stairs to the first floor. The fire department has been dispatched."

*Damn it.*

"I'm on my way." Kyle grabs his keys and jumps in his truck, turning on the ignition as his Bluetooth connects his cell. "I'll get in touch with the plant operator or custodial staff so they can unlock the valves and shut off the water."

"Why wasn't one of your guys here to supervise, Kyle? And why didn't the PM pick up his phone?" Justin demands.

"I'll get to the bottom of it, Justin. First, let me get a hold of the plant operator so the valves can be unlocked and the water shut off. I'll call you as soon as I speak to them. I'm about fifteen minutes away from the site."

"This is going to cost you, Kyle."

"I understand. Talk to you soon." Kyle disconnects the call, then tells his Bluetooth to call the plant operator.

"Hey. What's wrong?"

"Don, you've got to get someone to unlock the water valves at Charles Street and shut off the water. We've got a flood."

The expletives Don recites are numerous. "Good thing I'm heading in early today."

"Don, I'm about ten minutes out. Where are you?"

"Turning in now. The fire department is here. There are going to be fines."

"I know." Kyle can't even think about how much this screwup is going to cost his company right now. "Get the valves shut off, and I'll meet you there. I need to make some more calls."

Kyle hangs up and again uses his hands-free to call Tim, the superintendent who was supposed to be on-site, and gets his voicemail. "Call me immediately, Tim. I need to know where you are and why you aren't at Charles Street."

Next, Kyle calls his project manager, Ben. Again voicemail. "You've gotta be kidding me." Unfortunately, this situation is no joke. It's a nightmare.

At the beep, Kyle leaves a message for Ben. "We've got a major emergency at Charles Street and neither you or Tim are on-site or answering your phones. Call me ASAP."

Kyle pulls into the parking lot just in time to see the custodian running out of the building and Don, the plant operator, speaking with several firefighters. Kyle runs over in time to hear the word "fine."

Not as in *everything is fine*, but that *Sanders Construction* is being fined. Kyle speaks to them and takes the fine, then enters the building, trudging through water to inspect the damage with his flashlight. It's good that the electricity hasn't been turned on yet. Wading through about two feet of water, he still can't find any of his own guys, let alone the drywall contractors responsible for this mess.

When he's on the third floor, he searches for the broken sprinkler head, and sure enough, it was knocked off with a ladder. Flood doesn't begin to cover the mess. Kyle calls the owner of a remediation company that he's used before.

"Hey, Kyle. It's early."

"Thank God you answered, Keith. I need you down at my Charles Street site. We've got a flood from the third floor to the first. I'm surveying the damage now."

Rustling meets Kyle's plea, then Keith says, "Give me the address. I'll send a crew now."

"We're going to need crews, buddy. Plural." Kyle clenches his fist, noting the fresh drywall that's soaked through, as he gives Keith the address. "Let me make another call."

"I'll meet you down there ASAP."

Kyle thanks him, then calls his client. "Justin. I'm here now, the water is off, and I'm assessing the damage."

"I'm on my way, too."

"Listen, I've already called the remediation company and they're going to be here ASAP. It will be taken care of. I promise."

"This isn't like your guys not to be on-site, Kyle."

Justin's right. Kyle prides himself on his stellar reputation, and his company's. "I know. I'll fix it and make sure it never happens again, Justin."

Expelling a sigh, Justin adds, "If this happened to anyone but you, they'd be tossed off the project."

"I understand, but you know me and I'm on it. I'll make it right."

After his call with Justin, Kyle waits for the remediation company to arrive. They have a master agreement. He also finds the drywall subcontractor's vans, with the employees sleeping on the job inside.

It's their screwup, but Kyle's employees should have been on-site.

Thankfully, he'll be able to back-charge the drywall company for the damage and repairs, but it all comes out of his pocket first. Then there's the fact that neither the project manager nor superintendent assigned to this site have returned his call.

Dialing another of his project managers, Kyle asks him for help. "We need all hands on deck. Get to Charles Street as soon as you can, and call the rest of the office in."

"You've got it, boss."

*Boss...* Right now Kyle hates hearing that word. Because it means that the buck stops with him, and he has a client to answer to, along with a company reputation to uphold.

He's going to have to fire someone. There's no excuse for at least one of his guys not to be supervising the drywall company. They know this. Kyle taught them better than this.

Sometimes, being the boss just plain sucks.

This is definitely one of those times.

# Chapter 25

I'm here.

No sooner does Amelia read Kyle's text than she opens her front door. It's dark, the street illuminated by streetlights, while her own interior lights are dimmed because the kids are already asleep.

She motions for Kyle to enter with her forefinger over her mouth in a silent shush, then notices the dark circles under his eyes, evident even in the dim lighting. He texted that he needed to talk, but judging by his wrinkled slacks and filthy polo shirt, along with the worry lines etched in his forehead and around his eyes, this is going to be a rough conversation.

"Outside or in?" she asks in a whisper.

"In, if possible. I've been in the heat all day and don't think I have it in me to sit outside. Is that okay?"

She nods, entering her kitchen and grabbing two beers from her fridge, along with a bottle opener. "Have a seat on the sofa."

After sitting beside Kyle in her dimly lit living room, she pops both bottles open and hands him one. "Did you know that bottle openers are also called *church keys*? I read about it once. Someone thought they resembled the keys to church doors."

Kyle chuckles, softly so as not to wake the kids. "How can you make me smile when that's the last thing I want to do?"

"That's one of my many superpowers." She winks at him.

"Your children do believe you're the Scarlet Witch." His grin is wide, though his eyes have lost their usual luster.

She reaches for his arm. "What happened today? Talk to me."

"I had to fire someone today. One of my superintendents, who was supposed to be supervising a high-profile project. He left the site and there was a flood." Kyle sighs. "I handled it, and we're repairing it. I had hoped I could just give him a warning, but when he showed up on-site today in the middle of the chaos, drunk… I had no choice."

"I'm sorry, Kyle." Amelia squeezes his arm.

"I hate firing one of my employees. I always try to mentor people first, but I couldn't excuse this."

"You did the right thing."

"Yeah, I know. But then there's my project manager. He wasn't answering his phone either. The client called me this morning, and I've spoken to him all throughout the day. He saw the site, saw the damage, and saw how I've ensured it will be fixed. But…"

Amelia waits in silence as Kyle peels the label on his beer bottle with his fingernail. "My client wants my project manager fired. I planned to remove him from this particular project, but that's not enough for this client."

"Okay. So your client wants that. What do you want?"

Kyle meets her eyes for the first time since he began speaking. "This is a kid, Amelia. I hired him straight out of college, trained him, watched him grow into a great employee. He's newly married with a baby who was sick last night. When he finally returned my call, Ben explained that he was taking care of his child and his phone was on silent. It's not a habit of his."

"Of all nights, right?"

"And with all clients." Kyle grimaces, squeezing his eyes shut. "I don't want to fire Ben…" Kyle's voice is rough and trails off.

"And if you don't, you'll lose your client?"

Nodding, Kyle meets Amelia's worried gaze. "Yeah. And I make a lot of money from this client. Profit I use to pay my staff. The thing is… I can't fire Ben. Give him a warning, yes. Teach him how to handle things like this in the future—like letting me know and forwarding his calls to me, yes. But fire him? I don't agree with firing him. After all, it's my company and ultimately the mistake falls on me."

Leaning into Amelia, Kyle whispers, "Am I wrong? Am I being...I don't know—"

"Emotional?" Amelia counters.

His exasperated sigh is all the confirmation she needs to continue. "No. You're being a good boss, who wants to use this as a teaching moment for a young employee who made a mistake."

She tips his chin towards her. "You're a good boss, but even more importantly, you're a man with integrity and empathy. Kyle, you're risking losing a major client because you see the humanity in this situation. Your employee had a sick baby and made a mistake. Explain that to your client. Maybe he will understand."

"You think so?"

"I understand, and I respect you for it." Amelia chucks him on the chin. "You're one of the good guys, Kyle Sanders. And if this client can't see that, others will. Remember, you have to be able to look in the mirror each day. And staring back at you is a guy who cares about his employees, his community, and so much more."

Kyle grins, flattening his palm against her cheek. "I believe that when you say it."

Amelia leans into his hand, which is warm and strong. So much so that she could forget about friend-zoning Kyle, could overlook the risk, except... She glances at the pictures of her children on her fireplace mantel. Their faces remind her of why she can't get involved with Kyle.

"You should believe it, because it's true." She pulls away from his palm, feeling slightly empty as she meets his eyes. "I meant every word."

"We could be something, you know." Kyle shoves his fingers

through his hair. "Maybe it's my exhaustion talking, or the fact that you're the brightest light in this horrendous day, but I see it clearly. We could be something."

Pressing her forehead against his, Amelia exhales. "You could be right. Actually, I think you are right about that. But I can't. I'm sorry."

He exhales, his warm breath fanning her cheek. "I know. Me too."

Again Amelia breaks their connection, this time by leaning back. "Did you want to talk about anything else? I'm here for you. That's what friends are for and all." She sounds like she's reciting a greeting card.

"I'm good, but thanks for listening. And for the support."

"Any time." Amelia offers him a grin. "I mean that."

Kyle nods, then stands, taking a swig of his beer before carrying it into the kitchen.

"I'll take care of that." Amelia follows him, placing her own bottle in the sink along with his.

Kyle turns to head out of her kitchen, and she grabs his hand. Instinctively, without thinking, she embraces him. "You seem like you could use a hug. And, as Chloe learned from *Frozen*, warm hugs cure everything. Let's see if Olaf was on to something."

With a chuckle, his shoulders relax as his arms encircle her waist. "Yeah. Thanks. That snowman might be on to something." He embraces her a little tighter, before adding, "That snowman was definitely on to something. I don't suppose you'll be there to give me one of these when I discuss my decision with my client."

Only after inhaling a shaky breath does Amelia counter with, "I guess we could arrange that. You have supported me through so much, it's the least I can do."

Kyle kisses the top of her head, then pulls away and heads towards her front door.

When he places his hand on the doorknob, he turns to face her, with a raspy laugh. "We're grown adults who just took advice from a fictitious snowman."

Chuckling, Amelia nods. "Yep. Welcome to my world."

His grin turns brighter.

"At least it made you smile." She reaches for his arm and gives it a gentle squeeze. "Stand by your decision. Just do what you believe is best, and trust that it will be okay."

"I will. You, too." He opens the door, as Prince prances down the hallway. "See you for guitar lessons. Good night, Prince."

His words linger, even after he's closed the door, and he's pressed the button so her lock turns. Again, for the second time. Protecting Amelia and her children. The first time wasn't a fluke.

*Do what you believe is best...*

That's what Amelia's been doing. So why is it suddenly so difficult?

Because Kyle is about to risk his company to do what he feels is right and protect an employee. That speaks volumes. As does her ex-husband's silence. Daniel is still ghosting their children.

It all falls on Amelia. To be strong, to be loving, and to be unbreakable. She can't afford to lose her way or be distracted. Amelia may not know where she's going, but she knows it's forward. With her children.

She picks up Prince and pets him behind his ear. "Never underestimate Mom power, little one. If that's not a hashtag, it should be."

At the very least, it will be Amelia's new mantra.

Prince meows, as if in agreement.

"That's my boy!"

# Chapter 26

Sitting at her dining room table with her laptop, Amelia organizes her research for the upcoming HOA meeting, though she still doesn't know what to use as her primary reason in her bid to oust Carla from her position as Castle Rock's management representative. Amelia has included the picture she took of Carla smoking beneath the NO SMOKING sign that she took at the pool during the Easter egg hunt, though she isn't sure if it's a low blow to use it.

Time's still on her side, and her brain has been working overtime researching ways to request a new representative. One is a petition, which Amelia has created, though she hasn't distributed it yet. Reason: Carla being rude and power hungry are Amelia's opinions, not facts to support a representative being reassigned. She jots down a note on her legal pad about this and circles it with an arrow.

Moving on, she continues organizing her bullet points for her hand outs, while Kyle, Jacob, and Chloe sit on her living room sofa. It's their first guitar lesson, with Kyle doing most of the work.

"You're getting it. Look at you. You're naturals," Kyle compliments both children.

Even to Amelia's nonmusical ear, Jacob seems to remember the chords, and Chloe is great with timing.

"Great job, sweeties!" she adds, smiling, before getting back to Operation Gnomegate.

She's facing the scene in the living room, and is keeping her gnome work under wraps. It's not that she doesn't trust Kyle, it's that she wants to leave him out of this. It's her battle to wage, and wage it she will.

"Do you know any Justin Bieber songs?" Chloe asks.

Laughing, Kyle shakes his head. "Justin? No, sorry."

"How about Billy Joel?" Jacob's a boy after Amelia's own heart. He loves the classics—classic rock, that is.

Strumming some chords to "Piano Man," Kyle tells Jacob he's got style. "Your mom taught you well. A ten-year-old who likes classic rock is rare."

"Oh! How about Taylor Swift?" Chloe counters.

There's no way Amelia's excited little girl is giving up on her pop icons. That much is obvious, as Kyle shoots Amelia a wry grin over his shoulder. After strumming "Piano Man," he pulls out his cell and looks Taylor up on YouTube. Kyle then asks the kids to choose a song.

At this, Amelia's attention is drawn to the scene in the living room. Kyle plays a portion of the video, pauses it, and tries to repeat what he heard with his guitar, making a ton of mistakes along the way. Jacob and Chloe laugh at each one of them, as does Kyle.

"I should leave the guitar playing to Taylor." Kyle must be making funny faces at the kids, because Jacob and Chloe laugh louder. Amelia can't help but smile. A thunderstorm watch alert vibrates on Amelia's cell, and she saves her work before heading to the tadpoles and dragging their large tub beneath her covered back patio. Prince watches her from inside the glass back door, ensuring all tadpoles are safe.

When she reenters her home and shuts the back door, Jacob asks, "Can we have dinner together, Mom?"

"With Kyle," Chloe clarifies.

Amelia arches her brow, studying Kyle's smile.

"I thought we could get pizza and celebrate our first guitar lesson.

As friends." He exaggerates the word "friends." "How about Umberto's? Table for four."

"A meal with my children, in a restaurant. Oh, Mr. Sanders, you have no idea what you're getting yourself into."

Kyle shrugs. "I'm a brave man."

"Please, Mom. Please!" Chloe and Jacob plead, until Amelia relents. The kids jump up and down, whooping and hollering. From the surprised look on Kyle's face, he's never known hyper like this until now, when Jacob and Chloe's energies are off the charts. Once the sound has reached an earsplitting crescendo, Amelia reins them in. "Let's be calm, please. Chloe, please make sure Prince's bowl is filled with crunchies. Jacob, please make sure Prince has enough water. Then get your shoes on and make sure we have everything—tablets and earbuds included."

Kyle places his guitar in its case, while Amelia carries her tote bag through the house, checking items off her imaginary list, announcing, "Tablets, check. Earbuds, check. Chargers, check. Chloe, sweetie, your shoes are on the wrong feet. Oh, and please remember a hoodie in case you're cold."

Chloe does as instructed, while Jacob smiles at Kyle. "This is cool, huh?"

"Yeah, very."

Amelia's not sure who is smiling wider as they say "See you later" to Prince and head out the door, which she locks behind them. "Let's take my car."

"I want to see Kyle drive!" Chloe shrieks, as Amelia plugs the tablets into the charging stations in the back seat and the kids hop in. Amelia then offers Kyle her keys. "Would you like to drive, and make all of Chloe's dreams come true?"

"First things first." Kyle escorts Amelia to her passenger door, opening it for her.

Leaning into Kyle, Amelia whispers, "This isn't a date. We're just friends."

"Friends are a big deal." Kyle responds in a serious tone. "I'm not 'just friends' with anyone. Friendship should be celebrated, like guitar lessons."

"Do you open the car door for all of your friends?" Amelia's skepticism is on full display.

Straightening his shoulders, Kyle responds, "What if I do? Is that a crime?"

He's deflecting, which is a sign that she's right. "You are such a—"

"Swear jar!" Kyle enunciates in mock horror. "What will your children think?"

Amelia opens her mouth to speak, however decides against it. Instead, she slides into her passenger seat. Once Kyle is behind the wheel, she mutters, "You're a gentleman. How did I miss that until now?"

Her smile is sweet, in spite of her teasing, or perhaps because of it. The parking lot for Umberto's isn't too crowded, due in part because they've arrived before the dinner rush. Between perfect timing and the fact that the owner and his wife are clients of Kyle's, there is no problem getting a table for four.

Theirs is a New York-style Italian restaurant, with Billy Joel, Frank Sinatra, and some other New York greats singing through the acoustics. Accentuated with rich red and white checkered tablecloths and murals of Italy painted on the walls, as well as candles on every table, the restaurant exudes old-school charm and an inviting ambiance.

"Did you build this restaurant, Kyle?" Jacob asks.

Kyle nods. "I did. And their other two."

"Wow! That's so cool!" Chloe studies her surroundings. "Did you paint that, too?" She points to the large mural of an Italian street with brick walls accentuated with vines woven through trellises.

"Afraid not. It's pretty though, isn't it?"

Chloe agrees as the owner stops by to greet Kyle, who introduces Amelia, Jacob, and Chloe as his friends. Amelia can tell that Jacob and Chloe feel important, and that Kyle is going out of his way to ensure that. It's endearing.

Over the course of their dinner, both children crack jokes. Neither understands the art of telling a knock-knock joke, and nothing they say makes any sense whatsoever.

"Knock knock." Chloe smiles.

"Who's there?" Amelia and Kyle ask for what must be the fifth time.

"Amazon."

Amelia blinks. "Amazon who?"

"Amazon you," Kyle says with Chloe. Apparently, he's learned the pattern of her knock-knock jokes. Everything is *who*, then *you*. No matter what she throws in there. The kids peal with laughter and think they've got this down.

Kyle leans into Amelia, pleading in a low baritone, "Can I teach your children how to tell a knock-knock joke? Please."

She laughs. "Absolutely. I've tried and failed miserably."

"Knock knock," Jacob says.

"Hold up. You're about to be taught the mastery of telling knock-knock jokes by Kyle." Amelia winks at her kids.

Both Jacob and Chloe stare at Kyle with wide eyes and spaghetti sauce all over their mouths. Amelia keeps reminding them to use their napkins, though somehow the sauce multiplies.

"Okay, so the thing about these jokes is that they need to make sense." Kyle studies the reaction of Chloe, then Jacob, confusion etched in their precious features. "Yours make sense, but we can do better."

"Like what?" Jacob asks, sitting back, surveying Kyle with skepticism.

Kyle tells a tank joke. "'Tank you' means 'thank you.' Get it?"

The kids stare at him blankly.

"I don't get it." Chloe tilts her head to the side.

Undaunted, Kyle tries again. "How about the Nobel joke? Who's there? Nobel. Nobel who? There's no bell, that's why I knocked."

Jacob grins, as if humoring Kyle. "That's funny."

"I like ours better, though." Chloe looks at her brother, who nods in agreement.

"Thanks for the lesson, Kyle. Maybe we can teach you sometime?" Jacob offers.

"You tried." Amelia's shoulders shake, as do Kyle's, as they laugh.

"This is one tough crowd," he mutters, clearly amused.

Amelia grabs her leather tote and reaches into it. "Which brings me to our gift for you. You ready, kiddos?"

Chloe and Jacob beam with excitement as Amelia pulls out a rectangular gift wrapped in tissue paper.

"What's this?" Kyle asks, his expression animated, which makes the kids laugh.

"Your payment for the guitar lessons, since you refuse to accept an actual payment." Amelia smiles as he tears open the tissue paper revealing a framed picture of the one taken when Kyle posed with them as the Easter Bunny.

"We didn't have another picture with you, so we chose this one," Jacob adds.

Chloe stands, pointing over the table to the frame. "Yeah, so it's you as the Bunny's helper with us. Friends have framed pictures of each other."

"This is great!" Kyle seems genuinely surprised, and touched. He looks from the framed picture to the kids. "Thank you so much, you two."

"It was all Mom's idea," Jacob admits.

Kyle points at Amelia. "She's got great ideas. Your mom gave me some advice about a client, and it worked."

"Really?" Amelia all but shouts. "Your client stayed with you?"

Kyle nods. "He appreciated my integrity."

Amelia turns to her kids, "That's great news!"

Jacob and Chloe look deflated.

"I love this picture, you two. Thank you so much!"

"He loves it!" Chloe claps her hands together. Clearly, Kyle knows how to read her kids.

Jacob nods. "Let's get a picture with just you and us. All of us, just not the bunny this time."

"Sounds like a plan." Amelia reaches for her cell as Jacob and Chloe stand behind her and Kyle. They pose and Amelia snaps a selfie, or twelve. Honestly, she doesn't count, instead continuing to take photos while Jacob and Chloe laugh.

"Let me see!" The kids say in unison.

Immediately, she shows them the pictures. They're in front of the wall with the large mural, and it looks like they're in front of a rustic building in Italy with bricks and vines. Everyone is smiling or laughing.

Amelia wipes sauce from each child's face, and kisses each of them. "Do you want one without sauce?"

"Nope." Chloe shakes her head.

Kyle smiles. "I'll definitely frame one of these, too."

"So will we!" Jacob agrees as he and Chloe return to their seats.

The children return to eating as Kyle's eyes hold Amelia's in a long, hard look. "Thank you. That picture that you framed, and the ones you took tonight, are perfect. In truth they're beyond perfect, if such a thing exists. They represent the fun that was tonight, and the kids' exuberant personalities." It's more of a rugged whisper, difficult to hear above the many conversations taking place around them.

"You're welcome. I wanted to remind you of how much you do for the community, and how much you are appreciated." Amelia's words are heartfelt, and if she didn't know better, she'd say Kyle was touched by them and the gift.

"Would you like me to keep the frame in my purse?" she asks, as Kyle stares at the photo.

He reluctantly agrees. "As long as you return it."

"I will. I promise." Amelia winks at him.

The drive back to Castle Rock is spent with Chloe singing to each song on Amelia's playlist titled Winding Down Songs, while Jacob comments that each song is his favorite. The playlist is old school and fits Amelia's eclectic vibe.

"You've got great taste!" The fact that her kids like the old-school music seems to amaze Kyle.

Before reaching their subdivision, they stop at a traffic light that's blinking, while the surrounding streetlights are dark on the main drag. Both are signs that the power's out. Sure enough, when they turn into their neighborhood, it's engulfed in darkness, with the exception of scarce lights emanating from the spattering of homes that have generators.

Amelia logs in to their electric company app. "Power's out for at least four hours, which probably means six to eight."

Kyle agrees. "Say what you will about our electric company, they're consistent in never anticipating a correct time that the electric will be back on."

"I'm scared," Chloe says.

"We'll be okay. We've got candles, and flashlights." Amelia's soothing tone does nothing to alleviate Chloe's anxiety.

Jacob moans. "I hate the dark."

"Want to hear something cool?" Kyle asks the kids, taking their silence as encouragement to continue. "When I bought my house, it needed a lot of work, which I did."

"Because you're in 'struction?" Chloe asks.

"That's right. I'm in construction, and knowing that we get a lot of storms in Houston, I put a generator in to power my house in case of outages like this. It's a whole house generator, and kicks on when the power goes out." He glances at Amelia, who nods. "Want to see how it works?"

"Please," Chloe answers, her usual excitement replaced with fear.

Jacob adds, "I do!"

Kyle parks in his driveway, where the lights accentuating each side of the garage door are lit. When he presses the button for his garage door opener, the kids gasp as the door opens and his garage light turns on.

"This is so cool!" Jacob's enthusiasm is contagious. "Do you have a TV?"

Kyle nods. "Yep. I have TVs and air conditioning."

"No way!" Chloe has recovered from her fear. "Wait. Will Prince be all right? And the tadpoles?"

Amelia smooths her daughter's hair. "They're fine. Prince has plenty of food and water, and the tadpoles are safe."

"Can we sleep over?" Jacob asks. "We have sleepovers at Aunt Bridget's all the time. This will be awesome."

Jacob's glee when Kyle turns off the ignition and exits Amelia's Explorer is full force. He runs into Kyle's garage, scanning his work bench, tools, and lawn equipment. "Is this all yours?"

"It is." Kyle helps Chloe navigate his garage as Amelia reminds Jacob to be careful.

"I so need this stuff when I grow up. Along with the cars and trucks on my list."

Chloe sighs. "His list keeps growing."

Kyle presses Amelia's key fob, which causes the single honk of her horn that means that her car is locked and that the alarm is set, before shutting his garage door and entering through his mud room and into his kitchen, where he turns on the lights.

"Wow!" Jacob runs into the living room, surveying the walls. "You've got lots of guitars."

"Okay, kiddos, let's set some ground rules. No touching Kyle's guitars—as a matter of fact, no touching anything without permission, okay? And no running, no jumping, and no to anything not mom approved." Amelia rubs Jacob's back as the little boy nods.

Chloe studies the room in awe. "How are the lights already on?"

Kyle bends down in front of her. "I installed a generator that has what's called an automatic power switch. It's set to run after the power goes off and stays off for a certain amount of time, and it's connected to my natural gas line."

"That's totally cool." The little girl is smiling at Kyle like he created electricity.

"Glad you like it," says Kyle.

Chloe yawns. Her one yawn sets off a chain reaction, as Jacob follows suit.

"How about we take your shoes off, use the restrooms, and then we can get you on the sofa?"

"With TV?" Jacob stops dead in his tracks.

Amelia runs her fingers through his buzz cut. "Yes, with TV. But only if you do as I've asked."

After showing them where the bathrooms are, Kyle returns to Amelia. "My guest room is upstairs, but I don't want Jacob falling down the stairs in his sleep. They can take my bed downstairs—so can you."

Thunder rumbles, and Chloe squeals, running into the living room, straight to her mom.

"It's okay. You're okay." Amelia hugs the little girl.

Jacob comes running. "I hate storms!"

Heavy rain begins to lash against the windowpanes, as Amelia suggests, "How about we watch a movie in Kyle's room?"

"Do you have *The Avengers*?" Jacob asks.

"Of course I do." Kyle leads them to his room and flips on the light switch, dimming it before picking up the remote. Amelia and the kids are quick on his heels. His master bedroom overlooks his backyard, though Kyle's blinds are closed. It's a man's room, that much is obvious. The bedding, a steel-gray and black combination, matches the curtains, while a row of large framed sepia photos of buildings hang on one of the walls.

"Are these yours?" Amelia studies the photos.

Pausing with his remote in hand, Kyle smirks. "It's obvious that I take my work home with me, huh?"

"Wow." Jacob points to one particular building—a skyscraper. "What's this one?"

"That was one of my most high-profile projects. I didn't design it, but my company constructed it. That building secured my place in the Houston skyline, though most won't know unless they see the name of my company on a brass plaque in the lobby." There isn't an ounce of bragging in Kyle's explanation, though it's obvious he's proud of his achievement.

Amelia surveys the rest. "You built all of these, then?"

"That I did. The one at the end was my very first project." Kyle pauses, deep in thought. "These remind me of where I started, and how far I've come. Also, how far I still have to go. Silly, right?"

"Not at all. I'm truly impressed." Amelia smiles.

Kyle wrinkles his brow. "Really?"

"Yes, really. This compass I wear." Amelia reaches for it. "It reminds me of the same things. It was a deliberate purchase."

"We're more alike than I expected," Kyle comments.

He is a great guy. He's compassionate, he's generous, and he's humble. That's a lethal combination right there. "You don't give yourself enough credit. I guess we have that in common, too."

Jacob yawns again as he heads to the bed. "Your buildings are really cool, Kyle. Do you wanna sit next to me?"

"I can watch from the chair. I'll pull it over." There's a small sitting area in Kyle's bedroom. He carries one of the chaises over to his bed and uses the remote to turn the movie on.

Rain continues to lash against Kyle's windows, and thunder rumbles. Amelia snuggles between Jacob and Chloe, watching the credits roll on the first Avengers movie.

"Who's your favorite Avenger? Cap or Iron Man?" Jacob asks Kyle, his words slurred, his eyes heavy with sleep.

Kyle, who has put his legs at the end of the bed, shrugs. "I don't know. Both are cool. Who's your favorite?"

Jacob snorts, a sure sign that he's out.

Chloe takes a little longer to fall asleep. It's clear that she's a fan of the Black Widow. "I like her hair."

Even though Kyle has lowered the volume for the children, Amelia expects him to be watching the movie, but he isn't. Instead, his smoldering gaze is intense as he studies Amelia. It's as if this moment, the four of them taking refuge from the rain and a neighborhood power outage, holds a special significance. And she supposes it does. Because this is where Amelia wants to be. In spite of all proclamations about remaining friends, she saw a glimpse into Kyle's soul tonight, and his kindness is like a balm for her own bruised heart and battered soul.

Resting her head against the pillow, Amelia whispers, "Hi." Her voice is barely audible, though Kyle grins, his response warm and achingly tender.

"Hi." His response, a mere whisper, feels…right. "Can I tell you a secret?"

Unable to trust her voice under his intense gaze, Amelia nods.

"I never thought a night of pizza, bad knock-knock jokes, and a power outage could be so much fun." He's displaying a boyish grin, like this is something that embarrasses him. Perhaps it does. "You're beautiful. Inside and out. So are your kids."

Amelia's cheeks feel warm. "I'm glad you think so, because I placed the photo frame on your fireplace mantel. Between a bowl of rocks and the tractor clock. I told you I'd return it, and I always keep my promises."

"I'm not one for pictures. Buildings, sure. But not mementos, not pictures depicting memories. That photo is the exception." Kyle admits, resting his head against the chair, but refusing to release Amelia's gaze.

"What about the rocks on your mantel? Surely, they hold a special meaning." she asks, knowing they do. She doesn't know how, she just knows it.

Kyle nods his head. "They're from the ground where my first project was built."

Her grin widens, and she feels warm, feels safe. Kyle exudes a strength, intermingled with a tenderness that is a complete contradiction, yet it is completely like Kyle, once one gets to know him. "You have a big heart, Kyle Sanders."

"That's not something I'm used to hearing, but I certainly wouldn't tire of hearing it from you." His admission makes her heart beat faster, causes it to skip a beat even. Or maybe it's just the realization that he could be more than a friend, so much more…if she allowed it.

She could allow it. But should she? Would it be fair to her children?

"How are you so good with children? Do you have nieces, nephews, Godchildren? What's your trick?" she asks.

Kyle's grin loses some of its luster. "I had a couple of girlfriends who had children. One relationship lasted two years. When she ended it, it cut like a knife, in no small part because I had grown so attached to her son. It's why I don't date women with children anymore. The breakups are heartbreaking on too many levels."

He studies her, as if waiting for a response, or for a reaction. Amelia watches him, her gaze steady and brimming with understanding.

"What are you thinking?" Kyle shifts uncomfortably in his chair, adding in a rough whisper. "Did I just spill too much?"

"No. Quite the opposite. I'm speechless." Amelia cuddles with her children, her eyes focused on Kyle in the dim lighting. "You make me speechless."

"There's a first time for everything," Kyle quips. "You know what I'm thinking?"

Muttering a faint "No," Amelia waits for him to elaborate.

Kyle doesn't disappoint. "That this feels right—that the four of us feels right. And if I were a betting man, I'd bet that you feel it too, deep down, if you search hard enough."

He's right, though Amelia can't admit it. Not yet. Perhaps never. So, she remains silent.

The lights dim and the power surges for a brief moment.

"Power's back." Kyle checks his phone. "Earlier than anticipated. Wonders never cease."

Standing, Kyle walks to his bedroom door. "I'll sleep in the guest room. You get some rest."

Amelia snuggles with her children, her mind racing. No, she's not going to get any rest tonight. Kyle's said enough to keep her awake all night and then some.

She and Kyle are friends. It's all they can be. But, darn it, she wishes they could be more. Maybe…someday.

Jacob tosses and turns, until he smacks Amelia in the jaw with his fist, jarring her back to reality. This is her reality. It reminds her to take today as a fun day and leave it at that. She and Kyle share a friendship. Nothing more.

Remaining friends was Amelia's decision.

It's too late to turn back now.

# Chapter 27

AMELIA'S EXPERIENCED QUITE A FEW DAYS IN THE WIN COLUMN, but if life has taught her anything, it's that she can't get too comfortable. Case in point: after dropping Chloe and Jacob at school and grabbing her mail, she kicks off her workday by settling into her office chair and checking her email, where she reads an email from a client demanding some dramatic changes to his website after having agreed to the design beforehand.

After working on the changes for several hours, she takes a coffee break and sorts through her mail to find another violation notice from the HOA management company, containing a black-and-white photo of her gnome after the storm, with her small flag clinging haphazardly after the tape gave out.

"Seriously, Carla. You could only have gotten this angle by walking on my lawn," Amelia says to herself, tossing the letter on her kitchen counter.

Though out of sight, the letter isn't out of mind. Amelia is all too familiar with the bylaws by now and Carla has no right to step onto Amelia's yard, gnome or not. That violation picture is proof that Carla trespassed on Amelia's property and has abused her authority. Amelia's rage rises as she returns to her office and tackles her next set of emails and the next project in her queue.

The sound of twigs snapping outside her office causes her to whip around in her chair and look out the row of three windows, one at a time, to see where the noise came from. Through the window in the center, she sees...

*It can't be. Would Carla be so brazen?*

Amelia scans the site of her gnome to find Carla with her cell in hand, taking more pictures, no doubt.

Racing to her front door, Amelia catches Carla red-handed, or at least cell phone-handed—crouching down in Amelia's front yard flower bed, taking a picture of Amelia's gnome.

"One violation letter wasn't enough?" Amelia slams her front door behind her, confronting Carla. "You had to return to my property one more time? I just got your latest notice this morning, Carla."

Straightening her shoulders, Carla stands her ground, even though the property doesn't belong to her. "I'm just being thorough."

"No! You're trespassing on my property. That's illegal, and unethical. You're not allowed to set one foot on my property, especially as an HOA management representative." Amelia studies Carla's reaction, or lack thereof.

The woman shows no signs of shame or remorse. Just a cocky smirk and condescending tone. "You're breaking the rules, Amelia—"

"That's *Ms. Marsh* to you." Forget playing nice, Amelia's done. "And out of all the violation letters you sent me, this is my only actual violation. It's felt like harassment for quite some time. Now get off my lawn."

Carla's cheeks turn crimson, visible even beneath her thick layer of foundation. "You can't speak to me like that."

"I can speak to you however I damn well please. You're trespassing on my yard." It's a good thing Kyle added extra cash to Amelia's swear jar, since she just swore. That swear word was prepaid and well overdue. Carla deserved that curse word, which makes it feel incredible to voice it. Carla's expression alone is worth the price of swearing.

"Amelia, is everything all right?" Mrs. Bass from next door stands in her driveway, in her yoga clothes. Arms crossed, it's clear that she's acting as Amelia's witness, and possibly her backup.

"No. Carla is trespassing on my property." Amelia's tone is sharp as steel, her expression menacing as she stares Carla down.

"I saw her on my security cameras. I'd be happy to supply you the footage if you need it." Mrs. Bass is helpful and resourceful.

*Gotcha!*

Carla's lip twitches ever so slightly. She's trapped, and she knows it. "You're breaking the rules."

"So are you. And I have proof." Amelia refuses to back down. "See, Carla, you and I have been dancing around this power play of yours since the Easter egg hunt. You make some snide comments about me, about my parenting skills, about my gnome, and gossip about me while I try to kill you with kindness. That does nothing but embolden you to the point where you're squatting on my lawn taking pictures of my gnome. Let's be honest, shall we?"

Amelia doesn't wait for a response. "You are unprofessional and, worse yet, you abuse your power. I have plenty of proof and will have more by the time we meet at the end of this quarter. This isn't just about my gnome anymore. It's about *you*. And I am going to get you removed from managing our community."

"You—you can't do that," Carla stutters.

"Watch me." Amelia squeezes her hands into tight fists. "Now get off my lawn! I won't repeat myself again."

Carla glances from Amelia to Mrs. Bass, then returns her attention to Amelia. "You have no authority over me. As a matter of fact, I'll tell Kyle—"

"Please do. Please. Save me the trouble. Tell the entire board, and tell your boss at the management company. I have nothing to hide and am fully prepared." Amelia marches towards Carla, who takes a step back with every step Amelia takes forward, until Carla is off her front lawn and standing on the sidewalk. "Don't you ever step one foot on my property again."

Amelia glares at her nemesis as Carla returns to her car, then fumbles with her keys before starting her ignition and driving away faster than the speed limit. Another instance of Carla breaking the rules, breaking the law.

A clapping noise from behind her causes Amelia to turn, noting that Mrs. Bass is smiling. "It's about time someone put her in her place. Well done."

With her temples pounding, Amelia manages a nod. "Will you be home for a while? I have a petition I'd like you to sign. To remove Carla as our HOA representative."

"Oh, honey, not only will I sign it, I'll help you get signatures." Mrs. Bass smiles. "It would be my pleasure."

"Thanks, Mrs. Bass." Amelia grins, her rage still palpable. "Also, thank you for placing that gnome in your yard. I appreciate your support."

"Don't mention it. Call me Evie. And make sure I've got your cell number. We're going to be great friends." Amelia's neighbor winks, then heads into her home and out of sight.

Did Amelia just confront Carla and yell at her to get off her lawn like some grumpy curmudgeon? Yes! Yes, she did. And it felt good. No, it felt fantastic! Riding that high, Amelia reenters her home to find Prince perched in the nook of the floor to ceiling narrow window next to her front door in her entry foyer, waiting for her. "I take it you witnessed my temper tantrum, huh?"

Prince jumps down and weaves his way through Amelia's calves, rubbing his face against her with loud purrs. She pets the feline who has wormed his way into her heart, before sitting at her desk. Prince joins her on her lap as she revises her petition and prints copies for herself and Evie. Once done, she tells Prince she'll be back and heads to Evie's house, clipboard in hand, and gets her neighbor's signature.

One down, an entire community to go.

Amelia walks down her block, knocking on doors and gathering support. Not only do her neighbors sign the petition, they provide Amelia with their own violation letters that include pictures proving by the camera angles that Carla has been trespassing on quite a few yards.

Every neighbor Amelia meets with has a story or some neighborhood gossip. Most pertain to Carla's behavior, but aren't limited to that. Amelia is bombarded with news of a car break-in, a neighbor's speeding ticket, another neighbor's divorce.

Who knew Castle Rock was such a haven for gossip?

As Amelia tries to keep the conversations to her petition and the residents' violations, more and more come forward to join her cause. Little did she know that Operation Game of Gnomes would morph into a community supported petition to oust Carla.

Now that Amelia has proof, this will be one heck of an HOA meeting coming up.

Her swear jar might be full by the time all is said and done, but it will be worth it if Carla can no longer bully their community.

# Chapter 28

DRIVING THE KIDS HOME FROM SCHOOL IS NOT THEIR USUAL family carpool karaoke and talk fest. Instead, Jacob is silent and pensive. Though Amelia asks what's wrong, Jacob insists it's nothing. Stopping to pick up her mail from Castle Rock's communal boxes, Amelia realizes just how much she misses having a mailbox in front of her home. It's old-fashioned, but she still misses it.

Sifting through the mail in her driver's seat, she notices the HOA management company's name and return address. Ripping open the envelope, an "ouch!" escapes her lips as the paper slices into her finger. It doesn't bleed right away but slowly, gaining momentum. Grabbing a tissue from her purse and placing pressure on her wound, Amelia reads the letter, which states SECOND NOTICE in all caps and features another black-and-white close-up picture of her gnome.

Back-to-back letters? Really? "What the heck, Carla?"

The kids stare at Amelia.

"What's wrong, Mom?" Chloe asks.

She expels a deep, ragged breath before answering. "Another letter from Carla about our gnome. It's from when she trespassed on our lawn earlier this week."

Even though Amelia called Carla out, she still sent the letter. Of all the nerve. This is Carla's way of saying she isn't afraid of Amelia, or of blatantly breaking the HOA bylaws and state law.

Bleeding, cranky, and more determined than ever to fight Carla, Amelia drives her children home and starts on dinner after cleaning her cut and wrapping it with a Band-Aid. Jacob and Chloe begin their homework at the kitchen table.

On the menu tonight is spaghetti and a salad. It may not be a gourmet meal, but they've got tomatoes in the form of sauce, and salad fixings. While at the table, Jacob and Chloe take turns reading aloud to Amelia, who pops the cork on a bottle of white and pours herself a large glass as the pot of water begins to boil.

Helping her children with the big words, Amelia provides lots of encouragement. Chloe's book is about kindness, causing Amelia to think about Carla and the woman's lack of empathy. That's what started Gnomegate—Carla's lack of tact and her mean-spirited comments. Had she been kinder and less judgmental during their introduction at the Easter egg hunt, Amelia might not have fought the first violation letter or the bylaws.

Carla's passive-aggressive attitude ignited the fighter in Amelia—the rebel with a cause. Her trespassing on Amelia's property and subsequent flaunting of it is currently fueling the flames. She must be stopped. And Amelia's the one to do it, with the help of an army of neighbors looking for the same outcome.

Since her life is all about multitasking, Amelia types search words about laws regarding HOA representatives and homeowners' rights, using her laptop on her kitchen island. In between searches and reading with her children, she prepares dinner and drinks more wine as they eat dinner and catch up on the day's drama. Elementary school can be brutal, and one of Chloe's friends was mean to her.

"She said I was wrong, but I wasn't and I told her so," Chloe says, with spaghetti sauce on her face, as she washes it down with a gulp of milk.

"What did your teacher say?" Amelia asks.

Chloe uses her napkin, then adds. "Mrs. Thompson said I was right and gave me a lion ticket."

Lion tickets represent Jacob and Chloe's school mascot and are given out as rewards. Mrs. Thompson stood up for what was right. So has Amelia. Gnomegate is now about fighting Carla and her intrusions. Amelia has read enough about the community's bylaws and researched enough Texas homeowners association laws to know Carla invaded Amelia's privacy by trespassing in the search for a violation, which is illegal, underhanded, and unethical. Of course, Amelia has quoted the law verbatim in her handout document.

As Chloe continues to fill Amelia in on her day, she learns that some boy named Mason asked Chloe to marry him at lunch, then at recess Mason announced that he's marrying Chloe's friend Allison instead. So turns the days of our elementary school lives.

"You're too young to marry, sweetie," Amelia teases her daughter with a bright, reassuring smile. "Besides, if this Mason boy doesn't see how wonderful you are, I won't allow him to marry you."

"Agreed!" Jacob replies forcefully. "You're my sister and I'll protect you."

Amelia loves that her children love each other and have each other's backs. "I love you both to the moon and back. So, Jacob, how are you, buddy?"

Her son contemplates her question in silence. "Some kid in my class told me I don't have a dad."

"What?" Amelia rushes to her son, plopping beside Jacob on the bench. "What happened?"

Jacob pretends to be chill, but Amelia knows him, and his eyes have lost their luster. "We read a book about family in class and this kid, Jackson, said I don't have a dad. He's right. Dad left us."

"It's true that your dad hasn't been in touch, but you do have a dad—you will always have a dad." On this Amelia is adamant. He may be a grade A jerk, to put it kindly, but Daniel is their father. "Not everyone we love loves us the same. Your dad tried in his own way."

"It just hurts." Jacob pushes his plate aside, squeezing his eyes shut. "Dad treats us like we don't matter, like he's a stranger. What that kid said today was right. I don't have a dad and it hurts a lot."

"I know it does." Amelia understands this, and it's her greatest source of rage and resentment towards her ex-husband. She wraps her arms tightly around Jacob, embracing him in a tight hug as Chloe jumps on top.

"Hug sandwich," Chloe jokes. "I'm the bread."

Amelia squeezes them harder and tickles them until they laugh. "Both of you, look at me, please." When her children have done so, she speaks to them with all of the conviction she possesses. "You are not to blame for your dad's behavior. And you are loved. I love you, your grandparents love you, Bridget, Lily, and their kids love you. Prince loves you. Those tadpoles love you. You are loved. Always remember that."

"We know, Mom. Can we have another hug?" Her son smiles, and the light is back in his eyes.

"Oh, I love your hugs. I will never get enough of your hugs." Amelia inhales a sharp breath, giving Jacob and Chloe all the love and support she can. She would do anything for them. Even if it means reaching out to the one person who has hurt them more than anyone in the world.

After finishing dinner and going through their normal nightly routine of loading the dishwasher, the kids' showers, hair drying, getting clothing out for the following school day, signing class progress sheets, and making sure all homework is completed, Jacob and Chloe's bedtime arrives and soon both are out like little lights. Elementary school is tiring.

Amelia takes time to unwind in a hot shower, then twists her wet hair in a messy top bun, and dresses in casual black leggings and a matching UT Austin jersey with LONGHORNS and the mascot in bold orange on the front and stripes on the sleeves. Then, with her glass of white wine freshly refilled and in hand, she heads to her backyard, the well-manicured grass coarse beneath her bare feet until she plops on her hammock swing and stares at her cell, mentally preparing to call Daniel.

What are the odds he'll actually answer, she wonders? He hasn't responded to any of the children's messages or calls. But that's just the latest in his list of bad parenting. He began distancing himself from the children years ago in Austin, before he took up with his mistress. He was a bad husband, but he was a worse father. And he keeps digging himself deeper into that dark ditch of neglect, of cruelty, of deep-rooted selfishness.

Thanks to some mean kid, her son is hurting more than ever and the absence of Daniel is looming like a dark cloud over her children. There's nothing worse than watching your children suffer. Amelia would make a deal with the devil himself if it would help Jacob and Chloe. Unfortunately, Daniel is that devil.

The thought of speaking with him causes Amelia's rage to rise, making her queasy as she leans back against the cushioned swing. Terra cotta in color, with an awning and matching pillows and cushions, it seats two. Jacob and Chloe love it, as does Amelia. Especially on nights like this when there's a nice breeze, and she can inhale the strong, sweet scent of jasmine that climbs the trellis behind her home. The view is lush, with tall shrubs hiding the six-foot wooden fence around her backyard.

She's already lit some citronella torches, and her children know that she sits out here sometimes, after bed. All bases are covered, including privacy from little ears. The kids are safely sleeping, and Amelia is enjoying a slightly numb feeling thanks to delicious white wine and the nature sounds that surround her, when she opens Daniel's contact info.

The full moon is high, and her mosquito zapper is busy electrifying the annoying little bloodsuckers. Confronting her ex-husband to the tune of a mosquito zapper seems appropriate. Of course, as she predicted,

Daniel doesn't pick up. Instead, she goes straight into voicemail, as if he's blocked her number.

*Hi. You've reached Daniel Marsh. Leave a message and I'll call you back.*

After the beep, Amelia gets straight to the heart of the matter. "Daniel, it's Amelia. I'm calling about Jacob and Chloe. It's important. Call me as soon as you get this." She pauses, before gritting her teeth and adding "Please." Like pleading with the man will make him return her call.

Amelia takes another sip of wine, followed by another. There's one last option, the nuclear option. Searching her contacts, Amelia pulls up Jessica—Daniel's mistress turned fiancée. Before Amelia and the kids moved away from Austin, Jessica had called Amelia and insisted she keep her cell number. In case Amelia ever needed to reach Daniel.

It seems that even the future second Mrs. Marsh knew that Daniel was abandoning his two children, and didn't like it. After another gulp of wine, Amelia presses dial, her rising blood pressure pounding against her temples as the line rings.

"Hello," a female says on the third ring.

"Hi, Jessica. It's Amelia." Though her voice is calm, and her tone is friendly, Amelia's emotions are heightened, and her every nerve on edge.

Here she is, calling her ex-husband's mistress, the same woman he is creating a new family with. And she is being friendly to her. The irony is high, while Amelia's confidence is nonexistent. "I need to speak with Daniel. It's about Jacob and Chloe."

Faint, warbled voices that Amelia can't understand cause her to realize that Jessica is covering the cell speaker so Amelia can't hear their discussion.

"Hey, Amelia. He's at the office." Jessica's tone is apologetic. Like even she is uncomfortable with this lie.

Exhaling a jagged breath, Amelia's heart drops and her breathing is labored. Her emotions cloud her eyes, and she blinks back tears, refusing to show weakness. Still, in spite of her best efforts, Amelia's words do just that. "I need to talk to Daniel, Jessica. I'm pleading to you as one mom to another. It's about Jacob. He's in pain and he needs his dad. I wouldn't have called otherwise."

"I understand." Jessica's tone is brimming with…what? Pity. Yep. Just when Amelia thought she had hit rock bottom, the fact that Daniel's mistress is showing her a kindness her own ex-husband is incapable of causes one tear to slip, then another.

Wiping her face, Amelia expels her breath in a whoosh. *Stay composed. Don't fall apart.* It's her inner mantra as the thick silence at the other end makes her wonder if the call is still connected. Just when Amelia's about to check her screen, she hears some back and forth between Daniel and Jessica. They're arguing. No one is muting or covering the speaker anymore.

"Hang on, Amelia." Jessica's tone is gentle.

Daniel says something inaudible in the background, though he's met with Jessica's hardened tone. "Tell her yourself."

"Amelia. Why are you calling me?" Daniel's voice…that same voice she's known so well for so long, suddenly seems foreign to her.

"Jacob and Chloe are hurting. I've tried to help them through this separation, but they're young children, Daniel, and they don't understand why you aren't part of their lives anymore. Can't you call them? Please, just show some interest in them." Amelia has sunk to a new low, pleading with her ex-husband to do right by their kids. She'd beg him on her hands and knees if it would take the pain away from her children.

Daniel sighs, his words clipped, dripping with impatience. "I can't. Why are you incapable of unders—"

"Jacob was told by a child at school today that he has no father." This shuts Daniel up. "Our son is hurting. *Our* son, Daniel. He's our son—*your* son. And all you need to do is make one call. That's all. One call to speak to Jacob and Chloe. Fake interest if you have to. Please."

A long, drawn-out pause follows Amelia's admissions. "Daniel?"

"I'm sorry, but I can't."

She tried playing nice, to no avail. Now it's time for some honesty. "You never could. You were distant, you kept our children at arm's length for years. That's why it doesn't surprise me that you're ghosting them now. What does surprise me is that I have told you the pain Jacob is suffering at the hands of a bully who is using the fact that you couldn't care less about our children against our son, and you still won't take a few minutes to call your son and fake interest."

"I can only handle one family at a time, and I've made my choice, Amelia." The man she married proves once again what a selfish a-hole he is.

"Your choice?" Amelia scoffs, aware Daniel will hang up at any moment. "Yes, you've made your choice, but your children exist. In spite of you, they are sweet, smart, and incredible. All you have to do is make one phone call to them. Just one."

She's met with silence, but that fails to deter her. Amelia is determined that Daniel hear the cold, hard truth. "They loved you, Daniel. That love has diminished with each passing day. In spite of my best efforts, your children know that you abandoned them. They saw it in Austin, and they face that fact every day between mean kids at school and the fact that you don't care enough to get in touch with them or even return their texts. Chloe doesn't miss you, and Jacob has realized that he has no father thanks to a school bully. This is your last chance— your only chance to stop Jacob and Chloe from moving on from you. It's happening, and I can't stop it. No matter how hard I try, and I do try for them. If you feel anything for Jacob and Chloe...any love, any bond, this is your last chance to hold on to their love. And let me tell you, their love is everything. You will miss out, whether you want to admit it or not."

Silence follows and Amelia looks at her screen, sees the seconds ticking by, and knows the call is still connected. Perhaps she got through to Daniel. Stranger things have happened. Or he's about to hang up on her.

"Don't call me again. It's over, Amelia." With that, he disconnects the call.

Sitting in the dark under a crescent moon, Amelia stares at her cell screen.

She receives a text from Jessica: I'm sorry. I tried.

How is it that this woman can show more empathy to her than Amelia's own ex-husband? Seconds pass, then minutes. Until Amelia's screen goes dark, and she squeezes her eyes shut.

Did she honestly expect Daniel would change his mind? No, but she had hoped he would. For the sake of her children. Because they want a dad, and they lost the lottery when it comes to fathers.

Sharp, searing pain brands Amelia's soul like a hot poker along with the rage that Daniel could be so selfish, so heartless, as to ignore his own children's agony. Meanwhile, the aftermath rests solely on Amelia and she must pick up the pieces, though those sharp shards are beginning to pile up. Taking several large gulps of her wine, she empties her glass.

Looking back, she can now see the stages of Daniel's desertion, though she will never understand how he can be so callous to his own children, nor will she ever forgive him. Her fury is so palpable that her hands begin to shake.

Her cell vibrates, and it's a message from Kyle: Are you awake?

Amelia clumsily types that she's in her backyard. No sooner does she send the text than her back gate squeaks on its hinges and Kyle steps into her backyard.

"Wow. It's nice back here when the torches are lit. I couldn't see that much during our tadpole rescue. How are they?" Kyle's in jeans and a polo shirt with his company logo on it, and he stops where the tadpole tub is sitting on Amelia's back patio. Though it's dark, the citronella lamps illuminate the patio enough. "Look at them. They're thriving."

Yep. The tadpoles are thriving. So is the kitten. As for Amelia, she's self-destructing. All of the positive force she used to keep the kids together through the divorce and their move is draining from her, slowly unraveling as she wipes her face with her free hand. Kyle sits beside Amelia, then hands her a box with a ribbon around it. "Here, I'll swap with you."

Taking her empty wineglass, he watches as Amelia tugs on the ribbon and lifts the lid of the box. Wrapped in plastic packaging is her favorite perfume.

"I noticed that you were running low when I showered here." His gesture matches his tone—considerate and sweet. It causes an ache deep within Amelia's heart. How can this man be so inexplicably compassionate and so close to perfect when Jacob and Chloe's own father can't be bothered to call them?

Staring at the box, Amelia's vision begins to blur. "Jacob and Chloe chose this scent for me at T.J. Maxx before Christmas, when we were purchasing a few things for our new home. They said I deserved something nice after our move. Later, we researched the fragrance together and discovered that the base notes are a combination of orchid, plum, vanilla, and sandalwood. At the time, they spritzed it on themselves and sang 'Last Christmas,' my favorite Christmas song, under the false assumption that perfume base notes meant music."

Kyle chuckles. "That's sweet. I had no idea."

Swallowing hard against the lump of emotion forming in her throat, Amelia blinks rapidly as one mean kid and one final conversation with her ex threaten to taint the happy memory. She can't go there; she can't fall apart in front of Kyle. Instead, she plasters on a smile.

She's worn her brave face before—throughout her marriage, through all of the changes that followed the divorce proceedings, and during their big move. She can certainly do it again tonight.

"*This* is sweet, Kyle. Thank you." Placing the box beside them, she reaches for her wineglass, her hand grazing Kyle's, albeit briefly. Amelia ignores the spark that flares when they touch.

"Thank you." He emphasizes the word *you*. "You listened when I needed it, offered some advice, and everything worked out. I don't know if I would have caved to my client's demands without you."

"You wouldn't have caved." This Amelia knows. Kyle's just not that type of guy. Unlike her ex-husband…

In spite of the sticky Houston weather, chills travel up her spine, splintering through her limbs. "Truly, this was very thoughtful."

"Are you okay?" Kyle's brows furrow. "You look pale."

Does she really want to lie to him? Does Amelia even possess the energy? Her body shudders as she admits the truth. "I'm anything but all right. Jacob was teased at school about not having a father and I called Daniel hoping he'd do something for the kids. But he won't. And I can't take their pain away, no matter how much I try."

Tears cling to her eyelashes. The dam has broken, and Amelia can't control them. "I'm sorry that I'm dumping all of this on you. I just can't hold it in anymore." She sobs.

Kyle places the empty wineglass in the grass, and the swing sways, causing Amelia's head to spin.

"It's okay. Talk to me. I'm here." Kyle wipes her cheek with the pads of his fingers.

Replaying her ex-husband's many betrayals to their children, Amelia comes to a realization. "Jacob and Chloe deserve so much more than Daniel, and I don't know if I'm enough. There's so much broken, so much to repair. It's all on me."

Wracked with chills, Amelia can't control the sobbing, the shaking, or the nausea. "I'm going to throw up." Covering her mouth, she runs into her house and straight to her master bath in time to lift the toilet lid and dry heave. Then she vomits, her white wine now a bitter bile.

A strong hand rubs her back. "It's okay. You're going to be okay."

The last thing Amelia wants is for Kyle to see this, but it's too late, as she heaves and coughs again. Reaching, she pulls on the toilet flusher.

Kyle walks away and she expects that he's just as grossed out as Amelia is. If he's smart, he's running from her as she dry heaves. The sound of her bathroom faucet running grabs her attention and after a minute or so, Kyle kneels beside Amelia, placing a cold, damp facecloth on her forehead while his other hand rests on her back, rubbing it in soothing circles.

"You're okay."

"Yeah, if you categorize *okay* as bending head-first over my toilet." Bright side: at least it's a clean toilet. Sparkling clean. So clean that Amelia can smell the lemon-scented cleaning product used this weekend on her whole bathroom.

The commercials lie. There is no cleaning product in existence with a lovely fresh scent that makes you want to dance while cleaning. Instead, she has a pounding headache from the chemicals. And the wine.

As for the wine. She will never drink another glass of white after this.

Grabbing the facecloth, Amelia wipes her face with it. The worst has passed. Closing the lid, she leans against the toilet, weak and shaky. When she's ready, Kyle helps her up, and she washes her face and brushes her teeth.

He doesn't leave Amelia's side. Not once. Her humiliation is strong and has multiplied by at least one hundred when she catches a glimpse of herself in the mirror. Her face is ashen, with dark circles under her eyes. LED lightbulbs are a blight on females everywhere. Especially when the females are sick.

"It's official. You have witnessed me at my worst." At least the worst he'll ever see. She's pretty sure nothing can match a C-section, and she's had two of those.

After scrubbing her hands, she dries them with a towel. "I need to get some water."

Kyle grabs her elbow. "Lie down. I'll get it. But first, you need something else to wear."

Pointing to her large dresser, her humiliation is amped up at least a thousand percent when Kyle opens her top dresser drawer, which is full of underwear and bras, both of the sexy lace and mom cotton variety.

"Middle drawer," she manages, though her hoarse voice sounds like she's swallowed sand.

He pulls out a cotton shirt and tosses it on Amelia's bed along with her cell. She must have left it outside when she was running for the toilet.

"I won't look. I promise." Kyle turns away, gently tugging Amelia's Longhorns shirt over her head.

"You don't have to—"

"Shush." One word… Is it a word? Amelia's not sure, but she's too weak to argue, as Kyle helps her into the clean shirt he laid out.

Amelia is a hot mess. In contrast, Kyle is gentle and compassionate. Much more than she's ever experienced.

Escorting Amelia to her bed, Kyle folds the bedding back, and helps her lie down. He then pulls the covers over her, and places Amelia's cell on her nightstand. "I'll get you some water. Stay here."

He dims the light above the bed, which soothes her sore eyes. The faint sound of ice clinking in a glass travels from her kitchen. It's muted, conveying Kyle's best efforts not to awaken Jacob and Chloe, which makes Amelia realize that while their dad won't call them, this man she's friend-zoned cares enough to be quiet for them while they're sleeping.

Once he returns, Amelia apologizes, though Kyle doesn't acknowledge it. Instead, he hands her the glass of ice water, setting the remainder of the water bottle on her nightstand, and asks if she has aspirin or Tylenol.

"Medicine cabinet," Amelia croaks, taking a sip of water.

Returning with two Tylenol, he hands them to her, and she swallows the pills with more water.

"Go slow." Kyle places a garbage bag next to her. After all he's witnessed, he's giving Amelia a garbage bag to puke in. "Just in case you need to…you know, and can't make it to the bathroom in time."

Exhaling as Kyle puts her water glass on the bedside table, Amelia squeezes her eyes shut. "I am so sorry, Kyle. You shouldn't have to take care of me."

"I'll be right back." Kyle leaves the room, followed by the sound of Amelia's back door closing. It's a faint sound, barely audible. She rubs her eyes and her forehead until she feels the other side of her mattress sink. Opening her eyes, Amelia finds Kyle sitting beside her.

Amelia rolls onto her side, and he strokes her cheek. "I saw an empty bottle of wine on your island. Oh, and I snuffed your torches outside. Do you want to talk?" His mossy gaze is clouded with concern, confusion, or both.

"Jacob is still being made fun of at school, and I had it out with Daniel tonight." That's it. That's all she can manage. Though it's the truth, it still isn't any easier to swallow.

"I'm sorry, Amelia." Kyle's smooth baritone is comforting.

"To add insult to injury, Carla sent me another violation. The picture was taken when she was trespassing—when I confronted her on my lawn." She remembers the war she has waged. "I'm failing my children on all fronts."

"No, you're not." Kyle's smooth jawline tenses as a vein pulsates in his neck. "I will handle Carla. As for Daniel, I'd have to dump my entire savings account into your swear jar if I told you half of what I think about him."

Kyle's loyalty is sweet and is something Amelia didn't know she needed until Kyle gave it to her freely.

"I know how difficult calling him must have been for you. It proves that you'd sacrifice anything, including your pride, to make Jacob and Chloe happy."

A lot of good that did. "Yes, and I failed."

Kyle gently caresses Amelia's cheek. "You tried."

"I'm such a mess, Kyle. Run while you can, while I lie here like a slug." Amelia tugs her bedding over her head.

"Using my favorite movie line against me won't work. I'm not going anywhere, at least not until you're asleep." How can this man's voice be so soothing?

Amelia peeks over her comforter. "You had your chance."

Grinning, Kyle studies her with a burning intensity. "You try your best to act fierce, but you're not as tough as you want me to believe. No one can be strong and unflappable 24/7, you know."

He's right. "You're a good friend."

It's true. Amelia is vulnerable with Kyle, or maybe because of him. He sees through her facade and that frightens her like nothing else. "You really don't have to stay. I'm fine now."

Kyle pats her bed as he stands. "I'm not going anywhere. What kind of a friend would I be if I left after you were sick?"

"A smart one?" Her attempt at humor falls flat.

"Nope. Not even close." Kyle turns off the bathroom light and dims

Amelia's bedroom light further. "I'll lock up, after you fall asleep. Then I'll call you tomorrow morning, so I can make breakfast for the kids. Don't argue. I don't have any early morning meetings, no fires to attend to, and can head into the office a little late."

"Who am I to argue? In truth, I have no fight left in me. Not right now." Instead, Amelia burrows beneath her warm bedding, her body feeling weak and exhausted. It's silent, short of the AC and some mosquitos being zapped in her backyard.

Kyle stands in the doorway to her bedroom, his tall, broad-shouldered silhouette waiting for her to sleep. But her mind won't quiet. "Go home. I'll text you the time the kids wake up and appreciate the help tomorrow morning. I really can't sleep and need some time to clear my head."

"Are you sure you're all right?" Kyle asks, adding. "I can wait on your living room sofa. If Prince will share it."

Nodding, Amelia admits, "The worst has passed. I just need to process what happened tonight and think of how to proceed with my children."

"Those two kids are lucky to have you fighting for them. I can't think of a better advocate for them." Kyle steps forward and kisses Amelia on the forehead.

Before she can fully comprehend his actions, Kyle adds, "A friend would normally hug you, but since you're buried in tons of damask, I thought a kiss on your forehead would be more appropriate. Was I right?"

"Yes," Amelia agrees, noting how much that forehead kiss meant to her. "Thanks for taking care of me, and for being so kind. You're a really good guy, Kyle."

She doesn't ask him how he knows her bedding is damask, though she is impressed with his knowledge. Instead, she burrows deeper beneath her comforter as Kyle bids Amelia a good-night, and promises to lock up behind him.

Amelia lies on her back, the room spinning from the wine, the heat, or a mere kiss on the forehead. Maybe it's because of Kyle's kindness. Or all of the above.

The mating croak of a frog emanates from her backyard. "Oh, for heaven's sake, no more tadpoles!" She pounds her fists against her mattress.

Her life is too chaotic as it is.

*How much more can I take?*

Immediately, she realizes that's a question she never should have put out into the universe. Darn it! She just jinxed herself. Like breaking a mirror, or walking on a crack in the sidewalk. Amelia just sent the dreaded *how much more can I take?* question into the universe.

With any hope of sleep now lost, Amelia sits upright and grabs her laptop, doing some work and fearing the worst. Because she fears that she hasn't hit rock bottom yet.

Not even close.

# Chapter 29

AMELIA WARNED KYLE THAT HER SCHOOL DAY BUSTLE BEGINS before dawn, and she wasn't kidding. No sooner does Kyle pour pancake batter onto the skillet than Chloe stumbles into the kitchen, her long brown hair tangled in what is best described as bed head at its wildest and most adorable.

"You're not my mom." She yawns in her purple polka dot PJs.

"Nope. Your mom is moving slowly this morning." Kyle smiles at her. "I came by to help out because she wasn't feeling well last night. She's fine now, though. There's nothing to worry about."

Chloe tugs on his shirt and Kyle picks her up, holding the little girl against his hip while she watches him flip the pancakes. She laughs. "That's my favorite part."

Jacob bumps into Kyle, rubbing his eyes. "Where's Mom?" He takes a step back, searching the kitchen through sleepy eyes.

"Running late," Chloe answers.

"I came by to make you pancakes for breakfast."

"You know how to make pancakes?" Jacob asks. "This I gotta see."

"Lay your eyes on this. Technically, I'm more of a grilling guy, but I do make a mean batch of pancakes."

Kyle flips another pancake, and Jacob shrieks, "That's awesome!"

In the eyes of Amelia's kids, Kyle is a master chef and they watch with rapt attention as he makes sure the batter is cooked and stacks the pancake disks on the plate next to the stove.

"Are you excited for school?" Kyle asks, like this is a usual everyday occurrence for him: making breakfast for two children.

Jacob stretches. "School is okay, though some kids are mean."

"Yeah, they are," Chloe agrees.

Before Kyle can ask Jacob to elaborate or offer his support, Jacob changes the subject. "I hope we read a book about transportation today. Oh! I have a hundred lion tickets, and the prize cart should be full."

*Lion tickets. Prize cart.* This is foreign to Kyle. "That's awesome. What are lion tickets?" *And what's a freaking prize cart?*

"Lion tickets are what we get for being good and helping others," Chloe answers. "They call them lion tickets because our nascar is a lion."

Kyle shoots her a confused look. "NASCAR?"

"Mascot, Chloe," Jacob helps his sister, shaking his head at Kyle when she's not looking.

Chloe, on the other hand, places her head on Kyle's shoulder, moving past the NASCAR mascot debacle. "I don't want to go to school today."

"Why not?" Kyle sets the bowl of batter on the countertop and studies the little girl in his arms. Her pout would be adorable, if he wasn't so concerned about her. "What's going on at school?"

Jacob throws his hands in the air with a flourish. "Okay. Here's what's happening. This kid, Mason, said he was going to marry my sister, then he told Chloe he doesn't like her anymore and that he's marrying Allison. Her friend."

"Seriously?" Kyle wants to beat the you-know-what out of this Mason guy, until he reminds himself that Mason is a kid. Looking at Chloe—still straddling his hip—whose eyes are now welling with unshed tears, Kyle says the first thing that comes to mind. "Mason is an idiot."

"That's what I said, but Mom told me I couldn't use that word." Jacob smacks his forehead with his palm. He's got drama club in his future, that's for sure.

"Right. Sorry. I won't say he's an idiot, even though that kid's clearly an idiot." Kyle glances at Chloe again. "Aren't you a little young for marriage? Besides, if this Mason kid doesn't appreciate you, he's not someone you should consider marrying."

Chloe wipes her eyes. "Mom said that, too."

Turning off the pan, Kyle studies the little girl in his arms. Her heart-shaped face reminds him of her mom's. "You are much too good for a guy who can't make up his mind. Don't ever sell yourself short. No guy is worth that."

The little girl rests her head on his shoulder again. "Thanks, Kyle." She tightens her grip around his neck in a hug. Like that, in one instant, Kyle's heart has swelled to the size of the entire Lone Star State.

"Question: What is this, elementary school or *The Young and the Restless*? I may be a man, but I've had watercooler and lunchroom conversations with enough employees—male and female alike—to know my soaps." Kyle is truly interested, and wonders if this what it's like to have a family and kids. Granted, there are tantrums, he's sure. More soapy drama at elementary school and those dreaded teenage years, but if this is what a real family is like, then…

"Mom!" Jacob's voice is animated as he runs into the living room. "Kyle's making us pancakes. Not the cereal you usually make on school days."

Kyle turns to see Amelia studying him with a look of wonder as she gives Jacob a good morning hug and kiss. How much of Kyle's conversation with Chloe and Jacob did Amelia hear? Something tells him it was a lot. And she probably knows that Kyle called some kid an idiot…at least a few times. It's clear that Kyle fails when it comes to being a positive influence.

"How awesome are these pancakes going to be? They smell delicious." Amelia smiles at Kyle, radiating warmth and light. Dressed casually in a tank top and leggings, she's a knockout. Always, even after being ill the night before.

Carrying the plate of pancakes to the table, where Kyle has laid out the plates for the kids along with one for Amelia, he sets Chloe down on one of the benches.

Amelia stands in front of the table and Jacob sits across from his sister. "So, Chloe. About this Mason thing… You're eight and much too young to consider marriage. Besides, your fiancé must meet me first, and have a job with a steady income. Otherwise, how will you pay for your monthly Wi-Fi and Netflix subscriptions, not to mention food and shelter, electricity, and water?"

Chloe tilts her head to the side. "We can't live with you?"

"Not if you marry Mason. He's not good enough for you." Amelia pats her daughter's head. "Let Allison have him. Besides, I bet he'll move on to someone else."

This whole thing is amusing: Their morning routine, their banter about a child proposing marriage to every girl Kyle knows of. Even the fact that as Amelia serves her children breakfast, she somehow knows just what they like—from the perfect amount of syrup to suit each of them, to the sizes and shapes that their pancakes should be sliced into. Each child has a preference, of course, and Amelia's got this down.

Jacob takes a bite. "These are the best pancakes ever."

"They aren't even burnt like Mom's," Chloe chimes in.

Amelia walks towards Kyle, rolling her eyes. "Pancakes aren't my specialty. I do make a mean frittata, though."

"How about we make a trade: I can teach you the art of pancake making, and you can teach me the whole frittata thing." He winks at her.

"You've got yourself a deal." She turns, watching Jacob and Chloe chow down, then her eyes lock with Kyle's, and her voice is hushed. "Thank you. For taking care of me last night and for coming back this morning and making them breakfast."

"Don't thank me. I wanted to be here for you." So much remains unsaid, and the meaning behind his words is so intense that a swell of emotion jolts his senses, sparks all of his neurons, taking Kyle by surprise. He's wired, and raw…

So very raw.

"How are you feeling, Mom?" Jacob asks with his mouth full.

Amelia grabs a thermal tumbler from one of the cabinets. "Good as new, sweetie."

"Are you hungry?" Kyle chimes in.

"Nope. Thank you. Hydrating helped last night, so I'll have some tea. Would you like some? I also have coffee." She places her travel mug under the Keurig and pops in a K-cup.

Kyle motions to his mug on the counter. "I helped myself."

"Good." She smiles again, then glances at her children, who are talking about school and their teachers. Their attention remains on each other. "Thank you for this morning. They needed this. So did I."

A Bruno Mars song begins blasting from Amelia's cell. It's the one about Michelle Pfeiffer, though it's not Bruno singing.

"It's Kidz Bop time, and you know what that means." Amelia dances to the beat. "It's time to get ready for school!"

Jacob and Chloe shove a few more forkfuls of pancakes into their mouths until they've finished their breakfast, then bring their plates to the sink.

"Don't forget to brush your teeth and wash your faces," Amelia sings along with her phone, adding sweetener to her tea as Jacob and Chloe race to their bedrooms. She then turns off her alarm.

"Jacob, I'm first!" Chloe shouts.

"No, it's my turn!" Jacob counters.

Amelia grabs the empty batter bowl and raises her voice. "Please stop bickering. Chloe, you went first yesterday. Give Jacob his turn today. He's first in the bathroom and you're first in the car."

"How do you keep that straight? My head throbs just thinking of it." Kyle savors another gulp of his coffee.

"It's a mom thing. Welcome to school day chaos and my mom voice." Amelia flashes him a mischievous grin. "This is how we roll on school days."

Kyle chuckles. "I like it. It's impressive."

Chloe and Jacob bicker again, though they're talking over each other.

"Knock it off." Amelia's mom voice has kicked into high gear. "I've got to gather the troops and drive them to school."

"I'll let myself out." Kyle places his mug in the sink. "Keep me updated on the whole soapy kid dating thing. Chloe really can do better."

Amelia smiles, and it brightens the room like a ray of sunshine. "I will keep you apprised. Talk to you soon, Kyle."

When Kyle reaches his truck, he pauses, only to realize that he'd been holding his breath. Amelia is sending his senses reeling, shaking him to his very foundations, without even trying. He's in trouble, and he knows it.

He texts his best friend, Wil. Need to see you. Can we have lunch?

Kyle's in trouble all right. He's falling hard, for a friend, who has no intention of being anything more, and that means one thing: heartbreak is inevitable.

If anyone can talk Kyle down, it's Wil.

His friend texts back: When and where?

It can't be soon enough.

# Chapter 30

Since today was a late day for him, Kyle makes up for it by making calls, talking strategy with his employees, and having an office meeting where he and his employees discuss all of their current and upcoming projects, as well as those they are preparing to bid upon.

To some, all of this is boring, but for Kyle, it's exhilarating. He loves his job, and the more challenging a project is, the better. He's got the experience to manage it, and it's something he's proud of. After a meeting with one of his subcontractors, Kyle heads downtown to meet Wil for late afternoon coffee.

Wil's finishing up a call when Kyle joins him at a table. They order and bring their drinks to the park across the street. It overlooks the skyscraper that Kyle built which, coincidentally, is where Wil's law office is situated. Six degrees of Kyle Sanders.

"How are you doing?" Kyle asks, sitting on a park bench with his best friend of more years than he can count.

Staring straight ahead, Wil inhales a slow breath. "Surprisingly well. Theo's adjusting to the move. We both like the new neighborhood, and he'll be transferring schools next year, which he's okay with. His current school reminds him too much of his mom, so he's ready for a break." Wil moved not long after his wife died. He was grieving, and being in their home caused him too much pain.

"And you?" Kyle asks. "You've got a lot of new stuff going on, too."

Glancing at Kyle, Wil grimaces. "Yeah. You know that I was in survival mode, Theo and I both were. I did what was best, though I do miss

Castle Rock, and I haven't seen enough of you lately. Now I'm in the middle of a big case, so that's keeping me busy. How about you? How's business?"

"I've had some challenges lately. More than usual. A couple of employees made some major mistakes, and I almost lost one of my big clients. Thankfully, Amelia supported my decision to go against what I was being told to do. In the end, I convinced my client to stay with me."

"Amelia… Ah. Are we going to talk about her?" Wil takes another swig of his coffee, waiting for an answer.

Kyle grins. "When it comes to that topic, I'm pleading the fifth. At least for now. First, let's talk Carla—"

"Oh yeah! I love talking about Carla. What's she done now?"

"Carla has sparked a gnome revolution. As you know, it began with Amelia's gnome, and transitioned to Amelia protesting. Since then, about two-thirds of our subdivision has placed a gnome in their front yard in solidarity with Amelia's petition to oust Carla as our management rep."

Wil coughs. "I can only imagine Carla's reaction. Is there enough paper, let alone postage, in the HOA's budget for all of those violation letters?"

Both Kyle and Wil laugh.

"Poor Carla is beside herself. Ms. There Are Rules has never experienced such an open display of rebellion." Kyle claps a hand on his friend's shoulder. "See what you're missing?"

"Trust me, my friend. The last thing I miss is dealing with Carla." Wil was on the board before Kyle. As a matter of fact, Wil asked Kyle to run for his seat when he had to resign due to his wife's illness. "So, Amelia's given up on challenging the HOA, then?"

Shaking his head, Kyle admits that Gnomegate is still a thing. "She's not going after the board, but she is fighting the bylaws and the management company. Carla's crossed the line. Amelia caught Carla trespassing, and Carla has ignored my warnings, so I've emailed her supervisor, demanding a formal reprimand. Her boss called me today to inform me that Amelia's been collecting signatures to oust Carla at the next quarterly HOA meeting. Apparently, some impatient residents are calling the office, demanding a change in our representative before the next meeting."

"Look at Carla making friends." Wil finishes his coffee, and places the empty cup in the trash can beside them. "She doesn't change, does she?"

"Does getting worse count? Carla is abusing her power and I told her boss that. I see her driving through the neighborhood much too often, which has led to another reprimand and my repeated requests that Carla be replaced. I've got the rest of the board members on my side."

"Good for you." Wil nods.

"We'll see what happens. The meeting is coming up soon, and it will be explosive. You resigned at the right time." Kyle surveys his friend. "Thanks for leaving me with Carla."

Wil laughs. "You're very welcome. Though it seems to me that there's a new neighbor to occupy your time."

Wil shoots Kyle one of those *I know you're into her* looks.

"Don't go there. Amelia is a good friend. That's all."

Wil arches his brow, loosening his tie. He's an attorney and dresses impeccably. "Whatever you say."

"Please," Kyle scoffs. "I'm her friend, which isn't a bad thing."

"What's the problem, then?" Wil asks.

"That's the million-dollar question, isn't it?" Kyle taps on the lid to his coffee, his anxiety mounting. It's a good thing he got decaf. Meanwhile, Wil remains silent, as the sound of a horn blares from across the street. "The problem is that *if* I wanted it to be more, it couldn't. For many reasons. She can't... The timing just isn't right. Besides, I don't have the best track record with relationships, especially with women who have children. You've had a front row seat. I get attached, and they move on without me. Another relationship going down in flames isn't what I want or need. Especially when I care about Amelia and her kids—as friends, I mean."

Wil grins. "There's one flaw in your theory, Kyle. You are great with kids. It's what makes you my favorite babysitter."

"That and free babysitters are hard to find." Kyle notes that Wil ignored his admission that he cares about Amelia.

"Hey, I supply pizza, don't I?" Wil studies his friend. "Seriously, though, you *are* great with kids. And those ex-girlfriends, as nice as they are, weren't right for you."

"True." Kyle hates to admit it. "You're right. I rock at babysitting."

"And deflection."

"Who are you, Dr. Phil?" Kyle shoots Wil his own look—*Don't test me.*

"Dude, you're my friend and I've known you longer than anyone with the exception of your parents. You can't fool me." Wil turns towards the skyscraper Kyle constructed and points. "If you can pull off building that skyscraper from the ground up, you can do anything you set your mind to. If you put in the work. Generally speaking, of course."

"Well, generally speaking, I never shy away from work." Truer words have never been spoken. And what is a relationship—friendship or not—if it doesn't require at least some amount of work?

Once he and Wil finish catching up, Kyle calls Amelia from his truck. The picture of them with her kids at Umberto's pops up on his dash. It's his contact photo for Amelia.

"Hi. This is perfect timing—Jacob and Chloe are eating dinner, and guess what I found out." Amelia's tone is upbeat.

"I give up. Tell me."

"Well, Mason decided that he wanted to dump Allison for Chloe today at lunch, but Chloe refused him and played with Allison at recess instead."

"Yeah! Girl power!" Chloe yells in the background.

"It's about time!" Jacob adds.

"That's great. I'm glad to hear it." Kyle's smiling so much that his cheeks hurt. Amelia and her children have that effect on him. "So, I know you're busy, but I'll get to the point. Would you like to have lunch with me sometime next week? When the kids are in school. If you're free and can swing it between work and everything else you've got going on."

"Sure, lunch next week sounds great," Amelia agrees without hesitation.

That's got to be a good sign.

"Guitar lessons, too, please!" Chloe shouts.

"You're now on speaker," Amelia advises Kyle. "No pressure about the guitar lessons."

Kyle laughs. "We will continue guitar lessons. This week is packed, and so is this weekend, with a project nearing completion. How about next weekend?"

"Yes!" Both children holler in unison.

"Great. I've got two very hyper children to calm down." Amelia pauses. "You're now off of speaker. Would you like to text me when you're available for lunch? Any day but Monday works for me."

This was easier than Kyle expected. "Sounds good. Will do."

Amelia's bubbly, "Okay, have a good night. Bye, Kyle," sends pure adrenaline through his system.

They're going to lunch. Just Amelia and Kyle. Is it a date? Darned if he knows. But it's time alone with Amelia and that's just what Kyle wanted. Things are looking up. Maybe, just maybe, he has a chance with Amelia after all.

Stranger things have happened, right?

# Chapter 31

JACOB, CHLOE, AND AMELIA ARRIVE AT LILY'S HOUSE EARLY. IT'S a yearly tradition marking the death of Bridget's husband. This day is always difficult for all of them, and each year, Lily hosts this particular gathering so there won't be cleanup at Bridget's. Also, Bridget has said that it helps both her and her children; they visit her husband's grave and then head to Lily's. It's sad, and Bridget says her children need a release before they return home. They miss their dad, and always will. Grief is a part of their lives, and this day is more difficult than any other.

Afterwards, Amelia and her children have a sleepover at Bridget's. It's usually solemn, though tickling the children helps, as does watching some movie involving one of the three most important Chris actors: Hemsworth, Evans, and Pine. Laughter helps, as does friendship and family.

Tonight, they're not serving pizza. Instead, they ordered from a popular Mexican restaurant. Chicken quesadillas, lots of guacamole, chile con queso, and tortilla chips. Then there are the margaritas for anyone who dares. Lily makes a mean margarita.

When Bridget and her children arrive, they're met with hugs. Amelia heads straight for Bridget's three children. "Hey, sweeties."

They run into Amelia's arms and group hug. Then Jacob and Chloe join in, along with Lily's daughters, Ivy and Violet. Jacob offers to tell them all about Kyle's generator, and the kids are off, racing into the fenced backyard where Lily already has children-appropriate songs playing on her outdoor speakers.

"Let me dish out the food," Lily offers.

Amelia hugs Bridget, and her friend shudders. "It never gets easier. No matter how strong I pretend to be. With the kids, with you and Lily... Just help me through this, please."

"You've got it. Lean on me." It's always the same, though there are different stages of grief. It isn't until Bridget and Amelia are alone that she can let her strong façade drop and be honest.

Lily places the food on the large antique coffee table in her living room, also known as the great room, where she's setting up an indoor picnic for the adults while the children will eat outside. This allows the adults to speak freely.

Putting the disposable plates on the table, Amelia can't help but comment, "How do you have antiques with kids around?"

Lily shrugs. "Maybe it's easier with two girls, or the fact that their dad has them every other weekend. Less time to do damage—oh, I'm sorry, Bridget. That was insensitive of me."

"Don't be sorry that your children have a father in their life. Never apologize for that." Bridget shoves her hair behind her ears. "Just because my husband died doesn't mean you have to walk on eggshells around me. We agreed, remember?"

"Yes, we did. And we're sticking to that because it's what you want." Amelia smiles, then motions to the large margarita pitcher with a flourish of her hand. "So, who wants one of Lily's famous margaritas?"

"Or wine. I have white wine." Lily pops open the cork. "Amelia, do you want wine?"

"No!" It comes out more forcefully than Amelia had intended. In truth, she's not ready to go down that wine-induced rabbit hole again. "Sorry. Wine made me sick the last time I drank it. I'll stick with a virgin margarita, please."

That's why Lily's margaritas are famous—their lack of booze, to start. She adds tequila if her friends want. It's up to each of them.

Bridget scoops guac onto her chip. "Same for me, but with tequila, please. How did you get sick from wine, Amelia?" she asks before devouring her chip.

After filling her friends in, Amelia adds, "Turns out, white wine isn't a major food group."

"Daniel is such an A-HOLE. In all caps." Lily's assertion is so out of character that Bridget and Amelia gape at her. "Sorry, am I not allowed to curse in this group?"

Bridget waves her hands in surrender. "Curse all you want. Curse like a drunken sailor if you wish."

"I cursed at Carla, and it felt great," Amelia admits, then adds, "I won't do it at the meeting coming up. But when she was trespassing on my front lawn, all bets were off. And get this: more than two-thirds of our subdivision have signed the petition to have her removed, not to mention more gnomes than I can count are popping up in front yards."

Lily takes a gulp of her virgin margarita. "That's a good sign."

"I just need to finish getting my handouts printed, and add some final touches, but I'm ready for the meeting." Amelia is proud of herself.

Bridget gives her friend a reassuring wink. "I haven't had as much success with my endeavor. It turns out that internet dating is a land mine meant to strip one entirely of her confidence."

"Why? What happened?" Lily asks, her tone deadly. Like she's ready to take down a dating site in record time.

Bridget eats more guac. "As it turns out, there's nothing attractive about me when my online date finds out I'm a widow. Unless he's a creep."

"Ugh. I'm sorry." Amelia pours more tequila into Bridget's cup, as Lily pours some into her own. Two out of three moms are no longer in virgin cocktail territory, proving that this topic has hit a nerve, or several.

"Tell us more about Kyle." Lily takes a sip of her drink.

"Here's the deal: Kyle and I are friends. He held my hair while I was leaning head first into my toilet bowl." Reliving it is humiliating, even with friends who Amelia trusts with her life. The same friends who are grimacing at her, revolted. "I probably shouldn't have admitted that while we're eating."

"Yeah, that puts a damper on things." Lily places her uneaten tortilla chip back on her plate. "It was clean though, right? Your toilet bowl, I mean."

Amelia nods. "Thank heaven for small favors, though the lemon-fresh scent of my cleaning products still makes me want to retch."

Bridget studies Amelia. "Repeating my previously unanswered question, did Kyle run or is he a good guy?"

"He's a really good guy." Shivers shoot through Amelia's body as she makes the admission. Because it's true, and because she never knew someone so sweet existed, let alone would ever enter her life. "He's kind to me and my children. He even came back the next morning and made Jacob and Chloe pancakes before school."

"Aw, he sounds perfect." Lily rests her chin in her hands. "What's the problem, then? You look worried, like there is a problem."

"He is amazing, and he's also friend-zoned—"

"No!" Lily gasps.

It's easier for Lily. The pain isn't as fresh, and the circumstances are much different. "Yes. While it's true that Kyle is amazing with Jacob and Chloe, I just can't commit to a relationship with him no matter how much I want to. I can't risk my children getting hurt."

"It's okay to admit that." Bridget offers Amelia a faint grin. "Downright honorable in fact. You're a good mom."

"We're all incredible moms," Amelia is quick to add.

Lily and Bridget agree as they raise their glasses in the air. "To us."

"To us," they all say in unison, clinking their colorful margarita glasses. No red Solo cups for them today. Not for this occasion.

Their conversation shifts to Lily's most recent Netflix binge, then to Amelia's tadpoles, and back to Lily's latest malfunctioning appliance. Each friend makes an effort to keep things light, understanding that Bridget doesn't have the emotional bandwidth to carry anything heavier than a lighthearted conversation right now.

Later, when she's ready, Bridget and Amelia will have a meaningful conversation. It will be rough, and it will be raw. That's what friends are for.

# Chapter 32

"I DIDN'T CRY TODAY. NOT ONCE," BRIDGET ADMITS, AS SHE LEANS back in her bed, propped up by pillows galore, with iHeartRadio streaming the 80s station.

Her kids are camping out in the media room along with Jacob and Chloe, fighting sleep while a Marvel movie plays for them. Meanwhile, Amelia and Bridget eat mint chocolate chip ice cream in their PJs and messy buns, singing along to classics.

This is the first thing Bridget has confided, and Amelia places her bowl of ice cream on the nightstand next to her, waiting for Bridget to continue.

Bridget traces the rim of her white ceramic bowl with her fingertip, studying it intently. "This is the first year that I didn't cry. Not when I woke up, not at the cemetery, not even with the kids."

"Grief has stages." Amelia dares not say she's ready to move on. That's for Bridget to decide on her own. According to the grief scale, acceptance would be her logical next step.

After setting her bowl of ice cream on her nightstand, Bridget finally meets Amelia's eyes. "I've been playing around with online dating, thinking I'm not really into it and not trying to impress anyone because I'm not ready to move on, but today I realized that I am moving on, in spite of my best efforts not to."

Bridget's hand is cold as Amelia takes it within her own, offering support. "There's no right or wrong when it comes to grieving. Sean loved you, and yours was a romance for the ages. He would want you to be happy. It sounds so trivial when I say it, so cliché, but we both know it to be true."

"I felt something today, like he was letting me go, or already had. That's ridiculous, right?"

"To the contrary." Amelia rests her head on Bridget's shoulder. "You deserve to be loved, and if you want to move on, you deserve to find someone who makes you happy."

"How many soulmates are there for one person?" Bridget stares at their hands.

"Do best friends count?" Amelia sits upright, studying the determined planes and contours of her friend's fair face.

"Absolutely!" Bridget fires back, her determination and strength in full force.

"Then as many as you deserve. And you, my dear, deserve as many as you want."

Exhaling a long, protracted breath, Bridget's expression softens, her vulnerability on full display. "Do you really think I can find love again?"

"To quote a dear friend of mine, 'absolutely!'" Amelia hugs her friend.

"This is the acceptance stage, isn't it?" she asks, squeezing Amelia tighter.

Nodding, Amelia manages, "Yep. I googled it. You did, too, didn't you?"

"Of course I did. You know me." She releases Amelia.

"I do know you. That's how I know you're going to be okay. You're a fighter." Amelia means every word. This woman survived the sudden death of her husband in an auto accident, and has raised three children, supporting them through their grief—and hers. "You're a warrior."

Bridget grabs her bowl of ice cream and motions for Amelia to do the same, then clinks her spoon against Amelia's in an ice cream toast. "It takes one to know one. Now, what's really going on with Kyle?"

"Other than the fact that he seems like the real deal, and has asked me to lunch this week? Nothing. We're friends, though sometimes I wish it could be more." Amelia's brutal honesty hangs heavy, in spite of the upbeat Wham! song playing in the background.

"Does this have anything to do with Gnomegate?" Bridget asks.

Amelia smacks her friend with a pillow, albeit playfully. "No! I've learned to separate Kyle from my battle against the bylaws. I'm tackling my own rage against Daniel, fears of being hurt again, and fears of the kids being hurt again. I'm also battling the management company, more specifically Carla. You should have seen her face when I ordered her to get off my front lawn. I still can't believe I went all crotchety like that."

"Maybe I should channel some crotchety Amelia Marsh during my PTA meetings?"

"Are they that bad?" Amelia asks, humming to "I'm Your Man."

"You've got the HOA, and I've got the PTA. Both are pains in the you-know-what," Bridget announces with mock severity, before adding. "There's this one mom... I just can't. Not today."

Amelia's cell vibrates, and Bridget studies the screen. "Would you look at that! Kyle's texting you. Mr. Sexy Bunny says that he's thinking of you. What could that mean?"

"It means he's thinking of me. Don't make too much of it." Amelia grabs her phone from Bridget.

Reading Kyle's text, Amelia notices that Bridget has changed Kyle's contact name to *Sexy Bunny Abs*. "That's just wrong. Bad Bridget!" Amelia chides her, as she edits Kyle's name in her contacts.

Bridget swallows another spoonful of her ice cream, then chuckles. "You love me."

"That I do."

Journey begins to play on the Bluetooth and Bridget turns up the volume, as she and Amelia start singing.

*Just a small town girl...* By the time they reach the chorus, their children enter Bridget's bedroom and sing with them. "Don't Stop Believin'" is perfect for this moment, and everyone is belting the song at the top of their lungs.

Seth and Ava stand on Bridget's bed, while Chloe, Jacob, and Liam dance on the floor beside it. Singing their hearts out, the friends burst into laughter at the end of the song, before Bridget and Amelia begin tickling the children. Bridget starts with her two on the bed, while Amelia makes a beeline for the three standing beside the bed. Peals of laughter fill the room, encompassing them in love.

Afterwards, all gather on the bed. It may be cramped, but neither Amelia nor Bridget would have it any other way as the kids request *Jumanji: Welcome to the Jungle.* Just like that, all it takes is one amazing song and a movie starring The Rock and Karen Gillan to turn what was once one of the saddest days into one of the happiest.

Poignant, yet sweet and adorable. This is the life.

*Mom goals: keep our children happy.*

Amelia smiles. So far, it's working, and things are looking up.

# Chapter 33

AMELIA AND KYLE AGREE TO MEET FOR AN EARLY LUNCH DOWN-
town, someplace easy for both of them to drive to, with Kyle driving
from his office and Amelia heading out of their subdivision. Her phone
rings, and the screen on her dash states it's her children's school.

"Hello," she answers through the car's Bluetooth.

"Ms. Marsh, this is Holly Hamilton, the principal at Lakewood
Elementary. I need you to come to my office, please—"

"Why? Are Jacob and Chloe all right?" Amelia's heart beats at a frantic rate.

There's a long pause, and the principal says quite simply, "I must
discuss this with you in person."

She has a strong southern twang, and is normally kind. This refusal
to answer Amelia's simple question, however, is torture as Amelia makes
a U-turn and heads to Jacob and Chloe's school campus. "I'm on my way.
Just tell me if my children are safe, are they injured?"

Numerous scenarios race through Amelia's mind, each more awful
than the next. "Please tell me if my children are all right."

"They are uninjured. When will you be here?" the principal asks, as
if annoyed by this whole conversation.

"Ten, maybe fifteen minutes depending on the traffic lights. I'm
already on my way." Amelia tries hard to calm her nerves, gripping her
steering wheel until her knuckles turn white.

"Please tell the receptionist that I'm waiting for you. We will see you
soon." The call disconnects before Amelia can ask any more questions.

What happened to her children?

She makes a right and calls Kyle to tell him she has to bail. The line rings once.

"Hey, I'm on my way and will be on time." He sounds happy, and Amelia hates to disappoint him.

"I'm not going to make it. There's some sort of emergency with the kids. I don't know what's happening. All the principal would tell me is that they're not injured, and that I'm to see her in her office."

She checks her speed and notes that she is going over the limit. When she hits the school zone, she slows to the posted speed. "I'm about to turn into the parking lot now. I'll call you later. I'm sorry, Kyle."

Hanging up, she finds a parking spot and sprints into the school, purse and keys in hand.

The receptionist makes her wait about fifteen horrendous minutes, until Mrs. Hamilton makes her appearance behind the administration doors, ushering Amelia into her office. Chloe is waiting, seated in a chair, her eyes swollen and her cheeks red, with tears flowing.

Amelia rushes to her daughter and hugs her. "Are you all right? What happened?"

Before Chloe can speak, Mrs. Hamilton interjects. "Your daughter is fine. The boy she punched is not."

Amelia turns to Chloe. "You punched someone?"

"That kid, Jackson, was making fun of Jacob again." Chloe cries, her shoulders shaking.

"Punching someone is never the answer, Ms. Marsh." Mrs. Hamilton is stern.

"Chloe, you know not to punch anyone. We discussed this." Amelia looks at her daughter once again. The little girl is hiccuping and crying to the point of sobbing.

Rubbing her eyes, Chloe mutters, "But—"

"There are no 'buts.'" Mrs. Hamilton is quickly becoming a pain in the grass.

Amelia ignores the woman, her full attention aimed at her daughter. "But what, Chloe?"

"I did what you said, and told the teachers in the cafeteria that Jackson was making fun of Jacob. They didn't do anything. After the bell rang, Jackson tripped Jacob and knocked him down in the hallway." She shudders. "I was protecting my brother."

Rubbing her daughter's back, Amelia sets her sights on Mrs. Hamilton. "I need to see my son."

"We looked at the camera footage, and Jacob tripped." The normally sweet Southern belle is rigid and unyielding.

Meanwhile, Amelia's in Mama Bear mode. "I appreciate what you're saying, but I want to see Jacob now, and I want to see that footage."

"We can bring Jacob here, and have you come back to see the footage at a later—"

"I'm sorry, but I'm not leaving until I see what happened." Whether Mrs. Hamilton is having a bad day or not, Amelia refuses to back down. "Chloe doesn't lie. Until I know what transpired, until I see it and my son with my own eyes, you and I can't discuss anything in detail, including disciplinary action. I must have all of the facts. Surely, you understand."

The principal shoves her dark hair peppered with streaks of gray behind her ears. Picking up her phone, she rings Jacob's teacher and asks for him to be sent to the office, then pulls up the security footage.

Amelia watches as the boy Chloe mentioned, Jackson, does indeed trip Jacob, sending him flying face first onto the hallway floor. The child then laughs and walks away. Chloe sees if her brother is all right, then runs up to the older boy and punches him in the back. Small but mighty, Chloe made the larger and older boy cry.

When Jacob enters the principal's office, Amelia runs to hug him, noting that his cheek is red, while his bottom lip is cut and swollen. "Honey. Have you seen the nurse?"

"Yes, Nurse Reeves gave him an ice pack. She is on her way in to speak with you," Mrs. Hamilton answers.

Amelia tells Jacob to sit next to Chloe. "What is being done with the other boy?"

"It was an accident. He said that he didn't mean to trip your son—"

"Is that why he's laughing on camera afterwards?" Amelia's rage is rising. "That is the same boy I emailed you and Jacob's teacher about—the one who made fun of my son, the same one who told him he didn't have a father because we're divorced. When I emailed you, I was promised it would be taken care of and that Jacob would be safe. A fat lip and swollen cheek isn't safe."

"Your daughter punched that child from behind, Ms. Marsh. That results in suspension due to a zero-tolerance policy."

"I can't help but notice that you didn't address anything I just said. Is there a reason for that?" Amelia's losing her patience.

"Your daughter punched a child. We have a zero-tolerance policy—"

"Yet you were warned about the other boy, promised you'd watch him, and did nothing to protect Jacob today." Amelia stares Mrs. Hamilton down. No one messes with her children. Not even an elementary school principal. "The other child tripped my son and laughed, meaning it was deliberate. If Chloe is suffering the consequences, then so should that Jackson. Will his punishment be the same as Chloe's?"

Mrs. Hamilton remains silent.

"His mom works at the school," Chloe mutters.

Amelia does a double take. "Is that true?"

Mrs. Hamilton's behavior is finally making sense. She doesn't want to discipline a staff member's child.

Looking down at her perfectly manicured nails, studying the art deco shapes that must have been done at a nail salon, Mrs. Hamilton admits, "Yes. His mother works in administration."

"So, my communicating with both you and Jacob's teacher about the first incident did nothing to make him safer, because the other boy's mother works here?" Amelia's mind is working feverishly to process this information. "That is unacceptable, Mrs. Hamilton."

The principal inhales deeply. "He will also be suspended, in light of the response you brought to my attention. That wasn't visible at the camera angle I previously studied. I do apologize."

*Suspension.* "How long is Chloe suspended for?" Amelia asks.

"One week." Mrs. Hamilton shoves a piece of paper across her desk along with a pen. "You will need to sign here, acknowledging her actions."

Amelia reads the document. "I'll be happy to sign once it is complete. The new information, about the boy tripping my son and laughing before the incident with Chloe, must be included."

"Of course." Mrs. Hamilton nervously dials her secretary and asks for the revisions. Amelia has her on the ropes.

"Now, how will Jacob and his sister be protected in the future? This isn't the first incident with Jackson. You were made aware and promised me you'd protect my child, which you didn't." Amelia won't leave until she has a plan in place, one they will actually follow. "I want to be assured that when my children go to one of their teachers, that they will be protected. This is now a pattern."

This is why Amelia's ex said she should have been an attorney. Because she is relentless, and fights for what's right. Even Mrs. Hamilton is looking at her differently, with wide eyes and a fearful expression. Perhaps she knows that Amelia could complain to the district. No matter what she must do, Amelia will protect her children.

"I promise you that I will meet with every staff member involved.

Tell me where the incidents occurred, and I will make sure the teachers watch Jacob, Chloe, and this other boy carefully."

Jacob speaks up. "At lunch, gym, and recess."

"This will never happen again, Jacob. I'm sorry I didn't see what happened earlier." Mrs. Hamilton seems sincere, and Jacob even offers her a grin.

Chloe hiccups, still crying.

"I was hard on you, Chloe. I see now that you were trying to protect your brother, but you still punched a boy twice your size. Not only was that wrong, but you could have gotten hurt if he hit back."

"My daughter and I will have many conversations about this, and it will never happen again." Amelia looks at Chloe, her heart breaking. Both of her children are wearing frowns, and tears are clinging to their lashes. A sharp pain seizes Amelia's chest, which is already heavy with guilt.

Once the paperwork has been revised and signed, Amelia takes both children to urgent care. She wants to ensure Jacob is all right, since his cheek and part of his nose are turning purple. After getting a clean bill of health and a list of things to look for if he has a head or nose injury, they head home.

Amelia remains silent through the ride, her mind racing, her rage stewing. She is angry at Chloe for disobeying her—Amelia did tell her not to hit anyone. Amelia's also mad at the child who bullied Jacob. But among all of them, Amelia is most enraged with herself.

Yes, Amelia thought things were going smoothly. All the while, Chloe was still angry at school and Jacob was still being made fun of. Between her own business, the work she was doing to take down Carla and fight the bylaws, and her time with Kyle, Amelia was distracted. She spread herself too thin.

What transpired today happened on her watch. And for that she will never forgive herself.

When she parks in their driveway, Amelia leaves the engine idling and turns to her children, each appearing wan and exhausted. "I'm sorry. I thought things had gotten better, I thought you were safe. I won't make that mistake again."

"Does this mean you're not mad at me?" Chloe asks, her voice cheery.

"No, little miss. I am angry with you, considering I did tell you not to hit anyone. But I understand that you tried to get help. It doesn't make what you did acceptable, just more complicated. You and I will be having a lot of discussions during your week suspension."

Chloe rubs her eyes. "I'm sorry, Mom."

"Me, too." Jacob mutters.

"This can't ever be repeated. Do you understand me?" She looks straight at Chloe.

The little girl nods, as does her brother.

"We have a lot to work through. All three of us," Amelia admits. "You've got my full attention, and you might get sick of me, but we're going to get through this together."

The kids mutter, "Okay."

Amelia's nerves are in overdrive. "I want you each to shower. Jacob, you can use my bathroom, Chloe, use yours. Then we'll talk some more over dinner."

They disembark from Amelia's SUV and enter the house. Even Prince can't lift their spirits. Just when Amelia thought life was looking up, she's pummeled by reality—hard and unrelenting.

Her focus must be on healing her family. There can be no distractions, which means she must put an end to this Gnomegate/Carla battle. It also means no more Kyle. He's kind, he's incredible, and he's also a distraction. One she can't afford.

Now she's got to tell him.

That's a conversation she dreads with every fiber of her being, but it's a conversation that she can't avoid. Better to get it out of the way, while the kids are showering.

Amelia pulls her cell from her purse. She's failed her kids. And now she's about to fail Kyle.

The best is yet to come, though, because after her conversation with Kyle comes repercussions for Chloe, not to mention lots more to discuss and dissect. With Chloe suspended, she's got the time and she must put in the work.

Her family needs a lot of fixing. If Amelia's being honest, so does she.

# Chapter 34

"HI, KYLE." AMELIA SITS IN HER FRONT OFFICE, IN HER DESK chair, staring at her blank monitor.

"How are the kids? I've been worried. What happened?"

Taking great care to listen to Kyle's baritone, that same baritone that usually comforts her, Amelia notes that there is no such relief during this conversation. "That's a long story."

"I've got time. Talk to me." He's so supportive. Always.

Amelia inhales deeply, then exhales…slowly and purposefully, before she trusts her voice. "Chloe was suspended today for hitting a boy twice her size. This boy tripped Jacob deliberately, and Chloe swooped in to save her brother. She got physical, even though I've told her not to, and is now suspended for a week."

"I'm sorry, Amelia. Is Jacob all right?"

"He's bruised, and has a busted lip, but he'll be okay. I took him to see a doctor." Amelia doesn't mention her argument with the principal, or the fact that the other child almost got away with bullying Jacob.

Nor does she mention how much Kyle's friendship means to her, or how ready she was for a lunch date with him. Nervous, yes. But, also ready to let him in. Until this latest turn of events.

"I'm sorry about lunch." It's all she can manage.

"Don't be." On this Kyle sounds adamant. "Your children are more important. We discussed this—your kids will always come first. Period. I knew what I was getting into."

This man is perfect, or as close to perfect as a person can get. That's why hitting stop affects her to the point where her hands begin to shake. Because under normal circumstances, Kyle would be a man she'd take a chance with. He is the opposite of her ex, he's someone who she'd be attracted to, who she wants to get to know better, and above all he is a great role model for her children. But they need more of her—

Jacob and Chloe need all of her.

"I've picked the wrong battles. I chose to take on the HOA management company and thought I was showing my children how to fight for what's right. Instead, Chloe's resorting to violence, and I feel like it's my fault."

"Amelia, none of this is your fault—"

"Maybe if I spent less time fighting Gnomegate and more time with my children—"

"Don't do this," Kyle pleads with her. "You are being much too hard on yourself. You did your best."

She grins. He's still protecting her, standing beside her, supporting her. "My best doesn't seem to be good enough, and I need to fix that. Immediately. It may seem to you like I'm taking the easy way out, but there's nothing easy about this for me."

Silence hangs heavy between them. He knows what she is referring to. He must, but still she admits, "You deserve better. You deserve all the happiness in the world. Right now, I've got to fight for my family, and help my children heal."

"I understand. I do." He sighs. "I had this feeling that I was falling for you much harder than you were for me. Still, I couldn't walk away. I didn't want to."

Falling for her? Time to be honest… "It's reciprocal, Kyle. For the first time in forever, I saw a future with someone. With you, but the timing was off."

"Look, you were honest with me. Your children come first. Now and always." Kyle's voice becomes rough with emotion. "That's one of your best qualities. I wouldn't change that about you. Not in a million years."

"Kyle, I hope we can still be friends when this all settles down." Amelia's heart all but stops beating as she awaits his response. She holds her breath until...

"I think I'm in too deep to go back to being just friends. I thought it would be enough. And it was, for a while. Until today, when all I want to do is support you, run over there and help you and your children through this. Knowing that I can't, that you're shutting that door... I can't rewind how I feel about you, and about Jacob and Chloe."

She's blown it with Kyle. "I'm so sorry. This is the last thing I wanted."

"It's the hand we've been dealt, and you have your hands full. I get it." Kyle pauses. "I'll always be here for you. If you need me, call me. I'm not abandoning you, but I am giving you the space you asked for; I'm respecting your wishes."

Respecting her. Something her ex-husband never did.

"Tell Jacob and Chloe that I care very much about each of you. That will never change."

Amelia squeezes her eyes shut, allowing herself to breathe. What does she want Kyle to know? Deep down inside, how does she really feel about him?

"I understand why you can't go back to being friends, and respect that. Asking you to wait for me wouldn't be fair to you. But please, Kyle, if you can, or maybe I should say if you *want*...don't give up on me completely just yet." She stands, proceeding into her living room. "As overwhelmed as I feel right now, I am determined to right the pieces that are out of place in our lives. We will be whole and ready to move forward. I'd like to think that when we get there, you might give me another chance. If you want, that is."

"Are we talking dating, Amelia? I need some clarification. I think I deserve it." There's no censure in his tone, nor judgment. Just confusion.

Walking to her fireplace mantel with Prince circling her legs, Amelia studies the framed picture of her, Kyle, Jacob, and Chloe at the Italian restaurant.

"Yes, I am." She expels a deep breath at her admission. "I'm contradicting myself, aren't I? I promise I'm not trying to jerk you around and don't expect you to make any promises. Just know that I care about you more than I thought possible. I'm truly sorry, Kyle."

Before he can object, Amelia disconnects the call. There's still much unsaid, but hopefully, she'll have a chance to rectify that in the future. First, Amelia must get Jacob and Chloe the help they need, along with the help she needs. It will be difficult, but worth it.

One thing Amelia has realized is that she isn't enough. She needs to provide her children more help than she can offer. After showers are completed, Chloe's hair is dry, and dinner is eaten, Amelia searches for a family therapist who specialize in the issues her family is facing.

Time to start the hard work...the real healing.

It's also time to ask for help. There's no time to waste. Her children are counting on her.

# Chapter 35

"THANKS FOR THE PLAYDATE. WE NEEDED AN ESCAPE." AMELIA SITS on the playground bench watching Chloe play with Ava on the swings, then Jacob, Liam, and Seth at the jungle gym, which is wasp free thanks to Kyle, she's sure.

Bridget pats Amelia's arm. "How's therapy going?"

"It's okay. I'm seeing my therapist while the kids are in school, and that helps me be honest and emotional without worrying that they'll see my weaknesses."

"Feeling emotional isn't a weakness, Amelia." Bridget's concerned.

Nodding, Amelia agrees. "You're right. That's one of the things I've been working on. That, and the fact that none of this is my fault. Then there are the scars made by Daniel that I've had to unpack. On the bright side, the kids seem to be handling this better than me. They do art therapy and there are cars and dolls that help them communicate during their individual sessions. Their therapist told me that they are making strides. They no longer blame themselves for Daniel's desertion, and they've regained their confidence. The bullying has stopped, which is something else to celebrate."

"Hey, Mom! Watch this!" Jacob shouts, right before he slides down the curly pole on the jungle gym.

"That's awesome! Way to go!" Amelia's tone is cheery.

"How do you do that? Turn your emotions on and off?" Bridget studies her friend.

Amelia meets Bridget's gaze. "I have to. I don't have a choice. They've got to see me happy and supportive. Their therapist told me it's what they need most."

"You're going to snap, Amelia. You can't keep everything inside."

"I'm not. I speak to my own therapist—"

"Is that enough?"

Darned if she knows, Amelia tells her friend honestly. "We'll see, won't we?"

"When is the HOA meeting?" Bridget's tone is apprehensive.

"Tomorrow night. It's been a long time coming." Amelia sighs. "If not for that, maybe I would have seen the signs…"

Bridget grabs Amelia's hand. "I saw nothing, and I was at their school watching over them. The kid stopped picking on Jacob, until that one incident. You couldn't have seen that coming, Amelia. You're not a mind reader."

"I appreciate the pep talk, Coach." Amelia plasters a smile on her face, then leads Bridget to the playground.

"Who wants to play with Mom?" she shouts, and Chloe comes sprinting towards her, followed by Jacob.

"Let's tickle Mom!" Jacob suggests, and it quickly gains traction.

Amelia laughs as her kids tickle her and she tickles them back, then chases them around the playground.

At least her children are healing, and happy.

Even if Amelia is still in a dark place. Tomorrow's HOA meeting—a.k.a. the long-awaited Gnomegate showdown—will mark the end of one battle. She's prepared, though the one thing she didn't expect to feel was anger. Towards Carla, and the management company.

Her cell vibrates, and she opens a text from Kyle.

FYI: I have the board on my side to vote out Carla. Have been talking to her boss since Carla trespassed on your lawn. Just

wanted you to know I've been fighting on my end. Good luck
tomorrow.

Kyle's been fighting for her, even though she halted their relationship.
The realization makes Amelia even more enraged. Maybe, if she didn't
have to canvass the neighborhood getting signatures for the petition to
oust Carla while the kids were at school and prepare all of her handouts,
she would have been able to fit Kyle into her life. It certainly would have
freed up a lot of time.

With a newfound clarity, Amelia realizes that her rage is aimed
directly at Carla. She made this harder on Amelia, she caused Amelia's
life to be upended without one ping of remorse, let alone an ounce of
compassion.

Yes, tomorrow's meeting will be an explosive one. Because Amelia
won't hold back. Adult bullies are even worse than child bullies, and
Amelia won't rest until she puts Carla in her place.

Jacob's rolling in the mulch with his sister. Amelia joins them, noting
that her children are happy, so drain-clogging potential doesn't matter.
It's time for Amelia to find some peace, if not happiness.

Carla better be on her best behavior, because Amelia isn't playing.

Her Game of Gnomes isn't a game—not anymore.

# Chapter 36

AFTER ALL THE PREPARATION AMELIA HAS DONE, ALL OF THE research, and canvassing Castle Rock for petition signatures, the quarterly HOA meeting has arrived at long last. Amelia stacks her handouts along with the petition on her desk, then places them in a folder, shoving it into her laptop tote.

Is she factually prepared? Yes. Is she emotionally ready? Not at all.

Amelia's nerves remain raw. It's as if her every emotion has risen to the surface, exposed for all to see. Therapy has made her do a great deal of contemplation and soul searching. It all ends the same way: with Amelia feeling like a failure.

If tonight's her last stand, she might as well dress for the part. Putting her makeup on, she studies her reflection. Red lips, onyx eye liner, and a fierce black outfit. If she doesn't feel confident, she might as well fake ferocity.

Does she think she will win her fight for her gnome? No, she doesn't. Which is why she has tried not to get the children's hopes up. If she's being honest with herself, Gnomegate is lost. Though not technically, not yet, she feels it in her heart. But her battle is by no means over.

Her fight is so much larger than a beloved garden gnome sitting in her front yard. Her anger stems from her lack of control over the situation. Similar to her divorce, which was dictated by her husband's actions, his infidelity, and subsequent ghosting, Carla's actions and callous behavior dug up all of those helpless feelings. Carla picked at Amelia's open wounds by abusing her power.

Amelia handled Daniel. She stood up to him and said her piece. Now it's Carla's turn.

Carla… She is who Amelia is really battling tonight. Amelia refuses to forget that. She will remember who her real enemy is.

When her babysitter, Charlotte, arrives, Amelia kisses her children, tells them to be good, then heads to the HOA quarterly meeting at the community's rec center. Not in the best head space to begin with, Amelia is assailed with her own conflicting feelings as she parks in the busy lot. She's still coming to terms with being the mom whose eight-year-old daughter was suspended from elementary school for a week, and whose heartbroken ten-year-old son still feels like he doesn't have a father, though he's come to accept it. These are the things they must all learn to accept, but knowing that doesn't make it any easier.

As she gathers her things and walks to the rec center, anxiety sends shivers up her spine in spite of the humid early evening Houston weather. Because she dreads that every resident in attendance will see that she's not as strong as they thought, or that they will judge her…just like Carla did, just like Mrs. Hamilton, the children's principal, did at first. Just like Daniel always did. But if there's one thing therapy and self-refection has taught her, it's that their opinions don't matter. Time to put that new-found education to the test.

The door to the rec center thuds loudly behind her, echoing in her ears as those in attendance turn and stare at her. Amelia straightens her shoulders. *What they think of you doesn't matter.*

A tap on Amelia's shoulder causes her to turn and see the smiling face of Bridget. "I thought you might need a pep talk."

Lily approaches from behind. "You are a boss! Don't forget that," she says, grabbing Amelia's hand and gently squeezing it for support.

Amelia studies her friends as her heart swells with gratitude. "I didn't expect you to come."

"Honey, you are taking down the Wicked Witch of Castle Rock. Do you honestly think we'd miss it?" Bridget winks at Amelia. "Game of Gnomes or not, you will always be Khaleesi to me."

"Same holds true for Gnomegate," Lily says, hugging Amelia.

"I'm nervous," Amelia admits, her voice shaky.

Bridget gives Amelia a hug, "Lily's right! You *are* a boss and you can do this. You will do this. You will make a sound argument, and you will be convincing. You may not be able to win them all, but you know which battle is winnable. Keep that in mind, and you'll do great."

Hugging her one more time, Bridget's tone is strong as steel. "Go get them, Khaleesi. Just don't burn anything down. Literally, that is."

Amelia heads towards the front row, grinning at neighbors she knows and nodding at others that she's never met. It's a full house, but there are available seats in the front. Sitting, clutching her tote filled with her notes, Amelia looks over her shoulder to find her friends standing in the back. They're here to support her and aren't going anywhere. She smiles at them and murmurs, "Thank you," just as a door in the front opens with squeaky hinges.

The three board members enter the room, and Amelia's heart lurches at the sight of Kyle. He's more tan than the last time she saw him, and dressed in a polo shirt that shows off his muscular arms. His hair is different, too, buzzed at the sides and longer in the front. His new look suits him, and Amelia watches as he sits at a long table in front of the room, leaning in to talk to the board member seated beside him.

The mere sight of Kyle is a shock to her system. He hasn't jogged past her home ever since Amelia pumped the brakes, and she has missed him, though, to be honest, she wouldn't allow herself to feel the full extent of her loss. It would have been too painful. But now it's pummeling her like a ferocious storm, along with the rest of her regrets.

Scanning the room one more time, she sees that it is filled with

Castle Rock residents, most of whom want to see Carla's downfall, Amelia predicts. Carla calls the meeting to order and introduces herself. Seated beside her are two women who identify themselves as representing the management company. The board members are introduced, then Carla recites the agenda, upon which Amelia's petition is one of the final items.

Minutes from the last meeting are approved, there's some community news about getting a new landscaper, sidewalk repairs, and more benches being installed at the splash pad. Pool and splash pad hours are debated by a few residents, with Kyle listening to their concerns and compromising when he can. He's good at this. He listens to everyone, no matter how minuscule their beef with the HOA is. One man is incensed that he got a letter for hanging a tire swing from the tree on his front lawn.

"Look, if it were up to me, you could have your tire swing. I've seen it, painted to match the color of your garage. In my opinion, it looks great. But it is against the bylaws and until the builders have completed our subdivision and sold all of their inventory, we're stuck with the bylaws as written by the developer." Kyle's honesty appeases the man.

Next up are some residents who complain about their trash cans and the fact that they can't keep them in front of their homes. It's the same answer, and seems to be a topic that is discussed at every meeting.

The agenda proceeds, until Amelia is called. Having removed her paperwork from her tote, she hands packets of stapled copies first to the board, then to the management company representatives, followed by the residents in attendance.

She glances briefly at her notes before setting them aside to speak from her heart. This is her story, these are her truths. Amelia doesn't need notes. This is her life.

"I'm fairly new to Castle Rock, in comparison to many of you. But it is home to me and my children, it's our community. It's your community." She looks at the crowd seated behind her. "We're in this together, and we all want the same thing: a place to call home. These aren't just houses, they are homes, with a community that comes together for an Easter egg hunt or, from what I've heard, pictures with Santa.

"Many of you know me as the gnome lady, and I am. I'm a single mom who promised my children that they could have their gnome in our new front yard, just like we had it before my divorce from their dad. So, I defied the bylaws because I didn't want to break my promise to my children, who had lost so much already."

"You cannot have your gnome in the front yard," Carla interjects, her tone venomous. "It's against the bylaws, and I have discussed this with you many times."

"That's true, Carla. And I recognize that I've lost that particular battle. My gnome will be relocated to my backyard as soon as I leave this meeting. The thing is… This is about so much more than a gnome." Amelia's emotions swirl like a cyclone, picking up force. "What this is about is you, Carla, and the thing that I can't accept: your chronic disrespect towards me and the fact that you were rude and condescending when you chastised me about my gnome. When we first met, I told you its sentimental value, yet you dismissed me without a second thought, like you did just now, in front of my neighbors, the management company representatives, and the HOA board."

Carla's shoulders slump. She was so quick to react that she didn't even consider how it would look to all in attendance.

Turning to the crowd, Amelia continues, "I also overheard Carla calling my gnome trashy and heard her insulting me for dressing my children in clothes they felt comfortable in for the picture with the Bunny. She implied that a single mom can only afford thrift store clothing for her children, and she used the words 'tacky' and 'monstrosity' while gossiping with her friend."

Amelia returns her attention to Carla. "Did you know I was within hearing distance when you said all of that about me?"

Met with silence, Amelia tosses a piece of paper on the table in front of Carla, with a full-page photo of her smoking beneath the NO SMOKING sign at the pool. She then provides one to each management company representative and HOA board member, before handing them out to the residents.

"I broke the rules and must go home and admit to my children that I can't keep my promise to them." She points to the photo, holding it in front of her for all to see. "How are you accountable for breaking the rules?"

Crimson sweeps across Carla's cheeks.

"You openly questioned my parenting abilities at that Easter egg hunt. So, let me be honest. That trashy single mom you made fun of is the same person struggling to be everything for her children. I'm also the mom of an eight-year-old daughter who was suspended for punching a bully twice her size while trying to protect her brother."

Amelia searches the crowd. "I second-guess myself all the time. Am I enough for my children? I pray that I don't let them down. I'm not alone, though. Most of us in this room feel some sort of fear…of failure, of making the wrong decision, and then there's impostor syndrome. That's fun, right?"

A few people in the crowd laugh, while more nod in agreement with Amelia. "This is where you come in, Carla. You have a way of making residents feel awful about ourselves. Do you honestly think I need your judgment? I'm hard enough on myself."

The phrase *you could hear a pin drop* comes to Amelia's mind. Amelia's eyes lock with Kyle's, which emanate approval. He grins and nods, encouraging Amelia to continue.

This is her one chance, and Amelia will speak the truth. "Carla, you speed through our neighborhood, where our kids play. You trespass on our front lawns, and you ignore our community rules, while sending letter upon letter to us and heaping judgment upon the people who call this community home. Why don't the rules apply to you?"

Many residents mutter "yes" and "uh-huh" in agreement while Carla stares blankly, her cheeks now a brighter red than her lipstick.

"Your behavior is toxic and inappropriate. It's also against the law, Carla. As a stickler for rules, you should know that and show some humility." Pausing, Amelia allows her words to settle before adding, "It shouldn't be this difficult to live in our community. We, as neighbors, should be able to trust that our management company will hold itself to the same standards that are expected of us. Also, our management company representative shouldn't judge us. You work for us, your salary comes from our yearly dues."

Amelia swallows hard, staring straight at Carla. "How can I allow you to bully Castle Rock residents? My own eight-year-old knew that bullying was wrong. Granted, she shouldn't have punched the bully, but she knew instinctively what that child was doing was wrong. I'm following her example. You are a bully, and you must be stopped."

Amelia lifts the stapled stack of papers she handed out previously. "This packet includes a petition requesting that Carla be reassigned, and demanding that Castle Rock is assigned a new management representative, one who respects our community. In it you will find copies of homeowner violation letters with photos clearly taken on their front yards, photos taken from my neighbors' security cameras of Carla trespassing on my property, and a full-size photo of Carla smoking under the NO SMOKING sign at the pool."

"A petition demanding my reassignment. Are you serious?" Carla demands of Amelia.

"Quite serious. I know that my gnome must be relocated per the bylaws. That's on me and I take full responsibility for that. Now it's time for your day of reckoning." Amelia looks at the residents seated in the room. "We have a volunteer HOA board that tries to help us. We also have a management company, represented by Carla, that enforces bylaws. I understand that. Carla is not, nor has she been in, compliance with state law, let alone our community rules. For those reasons, we deserve a different representative to be assigned to our community because that's what Castle Rock is—a *community*. Neighbors helping neighbors, supporting one another. A community that comes together for Easter egg hunts and pictures with the Easter Bunny and Santa. We ask for a representative who will see us as a community, as homeowners, and not abuse us under some misguided power trip."

At this, the crowd applauds. Amelia glances at Kyle and he smiles, pride emanating from his bright green eyes. It's all the encouragement she'd hoped for.

"Our community has come together on this. Carla must be replaced. Per the petition, we have the votes, and we also have a quorum for a board vote, do we not?" Amelia scans the board and others at the table.

The management representatives, minus Carla, walk the length of the table to Kyle, whispering back and forth with him. He, in turn, whispers to his fellow board members, while the lead management company rep says something to Carla, whose incensed expression tells Amelia she's about to get one win today.

Kyle leads the vote to replace Carla. It is seconded by another board member and the management company acknowledges Carla's reassignment. While Carla radiates rage and resentment, the higher-up at the company apologizes to the residents and introduces those in attendance to their new representative, the smiling woman who sat beside Carla, who makes a speech about how excited she is to be representing Castle Rock.

Amelia's not heartless. To the contrary, she feels a pang of pity for Carla. It must be difficult for her to hear her replacement give such an uplifting speech. As the meeting winds down, Carla ducks out without any fanfare, and the meeting ends on a high note.

As Amelia stands, slinging her tote over her shoulder, her neighbors descend upon her, encircling her with congratulations and thank-yous.

"I knew you could do it," Dr. Bass says, as his wife smiles beside him. "Well done."

Amelia thanks everyone, and small talk ensues, until more time has passed than she expected.

The crowd thins, and Bridget gives Amelia a hug, whispering, "Ding dong, the witch is gone!"

"I think I said too much," Amelia admits.

"You were brave and honest." Bridget studies her friend. "That's who you are, so own it."

"We are so proud of you!" Lily adds with a hug, "I'm sorry about your gnome. When are you telling the kids?"

"When I get home." Amelia forces a grin. "They'll be awake."

"What are you going to tell them?" Bridget asks.

"The truth." Amelia can't lie to them, nor would she. "I tried, but ultimately, it is my fault. I never should have made that promise without all the facts."

"Sounds like a life lesson," Lily grimaces.

"It is. For them and me." Courtesy of a reformed mom who once overcompensated for her ex's desertion by trying to heal her children's pain all by herself, and with a little help from her friends. "I learned a lot about myself, and about my friends. You are remarkable women."

Bridget beams. "Right back at you."

"Group hug!" Lily laughs as they each lean into one another. "Call us if you need us."

Amelia promises to do so and watches her friends leave. Alone in the rec center, she exhales, dreading the upcoming conversation with her children.

"Am I interrupting?" Kyle's voice is hushed, as if not to interrupt Amelia's introspection.

She turns, offering him a smile. "Never."

"I just wanted to congratulate you. You did it. Carla's removal was a win." He shoves his hands in his jeans pockets.

"Thanks for your text, by the way."

Kyle grins. "I told you that I'd handle Carla that night you were sick. She was written up the following day. Between that and residents calling about your petition and demanding a change, it was a done deal. Still, you made it happen."

"With your help." He's had Amelia's back all along, even when she didn't know it. His devotion never wavered.

"The clubhouse was packed tonight. It isn't always standing room only. Clearly, people were eager to witness Carla's downfall." Kyle looks at the door. "We're about to go into executive session. I just wanted to congratulate you before you left. Nice seeing you, Amelia."

Returning his attention to his fellow board members, Kyle takes his seat as Amelia leaves the rec center, her heart heavy. There was so much she wanted to say to Kyle, but didn't. Because the timing was off, and because Amelia can't prolong her conversation with Jacob and Chloe any longer.

Being a mom is hard. It's worth it, but more difficult than she ever imagined.

It's time for some more life lessons.

# Chapter 37

FOCUSING ON THE RHYTHMIC HUM OF HER ENGINE IDLING AND the blue interior dash lighting, Amelia sits in her driveway. Though night has fallen, she looks out her driver's window, studying the spot where the gnome that started it all is defiantly guarding the gardenia bush, with a fake gardenia tied around its neck.

That poor, once-proud gnome has been reduced to wearing costumes. She'd laugh if the scene weren't so sad. The irony isn't lost on her. Jacob and Chloe created that gnome as a gift and it brought a great deal of happiness until…

Until the fog of her HOA battle known as Gnomegate.

Amelia turns off her engine and climbs out of her SUV, keys and purse in hand.

"I'm sorry." Amelia kneels in the grass, picking up the gnome. "I'm sorry it came to this. It was a valiant effort, taking on the HOA, but if I'm being honest, this was the inevitable outcome. I broke the rules, and you were always going to be moved. I just couldn't accept it before now."

*Wouldn't accept it*, Amelia reminds herself. This is her doing, and it's time to come clean to Jacob and Chloe.

"Mom!" Jacob and Chloe shriek, running down the hallway to greet her.

Amelia places her purse on the bench in the hall, along with the gnome, and gives each child a hug and kiss. "Hi, my loves. How was your night?"

"We watched Tom and Jerry!" Chloe's expression is animated.

Jacob wrinkles his brow. "Are the cat and mouse friends, or not? Charlotte called them friendimies—"

"Frenemies," the babysitter corrects him, carrying her backpack down the hall. "It was just my opinion. We had a huge debate, and then I told them they can make up their own minds."

"Thanks, Charlotte." Amelia forces a smile, reaching into her purse and pulling out the cash. Charlotte doesn't count it. She never does.

How nice it must be—to be so trusting. Then again, Amelia was once that trusting, and got hurt. Would she want to go back to that? No. If given a choice, Amelia would take the woman she's become over the too-trusting woman she once was any day of the week.

"How are you?" Charlotte asks. A harmless question from a high school cheerleader whose idea of a bad day is not making sectionals. Instead of snuffing her optimism, Amelia manages to sound like all is as it should be. "I'm great. How's school?"

"I have lots of homework, but it's going well. In addition to debating Tom and Jerry with Jacob and Chloe, we got some reading in tonight." Charlotte can be counted on to do assignments with Amelia's children, and she's worth every penny for the support she gives to Jacob and Chloe.

"Thank you for everything, Charlotte."

"No problem. I can use the extra cash." Shoving a large textbook in her backpack, Charlotte waves goodbye to the kids, then Amelia. "Have fun explaining Tom and Jerry."

"We'll talk the complexities of Tom and Jerry tomorrow," Amelia jokes, before bidding Charlotte a good night. "Drive safe, and thanks again."

When alone, Amelia caresses Jacob's cheek, then Chloe's. "Where's Prince?"

"He's sleeping in the living room. So, did we win?" Jacob asks, eyeing their gnome with narrowed eyes, like he suspects the truth.

Amelia picks up the gnome and leads the children to their backyard. "Let's talk about it outside. It's a nice night."

"That doesn't sound good," Chloe mutters as she shuts the back door. Protecting Prince from getting out has become second nature to her and her brother now.

Walking to the grass, Amelia sits, placing the gnome on the manicured lawn beside her. "Sit with me."

The kids do, Chloe on Amelia's lap while Jacob snuggles beside her, asking, "We lost, didn't we?"

"Shush. Just listen, and look…" The sounds of nature envelop them as together they survey their backyard. From the large bin still full of tadpoles and frogs in various stages of their evolutionary cycle on the patio, to the crickets and croaking of the older frogs in the darkness, it's the circle of life at Casa Marsh.

The moon is still in the east, emanating enough light to cast the backyard in shadow. It makes the truth easier to admit.

Wrapping her arms around them, she gently squeezes their shoulders. "When I promised you that we could have our gnome in our front yard, I didn't realize that I'd be violating community bylaws."

Chloe gasps. "You broke the law?"

"Are you going to be arrested? Will we see a police car in front of our house?" Jacob asks, almost giddy at the prospect of seeing a police officer, let alone an official police vehicle.

"No to both questions. Bylaws are neighborhood rules, not actual law, and I cannot be arrested for breaking them. But it does mean we have to move our gnome from our front yard." Both kids look crestfallen. She expected this. "I tried to fight it. I really did. However, the bylaws can't be changed, and in the end, I had to do what's right. So, I have a compromise. Let's place the gnome on our back patio, where we can see it from our living room."

The kids agree, though neither is happy about it.

"Hey. Our home is a home because we're together… We're a family—you and me. What's important is that we're together and we're stronger together than apart. That gnome is ours. It is a symbol of our family. Always and forever."

"Are Prince and the tadpoles part of our family?" Chloe asks.

Amelia smiles. "Absolutely. Prince, all of those tadpoles and frogs, and all of the other gnomes in our backyard. We're all family. Add Aunt Bridget, Aunt Lily, and their children, along with your grandparents, and we're doing great in the family department, don't you think?"

"Yes!" Chloe's excitement is infectious, though worry mars her features. "What happens after our tadpoles turn into frogs? Will they leave us?"

"Some will, others will probably stay in our yard. They'll have their own tadpoles someday." Amelia sighs, then addresses the hardest issue of all. "Now, listen, because this is important. Unfortunately, I lost my fight against the bylaws. One thing life teaches you is that you can't win all the time, no matter how hard you try."

Chloe places her head on her mom's shoulder, as Jacob snuggles closer.

"Even the Avengers lose sometimes." Leave it to Chloe to look on the bright side.

"Yeah, but it's our gnome." Jacob sounds dejected.

Amelia clings to her children tight, squeezing her eyes shut. "Yes, it is, and our gnome… This guy is special."

Reaching for the gnome that started Gnomegate, the same gnome she will always cherish, Amelia removes the fake gardenia. "He shouldn't be in hiding in our front yard, or incognito. He should be front and center on our patio."

"In-what?" Jacob shakes his head. "What does innito mean?"

Leave it to Jacob to question such a detail. "Incognito means 'in disguise.' Hidden by gardenias, wearing bonnets and bows."

"Yeah. I get it. Right, Jacob?" Chloe asks.

Jacob nods.

"We can have a wonderland of gnomes back here. And they won't need to hide. They can be front and center. Starting with this guy." Amelia hands the gnome to Chloe, as Jacob follows her to the patio. "Where would you like to place him?"

"We can see it from here," Jacob says, placing the gnome on their patio table, beneath the umbrella accentuated with warm white lights that illuminate the colorful gnome to perfection.

Chloe adjusts the gnome so he faces their back door and window. "He'll be safe here, too. From rain and stuff."

"Perfect." In spite of her encouraging tone of voice, both children are standing still, studying the gnome intently.

They're growing up so fast. She studies Jacob and Chloe, noting how strong, sweet, and smart they are… They always have been. Amelia's heart swells with nostalgia as she admits, "I'm sorry we had to move the gnome."

The children run to her, pouncing on her lap.

"It's okay, Mom. We know you tried," Jacob says.

"Yeah. You're like Wonder Woman, only better," Chloe adds. "Please don't cry."

Amelia didn't realize that tears had begun to fall. Wiping her eyes, she admits, "I didn't want to disappoint you, or make you feel like I won't fight for you. Because I will. I always will."

"We know, Mom." Jacob hugs Amelia tightly. "You fought for Chloe when she was suspended."

"I messed up." Chloe begins to cry.

"So did I," Jacob admits, as tears begin to fall from his eyes as well.

"No. You didn't." On this Amelia is adamant, as she hugs her children tighter. "I tried to replace everything you lost when we moved from Austin. I wasn't enough. That's on me."

Both children chime in with, "You are enough."

Chloe pulls away, and looks at her mom. "We're family. Always and forever."

The little girl is using Amelia's words against her. Or for her… She can't help but grin at her daughter's tenacity.

"And if one of us fails, we'll do that together, too," Jacob adds, quoting Captain America.

"It all leads back to the Avengers." Amelia can't help but chuckle. "You are both great at pep talks. That's something special."

Something that Amelia finds awe-inspiring. These are her children, who have an abundance of empathy and strength. "I love you both so much. You know that, right?"

The children nod, and the sounds of the great Texas outdoors envelop them once more. The frogs croak their mating calls, and Amelia wonders if another round of tadpoles will be her responsibility. She may never be able to get rid of that bin taking up a large part of her patio.

"It really is cool that our gnome isn't in hiding anymore," Chloe whispers. "Now he's guarding us."

"That's super cool!" Jacob agrees as a warm breeze tousles their hair. It's a nice night, a calm night, until Jacob breaks the spell. "Where's Kyle? Is he in hiding, too?"

"No, Kyle isn't in hiding. We've taken a little break, remember?" Amelia chooses her words with care. "Between everything going on at school, at home, and with therapy, I thought that you both needed me more than Kyle does."

"But you need Kyle." Chloe's astute comment floors Amelia.

She does need Kyle. But she prioritized her children. How does she explain that without making it sound like Jacob and Chloe are burdens, which they're not and never will be?

Jacob places his cheek on Amelia's shoulder. "It's okay to need someone, Mom."

Amelia grins. "You both have always been intelligent, but when did you become so...well, smarter than me?"

Jacob shrugs while Chloe says, "I don't know. Sometime after I punched Jackson, I think."

"Oh! Do you think if you hit Carla, we could have kept our gnome in the front yard?" Jacob asks.

Shaking her head, Amelia responds, "No! Hitting and punching isn't okay. We're not Avengers."

Her children nod, showing that they understand.

After a long pause, Amelia admits, "If I'm being honest, there was a time I wanted to hit Carla. When Carla trespassed on our front lawn. But hitting isn't the answer."

"What happened to Carla?" Jacob asks. "I don't like her. She never smiles back at me."

Amelia snuggles into their hugs as she announces, "There is some good news tonight. You ready?"

The kids nod in unison.

"Carla has been reassigned to another community. She won't come around our neighborhood anymore."

"Yes!" Jacob hisses. "You didn't need to hit her. You snapped her, Mom."

Okay, Amelia's children are too into the Avengers. "Jacob, we don't snap people. Thanos is bad."

"So is Carla," Jacob counters.

Amelia clucks her tongue. "You've got me there. Isn't it way past your bedtime?"

Chloe and Jacob sigh. "No."

"Yes, it is." She stands, holding hands with both Jacob and Chloe.

"What about Kyle?" Jacob asks, clearly unwilling to let this particular topic go.

"I can't promise anything, honey," Amelia admits. "All I can say is that Kyle cares about you both a great deal and that I'm going to try to make things better with him."

Yes, there's a lot to make up for with Kyle. For the first time, though, Amelia knows without a doubt that her children are ready. As is she. Hopefully, Kyle is, too.

What are the odds that he waited? she wonders as they reenter the house, met with Prince's soft mews.

A line from Han Solo comes to mind: *Never tell me the odds.*

Amelia's going to go with that for the time being. Even if the odds are stacked against her, she'll give it her all.

Yes, she will fight for Kyle, will humble herself to him. Because he is worth it, and so much more.

# Chapter 38

AFTER THE KIDS ARE ASLEEP IN THEIR ROOMS, AND A WELL-FED Prince is sacked out on Amelia's mattress nestled in her bedding, Amelia plops down on her front porch, watching the street, waiting to see if Kyle jogs by.

It's a nice night, with very few mosquitos. The sound of crickets chirping is a nice lullaby, uninterrupted by very few cars passing. Though Amelia is unsure how much time has passed, the moon is higher in the star-studded sky than when she first sat down.

Just when Amelia is about to give up, the shadow of a jogger approaches her block and turns, heading towards her driveway. She'd recognize Kyle's silhouette anytime.

Rising, she hurries to the end of her driveway, waiting for him.

"I was hoping you'd jog my way tonight." She manages a smile, though her admission sounds corny, even to her own ears.

Kyle doesn't react. Instead, he removes one of his earbuds. "After what must have been the most gut-wrenching HOA meeting ever, there was a lot to process. I've had a long jog tonight."

"Really?" Amelia studies Kyle and notes that he isn't perspiring at all. If she didn't know better, she'd think he jogged past her house and her house alone.

"You would not believe what happened." Kyle is animated, with lots of hand motions. "This neighbor had handouts with charts, graphs, and a picture of Carla smoking a cigarette at the pool, which is a complete infraction of the bylaws, not to mention a fire hazard. Carla was replaced to much fanfare. All residents were thrilled, even the guy who gives me grief about his garbage cans, and the one with the tire hanging in his front yard. It was genius. You should have been there."

Amelia laughs, "I was there. I ranted and raved, and was guilty of TMI."

"That was you?" Kyle asks with a grin.

Amelia nods. "Guilty as charged."

"You've had a rough time of it, then."

With a scoff, Amelia mutters, "You don't know the half of it."

"True," Kyle agrees, adding, "but I want to. If you'll let me. Besides, you are outnumbered if you count the kids, the cat, and the tadpoles. You kind of need me. Or am I being too presumptuous?"

He's right, of course. "I do need you. Even more so, I *want* you in my life. So do my kids. Can we do a reset?"

"A reset, huh?"

An uncomfortable silence surrounds them. "If you want. If—I mean, if you're not seeing someone. I would understand if you are. I did tell you that you didn't have to wait for me."

Amelia considers that Kyle might not have waited for her. Heaven knows she's given him every reason not to. Kyle proved to be more sensitive and kinder than Amelia ever thought possible. She took him for granted, and Kyle had every right to move on.

"I'm sorry, Kyle. I should have admitted this sooner, before...well, before it was too late."

"Too late?" Kyle sighs. "Don't tell me you're having second thoughts already."

Amelia takes a step closer to him. "No. I'm certain. I've always been certain that you are everything I have ever wanted. I just never felt like I was enough for my children, and let you go. I realize now that needing you, and wanting you in my life—in our lives—isn't selfish. I understand if you didn't wait, I just wanted you to know how I truly feel."

"Are you sure you're ready? For a relationship with me?" Kyle asks, smoothing Amelia's hair. "Because I want a friend, but I also want more, and I want it with you. I'm all in. Are you?"

Amelia flattens her palm against his smooth jawline. "I want to give us a try."

"Why?" One word, one simple word. Splintering the walls Amelia had erected around her heart when her husband betrayed her and their children.

"Because I could fall in love with you, Kyle Sanders." She leans closer to him, caressing his cheek with her thumb.

There it is—the truth of the matter. She could fall in love with Kyle, they could have a future with Jacob, Chloe, Prince, and a never-ending bin of tadpoles and frogs along with who knows how many other creatures.

"Then it's a good thing I waited for you. You see…" He takes a step closer, bridging the distance between them, encircling her in his warm embrace. "I think you've already fallen, and I'm not going anywhere. Though, technically, I'm not sure that we're compatible. My favorite Christmas movie is *A Christmas Story* and yours is *Die Hard*. Not exactly a perfect fit."

"It is if you watch *A Christmas Story* during the day, and *Die Hard* after the kids are asleep." Amelia's thought this through.

"Still, *Die Hard* isn't a Christmas movie, it's an action flick." Kyle's voice is gruff with emotion.

Amelia chuckles. "And I'm carrying a lot of baggage. Are you sure you can handle me?"

"Well, I may not have a Mercedes transit van, but I've got a truck that fits plenty of baggage." Kyle tugs her closer.

"Forget the Mercedes transit van, Jacob has moved on to a GMC truck." Amelia revels in Kyle's warmth and close proximity.

Kyle tilts his head to the side. "That's good to know."

"You might be right about me already falling in love with you," Amelia whispers, as they lean into each other.

"I know." Two words, recalling one of their previous conversations about favorite movie quotes, as Kyle quotes Han in *The Empire Strikes Back*. Then his lips crush Amelia's in a soul-fusing kiss.

There's a reverence to his kisses, and a hunger. Gentle, yet brimming with emotion and a yearning matching her own. Amelia doesn't know how long they kiss each other, but with each passing moment, she feels more connected to him.

A kiss like this should be the start of something spectacular. And it will be, because with a man like Kyle Sanders, all of the heartache and the difficult journey was worth it.

Yes, Amelia has fallen in love. And based upon their kiss, Kyle feels the same.

The future is filled with endless possibilities, but one thing is certain: with a kiss like this, the neighborhood gossip wheel will be spinning overtime.

# Acknowledgments

Thank you, Nicole Resciniti, for your boundless support and friendship. You're the most wonderful agent I could have asked for. More importantly, you're the most wonderful person, and I adore you.

A special thank you to Deb Werksman and the entire Sourcebooks team for all of your guidance, excitement, belief in me, and for welcoming me into the Sourcebooks Casablanca author family.

Thank you, Kait Ballenger, for being the best BFF ever! You were with me through this entire process, and I couldn't have done it without your friendship and encouragement.

I'd also like to acknowledge my readers. Thank you for taking the journey to Timberland, Texas, with me. I hope you've enjoyed it and appreciate each and every one of you. Until next time…

# About the Author

Tracy Goodwin is the *USA Today* bestselling author of uplifting women's fiction, captivating contemporary romances, and romantic comedies. In addition, she pens sweeping historical romances and vivid urban fantasies. Though the genres may be different, each story delivers her unique blend of passion, poignant emotion, humor, and unforgettable characters that steal readers' hearts.

To receive the latest news and information about upcoming releases, please sign up for Tracy's newsletter at tracygoodwin.com. There you will also find social media, BookBub, and Amazon links.

**If you love bright, sparkling love stories and heartfelt romance, read on for a look at Teri Wilson's second book in the Turtle Beach series:**

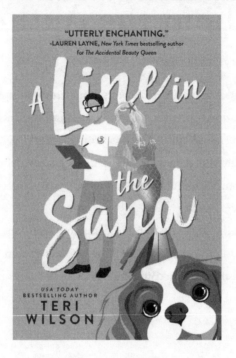

Available now from Sourcebooks Casablanca.

# Chapter 1

ON ANY GIVEN WEEKDAY EVENING, THE DOG BEACH ON THE SMALL barrier island known as Turtle Beach, North Carolina, was typically occupied by two Dalmatians, six or more octogenarians, and any number of canines of dubious origin.

Plus one mermaid.

Make no mistake, Molly Prince, the mermaid in question, was every bit as human as the aforementioned octogenarians. Mermaiding was simply Molly's day job, but sometimes she wore her costume home instead of changing out of her emerald-green sequined fishtail and clamshell bustier. For modesty's sake, the bustier was attached to a flesh-colored body stocking adorned with a sprinkling of rhinestone starfish and draped with no fewer than six strings of pearls. Getting out of the thing was no easy task.

Molly would get to that once she and Ursula, her Cavalier King Charles Spaniel puppy, got to the quaint oceanfront cottage they called home. Ursula was a recent addition to Molly's life and due to the puppy's extreme separation anxiety, she rarely left Molly's sequined-clad side. The little chestnut-and-white spaniel was also prone to bursts of the zoomies, hence their regular stops at the dog beach after work.

"Look at that little dog go." Ethel Banks, resident of Turtle Beach Senior Center and one of Molly's favorite octogenarians, peered over her purple-framed bifocals and grinned as Ursula charged at a flock of sandpiper birds chasing waves along the shoreline.

Three aluminum walkers were lined up in front of the smooth

wooden bench where Ethel sat alongside Opal Lewinsky and Mavis Hubbard—or, as everyone in town called their little trio, the OG Charlie's Angels. Nibbles, a teacup Chihuahua, sat shivering in the basket of the walker belonging to Mavis.

"Ursula really loves other animals," Molly said. "You should have seen her today at the aquarium. She sat right in front of the shark tank, totally rapt."

Opal snorted. "Like Mavis and her new boyfriend Larry every night when *Jeopardy!* is on."

Molly bit back a smile. Was it weird that her senior citizen friends seemed to have more active social lives than she did?

Mavis muttered something in response—laced with snark, no doubt—but whatever it was went into one of Molly's ears and right out of the other one. Her attention had snagged on a man wading knee-deep through the waves, just beyond the shallows where Ursula pawed at the tiny silver fish that always skittered through the foamy water.

"Do any of you know who that guy is?" Molly felt herself frown.

The dog beach was too close to the crest—local speak for the southernmost tip of the island—to be safe for swimming far from the shore. The surf close to the crest was rougher and the riptides stronger, due to warm water from the bay spilling into the salty depths of the open sea. Swimming past the sandbar wasn't allowed, for humans and dogs alike.

Opal, Mavis, and Ethel narrowed their gazes in the stranger's direction and then shrugged in unison.

"Where's his dog?" Molly did a quick inventory of the canines enjoying their freedom on their small designated strip of sand. She'd been here enough times to know precisely who each dog belonged to.

"All the pups here are accounted for," Ethel said. Clover the corgi woofed in agreement at her feet.

Weird. What was he doing at the dog beach, dogless?

"He's staring into the water like he lost something." Opal pressed a hand to her heart as a wave rocked into the man's chest. "He really shouldn't be so far out there."

Mavis shook her head. "Definitely not."

Ursula romped back toward them and spun in excited circles around Molly's mermaid tail.

*Oh, yeah…the costume.*

Super. Molly was going to have to go out there and warn the stranger about the riptide while she looked like Daryl Hannah straight off the set of *Splash* in 1984. Not ideal, but she didn't have much of a choice. Molly certainly didn't want the guy to drown, and she was currently the only person in sight who was fully ambulatory. The dog beach was dotted with more walkers and electric scooters than actual canines. Where were the Dalmatian owners? They always helped bring the median age at the dog beach down by a decade. Or three.

"He's drifting farther out," Ethel said. "Molly, maybe we should do something."

"I'm on it." Molly took a deep breath and headed toward the shoreline in urgent-yet-tiny footsteps, since her fishtail was almost as confining as it was glittery. The costume was never a problem on the turquoise vintage Vespa she used to get around the island. Of course, she didn't normally have to rescue swimmers on the way home from work.

Ursula romped after Molly, just like she always did.

"Don't worry. We're just going to stand right at the edge of the water and yell at that guy to come back to the shallows. We'll be on the couch in front of the *Great British Baking Show* before you know it," Molly said, not altogether sure if she was talking to her dog or herself. Possibly both.

But just as they moved from the sugary sand of the dunes onto the damp shore, the tide rushed in. The man bobbed up and down in the water, and he finally looked up as he seemed to realize how far he'd wandered offshore. A wave smacked him right in the face.

*Oh no.*

Molly's stomach tumbled. "Hey, are you okay?"

Ursula paced at the water's edge, leaving a trail of frantic, tiny paw prints in her wake.

Molly waited a beat for the man to resurface, but all she could see was sunlight glinting off something shiny floating in the water. She shaded her eyes with her hand. *Eyeglasses.* Not a good sign at all, considering they were missing the head that they belonged to.

"Wait here!" she said to Ursula. "I'm going in."

Hoyt Hooper, the senior center's bingo caller, rolled to a stop nearby in his mechanical scooter. His pug, Hops, sat in the scooter's basket, dressed in a Hawaiian shirt that matched the one Hooper was wearing, down to the last hibiscus. "That man's got to be in trouble. I'm calling 911."

Molly nodded. "Good idea."

But would they get to the dog beach in time to help him? Doubtful.

She glanced at the red Igloo cooler strapped to Hoyt's scooter with a bungee cord. "Hoyt, remember that safety demo the fire department gave at the library last year?"

He nodded. "Yeah, why?"

"I'm going to need your cooler." According to the fire department, a fiberglass cooler could be used as a flotation device in an emergency situation. And this was definitely beginning to feel like an emergency.

"Does this mean you're going in after that guy?" Hoyt grabbed the Igloo and handed it to her.

Molly dumped out the contents—three frosty cans of root beer and a pile of ice. "I sure am."

Ursula's tail wagged as she licked the spilled ice cubes.

"I'll watch your pup. Be careful, Molly," Hoyt said as he climbed off his scooter. "Please."

"It's going to be fine," she said, not quite sure whether she was talking to Hoyt, Ursula, or herself.

Molly waddled as fast as she could into the water while Hoyt scooped Ursula into his arms and the other seniors made their way toward the scene with their walkers leaving winding trails behind them in the sand. The dogs gathered round, barking at the ocean while their ears flapped in the salty breeze. Molly suddenly felt like she was in a very bizarre episode of *Baywatch*.

It occurred to her that she didn't even know if her costume was waterproof. She'd never actually gotten it wet before. Some mermaid she was.

She held her breath, dove into the waves and breaststroked her way with one arm to the place where the man had disappeared, clutching the cooler tightly with the other. The water this close to shore was murky, filled with tumbling seashells and stirred-up sand. Molly's eyes burned, and her chest ached. A wave splashed into her face, and she couldn't see a thing. Then she blinked a few times and spotted him.

The man's arms flailed at the waves. He gasped for air. Molly could feel the riptide pulling at her ridiculous fishtail, threatening to drag her out to sea. She clutched the cooler as tightly as she could.

No way. She was *not* going to die like this—costumed, while the greater senior citizen and dog populations of Turtle Beach looked on. Absolutely not. She flat-out refused.

"Grab my hand," she yelled above the roar of the waves and sea spray.

The panicked man's head jerked in her direction. Their eyes met, and his gaze filled with a combination of wonder and relief. Molly's heart thumped hard—adrenaline, no doubt. Still, there was just something about those soulful eyes that made Molly's head spin.

She only hoped it wasn't because they were about to drown together.

Drowning was nowhere on Molly's to-do list, and the stranger was far too cute to get lost at sea. She simply couldn't picture him with a Tom Hanks *Cast Away* beard, crying over a volleyball with a face.

Why on earth were these crazy thoughts flitting through her head? Was she drowning *right now*?

She reached for the man as hard as she could, kicked her mermaid tail against the current and yelled at the top of her lungs.

"Wilson!"

---

The first, and last, time that Max Miller had eaten a raw oyster, his first impression had been that it tasted like he'd just licked the ocean floor. Salty...wet...

And gritty. So *very* gritty. Max had not been a fan, nor had he been inclined to repeat the experience. Besides, oyster reefs were currently the most endangered marine habitat on the entire planet. Best to leave the poor, non-delicious things right where they belonged.

At the moment, though, Max was having some sort of gustatory flashback, because that highly memorable oyster taste was permeating his senses again—in his mouth, his nose, the back of his throat. Even his eyeballs, glued shut with sand and salt and any and all manner of fish excrement (sometimes being a marine biologist afforded a person with more knowledge than was preferable in moments such as this one), seemed to taste the oyster.

But when at last Max managed to pry his eyes open, there wasn't an oyster in sight. Just a mermaid, gazing down at him with worried eyes the color of a stormy sea while her lush, blonde mermaid hair whipped around her face. Max closed his eyes again. Mermaids weren't real. Maybe he was dreaming, or maybe he'd died. He certainly didn't feel particularly alive at the moment.

Salty bile rose up the back of his throat. He gagged and sputtered until someone—the imaginary mermaid, probably—rolled him onto his side and he coughed up what seemed like a gallon of seawater. An upturned Igloo cooler sat about a foot from his head for some odd reason.

Max groaned into the sand, and then a wet, warm tongue swiped the side of his face. Someone was attempting mouth-to-mouth resuscitation, but they were doing a terrible job of it.

"I'm fine," he said.

Max was *not* fine. His gut churned with equal parts nausea and humiliation. This was the first day of his new life in Turtle Beach, North Carolina. He'd hoped to slip seamlessly into the sleepy little town by the sea, not land with such a splash—pun definitely not intended. Max wasn't a punny person in the slightest. An ex-girlfriend had once told him that he had a Ph.D. in place of a sense of humor.

"Ursula, *no*," the mermaid said.

Max squinted at her through sand-crusted eyes, but all he saw was an extreme close-up of a face that was distinctly canine in nature, as opposed to mythical sea creature-esque. The dog, a tiny white-and-chestnut-colored spaniel, licked Max's face again in direct opposition to the mermaid's command.

Max turned his head. Three elderly women gripping aluminum walkers loomed over him. A dog the size of a squirrel sat trembling in the basket of one of the walkers. The block lettering on its identification tag spelled out the word Nibbles.

*Where on earth am I?*

Max had known that a small island like Turtle Beach would be different from Baltimore, but his Uncle Henry had in no way prepared him for how truly quirky it apparently was.

Mermaids? Little toy spaniels named Ursula? And why so many dogs? An enormous poodle with pink bows on its ears poked at Max with a narrow snout. He felt like Alice, falling down a very deep and uncommonly sandy rabbit hole.

Ursula came toward him again, pink tongue lolling out of the side of her tiny mouth. Max sat up in order to avoid another attempt of mouth-to-mouth. He coughed a few times, rubbed his eyes, and when he opened them, he found the mermaid staring down at him. Not a hallucination after all. And here he thought she'd just been an imaginary by-product of his near-death experience.

"You're from out of town, aren't you?" The mermaid jammed her hands on her iridescent, scaly hips.

The scales weren't real, obviously. They appeared to be satin, covered in copious amounts of sequins. Now that Max had gotten a proper look at the woman, he realized that she was in costume, of course. Still, how odd.

"Yes." Max nodded. "Just arrived today."

He didn't have the energy to say more. It took every last shred of energy to form words and pull himself to his feet.

"You're really not supposed to swim this close to the crest. The riptide is too strong beyond the shallows," she said.

Strands of long, wet hair clung to her face. Max had the absurd notion to peel it away from her eyes and kiss her full on the lips, right there in front of the growing collection of dogs and retirees surrounding them.

He angled his head toward her, searching her gaze. "You saved me."

It was a statement, not a question. She'd been the one who'd just pulled Max from the water. In his panic, he'd thought he'd imagined a mermaid coming to his rescue. She'd been real, though. Go figure.

"Indeed she did," one of the senior citizens said. She wore purple glasses and an identical expression to the corgi panting at her feet.

"It was the most romantic thing I've ever seen," the woman beside her—the Chihuahua enthusiast—gushed.

The mermaid rolled her eyes, and her porcelain face went seashell pink. She shoved his glasses at him. "It wasn't romantic in the slightest."

Disappointment settled in Max's gut, along with what felt like a liter of salt water. He wasn't thinking clearly at all. Had he hit his head on something in the ocean?

He slid his glasses in place. The lenses were hopelessly smudged so he removed them and tucked them into the pocket of his sodden dress shirt. As he did, a small fish leapt out and flopped onto the sand.

Max glanced down at it. The tiny critter was a *Membras martinica*, more commonly known as a rough silverside. He picked it up by the tail and tossed it back into the surf before returning his attention to the mermaid.

"You called me Wilson." Max felt his lips twitch into a grin. *Cast Away.* He loved that movie. "The name's Max, actually."

The mermaid eyed him with concern and crossed her arms. She started to shiver like Nibbles. "And you're okay, right? Do I need to call 911 or anything?"

"I'm fine," Max repeated. He'd already made enough of a spectacle of himself. The last thing he needed was to add sirens to the mix. He cleared his throat. "Are you okay, though? You look…" *Beautiful.* "Cold."

"I'm just peachy." She gave him a grim smile and wrapped her arms tighter around her torso, which was decorated with a sparkling assortment of strategically placed starfish, shells, and pearls.

Max did his best to look elsewhere.

The little spaniel yipped and came toward him with a full body wiggle. Max bent to scoop the dog into his arms. The tiny thing couldn't have weighed more than six or seven pounds, but he could barely lift her. He felt himself sway a little on his feet. Almost drowning was exhausting.

He nodded at the mermaid. "I get it now. Her name is Ursula—from *The Little Mermaid*, right? Your name isn't Ariel, is it?"

"It's Molly," Nibbles's owner said before Molly herself could chime in.

*Molly the mermaid.* Cute. "Well, it's nice to meet you, Molly. Thanks for the rescue."

Molly plucked Ursula from his grasp and hugged the puppy to her chest. "You're welcome. But really, swimming isn't allowed at the dog beach. The current is too strong out here."

This was a dog beach. Well, that certainly explained a few things. "Noted. Although for the record, I wasn't going for a swim. I saw something in the water—a *caretta caretta.*"

"A whatta whatta?" one of the older women asked.

"He means a sea turtle," Molly said. "Specifically, a loggerhead."

Max arched a brow.

Molly lifted her chin and tucked a damp strand of hair behind her ear. Highlights the color of pink cotton candy were mixed in with her mass of blonde waves. Tiny droplets of seawater starred her eyelashes. "That's right, I know the scientific name for a loggerhead sea turtle. I'm not a cartoon character. Don't let the costume fool you."

"I wouldn't dream of it," Max said. After all, she'd very probably saved his life.

"There are loads of loggerheads at this beach. Try not to chase any more of them out to sea. Deal?"

Max nodded. "Deal."

Loads of loggerheads? Now she *really* had his attention. He wanted to know more, but before he could utter another word, she scooted past him in the sort of quick, tiny steps that a mermaid tail necessitated. Ursula planted her little head on Molly's shoulder and watched him as the little pup's mistress carried her away.

Max stared after them until they became glittering silhouettes against the molten light of the setting sun. Then a throat cleared nearby and he turned to find every set of eyes on the dog beach, both human and canine alike, watching him with keen interest.

"Welcome to Turtle Beach." The woman with the purple glasses flashed him a wink.

She aimed her walker toward the dunes, and the rest of the retirees followed. A white-haired man and a pug in matching Hawaiian shirts zipped past on a motorized scooter. The man waved, while the pug seemed to smile at Max with his goofy pug face.

Max just shook his head. He and his uncle were going to have a nice, long chat—sooner rather than later. Uncle Henry had some explaining to do.

*Welcome to Turtle Beach, indeed.*

# Chapter 2

IT WASN'T JUST THE NUTTINESS OF THE DOG BEACH ENCOUNTER AND Max's near-drowning that had him rattled. Being back in Turtle Beach after so many years away somehow felt both familiar and surreal at the same time.

He climbed the steps of his uncle's beach cottage—now *Max's* ocean-front home—on shaky legs and plopped down onto a deck chair with a sigh. So far, the island was exactly the way he remembered it, from the rickety Salty Dog pier where Max had spent hours upon hours as a teenager fishing in the moonlight (catch and release, obviously) to the old-timey roller rink above the post office. Back when Max had summered on Turtle Beach, the floor of the small roller rink had been like a vinyl record album, worn with grooves from generations of summer skaters. How the place was still standing was a mystery he couldn't begin to fathom.

Nostalgia had washed over him like a tidal wave the moment he'd crossed the bridge from the mainland and seen the familiar boardwalk and the park by the bay, lit with twinkle lights. The Turtle Beach library, the bookshop that doubled as a coffee bar, the ice cream parlor where as a kid he'd consumed his body weight in chocolate malts were all still there. Aside from fresh paint jobs, the mom-and-pop local businesses looked exactly the same, as did Turtle Beach's modest downtown area on Seashell Drive. Max could hardly believe his eyes.

Where were the improvements his uncle had mentioned? In their phone calls over the past few months, Uncle Henry had made it sound as if Turtle Beach had been on the verge of becoming the next Outer Banks or Myrtle Beach. He'd known his uncle had been exaggerating, but the last thing Max had expected was to find the island looking like it had been lovingly preserved in a time capsule for the past twelve years.

Everything was going to be fine, though. Max hadn't given up a perfectly good job, home, and life in Baltimore because he thought he'd be moving to a booming beach metropolis. This was about more than that. It was about something he hadn't given much thought to in quite a while—family.

And the turtles, obviously.

Max could make a meaningful difference here. He hoped so, anyway. His uncle had assured him that he could.

*He also told you that Turtle Beach had a Starbucks now. And a Krispy Kreme.*

Right. So far, there wasn't a cup of Pike Place roast or a glazed donut in sight. The only visible difference between the modern-day version of Turtle Beach and the one Max remembered was the booming canine population. Why so many dogs? They even had their own private beach.

That was definitely new. As was the mermaid.

Max yawned. With the move and the drive down from the D.C. area in a rental car, he'd barely slept a wink in the past twenty-four hours. Everything that had just happened at the beach seemed like a fever dream—one he didn't care to repeat anytime soon. Or ever, for that matter. What Max needed most was sleep. He'd deal with his uncle, his mess of moving boxes, and the aquarium in the morning.

A sliver of moon hung high in the twilight sky, bathing the ocean with silvery light. Stars were already visible, glittering like diamonds against soft velvet. Max stood and leaned against the deck's railing, taking it all in.

How had he stayed away from the Carolina coast for so long? And why?

The fact that he had no substantive answers to those questions made his gut churn. After college and graduate school, he'd just gotten so caught up in his career that one year turned into two, two into three, and so on. But this was where it had all started—right here on this tiny, precious island. And just like sea turtles always returned to their birthplace to lay their eggs, Max had found his way back to where he belonged.

Did he belong, though? The jury was still out on that. Nearly drowning before he'd unpacked a single moving box or set eyes on his uncle didn't seem like a good sign.

Max sighed and raked a hand through his hair, salty and damp from his impromptu swim. It was too late for regrets. The deed was done. Surely things would seem more normal in the morning. What he needed most right now was a hot shower and a good night's sleep.

He turned to open the sliding glass door and step inside the weathered beach house, but just as he grabbed hold of the door handle, his gaze snagged on a flash of white in his periphery. Max squinted in the semi-darkness and realized it was a dog. Not just any dog—*the* dog.

"Ursula?" Max said.

The little spaniel's tail waved back and forth. She was standing on the deck of the beach cottage situated right next door, watching Max through the white lattice trim of his neighbor's deck.

It had to be the same dog, right? What were the odds of an island the size of Turtle Beach having two of those fancy toy-sized spaniels?

Max snorted. As dog-crazy as this place was, there was no telling. He walked toward the railing, hoping to get a better look, but the little dog turned away and trotted through the open French doors of the other beach cottage and disappeared.

Max told himself he didn't care one way or another if he lived next door to Ursula, but that night he dreamt he was underwater again. Sea foam and kelp danced around him as he tried to follow a bale of sea turtles, their flippers moving through the eerie darkness like graceful angels' wings. Beside him, just beyond his reach, was a mermaid. Her long hair danced in the water, obscuring her face. Max couldn't tell whether or not she was *the* mermaid. *His* mermaid. She seemed to grow fainter and fainter the closer he got to her, until he finally woke up in a cold sweat.

Max chugged a cup of black coffee from his uncle's ancient percolator and tried to shake off the dream. He was losing it. For starters, sea turtles rarely if ever swam in groups. And mermaids were definitely not real, recent events notwithstanding.

He threw on a pair of khakis and a light blue oxford shirt, grabbed the keys to his uncle's Jeep, and headed down the steps of the deck toward the gravel driveway, more than ready for a face-to-face with Henry. The automobile was old enough to be considered vintage, with a stick shift that required serious elbow grease. After stalling out a few times as he backed out onto the street, Max snuck a glance at the cottage next door and saw the Cavalier King Charles pup watching him from an upstairs window. Max wrestled the Jeep into first gear and looked away.

Mere minutes later, he knocked on the door of Uncle Henry's new residence at the Turtle Beach Senior Center. Henry's room was located just off the main lobby, where Max had passed a group of retirees who'd seemed to be gathering for some sort of exercise class. The shivering Chihuahua from the dog beach was nestled inside the basket of one of their walkers. Why did Max feel like he was being stalked by random canines?

"Max!" Uncle Henry looked him up and down as he swung the door open. He was exactly how Max remembered him—powder-white hair, eyes full of laughter, and a face weathered from a lifetime of island living.

The only thing missing was the scent of Captain Black cherry pipe tobacco. Henry had given up smoking a while back, but the sweet, aromatic scent had burrowed into the pine wood paneling of the beach cottage years ago. The absence of it here in Henry's new home was startling to Max.

As was the sight of a turquoise yoga mat rolled up and tucked beneath his uncle's arm.

"You made it. Good. Good." Henry nodded. "I'm glad you stopped by, but I'm afraid I don't have time to visit. Class starts in just a few minutes."

Uncle Henry stepped into the hallway, shut the door behind him, and began hustling toward the lobby.

Max blinked. *What the…*

"Wait." He chased after his uncle. "Where are you going?"

"Yoga," Henry said without missing a beat.

"Yoga." Max felt himself frown. "You do *yoga* now?"

"Five days a week. It's very refreshing," Henry said, as if a reclusive eighty-year-old scientist suddenly taking up group yoga classes was the most normal thing in the world.

"That's…um, great, actually." So much to unpack here, but first things first. "Look, we need to talk."

Henry glanced at him, but kept walking. "You got into the house okay, didn't you? The key was right where I left it?"

Max nodded. "Underneath the conch shell on the upper deck of the porch, the same place where you always hid it when I was a kid. Ace security. It's a good thing this island isn't exactly a hotbed of criminal activity. Getting into the house wasn't a problem at all."

"Good," Henry said as they rounded the corner into the foyer.

Max looked around at the room where he'd played bingo every Tuesday night of the summer visits when he was a kid. Now it was filled with rows of colorful yoga mats stretched from one wall to the other. A black-and-white spotted Dalmatian trotted from mat to mat, greeting the elderly yogis with a wagging tail, because of course.

Max sighed. "Uncle Henry, what exactly is going on here?"

Henry unspooled his yoga mat and flapped it onto the tile floor with a *thwack*. "I told you already—yoga."

"Good morning, everyone. Are we ready to get started?" The instructor, a woman who looked much closer to Max's age than Henry's, stood at the front of the room in leggings covered in a pink cupcake print. The Dalmatian romped in circles around her as she glanced around the class. Her gaze settled on Max and she paused. "Oh good, we have a guest."

Max shook his head. "No, I'm just here visiting my—"

"The more the merrier. Extra mats are over there." She pointed to a stack of yoga mats beside what looked like an official parking area for ambulatory devices. "Let's begin with pretzel pose."

Pretzel pose? Was that Sanskrit? Max wholeheartedly doubted it.

"Uncle Henry, I..."

"You heard her." Henry shrugged. "If you're staying, go get a mat. A little yoga would probably do you some good."

He could *not* be serious.

Oh, but he was. Uncle Henry sat down and proceeded to close his eyes and take deep breaths while Max stood there trying to process what was happening.

"Fine," he finally said, planting his hands on his knees and bending over to whisper-scream at his uncle. "But I'll be back tonight right after the aquarium closes, and we're going to talk."

Uncle Henry popped one eye open. "Sorry, no can do. Tonight is trivia night here at the senior center."

"Seriously?" Max arched a brow. "And I suppose you're busy tomorrow, too. What's on Tuesday's agenda? Pilates? Book club?"

"Don't be silly. Tomorrow night is bingo. You should know that." Henry frowned at him in a very non-Zen, non-yoga-ish sort of way.

Max sighed. He knew all about bingo night. Anyone who'd ever set foot on Turtle Beach did. It had simply slipped his mind for a second, what with the near-drowning and his uncle's total transformation into a different person.

"Hi, there. I'm Violet." The yoga instructor and her Dalmatian were suddenly standing right beside Max. Now that he got a look at the dog up close, Max realized her collar had tiny cupcakes printed all over it, just like Violet's leggings. "It looks like you're staying, so here."

She shoved a yoga mat at him, and Max had no choice but to take it.

"Okay, then," he muttered as he kicked off his shoes.

If this was the only way he was going to get some actual face time with his uncle, then so be it. Max situated the mat beside Henry's and plopped down into a pretzel shape.

"You lied," Max said under his breath, just loud enough for his uncle to hear him.

"About what?"

"Okay, everyone. Let's transition into rear view mirror pose," Violet called from the head of the class.

*Rear view mirror?* What kind of nutty yoga class was this?

The seniors all twisted to look over their right shoulder, so Max did the same. He took advantage of the posture to glare at his uncle.

"About *everything*," Max hissed. "There's no Starbucks, and there's no Krispy Kreme."

"Sure there are…just over the bridge in Wilmington." Henry cleared his throat and swiveled his gaze to peer over the opposite shoulder.

Max did the same. Maybe yoga wasn't a half bad idea. He was beginning to feel like his head might explode. "Wilmington is almost an hour away, Uncle Henry. You told me the island had changed. You made it sound like—"

"Like what?" Henry said, at last meeting Max's gaze head-on. "Like someplace important enough for you to visit?"

*Ouch.*

Max swallowed. He knew better than to issue a denial when his behavior over the past twelve years spoke for itself.

Then Violet's teacher voice rang out, mercifully breaking the tense silence that had just fallen between Max and his uncle. "Looking good, everyone. Let's move into secretly-checking-your-phone pose."

Henry and the other seniors all brought their hands into prayer-like positions and shifted their gazes downward. Max had to hand it to Violet. As bizarre as these pose names were, they were spot-on.

"I'm here, okay? And I'm not going anywhere," Max said quietly. It wasn't as if he had a choice. He'd tendered his resignation. Someone else was already sitting behind his desk at the National Aquarium—and more to the point, there was a new name etched on the aquarium director's door, and it wasn't Max's. That ship had sailed. Where else would he go? "You may as well tell me the rest. Is there anything else I should know?"

Violet called out another pose—downward facing Dalmatian. Henry shifted forward and shot Max an upside-down glance.

"There might be one little thing," he said.

Max pressed his hands into his mat, lifted his hips, and took a deep breath. *Whatever it is, you can handle it. It can't be that bad.* "And what might that be?"

"It's the aquarium," Henry said.

Max's heart pounded hard in his chest.

*Not the aquarium.* Anything *but the aquarium.*

"Henry, I love overpriced coffee and donuts as much as the next person, but the false promises of big city conveniences like Starbucks and Krispy Kreme aren't what convinced me to leave my life in Baltimore and start over here. You founded the Turtle Beach Aquarium nearly a decade ago and have served as the director since its inception. When you told me you were ready to step down, you *insisted* I was the only person who could step into your shoes."

Max had been reeling from being passed over for the promotion at the National Aquarium, and his uncle's offer had felt like fate stepping in to set everything right.

Why not take over Uncle Henry's job? There was something poetic about coming back to the island, back to the beach where he'd learned to love everything about marine life. Like a loggerhead finding its way home. *Caretta caretta.*

But Max wasn't a turtle, and as a scientist he knew better than to anthropomorphize. He should have, anyway.

"So, what about the aquarium?" Max craned his neck and studied his uncle's upside-down face.

Henry didn't even pretend to look Max in the eye. Something was wrong. Something big.

"The aquarium is about to go broke."

# THE UNPLANNED LIFE
# OF JOSIE HALE

Hilarious, heartwarming fiction from Stephanie Eding that reminds us it's always a good idea to expect the unexpected...

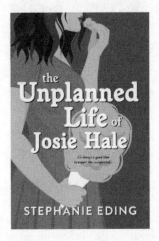

When Josie discovers that she's unexpectedly pregnant with her ex-husband's baby (darn that last attempt to save their marriage), she seeks comfort in deep-fried food at the county fair. There she runs into her two old friends, Ben and Kevin. While sharing their own disappointments with adult life, they devise a plan to move in together and turn their lives around. Soon Ben and Kevin make it their mission to prepare for Josie's baby. Maybe together they can discover the true meaning of family and second chances in life...

For more info about Sourcebooks's books and authors, visit:

**sourcebooks.com**

# LUCKY LEAP DAY

A whirlwind trip to Ireland is supposed to end with a suitcase full of wool sweaters and souvenir pint glasses—not a husband you only just met!

After one too many whiskeys, fledgling screenwriter Cara Kennedy takes a page out of someone else's script when she gets caught up in the Irish tradition of women proposing on Leap Day. She wakes the next morning with a hot guy in her bed and a tin foil ring on her finger. Her flight is in four hours, and she has the most important meeting of her career in exactly two days—nothing she can do except take her new husband (and his adorable dog) back to LA with her and try to untangle the mess she's made...

**"A fun and flirty read that I couldn't put down—
the perfect feel-good rom-com."**

—Sarah Morgenthaler for *Happy Singles Day*

For more info about Sourcebooks's books and authors, visit:

**sourcebooks.com**

# THE STAND-IN

A hilarious and heartwarming story of fame, family, and love

Gracie Reed is doing just fine. Sure, she was fired by her overly "friendly" boss, and no, she still hasn't gotten her mother into the nursing home of their dreams, but she's healthy, she's (somewhat) happy, and she's (mostly) holding it all together.

But when a mysterious SUV pulls up beside her, revealing Chinese cinema's golden couple Wei Fangli and Sam Yao, Gracie's world is turned on its head. The famous actress has a proposition: due to their uncanny resemblance, Fangli wants Gracie to be her stand-in. The catch? Gracie will have to be escorted by Sam, the most attractive—and infuriating—man Gracie's ever met…

**"A sparkly, cinematic adventure that combines emotional drama with hilarious and relatable moments."**

—Talia Hibbert, *USA Today* bestselling author

For more info about Sourcebooks's books and authors, visit:

**sourcebooks.com**

# LOVE, CHAI, AND OTHER FOUR-LETTER WORDS

Kiran needs to fall in line. Instead, she falls in love.

Kiran Mathur was the good daughter. When her sister's defiant marriage to the wrong man brought her family shame, Kiran was there to pick up the pieces. Nash Hawthorne had parents who let him down, so he turns away from love and family. After all, abandonment is in his genes, isn't it?

If she follows the rules, Kiran will marry an Indian man. If he follows his fears, Nash will wind up alone. But what if they follow their hearts?

**"A sweet story of finding love where you least expected."**

—Sonali Dev, author of *Recipe for Persuasion*

# I HATE YOU MORE

"Romance that blends heat, humor and heart" (*Booklist*), from author Lucy Gilmore. She'll show him who's best in show...

Ruby Taylor gave up pageant life the day she turned eighteen and figured she'd never look back. But when an old friend begs her to show her beloved Golden Retriever at the upcoming West Coast Canine Classic, Ruby reluctantly straps on her heels and gets to work.

If only she knew exactly what the adorably lazy lump of a dog was getting her into.

**"Romance that blends heat, humor, and heart."**

—*Booklist*

**"As appealing as a puppy."**

—*Publishers Weekly*, STARRED REVIEW, for *Puppy Christmas*

For more info about Sourcebooks's books and authors, visit:

**sourcebooks.com**

# WELCOME TO THE NEIGHBORHOOD

Funny and heartfelt romantic women's fiction about what lengths a mother will go to protect what's most important

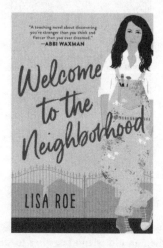

How did Ginny and her eleven-year-old daughter Harri end up in a town full of gossipy trophy wives and their mean-girl daughters? The short answer: Ginny Miller fell in love. Her new husband Jeff's lavish house in the suburbs had everything her little walk-up in Queens didn't—a huge backyard, lots of neighbor kids, and a great school system. It looked like the perfect place to build a new life. Then she met the neighbors...

When their secrets, backstabbing, and bad behavior take a devastating toll on her daughter and new marriage, Ginny must decide what really matters—and protect it at all costs.

**"A touching novel about discovering you're stronger than you think and fiercer than you ever dreamed."**

—Abbi Waxman, *USA Today* bestselling author

For more info about Sourcebooks's books and authors, visit:

**sourcebooks.com**

# A SPOT OF TROUBLE

A sparkling and fun opposites-attract romantic comedy
from *USA Today* bestselling author Teri Wilson

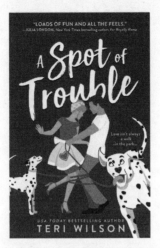

Violet March and Sam Nash are as different as night and day and have been enemies ever since Violet accused Sam of dognapping her beloved Dalmatian. Sam knows that would never happen—his well-trained fire safety demonstration dog never steps out of line, whereas Violet's problematic pooch has never met a command she didn't ignore completely, much like her bubbly owner. But by the time the Fourth of July Fireman's Ball rolls around, they begin to realize that sometimes love isn't so clear-cut, and a little puppy love might be just the thing they've been missing...

**"Teri Wilson is the Queen of Romantic Comedy."**

—Sarah Morgan, *USA Today* bestselling author,
for *The Accidental Beauty Queen*

For more info about Sourcebooks's books and authors, visit:

**sourcebooks.com**

# FOR YOU & NO ONE ELSE

A beautifully emotional and compelling contemporary romance from *New York Times* and *USA Today* bestselling author Roni Loren

Eliza Catalano has the perfect life. So what if her actual life looks nothing like the story she tells online? But when she ends up as a viral meme, everything falls apart. Enter the most obnoxious man she's ever met, and a deal she can't resist: if she helps Beck out of a jam, he'll teach her the wonders of surviving the "real world." No technology, no pretty filters, no BS.

Except what starts out as a simple arrangement gets much more complicated when their annoyance with each other begins to morph into an attraction that neither can resist. As complex feelings grow, this living-in-the-analog-world experiment threatens to get much too real.

**"Absolutely unputdownable!"**

—Colleen Hoover, #1 *New York Times* bestselling author, for *The One You Can't Forget*

For more info about Sourcebooks's books and authors, visit:

**sourcebooks.com**